KU-610-076

consumed

J. R. Ward

Piatkus
An imprint of
Little, Brown Book Group
Carmelite House
50 Victoria Embankment
London EC4Y 0DZ

An Hachette UK Company
www.hachette.co.uk

www.piatkus.co.uk

piatkus

PIATKUS

First published in the US in 2018 by Gallery Books,
an imprint of Simon & Schuster, Inc.
First published in Great Britain in 2018 by Piatkus
This paperback edition published in 2019 by Piatkus

13 5 7 9 10 8 6 4 2

Copyright © 2018 by Love Conquers All, Inc.

The moral right of the author has been asserted.

*All characters and events in this publication, other than those
clearly in the public domain, are fictitious and any resemblance
to real persons, living or dead, is purely coincidental.*

All rights reserved.
No part of this publication may be reproduced, stored in a
retrieval system, or transmitted in any form or by any means, without
the prior permission in writing of the publisher, nor be otherwise circulated
in any form of binding or cover other than that in which it is published
and without a similar condition including this condition
being imposed on the subsequent purchaser.

A CIP catalogue record for this book
is available from the British Library.

ISBN 978-0-349-42061-5

Printed and bound by Clays Ltd, Elcograf S.p.A.

Papers used by Piatkus are from well-managed forests
and other responsible sources.

MIX
Paper from
responsible sources

FSC

Waltham Forest Libraries	
904 000 00648512	
Askews & Holts	25-Jun-2019
THR	£8.99
6068873	

Waltham Forest Libraries

Please return this item by the last date stamped. The loan may be
~~~~ another customer.

J. R. Ward lives in the South with her incredibly supportive
husband and her beloved golden retriever. After graduating
from law school, she began working in health care in Boston
and spent many years as chief of staff for one of the premier
academic medical centres in the nation.

Visit J. R. Ward online:

www.jrward.com
www.facebook.com/JRWardBooks
@jrward1

WALTHAM FOREST LIBRARIES

904 000 00648512

By J. R. Ward

To Elizabeth and Steve Berry,
with all my love, respect, and appreciation.

1

Box alarm. One-niner-four-seven. Two engines and a ladder from the 499, responding.

Or, put another way, Anne Ashburn's Friday night date had showed up on time and was taking her to a show. Granted, "on time" was the precise moment she had sat down for a meal at the station-house with her crew, and the "show" was a warehouse fire they were going to have to chorus-line for. But if you judged the health of a relationship on its constancy and whether it brought purpose and meaning to your life?

Then this firefighting gig was the best damn partner a woman could ask for.

As Engine Co. 17 turned the corner onto Harbor with siren and lights going, Anne glanced around the shallow seating area of the apparatus. There were four jump seats behind the cab, two forward-facing, two rear-, the pairs separated by an aisle of gear. Emilio "Amy" Chavez and Patrick "Duff" Duffy were on one side. She and Daniel "Dannyboy" Maguire were on the other. Up in front, Deshaun "Doc" Lewis, the engineer, was behind the wheel, and Captain Christopher "Chip" Baker, the incident commander, was shotgun.

Her nickname was "Sister." Which was what happened when you were the sibling of the great Fire Chief Thomas Ashburn, Jr., and the daughter of the revered—falsely as it turned out—Thomas Ashburn, Sr.

Not everybody called her that, though.

She focused on Danny. He was staring out the open window, the cold November wind blowing his black hair back, his exhausted blue eyes focused on nothing. In their bulky turnouts, their knees brushed every time the engine bumped over sewer-access panels, potholes, manholes, intersections.

Okay, okay, she wanted to say to fate. *I know he's there. You don't have to keep reminding me.*

The hardheaded bastard was a lot of things, most of which carried terms you couldn't use around your grandmother, but he knew she hated the "Sister" thing, so to him, she was Ashburn.

He'd also called her Anne—once. Late at night about three weeks ago.

Yes, they had been naked at the time. Oh, God . . . had they finally done that?

"I'm gonna beat you at pong," he said without looking at her. "Soon as we get back."

"No chance." She hated that he knew she'd been staring at him. "All talk, Dannyboy."

"Fine." He turned to face her. "I'll let you win, how about that?"

His smile was slow, knowing, evil. And her temper answered the phone on the first ring.

"The hell you will." Anne leaned forward. "I won't play with you if you cheat."

"Even if it benefits you?"

"That's not winning."

"Huh. Well, you'll have to explain to me the ins and outs of it when we're back at the house. While I'm beating you."

Anne shook her head and glared out the open window.

The first tap on her leg she ascribed to a bump in the road. The second, third, and fourth were obviously—

She looked back at Danny. "Stop it."

"What?"

"Are you twelve?" As he started to smile, she knew exactly where his mind had gone. "Not inches. Age."

"I'm pretty sure I peak more like at sixteen." He lowered his voice. "What do you think?"

Between the sirens and the open windows, no one else could hear them—and Danny never pulled the double entendre if there was a risk of that. But yes, Anne now knew intimately all of his heavily muscled and tattooed anatomy. Granted, it had been only that once.

Then again, unforgettable only had to happen one time.

"I think you're out of your mind," she muttered.

And then they were at the scene. The old 1900s-era warehouse was a shell of its former useful self, sixty-five thousand square feet of broken glass panes, rotting beams, and blown-off roof panels. The outer walls were brick, but based on the age, the floors and any room dividers inside were going to be wood. The blaze was in the northeast corner on the second floor, billowing smoke wafting up into the forty-degree night air before being carried away by a southerly wind.

As Anne's boots hit the ground, she pulled the top half of her turnouts closed. Her ponytail was up high on the back of her head, and she stripped out the band, reorganized the shoulder length, and cranked things tight at her nape. The brown was still streaked with blond from the summer, but she needed to get it trimmed—so all that lightness was on the chopping block.

Of course, if she were a woman "who took care of herself," she'd get it highlighted through the winter months. Or so her mother liked to tell her. But who the hell had time for that?

"Sister, you sweep the place with Amy for addicts," Captain Baker commanded. "Stay away from that corner. Danny and Duff, run those lines!"

As Captain Baker continued to bark orders out, she turned away. She had her assignment. Until she completed it, or there was an insurmountable obstacle or change of order, she was required to execute that directive and no other.

"Be safe in there, Ashburn."

The words were soft and low, meant for her ears alone. And as she glanced over her shoulder, Danny's Irish eyes were not smiling.

A ripple of premonition made her rub the back of her neck. "Yeah, you, too, Maguire."

"Piece'a cake. We'll be back at pong before ten."

They walked away from each other at the same time, Danny going around to the stacks of hoses in the back, her linking up with Chavez. She liked being paired with Emilio. He was a four-year veteran who was built like an SUV and had the brains of a *Jeopardy!* contestant. He also did what he said he was going to do with no drama.

Godsend, really.

The two of them went to a compartment on the outside of the truck, threw up the protective metal panel, and grabbed for their air tanks. After pulling her hood over her head, she Velcro'd and buckled her jacket and loaded her oxygen source onto her back. She let the mask hang loose and put her helmet on.

Moving forward on the truck flank, they opened another compartment, and she strapped a hand axe on her hip and added her radio and a box light. When Emilio was ready, the pair of them gloved up and jogged across the frosted scruff grass, hopping over a debris salad of rusted-out car parts, random pieces of building, and weathered trash. The flashing red lights of the trucks made bulky shadows out of their graceless movements, and the clean air going in and out of her throat was the kind of thing she made sure to enjoy.

It was going to be a while before she had it again.

As they came up to a side door, the knob was locked, but the panels were loose as a bad fighter's front teeth.

"I got it," she said.

Turning a shoulder in, she threw her weight into the flimsy barrier, busting it wide open. As splinters fell in a clatter, she triggered the light beam on her helmet and looked inside. Not what she expected—which was the norm. You never knew what a building's interior was going to look like for sure until you got a peek at it, and instead of one cavernous space, she and Emilio were in a makeshift hall. Offices, narrow and short-ceilinged, opened off it, the repurposing transforming the warehouse into a den for administrators of some sort. Or telemarketers. Or day traders.

Of course, whatever it was had been a going concern a good ten years ago. Now, the place was uninhabitable.

She and Emilio took opposite sides, and as they progressed, she checked out a lot of old office equipment from the *Ally McBeal* era. Everything was busted up, water-stained, and covered with grunge, which explained why it hadn't been looted.

No scent of the fire. No heat. But the air was not clear.

The smell of rot, urine, and mold was dense as a solid.

They made quick time, going through the maze. As they went

along, their radios kept them updated, the alternating hiss and talk the kind of thing she took in without being aware of hearing it.

"—wind changing. Northeast."

"—getting that roof ventilation opened now—"

In the back of her mind, she noted the former, but didn't worry about it. The blaze had been small, the engine was on it with a good water source charging the lines, and they had plenty of ladder access from above. Plus, the place was so big, she and Emilio were a mile away from the hot spot.

As they came up to a staircase, she stopped. "You take the second floor, I'll keep going."

"That's no protocol."

"There's no reason to stay together. The fire's all the way over there—it's more efficient."

"But it's not—"

"Are you suggesting I can't handle myself."

Emilio shook his head. "I guess I'll take upstairs."

"I'll join you soon as I'm through down here. There's one more corner to go, that's it."

As Emilio headed up the tight, jury-rigged steps, she continued on. The farther she went, the more mold compromised the air quality, but she had thirty minutes of oxygen on her back—fifteen if she were exerting herself—and she wasn't going to waste it on a bad smell.

Up ahead, something flashed across the corridor, the figure scrambling in the darkness.

"Stop!" she called out as she took off after the person.

Anne went left, right, hit a straightaway, her lungs working, thighs churning, equipment bouncing on her body. In the helmet's jumping beam, the man or woman went in and out of phase with the illumination, a ghost dressed in rags.

They ended up in a shallow room with no door, no window, nothing but the archway they both entered through. The vagrant was muddy as a hound, his hair so matted he had tails growing out of his head. His breathing worried her. Very labored. And that flush, too. He was on something, and probably had pneumonia.

She put her gloved hands up. "I'm not the police. I just want you out so you don't get hurt—"

"I'll kill you!" he panted. "I'll fucking kill you!"

Stepping away, she put one hand on her short axe. "I don't care what you're on, or why you're in here. There's a fire in the building behind us. Do you know where the ways out are?"

The man nodded.

"Go then. I won't stop you."

"I'm not going back to jail!"

"That's cool. I'm fire, not police. But you have to get out of the building—if only because the cops will show up here soon. If you don't want to be arrested, leave now. I'm not in your way."

The vagrant took off, streaking past her and running flat out in his mismatched boot-and-shoe combo. If he had been saveable, she would have played a different card. But she was not going to get hurt trying to convince someone they needed help, and she wasn't going to waste time vouching for rehab and treatment when there might be somebody who was in medical distress two doors farther down.

Three minutes later, she was at the far end of the building. "First floor cleared," she said into her radio.

As she came back to the stairwell, she got her initial scent of smoke, that change in wind direction blowing the fire into its source of combustibles instead of away from it—

Bam!

The frontal impact was so quick and hard, she got blown backward off her boots, her body landing on her tank as gravity took her to the ground. With the air punched out of her lungs, her vision flickered, and she heard another of those vagrants disappear at a dead run.

Rolling off her air cylinder, she braced herself on all fours and looked at the wake of what had hit her. All she caught was a black shape disappearing around the corner.

"Sonofabitch."

With a groan, she got back to vertical and took a couple of deep breathers. Pain was registering on her spine, but other than that case of the owies, she was okay.

No reason to go after that addict. He or she had gotten the GTFO memo.

Pivoting around, her beam flashed along the graffiti'd wall and then penetrated the stairwell. Emilio must have flushed the person down from the second floor—

The explosion was so loud, her ears lacked the capacity to accommodate it as sound. Pain was what registered, and covering her head and going into a crouch was both instinctual and part of training. Her immediate thought was meth lab. They'd had something similar the month before, with the chemicals used to make the drug blowing a two-story duplex sky-high.

She grabbed for her radio. "Emilio. Are you clear? Emilio—"

"Roger that," he said over the connection. "I'm way off in south-west corner, second floor. What was that?"

Thank God, she thought. She did not want to lose him—

The rumble overhead started as a creak and a rattle. It did not stay that way. The collapse was as unexpected as it was fast, all kinds of heavy and hard landing on top of her, an avalanche of God only knew what raining blows on her body.

And then flames were everywhere.

Crushed under debris, pinned to the concrete floor, and without her air mask on, Anne had only one thought.

All her life, she had been determined to follow in her father's footsteps.

Now it looked as if she might die in the same way he had.

2

W here the *fuck* were you just now?"

As Danny Maguire went around the pumper truck for an axe, he shot a glare over his shoulder at Captain Baker. "Running lines like you told me."

"Then why's Duff working alone over there, Maguire."

"I was with Doc. We had a problem with the pump."

"You do what you're told, goddamn it! Doc can handle his shit!"

Captain Baker was in a nasty mood, and that was what happened when you quit smoking. But come on, man. Talk about handling shit.

"You want some Nicorette?" Danny muttered.

"No." Captain Baker walked away. Came back. "Yeah."

Danny went inside his turnouts and took two squares out of the ass pockets of his work pants. "Chew 'em both. Trust me. I got three between my molars and they're barely taking the edge off."

"I want you and Duff on—"

A loud explosion buffered out through the cold air, coming in waves that Danny could feel against his face. Over the captain's red helmet, flames and sparks burst out the second story of the abandoned warehouse, escaping through busted glass like fire through the nostrils of a dragon.

"Check in, people! Check in!" Baker said into the radio.

As firefighters started calling out their IDs, Danny lunged for an air tank—only to stop dead as a female voice came through. "Twelve-ten down. Base of north stairwell. First floor."

A cold flush went through him, his vision going tunnel on the blaze that had suddenly gone absolutely, positively really-fucking-complicated on him. He looked at Baker. "Send me in, Captain—"

"No, Maguire. I just called the six-one-seven for backup and I want you on the hoses. You're the strongest one we've got, and Duff's got that busted rib—" He put his face right into his captain's—and had to remind himself he was not going to tear the man's throat open with his canines. "*Send me the fuck in.*"

Baker punched at his chest. "You are on hoses. That is an order, and don't pull your shit with me!"

White-hot fury blanked Danny out, but before he could go rank stupid, a pair of heavy arms spun him around. Patrick Duffy, a.k.a. Duff, slapped him with an open palm and no emotion.

"Don't do this." The man grabbed his lappies and shook him. "Look at me, Danny. No one needs to add more paperwork to this bitch and you do *not* want to get suspended again."

Twelve-ten was the call number for Anne Ashburn, the sole female firefighter at the 499, and the word "down" meant she was trapped in the burn. Under normal circumstances, Danny would have given her his right arm if she'd asked him for it. The fact that she needed assistance and might be hurt—

Duff yanked his lapels again, and then hung off them so that Danny was forced to bend down from his six-six height. "Amy's going after her. You and me are getting on those hoses." In a lower voice, the guy said, "You gotta regulate yourself. This is not about Sol."

No, it was worse. If he failed Anne, that was going to make losing the stationhouse's sergeant look like a cakewalk.

The pair of them stayed nose-to-nose for a hundred and one years—that somehow passed in the matter of a moment.

Accept. Adapt. Change.

"Okay," Danny said. "Fine."

He shoved Duff off his jacket like the two-hundred-and-fifty-pounder was nothing but lint. Then he hooded up and strapped on that air tank.

"What do you need that for?" Duff asked.

"The wind just changed. I'm not going over there with a hose without an oxygen supply. That okay with you? Or do you want to try to make out with me again."

He didn't give the man a chance to answer that one. And everybody got out of his way as he went around to where he'd been assigned to go.

Firefighting followed in the military's chain-of-command boot steps. You took orders or you were out. Even if that meant leaving the love of your miserable wasteland of a life in the middle of a now two-alarm fire to get burned to death inside her turnouts.

Happy Friday night, motherfuckers.

Trapped underneath debris and fallen wooden beams, the first thing Anne did after checking in on her radio was get enough freedom of movement so she could secure her mask over her face and turn on the airflow. As she breathed that metallic-and-plastic swill of oxygen, she did an internal assessment of her body. Her left arm was wrenched up above her head, and one leg was twisted at the foot and straining at its knee joint.

Her helmet beam was off, and she pulled her right hand loose to feel around for it. No go. The unit had snapped off, and there was no reaching her box light.

"Check in, twelve-ten!" Captain Baker said over the radio. "Twelve-ten, what's going on?"

Forcing her lungs to work, she rasped, "It's getting hot in here."

In her mind, she heard Danny's voice: *So take off all your clothes. I . . . am . . . getting . . . so . . . hot . . . Iwannatakemyclothesoff.*

She thought about the hell she was going to catch when Captain Baker found out she had split up from Emilio. Although maybe the man would be dead if they'd stayed together down here.

"We're coming for you, Anne," the captain said. "Injuries?"

"Negative."

Twisting her head to the right, she only made it halfway around, her helmet getting crammed into something—

Through the visor of her mask, she got a crystal-clear on the field of orange flames roiling out of the stairwell and across the ceiling, the bubbling movement like a hundred rats fleeing rising water in a sewer, its escape the large hole above her that had been a ten-by-fifteen-foot section of the second floor, but was now the debris field trapping her in place.

Pushing against anything that was on her, she phoenix'd-from-the-ashes like out of *The Walking Dead*, a stiff, bad-angled version of herself rising from the floor. As she made it halfway to full height, it was a relief that her legs were fully capable of holding her weight.

That was the last piece of good news she got.

"Twelve-ten, check in," came over the radio.

"I'm okay." She looked around and tried to place herself directionally. "I'm up on my feet."

"Good girl—"

"Don't call me 'girl.'"

"Roger that. We're coming for you—"

There was a sudden shifting overhead, one of the old timbers groaning as it was forced to shoulder an unexpected burden. She glanced up. The fire was closer, and she could feel the heat more. Smoke was beginning to build, too, bringing with it a galaxy of cinder stars that floated around, innocent and beautiful as fireflies in a summer meadow.

Anne realized she was trapped when she attempted to fully straighten her spine. Her right side was fine. The left half of her came up only so far as her arm would permit.

Leaning back, she pulled against the tether. Her hand, fat from her glove, refused to yield, some triangulation of trash turning the extremity into a rope with a blood supply.

The pulsating orange waves licking above her threw off enough illumination for her to see the problem. Desk. There was a desk that had fallen through the ragged hole in the ceiling, and somehow, the thing had managed to mate with one of the massive ceiling beams. No, two old beams.

Her hand was the bad-luck hole-in-one in the middle of the tiddlywinks from hell.

Planting her gloved right palm on the closest length of oak, she braced her feet in her steel-toed boots and shoved hard.

Nothing.

She tried a different hand position on the beam. And then an alternate angle of counterforce. Her big-ass glove was the problem, and with no way of reaching over things to release it, she was stuck with a Popeye problem at the base of her wrist.

And all the time, the fire spread, eating its way down the flammable, ancient carpeting on the stairs, spreading through the beams still on the ceiling, consuming the cheap particleboard that had been used to make walls.

"Twelve-ten, hang on in there—"

Another collapse rumbled all around her, more sparks flying, another helping of debris added to her plate.

She pulled harder. Pushed more.

Inside her turnouts, something welled and river'd. She prayed it was sweat and not blood—and as much as she told herself to preserve oxygen, her lungs started to inflate and deflate like she was on a sprint, her cognition, her thoughts, fragmenting.

Talking into her radio, she tried to make like she was calm. "You guys almost here? Are you—"

The third collapse brought down a wooden beam that was breeding open flames two inches in front of her mask.

"Twelve-ten!" Captain Baker yelled through the radio. "Check in—twelve-ten!"

chapter

3

Fire Chief Thomas Ashburn stared over his messy desk at the two geniuses before him. Idiot number one, on the left, was a third-generation Italian firefighter, a stand-up guy who was built like a pro wrestler, never blinked in the face of death, and, aside from an intermittent off-duty drinking problem, had no red checks after his name.

If he had a dozen Chuck Parnesi's in his firehouses, he wouldn't be prematurely gray and divorced.

Okay, fine, he'd probably still be divorced. But his hair wouldn't be almost white.

Genius number two was the problem—and the carrier. Spike-haired and heavy-metal-loving Damian Reichmann was a walking hemorrhoid, the Typhoid Martin of Bad Behavior, a man capable of reducing even a relatively tight guy like Chuckie P to the lowest common denominator of a twelve-year-old at summer camp. Damian absolutely, positively measured his life's worth on how many people around him were pissed off. Nickname? Damnit. Because pretty much every time the asshat was addressed, it was along the lines of "Damnit, why did you . . ."

"I am too old for this shit." Tom glared at Damian. "And so the fuck are you."

Damnit's smile had fat-kid-loves-cake all over it. "What I do?"

Tom leaned back in his old wooden chair. And stared at the guy.

Damnit shrugged. "Look, Chuckie P got no game. I thought I was helping."

"You set up an eHarmony account," Chuck cut in. "And sent women to my house. To go on dates. With me."

"Did any of it work?" Damnit gave a two-thumbs-up. "Did we get it in?"

"They were fetish models!"

Tom had to give that detail a "huh." "I didn't know those type of women were on eHarmony."

Damnit shook his head. "It was an ad on Craigslist, actually."

"What the fuck!" Chuck glared at the guy. "People get killed off that thing!"

"Annnnd you're still breathing. Also haven't answered the question. What about that redhead who was into bondage—"

"Enough." Tom backhanded his neck to rub away the steel beam that was his spinal cord. "Look, I can't let this go. This is one too many times in the last month."

"Come on, Chief." Damnit smiled some more, flashing the gold canine he'd added last month. "It was a practical joke. That could possibly have gotten him a blow job—"

"Chuck, punch him in the junk, and you're even."

Damnit cut the shit and stood up straighter. "*What.*"

"I love you, Chief." Chuck put his hand on that heavily muscled chest, right over his heart. "And I mean that as a leader, a friend, an example of good works everywhere—"

Damnit double-clapped his happy tackle. "Seriously, I'll sue. I will sue you, the city, him, this firehouse. There are rules, you know."

"Oh, right." Tom reached back and took the city's human resources manual off his shelf. Cracking it open, he drawled his forefinger down the table of contents and then opened the thing at about the halfway mark. "I better make sure I follow procedure—okay, I'm supposed to give you a warning first." He looked up at Damnit. "Damian Reichmann, Chuck Parnesi is about to turn you into a soprano. Chuckie, g'head."

"Take it like a man, Damnit." Chuckie smiled like Jason on the right Friday of the month. "Besides, it'll help you hit the high notes in the shower—"

The clanging of the alarm bell going off was an eraser on the board, swiping away the fun and games.

"Back to work," Tom said as he pivoted and checked his computer screen.

"What we got?" Chuck asked.

"One-alarm that's now a two down on Harbor and Eighteenth. Looks like the four-nine-nine is already there."

"One of those warehouses?" Damian said.

"Yeah. They're only requesting one engine. You boys take the call. Ropes's still got that bum shoulder from last night—"

Vic Rizzo, a.k.a. Ropes, broke into the office. He had a cell phone up to his ear and one arm in a sling. "It's Anne. Your sister's trapped in there."

Tom knocked his chair over as he burst up. "Is she alone? Where's the rest of the crew?"

Later, Anne would wonder what exactly it was that made her look over her shoulder. It couldn't have been a sound because her heavy breathing in her mask drowned out even the roar of the fire. And it wasn't anything visual. She didn't have eyes in the back of her helmet. But some kind of instinct called her from behind, and she pivoted against her left arm, glancing toward a wall of fire that had spread down the vertical particleboard.

From the midst of the swirling red and yellow flames, a massive figure plowed through the partition, its force so great, things didn't so much break apart as powder into sparks.

And it had a chain saw.

There was only one person that size who would be insane enough to bring a gas-powered tool with him to rescue her.

As a lit part of the walling fell off Danny Maguire's enormous shoulder, his head beam hit her square in the face, and she looked away as her retinas squeezed tight.

Thank you, God, she thought as she blinked to clear her vision.

"I'm trapped, Danny! I'm stuck—" When she didn't hear her own voice over the radio, she realized her unit must have been compromised.

Pulling back against her hand, she pointed to show him what her problem was, and he nodded, that light of his moving up and down. With a powerful pull, he ripped the chain saw to life and came forward, wielding the twenty-five-pound piece of equipment like it was an empty coffee mug. Pumping the gas, a high-pitched whine rose and fell above the din as he assessed the wooden beam that had just fallen and was now part of the tangle. Moving herself to the side, she shoved something relatively light off her—a laptop, or what was left of one.

The blade and its chain came within inches of her facial mask, but

she didn't wince. As reckless as the man could be in real life, he was a
surgeon with anything that cut wood or building materials—

Without warning, a ten-foot-by-ten-foot section of the ceiling fell
on them, and she dropped her head, bracing against impact. When
she wasn't crushed, her first thought was that Danny was holding that
whole part of the building up—but no. That beam he'd been about to
cut had caught the load and was keeping it at bay.

But if he cut the length now, they would get buried.

The chain saw's engine went silent, and as he put it down at his
feet, she could tell he was cursing inside his mask, his eyes in a nasty
squint as he scanned the collapse. Then, with an arch to rival a bridge
span, he grabbed ahold of her jammed forearm. When she nodded and
sank into her legs, she watched the brim of his helmet dip three times.

One . . . two . . . *three.*

They both pulled and the pain that shot up her arm and into her
shoulder had her grinding her molars to keep from screaming. When
she couldn't handle it for a second longer, she shook her head and
bumped her body against his.

Danny released her. Looked around again. Behind his mask, his
mouth was moving; he was talking into his radio—and she could
guess what he was saying.

Anne gave a couple more half-hearted pulls. Then, with a curse,
she pointed at the wall he'd come through. "Go!" she yelled inside her
mask. "Leave me!"

Danny leaned over and grabbed her arm again, that cranking grip
of his locking on her so tightly her bones compressed. As he pulled
with his incredible power, her teeth clenched, and her breath shot out
of her ribs—and she took as much of it as she could.

"Stop! Stop!" She sagged as he relented. "*Stop . . .*"

Anne shook her head and motioned toward where he had entered. "Go! I'm done!" Moaning in her throat, she pushed at his huge body. "Go."

When that got her nowhere, she released her mask and shoved it aside. Hot, deadly air, the kind that toasted your esophagus and BBQ'd your lungs, closed her throat.

"Go!"

Behind his mask, Danny was furious and his gloved hands went to try to force her oxygen supply back into place.

"No! Get out of—"

Creaking over their heads made them both duck on reflex. As sparks rained down through the smoke, Anne weaved on her feet. "You're going to die in here! Go!"

Danny put his face in hers. He was ripshit and letting her know it behind his mask, and for a split second, she watched him from a great distance even though their faces were six inches apart.

I'm going to miss you, she thought. *Of all of the people I work with, and everyone I know . . . I'm going to miss you the most.*

Danny yanked his own breathing mask away. "Put your goddamn oxygen back on!"

"You're going to die!" she screamed.

"I'm getting you out of here!"

"It's too late for me! Go!"

As if the fire were excited by their yelling, a hot flare burst out next to them, roasting the skin on one side of her face. Danny cursed and forced her mask back on, and she was still hollering at him as he reestablished his own air and then bent all the way over to the floor. Picking up the chain saw, he backed away a couple of feet and went on a discus spin, releasing the Craftsman at the top of the arc, the tool flipping end over end into the wall of fire. Then he covered her with his body, forming a shield.

The explosion was loud and immediate, the gasoline in that tank heating up until it created sufficient pressure to blow the Craftsman apart, the bomb detonating with a brutally hot kiss.

Anne ripped her mask off again. He was barking into his radio, but the time had come and gone for plans, and rescues, and her salvation.

"You need to go," she ordered him. "Now."

Danny stopped talking, his face going still behind his clear shield. And then he removed his oxygen supply. "We die together, then."

He was every bit as resolved as she was, an unstoppable force meeting an immovable object. Exactly as it always had been between them. God, why did she think death would change anything? And the man wasn't going to leave her. Between his brother dying on the job three years ago and then him losing Sol twelve months ago, all of his nope-I-don't-have-PTSD was going to make it impossible for him to go through that kind of mourning again.

Anne looked down at her arm. It was her left one. Not the hand she wrote with. And she was never getting married, so it wasn't like she needed to worry about a ring finger.

Clean cut, she thought.

"Cut it off," she said over the crackle and spit of the fire. To help him understand, she pointed to her forearm. "Tourney and cut!"

Danny's blue eyes flared, and he shook his head as he looked around again, assessing all of their no-go options.

Anne released the straps on her tank under her pits and let the weight drop off her. Then she bit her right glove off and spit it out. The fastenings down her fire-resistant jacket released one by one, and she kicked the heavy folds off so that that one sleeve pooled the entire weight at her trapped wrist.

"Tourney!"

Shit, it was hot. She could feel her skin prickle in warning—or maybe that was her shirt melting into her arms. But she had other problems.

Danny released his mask and put his face in hers. "Listen, James Franco, this isn't fifty-seven hours!"

"The movie was *127 Hours*!"

"Are you *seriously* arguing about that right now!"

"Tourney me and do it!"

"That's it. I'm demanding backup—"

"Do you want to kill all of us? Either leave me or do it!"

She would have taken care of the problem herself, but the angle of the blade needed to be right . . . and oh, God, was she out of her mind? What was she saying?

"Cut my hand off or leave me!"

4

Danny was rank furious as he tried to get Anne's jacket back on
her. Was she out of her fucking mind—

A resounding groan escalated into a roar, and more of
the floor above collapsed around them, coming down the slope created by that panel held up by the beam tangle. Arching over Anne, he
protected her, bricks and pieces of particleboard punching at his
shoulders and crashing on his helmet.

When things stopped hitting him, he discovered an unexpected
bene. Smoke was escaping fast in a new direction, the rush-hour-
worthy evac suggesting a way out might have opened that hadn't been
there before. The flames were so thick, he couldn't be sure.

"Cut it off!" she yelled at him.

"Will you shut up with that!"

He kicked shit out of his way and attempted to get her mask back
into place again, but she fought him—even as consciousness began to
go in and out for her, her eyes rolling back, her weight weaving. And
still that goddamn hand of hers was squeezed in between a trap of
beams and crap that looked like pieces of machinery and a desk.

"Pull with me!" He wrapped himself around the back of her once more and took her forearm in his palms. "On three. One!" *Maybe this will work.* "Two!" *Please, God, let this work.* "Three!"

They both strained, her strong body bowing until her boots slipped out from under her and he had to catch her.

"Dan!"

As Anne barked his name, he refocused on her—and she put her free hand to the side of his mask.

"Do it, Dan," she said. "Or you have to go. I'm okay with dying. Honest."

He stared into her eyes through his facial shield. His breathing was a freight train in his ears. His body was shaking under his PPEs. His mind was racing through solutions, too many of them getting rejected.

Oh, wait, actually all of them getting tossed.

"Fuck," he said.

"I'm sorry."

Releasing his mask, he pushed it aside and locked eyes on hers without any barriers. *It wasn't supposed to end like this . . .* although even as he thought that, he wondered what the hell their other option was. He and Anne Ashburn were both death-wish idiots, the kind of people who pushed limits, and themselves, until shit got broken.

Danny looked around one last time. Then he shifted his eyes to her arm and wondered, *Can I do this?*

"It's the only way," she said into the smoke and heat. "If you won't save yourself."

He didn't make a decision. He just started moving. Because if he thought for a moment—for one goddamn *millisecond*—that he was going to hurt her? He was going to vomit the pepperoni-and-onion pizza, side of fries, two Cokes, and a cherry pie he'd had for dinner all over the fuck.

With hands that shook, he pulled off his gloves, unlatched the front of his jacket, and reached in through his bunkers to his woven nylon belt. When he brought the strap out, Anne closed her lids. And shrugged out of her heavy jacket again.

Danny drew the strap around her upper arm, busted the fork in the buckle, and pulled the length tight. She was right with him, reaching across with her good hand and taking the end, cranking it over until her bicep puffed up around the ligature.

Nope, he thought. If she lost consciousness and couldn't hold that tight, she was going to bleed out. Plus, he was going to have to carry her once she was free because chances were good she was going to go into shock—so he couldn't keep it in place.

Pushing her hand away, he loosened the length and made a slip-knot. "Brace."

When she nodded, he used all of his strength to make a self-holding tourniquet, and the grunt she let out went through the center of his chest like a bullet. But it worked. Even though her upper arm was well muscled, the nylon bit into her flesh like fangs, going deep and locking in.

With a yank, he pulled her PPE back up so she would be protected from the heat, making sure the tough fabric was flat and tight over her forearm for a clean cut—

Another warning creak from up above had him ducking and looking to the ceiling at the same time.

"Do it!" she yelled.

The long-handled axe was on his belt, and he popped it free and removed the head cover. The grip was insulated, certified to handle up to twenty thousand volts of electricity. Too bad the bitch was not rated to cover the shock of cutting off a piece of your partner.

Just so you could maybe, possibly, probably-not-but-still, save her life.

Anne stared up at him, unblinking, unafraid. And that steely expression on her face reminded him, not that he needed it, that she was the single most courageous person, man or woman, he had ever met.

I love you, he thought. Not for the first time.

"Put your oxygen on," he ordered. "Or I'm not doing shit."

When she complied, Danny closed his eyes, but only for a second. Then he masked himself and changed position so he could get a clear swing with good aim. Testing his angle, he lowered the blade so it rested on the PPE sleeve in the middle of her forearm. And then he settled his body into a stance, and thought about all the firewood he had been chopping for the winter.

This is no different, he told himself. *This is a piece of wood.*

If he thought for one second it was Anne's flesh and blood, he was going to lose his nerve and fucking maul her.

Clean cut.

One chance.

As Anne went numb, she watched from a great distance as Danny lifted the axe over his shoulder, his powerful arms rising high. For a split second, the reflection of flames on its polished steel blade made the metal glow orange.

She couldn't look away, but she couldn't watch it happen. So she focused on his face, the angry, strobing illumination of the fire making his features animated even as they didn't move behind his mask. She had thought of him as a surgeon no more than two minutes ago. Who could have guessed he was going to—

Raw human survival instinct made her open her mouth to tell him to stop—but she didn't get far. The ceiling across the room caved in with the sound of galloping hooves, bricks from an outer wall landing fifteen feet away from them.

She looked at that wedged beam. That slope. How much was above them. "Do it!"

Danny didn't move.

Until he did.

In a single, decisive surge, he brought the axe down. Blink-of-an-eye time. Nothing more than a quick inhale.

As she was freed, momentum from her pulling back carried her away from the trapping tangle, the blade . . . the hand that she left behind.

The hard landing reverberated not just in her ass but through her whole body, her teeth clapping together, her legs banging into the floor, one shoulder taking the brunt with a holler as her spine torqued.

The cut she did not feel whatsoever.

Anne brought her arm up, and her brain was so compelled by the absence halfway down her sleeve that even the fire and the danger went away. The PPE's tough material had been pulled tight as a result of her leaning away from the axe, and there wasn't any fraying of the fabric or insulation. There was blood, though, and—

Like time wanted to catch up to itself, everything went from slow motion to speed of light.

All of a sudden, Danny's grip was biting through her heavy jacket and he had her up off the floor and over his shoulder. As he took off at a run, she bounced around and tried to figure out where he was going—and then she saw it. The most recent collapse had wiped out a small part of the warehouse's brick shell, and though it wasn't a clear shot to an escape, it was better than the flames—

The world went tilt-a-whirl again as Danny swung her off him and started shoving her over a landslide of debris, through a ragged hole that was about five feet from the ground.

People reached for her. People on the outside . . . were reaching for her. Firefighters—it was Moose, Danny's former roommate, who helped pull her out.

Except then she did the math.

"No!" she yelled as she kicked and fought. "Not without him, I'm not leaving without—"

There were voices, a volley of talk around her as she was dragged over splinters of beams and hunks of metal and crumbles of bricks.

"Danny!" she yelled as she shoved her mask off. "Get Danny!"

A gust of wind pushed the smoke back into the building, and for a split second, his helmet and mask were briefly revealed, his arms pinwheeling as he tried to get over the avalanche. Their eyes met one last time, and even though they were separated by so much, she could make out the blue of his stare—or at least told herself she saw it—

The entire building collapsed without warning, the three floors dominoing down, ash, soot, smoke, and flames joining the rush of dusted concrete, brick and mortar, that exploded out of the hole.

"No!" she screamed. "*Danny!*"

5

Tom had been waiting for two years for this call. This screaming trip across town. This pull-up-to-a-scene with screeching
tires and sweaty palms, this choking panic, this paralyz-
ing fear.

This reality that his sister was trapped in a burning building.

The slide show in his head was single frame, from the past and
without a soundtrack: Anne at seven stuck up in a tree, jumping down
so he could catch her; her at ten pedaling like mad on her bike to keep
up with him and his friends; her at twelve with a jackknife slice across
her leg, telling him he needed to take her to the ER, but not to say
anything to Mom . . .

Her at their father's grave, dressed in black, sitting next to their
weeping mother in front of a hundred firefighters.

And then finally, her on her first day on the job, wearing the navy
NBFD shirt tucked into the same work pants he put on every morning.

From the moment he saw her in that getup, he had known that
this reckoning was coming. But good luck trying to get his sister to
slow down, ease up, chill with the risks. No matter what he had said to
her, she had refused to listen to him, and as he jumped out of his SUV

at the scene, he hated her to his core at the same time he would have given up his own life to save her.

Their mother had already buried one member of the family. Anne had always seemed determined to make it two.

Tom went dead run to the clutch of ambulances by the incident command post. The warehouse beyond was a roaring fireball, more like a meteor that had crashed to earth than anything built by man, and he prayed Anne was out of there.

As he came up to Chip Baker, he demanded, "Where is she?"

Before the IC could respond, the question was answered. As the warehouse collapsed, three firefighters burst away from the disaster like they were being chased out of the building by demons, their escape path accessorized by an explosive cloud of smoke and orange flames. Two of them were carrying someone.

"Sister!" Tom yelled.

As he bolted up to her, he wanted to do the medical assessment himself, and settled for searching her sooted, streaked face—or what he could catch of it. She was screaming and twisting against the holds on her arms and legs, the strobing effect of the engines and ambulances turning her suffering into stop-motion animation.

"Medics," Moose said as the men kept running. "We need medics!"

Anne just kept fighting the guys carrying her. "Danny!"

With a wrench and a kick, she nearly got free, one of her arms going flying and sending out an arc of blood into the air, the splash of red backlit by the flames.

Tom grabbed the firefighter holding her knees and shoved him away. "You're hurt!" *No shit.* "Anne, stop fighting, you're bleeding—"

"Dannnnnnnnnnny!"

The EMTs rushed over with a flat board and neck immobilizer, and he and Moose lowered her to the ground.

Tom knelt down by her head. "They'll get him. They're going to get Dannyboy. Sweetheart, look at me, I need you to calm down—"

Her wild eyes latched onto him through the tangle of her brown hair. "He's still in there!"

More of that blood spooled out from her left sleeve, and he grabbed her elbow and cocked the joint up—

When he saw the stump at the end of her arm, he couldn't process what he was looking at.

No hand.

Where was her fucking hand—

"We got this, Tom." One of the medics tugged him back. "Let us work on her."

"Where's her hand?"

But then the board was under her, the neck brace was in place, and she was being assessed.

Where the *fuck* was her hand?

"Danny?" she shouted. "Don't worry about me, you have to get him out of there!"

Tom looked toward the warehouse just as another collapse happened sure as if there were a controlled detonation taking the structure to the ground. If Danny wasn't out, he had to be dead. No one could survive in that debris field.

As Tom refocused on Anne, a cold numbness hit him on the top of the head and flooded down his body. The sleeve of her PPE had been cut at the shoulder and removed by the EMTs, and what was revealed made no damn sense. A makeshift tourniquet had been applied to her bicep, the red nylon belt locked in place by itself. Down below? A surgical slice, the white of the bones glowing against the deep red of the muscle and the pale stripes of sinew and skin.

The fact that she had been pushed roughly out of the building and jogged across the ground with that thing just looped on there like that made him want to yell at someone. What if it had unraveled? She could have bled out. And what the *fuck* had happened in there?

"Time to transport."

The EMTs got to their feet and picked up the board by the grips. Tom took the IV bag without being invited to, and no one tried to stop him. They knew that when it came to his sister, he was going to help, and he was going in the ambulance, and if anybody had a problem with this, they could go fuck themselves.

"Danny!"

As Anne continued to struggle, he spoke to her. "Stay tight, sis. You just stay tight."

That hand. Dear God . . . her days as a firefighter were over.

It was what he had wished for all along. But not like this. He didn't want it to happen like this.

Danny lay facedown and sprawled under a great weight, his body that of a soldier slain on a battlefield, his Personal Alert Safety System going off. Water was dripping on the back of his helmet and somehow finding a way into one of his ears . . . before it penetrated the cracks in his broken SCBA mask and got into his nose and mouth. It was definitely not blood. The shit moved too fast and it was cool—and it tasted like ash.

Yup, there was a big fucking crack in his mask, the seal broken, but at least the oxygen supply wasn't compromised and enough air got pumped that he had something worthwhile to breathe. Which was good.

The rest of everything was bad. He couldn't hear anything from his radio. And he had no sense of how long he'd been down. The air tank had a lifespan of about thirty minutes, and he'd been with Anne only six to seven—

"Anne . . ." he moaned.

Abruptly, his brain jammed with what he'd done to her, and he tried to reassure himself that at least he'd gotten her out. He'd seen her carried away. That was the last thing he remembered before he'd been hit—

Wait, what had happened to his PASS? Why was his alarm not going off anymore?

What motivated him to fight was the need to find out what had happened next. Had his tourniquet stayed in place on her? Or had the knot slipped or the length broken or . . .

Shit, he had to get out of here to make sure Anne was okay.

No vision, though . . . he couldn't see a frickin' thing and he couldn't feel anything below his waist. Paralysis? Shock? Weight on his legs? He was on his stomach, he knew that much, and one of his arms was bent at a very bad angle. He should probably sense some pain there, but that was evidently a no-go.

With a curse, he tried to move something, anything—nope. He was totally trapped. After a couple more tries, he managed to shift an arm around—the one that wasn't twisted like a pipe cleaner—and he strained to turn his head an inch. When he tried his legs again, they were immobile, and for a split second, he knew pure terror. Were they not moving because they were pinned, or had whatever had fallen on him severed his spinal cord along the way?

Refocus. Inside his PPEs, he was sweating, and maybe bleeding—he didn't know. But the heat wasn't bad, so he suspected the fire was at least contained. Also, the ambient noise level was down, although maybe that was his shock talking. Or not talking. Whatever.

He had to get to Anne.

"Help . . ."

Okay, that didn't carry far. He took a deeper breath. "*Help . . .*"

He had a glow stick and a whistle in his chest pocket. If he could just get to them, maybe he could make some noise, throw some light, that would give the crew something to find him with?

"Help . . ."

With dwindling strength, he gave the whole movement thing one last try, even though, assuming he had a spinal cord injury, that was ill-advised. Grunting, straining, he lifted his head and managed to free his left arm. It cost him, though. What little vision he'd gained on the fritz and something started to hurt in his chest.

Heart attack? Maybe.

He was young, but that was what his father and his grandfather had died of. Widow-makers were what the docs called those occlusions . . .

Not that he had anyone to make a widow.

Anne was the only woman who had ever held his interest longer than it took to have an orgasm. And she was never going to be the marrying type. Hell, she'd cut her own arm off before she'd let anybody put a ring on—

Oh, God, what had he done to her?

Groaning, he patted around with his gloved hand, feeling for something he could bang with or—wait . . . was this a pipe? No way of knowing, but it damn well felt like a cylindrical, super-hard object as he fit his palm around it.

With the speed and strength of someone a hundred and eighty years old, he managed to grip whatever it was and knock it against whatever he could find. Wet wood made a *thucking* sound that didn't carry more than his voice did, but the concrete floor?

He got a good ring out of it.

Danny hit the pipe over and over again, training all his focus on raising his arm the five inches he could and bringing it down repeatedly. With every strike, the thing weighed more and made less noise.

Eventually, he gave up. And realized he was having a lot of trouble breathing.

The oxygen feed was dead. His thirty minutes up. So he'd been unconscious for almost twenty.

And still nothing but that dripping. No voices calling his name. No sirens. No debris removal. Yeah, sure, there wasn't any more collapsing going on, but gravity had already won the grudge match against the warehouse and was doing victory laps around the ruins it had created.

It appeared he was going to die here—and what exactly did that mean?

As he posed the question, he waited for the slide show of his life to roll out, that whole flash-before-the-eyes thing that people talked about.

When his mental screen stayed blank, he thought, *Probably just as well.* There wasn't much he wanted to revisit. But shit, shouldn't he go out with something better than . . . nothing?

All right . . . fine. He was pissed he didn't know how *Game of Thrones* ended. And he was going to miss the taste of cold beer on a hot afternoon in August. And damn it, why the hell had he bothered to quit smoking?

He was not going to miss filling out paperwork, getting stuck in traffic jams, or his chronic bad elbow. He was glad his parents were already dead.

He really hoped he got to see his twin brother on the other side.

Yeah, it would be almost worth all this just to see John Thomas again.

Likely not in heaven, though, given the way they had behaved all those years. But Hell was more fun, wasn't it? And he'd sure as shit know more people down there.

He was never going to know who the next president was going to be, or whether that raise he'd put in for would have gone through, or if that mole on his back was melanoma or not. And his landlady was going to be pissed. Out of the original four of them who had rented her shit hole, Mick was in rehab, Moose had just gotten married, Jack was going to end up moving in with his sister . . . so it was just him left.

Who was going to get all his crap out?

Probably the boys on the crew, and they'd divvy up the good stuff—

Aw, fuck. He was going to get added to the list, wasn't he. That horrible list they lifted whiskey to at the end of a long off-duty night when they were saturated drunk and the emotions they liquored up to forget came plowing back through the buzz like charging bulls.

It was the list of the fallen who had died in the line of duty, the ones who were missed every day and night, the ghosts who followed them on each call . . . the regrets that didn't just have titles in all caps, but faces, clear as day.

Daniel Michael Maguire. Would they recite him in order as the newest one, or by his brother, John Thomas Maguire?

Anne would drink to him. Anne would raise her glass and think of this night and feel the tightness in her chest and the sting in the corners of her eyes. She would maybe remember the laughs. She would definitely think of working this fire.

And she might just recall that one time they'd made love.

In the end, though, he would be another thing she ran from.

If he could have apologized to her for that, he would've, and wasn't fate a bitch. He wouldn't be dying now if he hadn't saved her, so she could end up regretting him and carrying the guilt around with her for the rest of her life.

One-handed.

As Danny shut his eyes against the memory of that axe he'd swung, he had a passing thought that he should bang the pipe again.

And that was it.

The end.

6

Victor "Ropes" Rizzo got out of his truck and flicked his cigarette to the ground. Crushing it with his boot, he ignored the way his heart pounded in his rib cage. Up ahead, on the far side of a ring of frozen scruff, the barbequed remains of an old abandoned warehouse were like a corpse at the end of an autopsy.

Holes everywhere. Leaking bricks. Whole sections gone.

Fire trucks were clustered at the collapsed northeastern half, their flashing lights overlapping to form a surging red glow that showed little good news. Those brick outer walls had disintegrated into a slope that was tall enough to require climbing, and his first thought was that if somebody was under all that weight, they were going to need a pine box. But at least the blaze was wholly contained, the hoses off, the steam as yet rising into the night sky while smoke, its not-so-distant cousin, lingered like a specter of the dead in the cold, post-traumatic air.

As his nose tingled at the familiar scent of soot and chemical stink, his eyes tracked the movements of firefighters from both his 617 stationhouse and the 499 while they picked around the debris mountain, their bodies throwing shadows over bricks, concrete blocks, sections of wood.

He hitched his shoulder brace up a little higher under his parka and walked across the cracked asphalt. Incident command had set up post out of one of the engines, but he went right by the—

"You're not cleared for duty, Rizzo."

He shook his head at Captain Baker. "I'm going in. Sorry."

"You're med'd out."

"So file me under concerned fucking citizen."

"I am so fucking tired of all of you!"

Rizzo blew a kiss and marched across to the rescue efforts, his boots crunching over stones slippery from what had been sprayed and then frozen. A couple of the boys sifting through the pile looked at him, and one even spoke up, "No way, Rizzo."

Of course it was his fellow 617 Chuck Parnesi—but at least the 499's crew stayed out of it. Then again, you didn't get involved in another family's drama.

"Seriously, Rizzo—"

"Did I hear someone talking?" Rizzo started to climb up on the pile, his balance all marble-on-a-rickety-table because of his bum-ass shoulder. "I didn't think so."

"Your arm's in a sling."

"And again, I say, wouldn't it be a waste of a someone's time to comment on what is my fucking business."

As Chuck got into a debate with himself, Rizzo tripped and went down to his knees on the uneven slope—but a gloved hand presented itself to help him up. It was Robert Miller, a.k.a., Moose, from the 499. Danny's old roommate. The man's civilian clothes were soaking wet and covered with ash, and there was blood smudged down the front of his shirt. His eyes were pits of suffering, his face pale beneath his trimmed beard.

Rizzo didn't hesitate to take what was offered.

The 617 and the 499 houses were not friends. They were not buddies. They didn't mix down at Timeout Sports Bar; they didn't work out or do off-duty second jobs together; they didn't clap each other on the shoulders and yuk it up if they met in town.

Bust a beer bottle over your head was more like it. They were competitors: for resources from the city, recruits from the academy, performance on the job. Except here was the thing. Both sides suffered from ah-hell-no-that's-my-little-brother syndrome. They were allowed to pick on the other guy, but no one else could, and in this situation, when a fellow firefighter was buried in debris? As far as Ropes or any of the other guys at the 617 cared, it was one of their own—and nobody was going to stop digging until they recovered Danny Maguire . . . or his remains.

With grunts and curses, firefighters were hefting charred beams, toasted office equipment, and bundles of bricks still mortared together out of the warehouse, the metastases growing on either side of the massive hole in the flank of the three-story structure.

Ropes knew better than to try that shit with his arm, so he got busy with his flashlight.

Holy shit. So much of so heavy.

This had to have been a manufacturing facility first, before it had become a warehouse and then a crack den. But why would you put the machinery on the second floor? Lot of weight to crank up to a higher level.

But people were idiots.

As he picked his way through, being careful with where he put his boots, there was the sound of dripping water from all directions, the cold tears of the extinguishing effort falling from anything and everything. The going was uneven, dangerous, and even though the removal effort involved a dozen men and women, there was still so much that he had to mount as he shined his beam down.

Rizzo lasted about a nanosecond before he ripped off his sling. His bad shoulder, the one he'd popped out of the socket again, immediately protested the freedom of movement, but it could fuck right off with that.

Training the flashlight into the slick mess, he searched for a reflective flash, a wink of movement, a sign, a sound, a—

Too many lost.

The thought elbowed in and took over, replacing everything save his visual acuity. But goddamn it, how many more times was this going to happen? How many searches after how many accidents where good men and women were lost? As the crazy bell started to go off in his head, he did what he could to dim the noise; in the end, though, all he could do was ignore it and try to focus through the distraction.

That familiar mental effort was harder and less successful than ever, the opposite of a muscle exercised regularly: Instead of getting stronger, his ability to withstand the chaos in his head was weakening, and his terror was that he was burning out.

If he wasn't doing this job? What the fuck else was there for him.

More with the careful footsteps, higher on the mound of twisted, mangled, burned-out crap, harder with the going now. In his heart, he knew this was not a rescue situation but a recovery one, and he pressed on because he was very well aware that chances were better than not that someone was going to have to do this for him at some point—

"Ropes."

He stopped and glanced over to the left, expecting to see a guy wanting to get his attention. But no one was there.

He'd heard his name, though. He absolutely had heard his name.

Frowning, he turned in that direction, and thigh-high'd one knee to get over a crushed desk. His flashlight, as he trained it into the tangle, was so bright that the wet patches on the blackened metal and charred wooden beams sent strobes back to his retinas, making his vision dance.

An instinct that made no sense whatsoever drew him to a juncture between two more I beams and what appeared to be a printing press and some travel trunks. It was about fifteen feet back from the opening that he'd heard Sister had been pushed through—arguably out of range. From what he'd been told over the phone, the collapse had occurred right as Danny had been shoving her from the building, so no, Ropes decided. Not here—

The movement was so slight, and occurred just as he was swinging the beam away, that he nearly missed it. And even as he pivoted back and did a reexamine, he was convinced it had been a smaller piece of wood or metal slipping down to the concrete floor and catching the light.

Frowning, he squatted further and braced his good hand on something that was still warm from the fire.

And there it was. Way down in there. The telltale reflective flash from the sleeve of a firefighter's PPE.

Rizzo whistled loud through his front teeth as he got down on hands and knees. "Danny! Maguire! Danny! Give me a sign. Move your hand!"

As every single person in the collapse looked toward him, the wait for a response was forever. And then an eternity after that.

But it moved. It fucking moved.

"Maguire!" Rizzo shouted as the others fought their way in his direction. "Stay with me, Maguire!"

Come on, my man, he thought at the guy. *Don't die on me now.*

But that arm didn't shift positions again . . . as if the man's last action on earth was to get help that did not get to him in time.

"Stay with me, Maguire." Rizzo's voice cracked as people tried to get a strategy for lifting everything away without causing another collapse. "Goddamn it, man, stay with me . . ."

University of New Brunswick Hospital
Downtown New Brunswick

Anne didn't so much wake up as rock climb her way back to consciousness, her will using ethereal secures to pull herself to a surface breach of awareness and cognition. And with baseline awareness came dull pain, her body carpeted with sensations that had been filed down by the morphine she was on.

It had to be morphine. Percocet made her nauseous.

As she opened her eyes, her hearing tagged along for the ride, the soft beep-beep-beep of a heart monitor reassuring her that she was alive. The hospital room was the color of oatmeal and had all the variability of decor you'd expect from Quaker Oats: no extraneous furniture, drapes, or even framed posters. The mini TV was off, and the bed next to hers was empty—

Higher reasoning returned with the speed and aim of a boomerang, bringing with it that image of the smoke clearing to reveal the inside of that warehouse just before the deadly collapse.

"Danny!"

With a surge that was more will than wellness, she went to sit up, get up, go find him, except there was an IV line in her right arm—oh, screw that. She reached over to pull it out—

And brought up a stump.

A carefully bandaged, medically addressed stump. The wrappings were bright white, and there were more layers of them at the top, the end bulbing out in a reverse taper. Like she had fennel for an arm.

Shock, the medical kind, not the emotional variety, made the monitor go into an alarm, and thanks to her medical training as an EMT, she reached over and turned the noise off. Then she just stared at the stump, her eyes blinking over and over and over again.

As if that would change the channel to something less horror movie, more kid-friendly cartoon.

Except . . . nope. The batteries on the proverbial remote seemed to have kicked it. She was still looking at what was a very traumatic injury, even if it appeared to have been properly treated . . .

And there was pain, she realized, in a place that no longer existed. Her missing palm and fingers were registering a three-dimensional, resonant discomfort, the severed nerves still talking like there hadn't been a divorce of the nuclear family, as if Christmas morning still had the same five people at the table, around the tree.

Nausea swelled in her belly, a beast awakening, but thank God someone had anticipated that. There was a horribly pink plastic bedpan at the tips of her fingers—

Remaining fingers.

"Oh, God . . ."

As she grabbed the pan and tried to curl onto her side so gravity would help the evacuation, every muscle and bone in her body screamed, and tears made things wavy and indistinct. Not that her vision mattered. Memories came hard and fast, eclipsing the hospital bed, the anonymous room, the medical equipment, and even the pain.

Danny bursting into the hot spot to save her. Danny yelling at her through his mask. Danny . . . with the axe.

And then, once again, that last moment, her out through the hole in the wall, her savior staying behind.

There was no way he survived.

Anne's tears were hot on her cheeks as more images of Danny came to her, the weight of the loss increasing as the sediment layers of what they had shared grew higher and higher. Moose's wedding was the worst. When they had danced. When they had . . . done what they did later.

It was impossible not to view the series of memories as her brain's version of phantom limb pain, her yearning emotions like nerves now servicing that which no longer existed: Danny was gone. Whatever they had had together, those currents of connection and bolts of passion, were now tied to a void. For the rest of her life, be it long or short, all of that potential would never be answered, no Polo for the Marco.

"Danny," she moaned. "It's my fault—"

And right on cue, there he was, opening the door.

Not Danny Maguire, no. Her brother, Chief Thomas Ashburn Jr., the legend himself.

Tom was so tall and so broad that as he came in, the hospital room shrunk down to a shoebox, the ceiling shortening to mere inches, the walls crowding in until she couldn't breathe. He looked the same, with that prematurely gray hair, and the hard, handsome face, and the aura of power and authority—and yet he was not the same, at all.

For once, his eyes were not narrowed with suspicion. Far from it.

"Oh, God, Anne," he said hoarsely. "You're awake."

She looked away from his sympathy. There was a temptation to lean on him, to use his strength to help herself, to rely on her big brother to make all this better. But that was a getaway car with no brakes and a kidnapper behind the wheel.

"You never call me by my real name," she whispered.

"Tonight's different."

Closing her lids, she braced herself. "Did they find Danny's body? Be honest. I'd rather know now."

"They got him out alive. He's in surgery."

"What?" She sat up so fast, she went faint. "Danny? Danny—they rescued him?"

"Yeah. They did."

The trembling came on quick and with violence, and as she sank back down onto the pillows, Tom took a step forward like he was thinking of helping her. He stopped that before she could tell him to back off.

"Anne."

For once, his eyes were sad, and that was far from a comfort. The sympathy from him made her realize how there was no one in her life that she could trust.

"When can I see him?" she asked.

The door swung open, an annoyed millennial in a nursing uniform bursting in.

"Not now," Tom snapped.

The young woman stopped short and looked at him like he was suggesting she'd voted for Trump. "Excuse me?"

"I'm talking to my sister. I'll tell you when you can come in."

The nurse glared up at the mountain in front of her. "I'm here to check on the patient's vitals—"

"Her blood pressure spiked and is normalizing. Same with her pulse. No change on oxygen stats. IV lines running clear and her urine bag does not need to be emptied. Good-bye."

"I'm getting my superior."

"Do that." He pulled the door open and nodded to the corridor. "And I'll throw them out, too."

"I don't know who you think you are, but you're not in charge here—"

Tom leaned down and spoke slow, like he'd made a call about her IQ level and it was not a compliment. "I'm telling my sister about the man who nearly died saving her life. Who is currently being operated on for an internal bleed that, if it doesn't kill him from blood loss, will probably make him stroke out and leave him a fucking vegetable. So yeah, get your goddamn superior, get the hospital president, call the fucking pope—and I will throw every single one of you out of this room. Are we clear, or do I need to draw you a diagram."

The nurse stared at him with such shock, it was clearly the first time anyone had not provided her with a safe, supported, emotionally aware and nurturing, micro-aggression-free educational platform.

And also, Tom was being a total dick.

As the nurse tripped over her Crocs to leave, Anne closed her eyes. "You have *such* a way with people."

"I'm not apologizing."

"Yeah, why would you break with tradition." She lifted heavy lids. "How long did it take them to get him out? And where's he being treated? Here?"

"Why don't we focus on you right now?" When she just looked at him, his lips thinned. "Fine. They found him at the bottom of a ten-foot pile of beams and debris. He had all kinds of broken bones, a dislocated shoulder, ruptured spleen, lacerated liver, and the blood pressure of a corpse when they brought him in."

With all her EMT experience, she ran the profile on a patient like that. "He'll make it," she lied. "He's going to be okay."

Tom shook his head and stared across at the window. Things were pitch-black on the far side of the glass, and his mood matched the night's dense darkness.

"Why do you hate him so much?" she muttered, aware that she was too weak for any kind of confrontation. Especially against someone like her brother.

"It's you I care about."

"Well, I'm going to be fine, too. Give me a week and I'll be back at the firehouse."

"Doing what," he said tightly.

"My job." When her brother went quiet, she glared at him. "Don't start."

"Then don't lie to yourself."

"About what."

"Your career is over." Her brother looked at her. "You're done."

For a moment, she thought of the shocked expression on that nurse's face just now. Yup, her brother's timing was as terrific as his delivery: By all means, when someone was in a hospital bed missing part of a limb, let's bring up the job situation.

It would be rude not to.

"Christ, Tom," she said. "Could you have at least waited until I was released? And screw you, I can do anything."

"Are you even kidding me. Anne. Seriously."

"Then why are you so pissed off? This is what you've been waiting for, right? Me on the sidelines, like a good little girl, letting the real men do the work. These last two years, you've just been waiting for me to—"

"To get killed." He leaned forward. "You got it exactly right, Anne. I've been waiting for the night when I have to go to our mother and tell her that you're dead because—"

"I'm alive!"

"You lost a limb!"

"My hand! And I can still fight after this—"

"No," he ground out as he lashed his arm through the air. "You're med'd out. Permanently. And you know what? You deserve it."

Anne recoiled. "You fucking *bastard*."

"You never follow orders, Anne. *Never*. You violated safety protocol by sending Chavez up to the second floor instead of proceeding in your pairing—"

"So I saved his life. Otherwise he would have been trapped with me—"

"Or maybe he could have gotten you free before Maguire appeared with a goddamn chain saw in his hand." Tom shook his head. "You want to know why I don't like him? Fine. It's because he's just like you. He doesn't listen, and he thinks he's better than the rules. And that's how people get hurt."

"Guess you've done your homework. Did you interview everyone before coming in here just so you could stand in front of my hospital bed with your cloak of superiority and beat me over the head with the rule book?"

"No, I waited until I could talk to Maguire's surgeon personally. Because I knew that was going to be the first thing you wanted to know."

"Well, now you've reported your intel. So you can go."

"Don't get your back up with me. You were in the wrong. Maguire was insane. And both of you are in the hospital. The fact that it only cost you—"

"A place to put a wedding band," she snapped as she lifted what was left of her arm. "Right? You want me stuck inside and knocked up with some man's kid, being just like Mom, waiting for my husband to come home and justify my existence. That was the fucking fifties, Tom. People like me don't have to be barefoot and pregnant any-more—hey, have you heard they let us drive cars and even vote now, too?"

"Leave Mom out of it. And this is not about you being a woman—"

"You sure about that? Oh, and as for Mom, I will bring her into anything I want. I am *not* going to be like her. No goddamn way I am going to get stuck living her life of reflected glory for someone who didn't deserve the hype."

Tom went quiet. "I do not understand you."

"It's more like you don't understand our parents."

"Yeah, well, excuse me if I'm not in a big hurry to buy into your perspective. For one, you're in a fucking hospital bed because you did the wrong thing in a situation where your life and the lives of others depended on you following orders. And two, thanks for taking a shit all over the two people who raised us and worked their asses off so we could end up here, arguing in this hospital. Clearly, you're a great judge of character."

"Whatever, Tom." Unaware she'd sat up, she let herself fall back again on the thin pillows. "You've never wanted me to be your equal. Tack whatever vocabulary you want onto it, but that's what's really going on."

"The hell it is. You never will be like me and not because you're a woman. It's because you've got a chip on your shoulder that makes you impossible to reason with or trust on the job. But like I said, that's over now. You're out, Anne. Good work."

She stared down at the bandage and felt sick about so much. "You know what's funny? I can set my watch by you. You just have to kick me in the nuts, especially when I'm down—and don't bother pointing out that I don't have any. You've spent the last two and a half decades showing and telling me that over and over again. Your position is very clear on the subject."

"Maybe you don't like hearing the truth."

"Try telling it to me, just once, and I'll let you know what it's like."

There was another long, long pause. "You need to call Mom. She's worried sick about you."

"I don't have the energy to help her with that."

"Right. Because you're having too much fun being a burden."

"Does it look like I'm enjoying myself?"

"Call Mom."

Once again, a standoff. And as the two of them glared across the stark room at each other, she was reminded of pretty much every single interaction they had had since she'd entered the fire academy.

With that, she and her brother had become enemies.

"Leave," she told him. "Just get out of here. I'm tired, I hurt all over, and I'm sick of the sight of you."

"Call Mom. That's all I care about."

As Tom pushed his way out through the door, all of Anne's energy funneled from her body and she was left with a skeleton that ached covered by a bag of skin that had ants all over it. Closing her eyes, she was aware of her stomach rolling.

In the background, that alarm began beeping like it was having a seizure.

Or maybe she was having one?

Medical staff ran in, a swarm of blue and white. But as Anne thought about Danny, her brother, her job, her family, she was content to fade away and let them save her . . . or not.

She didn't really care one way or another.

8

And they did.

Save her, that was.

When Anne woke up the next morning, she turned her head to the window and looked out on a gray November day. It was impossible not to view the hospital room as a prison, with the wires and tubes going in and out of her as the shackles to keep her in place.

She had to pee. At least, she thought she did. Maybe it was the catheter irritating her?

Peeking under the sheets, she saw that the thing had been removed. Good to know—oh, that's right. She'd threatened to take it out herself sometime before dawn, and when the staff had challenged her to try, she'd done it with a yank.

Lifting her left arm, she stared at the bandage and heard her brother's voice in her head. Fear, an old, toxic friend, sidled up and joined in by whispering all kinds of things in her ear, too—and yet even that din was drowned out by the abiding sense that she might well prefer to be dead right now.

When surrounded by flames, and no alternative, self-mutilation had seemed reasonable. Now, in this hospital room, with nothing but the postnasal drip of smoke down the back of her throat and an un-seasonal first-degree "tan" on her arms, that imperative seemed a distortion of reality.

Which had condemned her to a life she couldn't even contemplate: an acute nightmare of imminent death traded for a chronic one mired in lack of purpose.

Except come on, she told herself. She was used to proving them all wrong. She would come back from this. She would return to the stationhouse and her crew and her job. Her life. There were prostheses, right? There were accommodations that could be made.

Hell, there were Paralympic athletes who were every bit as strong and powerful as the so-called able-bodied. Attitude to get to the altitude, she told herself. And that shit needed to start right now because she had a long road ahead of her.

On that note, she sat up and reached for the landline phone on the bedside table. Palming the receiver, she went to—

As she brought up the stump, she felt her head spin as she realized she had no fingers to push "0" with. Freezing in place, with that receiver off the old-fashioned cradle, she couldn't breathe . . . but then focus brought her back to life, and wasn't that always the case. Hitting the number with her right forefinger, she waited for an answer.

"Yes, ah—" She had to clear her throat. "What room is Danny—I mean, Daniel Maguire—in?"

When she got her answer, she hung up and sagged with relief. They didn't give hospital rooms to corpses, so he must have lived through his surgery.

After a moment of rest, she took off all the monitoring sensors on her chest and debated removing the IV. In the end, she kept that in, considering it was the source of her morphine and on a pole that had wheels. Both were going to make ambulation easier—

The nurse who burst into the room was going so fast, her crepe-soled shoes squeaked on the linoleum as she pulled up short. "What are you doing?"

Anne gave the woman a talk-to-the-hand—the only hand she had left. "I'm going to the bathroom. And then I'll be back."

As she shifted her legs off the side of the bed and lowered her weight onto her feet, the nurse seemed confused. "Back?"

"Yeah." She grabbed her IV equipment and started for the bathroom. "Like as in leave and return."

Man, her voice was hoarse, her breathing more asthmatic-going-up-the-stairs than twenty-five-year-old athlete shuffling across the floor.

"Ms. Ashburn, if you do not get back into bed, I'm going to call the attending—"

"G'head. Knock yourself out. But I'm just going to tell her the same damn thing."

Put like that, it was clear that her and her brother shared DNA. And like Tom, she was used to ignoring people, so she limped her way across the floor. From out of the corner of her eye, she was aware of the nurse hopping up and down and talking all kinds of whatever, but who the hell cared.

She shut the bathroom door on the noise.

Over on the left, mounted over a stainless steel sink, the mirror on the wall was like a crystal ball with bad news about the future, at once utterly avoidable and completely inexorable.

Good God, she looked like an anime version of herself, assuming her character had gone through a coal mine shaft while being chased by a demon throwing compression bombs at her. Her blue eyes were too wide, and there was soot and ash still in her matted hair and all over her face and neck. The hospital johnny she had on was a mismatch to the fire's temporary tattooing job, the cheerful pink bouquets on their white background making her seem like a trespasser in some grandmother's wardrobe.

The initial burst of I-can-triumph-over-this collapsed, a house of cards hit by the cold, hard gust of her reflection.

And what do you know, that all got worse as she turned away and hobbled over to the toilet. Her new way of life became immediately apparent when she tried to lift up the johnny. One hand. Only. Which meant sloppy, flappy, ends-of-the-hem everywhere, and then she couldn't hold the thing up and move the IV pole closer to the seat and settle her weight properly.

When she finally sat down, tears threatened to explode out of not just her eyes but her soul.

I can't do this, she thought as she awkwardly reached across with her right hand for the toilet paper while holding the johnny up, while peeing, while not passing out, while not getting tangled in the IV tubing, while being terrified about everything, while mourning her mother, her father, her brother . . . Danny.

The bathroom became so crowded with her mind's chaos and sorrow that the oxygen was forced out of it, her lungs pulling nothing in as she began to hyperventilate.

It was a while before she re-emerged. And she would have preferred to wash her hand and face first, but this wasn't a hotel. There weren't guest towels hanging to the side of the sink or little bars of soap. No bath mat to warm the soles of her bare feet or printed notice that there were toiletries available courtesy of the front desk if she forgot to pack something.

This was not a vacation. And there was going to be no getting away from what she had lost.

That hand that no longer existed was going to take up more space than it ever had when still attached to her arm.

Back out in the room, two nurses, a resident, and an attending were standing in a kick line, and they were singing the bars to an old familiar: "You're a Slip-and-Fall Risk, Please Lie Back Down."

Which was the theme to a little-known Disney movie, actually: *Why Can't She for Once Be F*cking Reasonable.*

Anne just walked out on that production. She already knew how it ended. Had the T-shirt, the download, and the book.

Heading down the hall with her IV pole, she discovered that she had to force her eyes to focus or she was going to lose her balance. Every step required tremendous concentration, her forward motion not anything that happened naturally, but rather a conscious orientation of legs, hips and shoulders that required constant maintenance.

The marching band of medical staff behind her was so annoying.

At the elevators, it took her a couple of tries to peg the up button, her forefinger trying to hit a moving target—which seemed a little weird given the fact that the hospital should have been a static inanimate, but whatever. She managed to light it up.

As the doors opened, she was just about to step inside when something hit her hard behind the knees—and as her weight went out from under her, she pinwheeled in a panic.

Only to land in the seat of a wheelchair.

"I told them this was a losing battle. So we were just going to have to roll with it."

Anne looked over her shoulder at the familiar voice. "Oh, God, Moose . . ."

Robert "Moose" Miller, Danny's former roommate, came around and lowered his heft down at her feet. His familiar, bearded face made her eyes water.

"Come here, baby girl," he whispered.

As he held out his arms, there were tears in his bloodshot eyes, too, especially as he looked at her bandage.

"Don't call me 'baby' or 'girl,'" she choked out.

"Okay, Anne. I won't."

She went up against his chest and held onto his shoulders, staring off at a corridor she saw nothing of.

"I was going to his room," she said roughly. "Danny's."

"I'll help you get there, but they may not let us in. He's in ICU."

"I want to try."

"Okay." When they pulled apart, he took a bandana out of his pocket. "Here."

She unfolded the red-and-black square and pressed the faded, well-washed softness to her hot, swollen face. "I don't want to look weak in front of him."

"You could never be weak, Anne."

Moose shooed away the medical staff, and then wheeled her into the elevator while she held her IV pole like it was the leash of a dog with biting history. They went up four floors, and then they were going down a hall with signage she couldn't seem to read and foot traffic that had only two speeds: fast and distracted or slow and somber.

"How bad is he?" she asked as they went along close to the wall. "Do you know?"

"Bad."

"Is he paralyzed?"

"They haven't even gotten to the part where they worry about whether he can walk."

As they came up to the nursing station, Anne was aware of the staff stopping whatever they were doing and staring at her, but she kept her eyes straight ahead as Moose did the talking—and they must have gotten clearance to proceed because they started forward again.

Passing by a number of glassed-in rooms, she saw patients swaddled in blankets, like caterpillars cocooned. On this floor, there were few visitors, and no one was coming and going with flowers or balloons. Death was what paced these halls, playing "eeny, meeny, miny, mo" with its bony finger, picking and choosing, at random or perhaps with a plan, who it would play with next.

Moose stopped them about halfway to the end and went around to open a glass door for her. "You want to go in alone?"

"Yes."

With resolve to get on her feet, Anne went to put both her hands down on the armrests, but as a bolt of pain lightning'd up her left arm, she gasped. No hand there. Only that raw open wound that had bandages for flesh.

Blinking back the agony, she thought, *I can't deal with this. What am I going to do with the rest of my life?*

Who am I going to be?

Pushing all that aside, she struggled out of the wheelchair and went to enter the room—

"Hold up. Don't forget this."

As she glanced at Moose in confusion, he moved the IV pole forward. "Oh," she mumbled. "Right, thanks—"

He didn't release it from his hold. "I need you to know that I tried to—I mean, we all wanted to get to him sooner. We worked as hard as we could to free him. But . . . oh, shit, Anne, he was under these beams that were so fucking heavy they'd crush a car and . . ."

She hugged the man when he couldn't continue, and it was a sad relief to be with someone who also felt guilt. "No one could have done a better job rescuing him."

"This is my fault, I should have—"

Anne pushed him back. "Stop it. How could you have gotten to him any earlier? And you didn't put him there. I did. You and the boys are heroes."

"What if he doesn't make it?" Moose dragged a hand through his hair. "I can't breathe every time I think about it. He's my best friend."

As she stared into his tortured eyes, she knew they were all crazy. Every one of them who got into turnouts, and took their bodies and their minds into open flames for little money and lots of risk, for strangers, for animals they didn't own, for houses they didn't own, for people they weren't related to . . . they were all insane. Because this was the other side of the adrenaline rush, the savior complex, the fight.

Tragedy was but a moment. Responsibility for it was forever.

And eventually, the latter turned you dark on the inside, molding over your emotions, making you toxic and uncleanable even as you looked the same on the outside. For every firefighter she knew who'd been hurt or died on the job, she knew even more who were corpses in their own skin.

They didn't tell you about all that when you were in the academy.

Good thing, too.

"Don't blame yourself," she said roughly. "You didn't let him down, and you're going to be there for him as he heals. And he will. He's Danny Maguire, for godsakes. He's unkillable."

"You haven't seen him yet, Anne. You need to prepare yourself."

She looked into the room. So many machines and wires and tubes—a reminder that the human body was an incredible miracle, its countless autonomic functions a gift when they were operating as intended, and a cumbersome nightmare to have to approximate when they were not.

Taking her IV pole, she entered the sterile space and the sound of the *whrrrring* and the beeping got her truly frightened. And then she actually looked at Danny's face.

Anne gasped. "Dear . . . God."

There were stitches all down one side, as if part of his cheek and half of his forehead had been stripped off. Everything was swollen and purple and red, the features distorted to the point where if she hadn't known it was him, she wouldn't have recognized him.

And then there were his legs. Both in casts, one elevated like the third side of a trigonometry problem. Also, his arm and shoulder were wrapped . . . and he'd been intubated at some point, a bandage at the soft juncture in the front of his throat between his collar bones.

She went over and sat on the edge of the bed because the floor was suddenly going whitecap storm surge on her. She tried to breathe. Failed.

Now she cried again, and fuck it. Danny wasn't going to know.

Taking his battered hand, she dropped her head and let the tears fall from her eyes to wherever they landed.

She had done this to him.

The loss of her hand she could live with as payment for her impulsive decision and rash behavior on scene. But this? This . . . catastrophic . . . injury to him? Even if he came through, she was never going to forgive herself and he was never going to be the same.

She thought of him saying that they were going to be back at the stationhouse, playing pong, before ten.

How wrong. How terribly . . . terribly wrong.

"Why didn't you just leave me?"

As soon as she said it, she regretted the words as they seemed to put the burden on him, and this really was all her fault—

There was a clicking sound.

Looking up, she recoiled. Danny's eyes were open, the white

around the left one blood red, the pupils unmatched and glowing as he stared at her and tried to speak.

"Shh," she said as he struggled to speak around the intubation. "No, please . . . don't talk . . ."

Things started to beep faster, and then alarms went off, and she shook her head. "Don't . . . it's okay—"

Medical personnel burst into the room, and they didn't hesitate to get her out of there, passing her shuffling, trembling body off to Moose, who held her up off the floor in the hall.

On the far side of the glass door they shut, she rose onto her tiptoes to see around the crowd to Danny. His face was turned toward her, and through the chaos of the staff, he still stared at her, his puffy eyelids and all the bruises making it a miracle he could focus even a little.

And then the doctors and nurses blocked her view of him.

Deep in her soul, she knew that was the last time she would see him. That it was the last memory she was going to have . . .

. . . of the only man she had ever loved.

ten months later

9

Harbor Street and Twenty-Second Avenue
Old Downtown, New Brunswick

As Anne turned onto Harbor Street, the tires of her municipal sedan crackled over the broken pavement and she winced at the blinding September morning sun. Putting the visor down didn't help, but there wasn't much to worry about hitting. There was no traffic, no pedestrians, and the commercial buildings in the neighborhood had been abandoned decades ago.

Two hundred yards later, she hit the brakes and stopped across from the singed ruins of what had been a warehouse.

At least up until the two-alarm fire the night before.

There wasn't much left of the structure, the mostly collapsed shell of the place painted black and gray from the blaze's soot and smoke. Wafting over on the autumn breeze, the complex, crappy bouquet of extinguished fire was so familiar, she actually took a deep breath and felt the sting of nostalgia—

The sneeze came out of nowhere, kicking her head forward—and as she righted things and sniffed, it was like her nose was out of shape. Waiting to see if there was another coming, she wondered exactly when her nasal passages had degraded into special snowflakes. Had it been in those brutal first couple of weeks of recovery . . . or later, during PT? Had it been as she'd raced to get into class to get certified as an arson investigator? Or how about when she'd been interviewing around for her new job?

Was it two weeks ago, when she'd been hired by the City of New Brunswick to fill a low-man-on-the-ladder vacancy in its Arson Investigation and Fire Inspection Division?

How about now, on her first official day?

She looked down at the lapels of her cheap office suit. The laminated ID card hanging off a silver clip had her picture on it, and she tilted the thing up so she could see her own face.

Her hair was the same. Sort of. Longer now and loose on her shoulders—and those blond highlights from summer a year before were long gone. Her face? Well, that was the same—actually, no, not at all. Her eyes were grim, and if she didn't know better, she'd say that they were all black pupil, no blue around any rim. Skin was as white and flat as wall paint. Hollows under the cheekbones were testament to the weight she had yet to put back on.

That pink lip gloss she'd thrown on out of some kind of duty looked ridiculous on the thin, straight line of her mouth.

Dropping the ID, she wiped away the Maybelline she'd put on before she'd left her house. She hated the way the stuff tasted, and come on, like it was fooling anyone? She wasn't a lipstick-and-perfume kind of girl, even if she was now a desk jockey.

Reaching for the door handle, her prosthesis *thunked* against the panel and she closed her eyes. Deep breath.

From out of nowhere, she remembered the morning after the fire that had changed everything for her . . . when she'd woken up in that hospital bed and tried to convince herself that she could go back to the stationhouse and resume her life as it was, a triumphant para-firefighter, just like those Paralympic athletes.

Yeah . . . no. Tom had been right. Her career was over.

But she had triumphed over lots of things in the last ten months, including a staph infection that had nearly killed her. Physically, that had been the worst, especially when they'd had to put her in a medically induced coma because her organs had been shutting down. The rest of the road forward had been mostly mental, with blocking and tackling solutions for her lost hand being sought at every turn.

Except as much as she could do now with her various prostheses, none of her skills included dragging a charged line into a fire and spraying down flames.

You can do this, Anne, she told herself.

When she was out on the pavement, she faced off at the warehouse that was her first assigned case and tried to ignore the fact that she was in a suit, not turnouts. That she was after-the-fact, not during. That there was nothing here to do, really.

"Origin and cause," she said as she started to walk across the road.

She was halfway to her goal when she realized she'd left her clipboard, her pen, and her voice recorder in the car.

Anne stopped. And could go no farther.

This whole length of Harbor Street was your typical used-to-be-necessary, nothing but a strip of asphalt accessorized on both sides by ragged scarves of abandoned, block-sized buildings that had, in their earlier, more optimistic and purposeful incarnations, housed manufacturing plants and shipbuilders. The facilities had been built of brick in the early nineteen hundreds, joist'd, rafter'd, and floored by wood planks and beams, and capped by tin.

Used until another pattern of profit motive had rendered them anachronistic.

As she blinked in that bright, blade-sharp sunlight, she found that memories took over and *Back to the Future*'d her to a different, but the same, structure—only this time it was night, and she was pulling up in the pumper with Danny, about to go into that one-alarm that had turned everything on its head.

"You *must* do this, Anne," she declared.

Digging down deep for more of the will that had kept her going, she was exhausted with propelling herself forward. Tired of punching through wall after wall of I-can't, I-don't-want-to, I'm-about-to-break. Life had become one trial after another, only the degree of difficulty and amount of failure what spiced things up.

"Origin and cause," she repeated.

Movement caught her eye and drew her attention to the right. A gray dog with a partially pit bull face, an ear blown up to twice its size, and a scar on its shoulder regarded her from around the burned building like it was sizing her up as a threat.

The two of them stared at each other—and for some reason, she thought of Danny Maguire. Probably because of the injuries the dog had.

She hadn't seen Maguire since that ICU visit. There had been a couple of times when she'd been in the rehab hospital that she'd been tempted to reach out to him, but between her recovery and his, they'd both had plenty going on. And then she'd heard that he'd gone back to work at the 499.

Which had hurt her for no logical reason. What, like her bad break had to be shared by him? Like she expected him to fall on the sword of resignation in her honor?

Come on.

There had been that one voicemail he'd left on her phone—like, three months ago. It had been in the middle of the night and he'd obviously been drunk, his words slurred and incomprehensible. And then a female voice had said his name with enough innuendo and invitation to melt paint off a car door.

So, no, there had been no contact.

"Are you hungry?" she asked when the dog didn't run away.

With slow movements, she went back to the car, got her bag, and brought it with her across the street to the broken sidewalk. Grabbing a Fiber One bar and her bottle of Poland Spring, she got down on her haunches and made what she hoped were encouraging noises.

The dog was slow on the limping approach, its head low, that swollen ear as flat back as it could get, one front paw obviously injured. The animal's ribs were so stark under its thin coat and skin that she couldn't bear to focus on them.

"Here," she said, breaking off some of the breakfast bar.

She tossed the piece right in front of the dog, and it eyed her with suspicion as it dropped its nose and sniffed. The first bite was taken slowly. The second went down a little faster. The third?

Gobbled.

She fed the dog the bar, bringing him or her ever nearer by pitching the pieces closer and closer. When she turned to get the Poland Spring opened, she lost ground, the animal flinching back and costing her a couple of feet.

Pouring a stream of fresh, clean water into her remaining palm was awkward, but she managed. And then she waited.

When the dog finally gave in to its thirst and she felt the first tentative brush of a rasping tongue, tears came to her eyes.

It had been months and months since she had cried. Not since that horrible stretch when the infection had really gotten its grip on her, the Grim Reaper's deadly handshake trying to pull her into her grave. She had had to choose. Did she live or did she languish? Did she fight and claw her way back . . . or did she give up?

"How about I help you?" she whispered as she sniffed hard. "I won't hurt you. I promise . . . I won't hurt you."

New Brunswick Firehouse No. 499
Harbor Street and Second Avenue

Goddamn, he hurt all over, Danny thought as he parked his truck behind the stationhouse and contemplated getting out and signing in for his shift.

Seemed like it was about three hundred and seventy-five miles to the back door. In reality? Probably only thirty feet. But when your head was thumping, your back had turned into a solid during your seven-minute commute, and the healed breaks in both your thigh bones and that fucking left calf of yours were aching because rain was coming, anything more than an inch and a half felt like a marathon.

As he opened the driver's-side door, his shoulder let out a holler and he thought fondly of his new girlfriend. It had been a mere six hours since he'd seen her—or maybe less than that? And he was starved for more of their connection.

On that note, he shoved his hand into the duffel bag on his passenger seat and fished around. When his palm hit what he was looking for, he smiled and pulled out a bottle of Motrin the size of his head. Across the front of the label, in black Sharpie, was written "BETTY FUCKING MAGUIRE."

Yup, he was dating a bottle of ibuprofen.

Popping the lid off, he thought once again that this was, in fact, the healthiest relationship he had ever been in. Betty never let him down, was always available, and improved his life immeasurably. Still, he was jealous over her, and unwilling to share her with anybody—not that she ever complained he was a smothering sonofabitch.

Shaking out six capsules, he took them on a oner, washing them down with some still-hot Dunkin'.

Looking at the back door to the stationhouse again, he breathed in. Someone was cooking bacon and eggs. He hoped it wasn't Duff. The bastard always under-did the former and hard-tack'd the latter—and for a guy who liked super-crispy and sunny-side up that was more tragedy than Danny could handle on a Tuesday morning.

To kill some time, he took out his Marlboros and lit one. Soon as he'd gotten out of rehab last spring, he'd taken the habit back up with a vengeance—but yet again, Betty didn't mind the secondhand smoke, and now that he essentially had no roommates, there was nobody around to complain about the ashtrays.

Perfect.

Sitting back, he closed his eyes. Firefighters in New Brunswick worked an unpredictable schedule, which was always tighter than the national standard of two days on, three days R&R—but with the city in a bad way financially, they had to cover the shifts. At least they were finally getting some newbs, although they were all going to the 617.

Chief Ashburn, who was now pulling double time as an IC due to budget cuts, always worked it so that he got the best of everything: the new stationhouse, the new apparatus, the extra help.

Must be nice.

Danny's lids cracked of their own volition, and his eyes shifted to his hands. There were blisters all over the insides of both, the result of him having worked with a chain saw and some clippers for five hours on Saturday and seven on Sunday. He must have been crazy to buy that old farm. The uninhabited house was crowded by trees and overgrowth, and the various outbuildings on the fifty acres were likewise choked with vines thick as tree trunks.

Shit might have gone easier if he'd used an axe, but he didn't pick them up anymore. Swing them. Cut things with them.

Anyway, at least the farm gave him something to focus on. If he didn't have that shitty property to go to between shifts, he would be clinically insane.

And hey, at least it kept him from dialing Anne Ashburn's number again. Jesus, he shuddered every time he thought about that drunken voicemail he'd left her.

From the moment he'd gotten out of rehab, he'd worked on reasons to call her, go over to her house, email her. You know, reasonable justifications that didn't involve him breaking down and getting all emotional over how he'd failed her in that fire.

The words hadn't come, even as the yearning had gotten stronger. So add too many beers and the fact that he'd memorized her number from the instant she'd given it to him almost three years ago—and you had a drunk dial that should never have happened.

She hadn't called him back. Why would she? And now hitting her up felt impossible.

Curling his left hand into a fist, he felt the worn spots burn and the heavy calluses protest at the contraction. Across the knuckles, there were countless cuts from the thorns on those bushes he'd ripped out, and then there was a bruise on the back of the wrist from when he'd clonked it on something.

He hated his left hand now—

"You comin' in for breakfast or just gonna hang out here and give yourself cancer?"

Danny glanced over at a screaming-yellow Dodge Charger that had black rims, blacked-out windows, and a red stripe down the side.

Moose was leaning against the quarter panel, arms crossed, mirrored sunglasses making him look like a bearded eighties action figure.

"I'll take the cancer if Duff's at the stove."

Moose frowned. "You shouldn't say shit like that."

"It's the truth." Danny deliberately took an inhale. "People need to stop being so politically correct."

"Got nothing to do with politics. It's bad luck."

Danny laughed with an edge. "Oh, I've already had my share of that. I won the shit out of that lottery, thank you very much."

As Moose just stared at him, Danny shook his head. "You got something to say to me?"

Although come on, it wasn't like he couldn't guess.

"Duff told me he took you home Saturday night."

"Jealous? Don't worry, we stopped at third base. And besides, you have your beautiful new wife to keep you warm at night."

"Still bitter about that, huh."

Danny opened his mouth, but he stepped off that ledge. His dislike of the human race had only intensified since last November. There were some things, however, that went too far even for him, and Deandra, Moose's new old lady, was one of them.

But he wasn't jealous of the marriage. Hell, if he were, all he had to do was snap his fingers and that gold digger would be on her back in his messy bed in a heartbeat. And Moose knew this. Which was why he'd insisted on putting a ring on it.

Like that meant she wouldn't leave him.

"Whatever," Danny muttered as he exhaled.

Moose looked away. Looked back. "You got a lot of people worried about you."

"That's on them." He examined the lit tip of his cigarette. "Have I been late for work, even once?" When there was no response, he glanced at his former roommate and cupped his ear. "Did I hear you say no? I think I did. And have I slacked on scene? Wait . . . is that another no? Why I believe it is."

"Your drinking is—"

"And here's a last one. Have I asked you, or anybody else, to comment on my fucking life?" He grabbed his duffel and got out. "We both know the answer to that one."

Taking a last drag, he blew the smoke over his shoulder. "So how about all of you shut up and worry about your own goddamn situations. I know all too well exactly how not-perfect your marriage is, for example, but you don't hear me going on about that, do you."

Before shit got way too real, he started to march off.

"How about you say hi to Anne for me," Moose bit out. "The next time you see her."

Danny stopped dead. As his hand tightened on the straps of his bag, he felt a rage that went so deep, he knew without a doubt that he could kill from it.

But what was behind the anger was even more toxic, a swill of pain and self-hatred that made all the crap he'd gone through with his brother's death and then losing Sol seem like warm-up exercises for the real challenge.

On the surface of his life, he was dragging through the minutes and the hours of the present. His reality, though, was stuck in that collapsing stairwell with Anne . . . and what he'd done with that axe of his. It was *Groundhog Day* 24-7, and the shit was wearing his ass out. But that was where some people ended up in life.

He did not need the reminder of his reality from his best friend, however.

"Fuck you, Miller," he said as he started walking again.

10

New Brunswick Firehouse No. 617
McGinney Street and Benedict Avenue

Behind the wheel of his city-issued SUV, Tom shifted his cell phone to his other ear as he made the turn onto McGinney Street.

"I don't know whether the mayor's serious or not . . . no, I don't. Get over yourself, Brent. She's a goddamn politician, and she's just announced she's running for a second term. She'll tell us anything we want to hear just to get the union endorsement. So no, I don't trust her." He let the union president drone on a little, and then had to cut that shit off. "Listen to me, do not confuse this woman's looks with virtue. She's charming you up and I'll be goddamned if I let us get pulled in a bad direction just because you like the smell of her perfume."

As he cut the call and tossed his cell onto the empty bucket seat in his Explorer, he thought . . . hell yes, this was his car. Even though the vehicle was issued by the city and in his possession only because of his job as chief, it was his personal property, damn it.

Then again, he considered all of the stationhouses and each one of the engines, ladders, trucks, ambulances, and all the marked cars as his.

The people, too. Which was why he needed to get Brent Mathison out of that job at the firefighters' union. The guy was too soft on the mayor and could not see the way she was manipulating him.

Stupid. But he didn't dislike Brent or anything. How could he? All the men and women in the fire service were . . . well, not his children, no. He was not parent material. And they weren't his family.

Even his family wasn't his family. Wife had hit the road. Anne was off the radar and out of the Christmas card photos. All he had left was his mother, and even with her, there was a lot of duty there—he was all she had.

And what she really wanted was her daughter involved in her life.

Thoughts of Anne put him in an even worse mood as he pulled onto the concrete pavers that went up to the four bays of his station-house. Everything was open, the sunshine glinting off the chrome and the glass and the red panels of the engines and the ladder trucks.

The 617 was the newest of the six houses in New Brunswick, functioning as the Fire Rescue Master Station. Built just six months prior, the four-story brick building had state-of-the-art facilities, including an office for him with a conference area, a restaurant-quality kitchen, a mess hall and rec room, a weight room, and, on the third and top floors, private suites for the overnighters.

No more common bunk room or communal shower. Which was good news.

With the divorce, this wasn't his second home; it was his only one.

And bonus—at least to the beleaguered city? The building had been erected as a gift by Charles Ripkin, a billionaire property developer, in thanks for the city's firefighters saving his daughter in a blaze. Now, if Tom had been asked, he would have preferred for the several million dollars to be apportioned around the five older stations for upgrades. But rich guys liked to make a statement, and the city was hardly in the position to turn that kind of cash down.

Heading around back, he eased the SUV in between Chuckie P's Jeep and Vic Rizzo's blacked-out F-150. Behind the shallow parking area, there was a lawn with a volleyball net as well as some picnic tables and a grill. The big, fat-topped trees that had been spared during construction had turned brilliant red and gold, and the grass was still green—although none of that would last. The grays of November and blue-whites of December and January were coming fast.

Just before he got out, he reached across and snagged his cell phone. The screen was cracked because he threw it a lot, and going by its current state of degeneration, he was guessing he had another month of functionality left, tops.

He hadn't expected to be so angry as an adult.

And as he thought about his sister, and how she wouldn't have answered if he'd called her, he decided he hadn't expected a lot about life.

He left his vehicle unlocked and went to the back door—

What . . . the *fuck*?

A shadow thrown on the lawn from the far side of the building suggested some douchebag was taking a piss on the stationhouse.

The bastard was *literally* planted there with his hand on his hose, a fine stream of urine arcing from the tip of his dick.

Tom marched over without screaming so he could catch the SOB and rub his nose in the mess like a fucking dog—

As he came around the corner, he stopped and became even more furious. The guy was wearing a New Brunswick FD navy blue T-shirt, navy blue work pants, and work boots. Everything was so new, there were no scuffs on those Carhartts, and both the shirt and pants still had creases from when they'd been folded at the factory.

"Goddamn it!"

The new recruit spun around, and his cock came with him, a golden stream fanning out so that Tom had to jump back.

You want to talk about pale? The FNG, who couldn't have been more than twenty, twenty-two, turned white as a Band-Aid pad. Then again, Tom's mug had been in the paper a lot, and there were few in town who wouldn't have recognized his salt-and-pepper hair.

Which was turning whiter by the frickin' second.

"OhmyGod."

"He pulled the lemonade trick, didn't he," Tom muttered.

"The bathrooms are out of commission! Chief, I swear, I—"

"Zip your dick up and get back inside—but first hose off my fucking house."

Tom left the recruit and nearly tore the door off its hinges as he went inside. Sure enough, front and center on the mess hall's table was a big fat jug of lemonade—that was three-quarters of the way empty. As well as a glass.

"Damnit!" he yelled. "You get your ass to my office right fucking now!"

Same shit, different day.

Across town, at Metro Emergency Veterinary Clinic, Anne stood up as the vet came in. She'd been waiting in this exam room for the last hour and she wiped her sweaty hand on the seat of her slacks.

"How're we doing?" she asked.

Dr. Delgado was a fifty-year-old woman with thick dark hair, no makeup, and the kind of face that made your heart rate ease up.

"Well," she said, "we're malnourished. We have worms. Fleas. Ticks. An infection in the ear flap and in the shoulder. A paw with a laceration in between the pads. There's a tooth cracked in the back of our mouth that will have to be removed. Do you want to come see him?"

"Ah . . . sure. Yes."

The vet smiled. "Come this way. He's been neutered, by the way, so he was owned by someone at some point."

Anne followed the woman out and down the corridor of exam rooms, the muffled barks and meows behind the closed doors suggesting the practice was a busy one. Entering a more clinical space, they proceeded over to a line of cages. The stray was down at the far end, curled in the corner as if he were terrified but used to being helpless.

"Hey, big guy," Anne murmured as she went across and got down on her haunches. "How you feeling?"

A tentative wag greeted her, just the tip of the tail moving.

"He recognizes you," Dr. Delgado said. "Anyway, you can pick him up tomorrow, assuming he does well on the antibiotic shot. I had to give him some powerful—"

"Pick him up?" Anne got to her feet. "I don't understand."

The vet's face grew remote. "I thought you were adopting him."

"I can't— I mean, no. I'm not a dog person. I'm not a pet person." She rushed on with, "But I mean, I'll pay for the charges. And his food and stuff until he's adopted."

"We're not really equipped to hold onto him after he's been treated."

"You must have people who want dogs, though."

"I'll do what I can. But he's part pit and that can be a problem. If we can't find someone, he'll have to go to a shelter."

Anne took a deep breath. "Okay, and someone will take him home from there, then." There was a pause. "Right? I mean, people adopt all the time. He'll find somebody to care for him."

"He'll have a week. If he's lucky. But again, with the pit in him, I'm not sure anyone will want him." The vet took a step back. "We have your credit card. I'll keep you posted on the charges."

"And how he is?"

"If you want"—the vet put out her hand—"I'll be in touch."

Anne shook the palm that was offered and then looked back through the steel weave of the cage. The dog stared up at her, his exhausted, pale brown eyes suggesting that all the things getting done to him and the stuff being pumped into his frail body was just one more scene in a nightmare that had started a long time ago.

"I'm sorry," she said to the dog. "I really am."

He wagged one last time and put his head down on the paw that wasn't bandaged. As Anne turned away, she got busy checking out the clinical space, everything so neat and clean, the techs and vets walking with purpose, the stainless steel tables and X-ray machines and clear-fronted cabinets of supplies as professional as any human-grade clinic she'd ever been to.

The next thing she knew, she was behind the wheel of the municipal sedan in the parking lot. Looking over to the front seat where the dog had been, she noted smudges of dirt and some stains she knew were blood. She was going to have to clean that all up.

As her phone rang, she jumped and fumbled in her bag. When she saw who it was, she cursed. "Hello? Mr. Marshall?"

"I told you, call me Don," her new boss said. "I just wanted to see how you're doing. Making progress?"

She stared at the outside of the vet office. "Yes, as a matter of fact, I am." Reaching forward with the key, she started the sewing-machine engine under the hood. "I should be back in the office in an hour. Or two."

"Well, that would be good, sure. But tell me, are you planning on spending any time at the scene?"

"I'm sorry?"

"The GPS on the vehicle you were assigned to is reporting you've been about seven miles away from the fire scene for the last hour and twenty minutes. I'm just curious what you're doing and where?"

Grimacing, she put her forehead down on the steering wheel. "I, ah, I found a stray."

"Bullet?"

"Dog."

There was a beat of silence. "I'd like you to come back to the office if you don't mind. I need to have a word with you."

"Yes, sir."

Don Marshall hung up, and Anne didn't waste time. Putting the sedan in drive, she lowered the window and took off, making her way back to the Fire and Safety Building. Traffic was pretty light, and it took her less than ten minutes to trade one parking lot for another.

As she was getting out and locking up, she composed a little speech along the lines of how seriously she was taking her new job and how much she wanted to work for—

Don was waiting for her at the front entrance of the sprawling black, steel, and glass building, the man standing in the sunshine, eating something. He was a tall, thin guy, built like the basketball player she'd heard he'd been, and his tightly trimmed Afro had all kinds of gray at the temples. Rumor had it he'd dropped out of Syracuse, where he'd been playing Division I college ball, and joined the Army. Considering how cut-and-dry he was, she could see him in a military uniform.

And he certainly had the been-through-it-all affect of somebody who had seen combat action.

"I'm so sorry," she said on the approach. "I won't ever get distracted again—"

"Walk with me," he ordered as he turned away, not waiting for her to catch up.

It was a bagel. He was eating half an onion bagel that had about two inches of cream cheese on it.

"So you know how many people wanted your job?" he asked as she fell into step with him on the sidewalk that made a square around the building.

"No, sir. I don't."

"Take a guess."

She thought about how bad the economy was. "Ten? Fifteen?"

"None." He stopped and looked down at her. "No one. The position was vacant for six months before you applied."

"Oh." Was she supposed to apologize? "I'm sorry."

"I think you and I need to be clear with one another." He put the last bite in his hopper and wiped his mouth with the napkin he'd been using as a plate. "I will fire you and go back to an empty desk before I put up with crap for effort. I took a chance on you—"

"Because of my arm," she said bitterly.

"No, because I know you don't actually want to work here." He resumed his long stride. "You'd rather be back on an engine, dragging hoses into a fire. The reality, however, is that you're out of that option, and I've got a backlog of cases that need to be looked at with only three investigators—one of whom is relocating because his wife took a job in St. Louis. Oh, did I mention another is pregnant and probably going on bed rest in a week? I won't have her back until after she's through with maternity leave. But allow me to reiterate. I would rather have an empty desk than someone who isn't getting work done. I don't care if I have to go out into the field myself. So you either get real and be serious about this opportunity, or you can file for unemployment for the twenty-four hours you've earned it for."

Anne shook her head. "You don't know me."

"Yeah, I do. You're someone who walks off the job site before she gets started. And lies to me when I call her and ask her how things are going."

"I'm sorry. That was the wrong thing to do, and from now on, I'm not going to let you down."

"Me? You're not going to let *me* down?" Don Marshall stopped again. "Wrong way to look at this. Someone died in that fire you blew off so you could make a trip to the vet's. A crime against property was committed, and in the course of it, somebody died. Maybe it was a vagrant. Hell, it probably was. But they had a mother and a father or they wouldn't be on the planet. What you fail to understand is that this job you think is a step down from your calling, your passion? It's actually justice at work. Unless there was faulty wiring involved—which is impossible because the grid to that block was shut down two years ago—someone walked in there, set a fire, and let the structure burn to the ground. I can't make you care about helping the police find that criminal. I can't wake you up to the fact that this work you no doubt consider a desk job is critical to making people safe. But what I *will* do is boot you out of my department if you don't prove to me you're worthy of my standards. You had your calling. This is mine. Are we clear?"

Anne swallowed hard. "Yes, sir."

"Now, get back in that car, and go back to that site, and try to do the job the taxpayers of this city are paying you for. And remember, you're a probationary employee for the next ninety days and I can fire you without cause or notice."

"Yes, sir."

Mr. Marshall nodded to the parking lot. "G'head. G'on now."

"Yes, sir."

Anne wheeled away and blindly walked off. She was halfway to the car when Don called out, "What about the dog?"

She turned back around. "The dog?"

"What did you do with it?"

"I, ah, I made sure it's at a good vet's."

"Better than the streets."

"Yes, better."

Lifting a hand, she returned to the car before she apologized again. Remade promises the man didn't want to hear. Got teary about an animal she was abandoning even though the thing wasn't hers in the first place.

God, she was so sick of life.

She really was.

11

Box alarm. Two engines and a ladder from the 617 responding to back up the 499.

As Tom arrived on scene, he pulled up behind the ambulance, and got out. The primary house on fire was a cheap, worn-out two-story—and its equally rundown next-door neighbor was looking pretty toasty as well, the wind carrying the flames across a tiny yard and onto siding that was dry.

It was a little unusual to smell the electric burn in the air. Still, faulty wiring wasn't solely the purview of 1920s bungalows and fifties-era cottages.

The plumes of water being used to fight the initial blaze were coming *out* of the windows on the first floor. Then again, the 499 was already on scene, and of course, those dumbass cowboys had dragged lines into the house, as opposed to extinguishing the flames via an external position.

Tom strode over to Captain Baker, the incident commander, and was not about to be diplomatic. "What the *hell* are you doing, Chip?"

The man held up a hand. "Don't start with me."

"Why are those idiots in the house?" He knew the answer,

though. "Chip, you gotta backbone this shit. Come on. You're in charge here."

"The fire's almost out."

Tom shook his head and opened his mouth—but then he caught the pisser recruit walking by.

Reaching over, he grabbed onto the sleeve of the kid's turnout. "Stop. This is done wrong."

The newbie halted and looked up with wide anxious eyes. His name was Reggie, but he'd already been given the nick of "Wedgie"—which, considering his last name was Boehner and it could have been "Boner," wasn't all that bad.

"You fold this side first, secure here . . . and buckle here. They taught you this at the academy."

As Tom made quick work of the jacket, the kid nodded and stammered something. And was cut off as glass shattered on the second floor.

Smoke billowed out—and then flames.

"Goddamn it," Tom muttered, "it traveled up inside the walls."

Wedgie blinked. "Huh?"

"Go help get the house next door wet." He shoved the kid forward. "Chip, get those boys out of there. Or I will."

"Bring those lines out," Baker barked into the radio. "Repeat, all lines and personnel out. Now. Reposition southwest exterior, six-one-seven fighters next door."

Three firefighters emerged from the open front door, dragging lines with them. Emilio, Duff, and Moose, Tom guessed by the body sizes.

"How many did you send in there?" he asked. When there wasn't a reply, he elbowed Chip. "I said, how many?"

"Four."

"And who's the fourth?"

The answer to that question presented himself by breaking a second-story window and jumping out onto the asphalt-shingled overhang above the front entrance.

Danny Maguire had a preteen girl in his arms, his oxygen mask over her face even as she struggled against him. "Medic!" he barked.

People ran over and held out arms. There wasn't a ladder truck free, but they didn't need one—at least not for this rescue. Maguire got down on his knees and handed off the victim—while keeping his mask tight to her face.

"Keep it on her!" He shrugged out of his tank. "Take this with her!"

The girl was thrashing and yelling about something, pointing back into the house.

"Don't you dare," Tom muttered. "Oh, hell no, you are *not* going back in there without your—gimme that!" He reached over and yanked the radio command out of Chip's hand. "Maguire! You are not fucking going back in there—"

Dannyboy didn't miss a beat. He stood up, turned away . . . and crouched down to shove his huge body back through the window he'd broken.

"Are you fucking kidding me, Maguire!" Tom yelled.

The fire coughed out a plume of gray smoke through the broken window, and then there was the telltale lick of flames. And Maguire was in there without his mask.

"Personnel, stay out of the structure." Tom held the radio so hard, the plastic casing cracked. "Stay out of there!"

The hoses were turned on again, graceful streams of water arrowing in on the hot spot. God only knew where Maguire was in the house or what he had gone back for. But at least the girl had been carried to safety to the lawn across the street, medics clustering around her as she coughed and struggled like she wanted to get back in there herself.

Cat or a dog, no doubt.

Fucking pets.

"Six-one-seven, you focus on the left for the spread," he commanded.

On cue, his boys snaked lines to the house next door that had caught the fire like a cold from a fellow bus rider who had sneezed: Kindling had a better chance of resisting an open flame, but that was eighties particleboard for you. The shit was right up there with birthday candles for getting lit up.

Wedgie was overwhelmed charging his line. But that was to be expected. First fire was always an eye-opener, and as much as the kid was trying to focus on getting the cap off a hydrant and screwing the hose head on, he kept glancing back at the first home.

Like maybe he expected Maguire to come out on fire.

"Maguire, can you respond?" Tom said into radio. "Maguire, get out of there, over."

He didn't expect any kind of reply.

"Maguire, where are you in there?" he said. "Over."

A fireball curled out of the window Maguire had broken, and Tom thought, *Well, isn't this great.*

"We need water to the second floor," he ordered. "Four-nine-nine, I want Chavez and Duffy on that. We're losing ground."

Off to the side, Chip Baker was pacing back and forth with his hands on his hips and his head down, like he was cussing his chief out in his head. Good thing Tom was used to people who didn't perform being pissed off at him when he took over. If that shit had bothered him?

Well, then he'd be Chip Baker, wouldn't he—

The crash came from the first-floor bay window, the glass shattering outward as something massive broke through it. But it wasn't a TV or an ottoman or even a love seat being used as an escape tool. No, it was Danny Maguire's shoulder first and then huge body afterward—which included his big, fat, empty, helmet-less head.

Because, somehow, he hadn't lost that. And really, wasn't that a miracle for someone who'd given away his air supply, his radio piece, and the part of his brain that processed risk assessment.

Actually, that last one was more like a birth defect in Maguire's case.

There was something in the man's arms, something he was protecting with the curve of his torso, although there was no way of ID'ing what it was.

Maguire landed. Stumbled. And fell face-first to the ground, collapsing from what was no doubt smoke inhalation.

"Medic!" Tom commanded. "Get me a fucking medic!"

———

Two hours after Anne arrived at the burned-out warehouse scene for a second time, she was back at her muni sedan and behind the wheel. Her notes were taken, her preliminary conclusions recorded, her plan for next steps outlining in her head.

But she did not return to the office.

She went a couple of blocks north, pulling up in front of a mostly bald lot that had been cleared with all the detail orientation and conscientiousness of a toddler. The debris, which was mostly building crumble and nonbiodegradable trash, was all small-piece and accessorized by weeds, the kind of stuff that would be there for a generation or longer.

Or until somebody built something else on the site, and when was that going to happen in this part of town?

Getting out, she walked across the street and stood on the sidewalk, hands on hips.

She could still smell that final fire she had gone into. Feel the weight of her turnouts and her air tank. See the flames and the smoke that had trailed away from the warehouse at first and then later, after the wind change, come inside. With total clarity, she remembered Emilio's voice as he reminded her of protocol, and how she had told him to leave her.

Walking forward, she triangulated what she recalled of the layout and stopped at what was her best extrapolation for where she had been trapped in the collapse. God, she could picture precisely that desk, the beam, the debris, the fire, and the smoke. The pulling at her stuck hand, the pushing at what had trapped her.

And then Danny Maguire breaking through the wall of orange flames, that chain saw in his hand.

No wonder they had worked so well together on the job. You were not allowed to bring accelerant directly into a known blaze, so gas-powered anything was a no-go. Except he'd known that she was trapped with time running out, and that the building had wood supports, and that a chain saw was so much faster than an axe.

She would have done the same for him.

Lowering her eyes, she stared at the prosthesis that was attached halfway up her forearm. It was her day-to-day one, the one that was a flesh-colored random hand, the one that people like Dr. Delgado, the vet, didn't always notice.

For no good reason, she lifted the thing and ran her real fingertips over the contours of the frozen digits, the static palm, the non-moving knuckles. She felt nothing—and not just on the surface, because there were no nerves to register sensation. She actually had no emotion about the thing, either. It was what it was, a part of her now that needed to be, by definition, as indigenous as all the stuff she had been born with.

What the hell did she have to get upset about?

On that note, she thought of Danny and wondered how long it would take before she didn't have an urge to see how he was doing. They were strangers now that they were no longer professional colleagues—after all, what did they have in common outside of fire-fighting? The fact that they both kept going in their separate lives made sense and it was arguably healthy after all the trauma: If you got into a car accident, it wasn't like you turned the burned-out, mangled shell of the totaled sedan into a planter in your front yard so you could revisit it every single day.

Besides, if the female in that drunken voicemail was any indication, it was pretty clear what kind of self-medicating he was using.

Whenever her guilt got to stinging, she needed to remind herself that Danny was just fine and so was she. And with the passage of all the hours, days, weeks, and months since that warehouse fire, their lives were in different places and that horrible eternity when she'd been trapped in that hot spot was gone.

You had to keep going.

Staring over the cleared site, she thought . . . yup, just as the remnants of the warehouse were gone, so, too, the events of that blaze had been struck out of the timeline of both their lives.

So, too, the connection they had once had.

Back behind her, her phone started ringing in the car. After a moment, she pivoted away and returned to her vehicle to answer it.

12

"You got a cigarette?"

As Danny tossed the perfectly reasonable inquiry out there, Emilio looked at him like he'd suggested the guy give him a block of cocaine.

"Is that a 'no'?" Danny muttered.

"You're sitting on the back of an ambulance—"

"So I'll light up over there."

"—and I'm treating you for smoke inhalation."

On that note, Emilio tried to put the oxygen mask back in place, but Danny was having none of that. Shoving the guy off him, he braced his dirty hands on his knees and leaned forward to give his lungs more space to inflate. The wheezing was not something he could hide, and to cut off conversation, he stared at the steaming pair of houses. They looked like a bomb had been dropped between them, the kitchen side of the one on the right and the living room side of the one on the left both blackened, dripping, ruined.

As the 499's pumper pulled out, he cursed. That was his ride.

Emilio gave the mask another shot. "Come on, Danny. You're wheezing—"

"No, I'm not—"

The coughing jag that hit him put liar to that one pretty good, but he was done with this. Getting to his feet, he yanked his turnout suspenders back on his shoulders and bent down for his insulated jacket.

"Mind if I catch a ride on the ladder?" He clapped the other guy on the shoulder. "Great. Thanks. I'll hang in the back—"

"You're not going to the stationhouse."

"The hell I'm not. Fire's out and I'm—"

"Heading for the ER."

"Amy, don't be codependent. It makes your ass look big."

"Don't argue and I won't have to be." Chavez pointed off to the side. "Besides, you got to deal with him now. Have fun with that."

Danny closed his eyes. And then faced off at what was coming on the attack.

Chief Tom Ashburn was bull-in-a-china-shop pissed off, his too-much-like-Anne's eyes glaring, his prematurely gray hair standing up straight as if he'd been dragging a hand through it, his target sight trained on Danny and Danny alone.

"Don't even start," the chief snapped as he arrived with all the subtlety of a grenade going off in a fireworks factory. "You will be seen at the ER. And now, not later."

God, he reaaaaaally wanted a cigarette. "You can't force me to do anything."

Tom ignored him. "Chavez, place the patient on a gurney and head to University's ER with him."

As Amy dropped an f-bomb, Danny shook his head. "I'm not going—"

"Yes, you are—"

"I'm fine—"

From under his arm, the chief brought out a singed folder. "No, you're off duty and on probation pending a psych evaluation."

Okay, that got his attention. "What the hell are you talking about?"

The yellow folder swung right up to his face. "You went back into that house for this. You risked your own life for papers—"

"It's her math homework. So I had to go and get it—"

"You risked your fucking life for nothing after you dumped your oxygen supply with her—"

"She's asthmatic! She couldn't breathe!"

"—and I'm tired of telling you the rules just to have you fuck them off because you have a death wish."

Danny dropped his voice and leaned in. "My roommate Jack has been out to this place twice in the last three months. And you know damn well he's fucking SWAT, not a beat cop. That kid has nothing but her homework, do you understand? Her father is in jail, and her mother's been skating the system. So hell yeah, I went back in and got it—and I would do it again."

"There's always a reason."

"That girl has nothing!"

"And you are out of a job unless you go get eval'd and are cleared."

Danny narrowed his eyes. "Look, why don't you just be a man about this, okay."

There was a beat of silence. And then Tom stepped forward and met Danny eye to eye. "Excuse me."

Danny glanced at Chavez, but the guy was no fool. He was shaking his head and backing off so fast, he tripped over his own feet.

Making sure his voice didn't carry, Danny said, "You're still pissed about what happened with Anne. Why don't you just admit that to my face instead of playing this backdoor-game shit."

The chief looked down at the ground, his jaw tightening. When his eyes lifted, they were cold. "I will not have a firefighter on my service that is a danger to himself and others. You will get that fucking psych eval or you can walk. Those are your two choices—and after that little crack about my sister, I care even less about the outcome. Chavez, get this fucking patient in the can!"

Abruptly, Danny blinked and saw only white, that rage of his coming back online with a hard-on.

The next thing he was aware of was Moose's bearded face. His old roomie was up close and personal, and he was speaking, that mouth moving.

Danny couldn't hear shit. It was like he was underwater, everything muffled.

"—to go now. I'm riding with you."

There was a pull on Danny's arm, and he glanced down, seeing Moose's hand grip his biceps and tug him toward the interior of the ambulance.

"Play the game," Moose said quietly. "You got too much to lose if you don't. You don't want to go out like this."

Chavez stepped up. "Come on, Dannyboy. The ER will fast-track you and then we'll be at Timeout. Okay?"

"Work with us," Moose urged. "As much as I've wanted to kick your ass since this morning, I don't want you taking a shot at the chief. You can't trust that voice in your head, Danny. I know that firsthand. The one that's talking to you now always steers you wrong."

———

Anne left her office at five p.m., taking the stairs from the third floor down to the first. As she funneled across the lobby to the glass doors, she joined a queue of fellow municipal employees, everybody walking out into the late afternoon sunshine and finding their cars in the maze of the parking lot. On the way back to her house, she stopped at Papa Joe's Pizza, a locally owned joint that she'd been going to since she'd moved into the neighborhood.

With her pepperoni-and-onion in the passenger seat, she continued on to Mapleton Avenue and hung a left. Her house, a nine-hundred-square-foot Cape Cod, was halfway down the street. Her garage was detached, and she parked in front of its single closed door.

Pizza in her good hand. Bag on her left shoulder. As she came up to her front door, she used the forefinger on her prosthesis to punch in a numerical code on the new lock she'd had installed a month after the fire.

When you had only one functioning hand, keys were a thing.

Inside, it smelled like home, a combination of Tide washing detergent, lemons, and something that was intrinsically 1404 Mapleton.

Kicking the door closed, she was abruptly exhausted.

The trip through the living space into the kitchen was a whopping twelve steps, and she ate the pizza standing up and next to the sink because she always washed her hand first and it seemed pretentious to set her Crate & Barrel table for one. She made it through half of the medium pie, put the rest away for tomorrow night's reheat in the oven—never the microwave, because that made the crust spongy when it was hot and tough as nails when it was not—and then she just stood there.

God, her place was quiet.

And the only good news was that it wasn't a Friday or a Saturday night. A random Tuesday was no big deal to be home alone with no other options than a CrossFit class, *Big Bang Theory* reruns, or cleaning a perfectly clean house. The weekends, on the other hand, were bad. All her buddies had been firefighters, but that was gone now—

and it wasn't that they didn't like her anymore, far from it. Even though she'd been the only woman in the boys' club, they'd never treated her as anything other than equal.

The trouble was, after things had changed for her, she'd become a reminder of the risk pool they lived in, a downer through no fault of her own. And besides, over at Timeout, the boys spent their time trading in-jokes, bad stories, and shit that had happened at work.

She was out of the loop for the last one, and as for the bad stories? She was part of a big one that didn't have a har-har at the end.

Anne looked down at her prosthesis. When she'd had the mold taken of her remaining hand, she remembered the guy asking her if she wanted the nails painted any specific kind of color. She'd thought he'd been serious, but it was a joke—and not a mean one. He'd been a veteran who was missing both his legs and walking very naturally around on his artificial limbs.

You can do this, he'd told her. *I promise you.*

"I can do this," she said to her empty house.

The lack of an answer back seemed a commentary on her life, and that made her think of her mother's latest bright idea. The woman was always offering to come over and "add a few touches" to Anne's place. "Spruce things up." "Make things more cozy."

So the woman wanted to bring over a ficus. And not a plastic one.

Anne had sent her an email saying no because that was more efficient than a phone conversation that had a one-minute hello and a nineteen-minute I've-got-to-go-now on her side. And as for the home stuff? Her mother had never understood. These four walls and a roof were like the refrigerator of someone who ate out all the time. Back when she'd been at the fire station, she'd only come here to crash and recover enough to go back to work.

Her home had been where her job was.

Besides, thanks to Mom, she'd had enough Laura Ashley in the nineties to last her twelve lifetimes.

When one of her ankles began to ache, she glanced across at the digital clock on the microwave. She'd been standing here for a good half hour.

Motivating herself, she went across to the year-round porch that overlooked her small fenced-in backyard. She'd set up an office in the space as a way to ground herself in her new reality, thinking that she'd need a home base as an investigator. A trip to OfficeMax had yielded a laptop and a scanner/copier, as well as a low-end desk and a cheapie black chair with rollers under the base.

As she parked it in front of the setup, she opened the laptop, but didn't turn it on.

She'd also bought herself some pens, document clips, a small pack of folders. Three legal pads and a ream of paper.

Looking around at everything, she decided it had been a waste of $400, just the vocabulary of an office instead of—

Anne frowned and focused on the laptop. Then she pushed herself back and regarded the desk. The scanner/copier.

The laptop again.

Office supplies. Bog-standard . . . office supplies. Like the ones that had been in the warehouse fire she'd lost her arm in. And the one she was working on now.

With a burst of energy, she got to her feet, flashed into the kitchen, and grabbed her bag.

She was in such a hurry to leave the house, she forgot to lock up.

13

The Timeout Sports Bar & Grill was a venerable establishment, with a founding date of 1981. Back then, when everyone had been calling 867-5309 because some chick had Bette Davis eyes and every little thing she did was magic, it had been cutting-edge with its video games in one corner, the pool tables in the back, and the pictures of Larry Bird, Bobby Orr, and the "Miracle on Ice" team fresh and unfaded.

Thirty-five-plus years later? The original posters were still up, but Nomar and Dustin, Tom Brady, and Cam Neely were flashing smiles along with the old greats, and the video games had been replaced by a booth section and more flat-screen TVs than a Best Buy's showroom. The pool tables were still there, however, and Carl's old lady, Terri, who ran the place after his death, would let you light up in the back as long as you popped a window and ashed in your longneck, not on her floor.

As with the evolving heroes in the frames, so, too, the clientele was a new generation of the same that had gone before. The firemen, cops, and detectives who were now sitting at the tables, playing pool, or hanging around the bar were the sons and nephews, the daughters and nieces, of the ones who had been there in the eighties, the nineties, the aughties.

"I bring you another one."

Danny glanced up at the waitress as she put a fresh Bud down in front of him. Josefina had worked there for a year now, and with her long black hair and her deep brown eyes, she was something to look at, for sure.

"You know me too well," he said.

"*Sí*, Dannyboy. I know you."

As the woman winked and headed to another table, Moose cursed. "Do you mind."

Danny took a pull and leaned back in his hard chair. "'Bout what."

"Why do you have to get every female in this place?"

"I haven't gone out with her."

"Yet."

"Nah." He eyed the dark-haired woman as she took an order from a homicide detective. "Chavez would kill me."

"Realllllllly." Moose sat forward, his bulk turning the sizable six-top into a Post-it note. "Amy wants her?"

"I don't know. Whatever."

"Come on, man. Tell me."

"I don't know nothing." Danny made a point of nodding toward the pool tables. "We're up next on number three."

"Yeah, after those Brads. Did they buy everything at the Polo outlet before they came here?"

Danny measured the loafers. The watches. Those haircuts. "Moose, buddy, those boys do not shop at outlets."

The set of four matching preppies, aged twenty-one to twenty-five, had sauntered into Timeout about twenty minutes before, and he was guessing they had boated into the New Brunswick Yacht

Club under sail, parked in a private berth, and were slumming it here after having dined on lobster thermidor and baked Alaska with Mumsey and Dads. No doubt they were hoping for some hot, raw townie sex before they went back to their oceanfront mansions and their two-entry-only Daughters of the American Revolution fiancées.

He'd seen the type before. And they'd come here again because these "Brads" were like the social equivalent of the rhinovirus: Bound to show up from time to time, but nothing that was terminal, and by reducing exposure, you had less of a chance of catching one.

So yeah, he was going to give 'em plenty of time at that pool table. Until they moved on their own.

"You drive me batshit."

He refocused on Moose. "Usually I just try to piss people off. I'm over-succeeding with you without meaning to."

"If you know something about Amy, why aren't you telling me?"

"Go talk to Chavez directly."

"He never goes into his personal life."

"So guess you're screwed."

"Fucker—"

A whistle broke through the argument, and both he and Moose looked toward the pool table.

"More beers," one of the frat boys said over the din. "Now, not later, *chiquita.*"

Danny frowned and sized the kid with the mouth up. He looked like law school material. Or med school—i.e., more forehead than jawline. With that gold watch and those Bermuda shorts, it was also an easy guess he had some Roman numerals after his last name.

Subtly turning his body in the direction of the pool game, Danny swallowed some beer and told himself not to get involved.

Two minutes later, Josefina walked over to the quartet with, oh, of course, some craft bullshit on her round tray—yeah, and the James Spaderses, circa *Pretty in Pink*, stared at her in a way he was sure Chavez wouldn't appreciate.

"Get anything good at the hospital?" a male voice said.

As Duff pulled a chair out, Danny nodded a greeting, and then realized the question was to him. "Nope. Just a co-pay I gotta get reimbursed by the department."

"You need any respiratory rehab?"

"Nope."

"Where's Chavez?"

"He's coming," Moose said. "It's early."

Danny refocused on the pool table—and watched Josefina bend down and pick something off the floor. As she made her way back to the bar, she was frowning.

"Oh, great, Rizzo's in the house," Moose muttered.

Sure enough, Rizzo and some of the 617s were filing in, and as usual, they went in the opposite direction, to the booths by the front windows.

"You want another one, Dannyboy?"

Danny looked up at Josefina. "I didn't know I was done. But yup, I do."

The woman smiled. "When you want me to turn you off tonight?"

"Not until I pass out."

"You make me sad, Danny." She put her hand on his shoulder. "You are with your friends, though. They always take care of you—"

"Hey! *Chiquita!* Where's our shots."

Danny slowly pushed his chair back a little farther from the table—but as he did, Josefina shook her head. "Danny, it's okay." More loudly, she said, "Coming. I bring them right out—"

"You better, or I'm calling ICE—"

Danny was up on his feet in a heartbeat. "What did you say."

Instantly, the other fifty people in the bar cut their chatter, nothing but the music filling the background. The yachtsman with the mouth didn't seem to catch that drift, though. The Brad smiled, flashing a perfect set of bright, pearly whites.

"I told her"—he emphasized each word—"to bring me our shots or I was going to get her deported."

A thick arm shot around Danny's pecs, and Moose's voice was low in his ear. "Sit down. We'll wait until they leave and catch 'em in the alley. No witnesses that way."

"Danny, it's okay," Josefina said. "It's not bothering me—"

"Apologize to her." Danny pointed at the exit. "And then get the fuck out of here."

"Do you own this place?" The rich guy looked at his buddies. "Your father must be *so* proud. Then again, he was probably a lawn guy. Garbageman. Oh, wait—was he a mason? 'Cuz maybe you could get him to work on that wall we need in this country?"

As the man nodded at Josefina, Danny lunged forward with such force, he snapped even Moose's hold.

The next thing he knew, he had the kid down on top of the pool table, his hands around that throat, his pumping arms driving the back of the asshole's head into the hard felted surface over and over and over again.

"You're going to kill him!" someone was yelling.

"Stop!"

And then Moose's more reasonable tone: "Christ, Danny, I told you—wait until we get 'em in the alley. It's cleaner that way."

—————————

Vic Rizzo hadn't even ordered his beer before the fight broke out, and as he looked over, he was not surprised that Dannyboy Maguire had mounted some yacht club member's son like the bastard was a sofa during Monday night football. And yeah, Danny was teaching the one-percenter about concussions firsthand.

Meanwhile, Moose, that fat fucker, wasn't doing a damn thing on the sidelines. Neither was the pretty boy Duff. Nope, those two geniuses were just going to let their buddy kill a guy in front of a bunch of cops—

"Yo, Italian."

He glanced over. Speak of the devil. "How you, Greek?"

Officer Peter Andropolis thumbed over his shoulder. "You going to let this go on over there?"

"Why is it my problem?"

"It's your boy."

"These are my boys." He nodded at the three from the 617 he'd come in with. "You know that's four-nine-nine over there."

"Whatever, Rizzo. We're going to have to arrest him if this isn't taken care of. As a professional courtesy, we're willing to let you handle it if you act now. Otherwise, we're going to take him in. Gotta be like that."

Officer Mikey Lange came over. "Well? What's it going to be, sparkers? And by the way, that's my favorite pool table. He's going to ruin the felt with the back of that asshole's head if he hasn't already."

As all eyes settled on him, Rizzo wondered why he was always the one who got called in when someone needed a babysitter.

'Cuz he despised children—especially the kind who had driver's licenses and problems with impulse control and alcohol.

"God*damn* it."

Rizzo slid out of the booth and plowed through the other patrons of the bar, all of whom were front and center with the fight. Given the money that was being exchanged, clearly there were bets being laid, but not on whether sailor boy was going to make a comeback. Nah, more like whether there were going to be manslaughter charges or a simple felony assault with grievous bodily harm.

As he passed Moose, he glared at the diesel, who was planted in front of a trio of tight-asses in Polo merch—crowd control for a wide-eyed peanut gallery unlikely to ever step in. "You should be dealing with this."

"I am."

Yeah, sure, by keeping those anemic reinforcements from helping their *Walking Dead*–candidate buddy. Big job.

Rizzo didn't waste time presenting the legal and rational arguments for Danny to release the choke hold. He just wrapped his arms around the man's diaphragm, balled up his left hand, and secured that fist in the palm of his right.

The Heimlich maneuver was the treatment of choice primarily in cases of stage IV steak- or pork-sphyxia. But it was handy in other situations, too.

Rizzo contracted his biceps, that reinforced fist of his driving up and in under Dannyboy's rib cage, expelling all breath, shocking the heart into a brief arrhythmia. The surprise of it made the lock on that throat ease up, and Rizzo step-two'd his evacuation plan with a backward yank that pissed off his bad shoulder.

Danny came off yacht boy and the table like a barnacle pried from the hull of a trawler. Momentum being what it was, they both pinwheeled. Balance-to-booze ratio being what it was, Rizzo recovered his footing. Danny not so much. The 499's firebrand landed on his ass.

But sure as alkies rallied during a bender, he didn't stay there. He was up like out of a toaster and he made as though he was just going to hop right back on his victim.

Rizzo stepped in the way. "No."

"Get out of my—"

"Time for an Uber, Maguire."

"Fuck you, Rizzo."

Annnnnnnnnnnnnnnnd that was when the next fight started.

14

It was after ten p.m. when Anne's cell phone rang. The old-fashioned ding-a-ling pulled her head up out of her laptop, but what she had been studying stayed with her both in her mind and on the screen as she answered.

"Hello?"

"Anne?"

She frowned. "Yes? Wait, Moose?"

"Yeah. It's me. Long time, no talk, right?"

"It's been a while." She cleared her throat. "Ah, how are you? How's Deandra?"

"Oh, she's great, we're great, I'm great. We moved into the house, you know. I got a new Charger, and I'm working on the engine already. You know, getting more horses under that hood. Guess I haven't changed, huh?"

"Guess not." She swung her eyes around the enclosed porch and wondered how she could end things without being rude. "So, um . . . what else is new?"

"So, yeah, so Deandra's really great. She got a new job at Avento Salon? It's that fancy place in the center of town. Did you know that

Reese Witherspoon showed up there for highlights last week? She was a good tipper. I think she's working on a movie somewhere around here. Deandra's just manning the front desk, but she's going to be a stylist soon. Did you know that she's got her cosmetology degree?"

Anne looked back at the laptop screen. The map that she'd been studying was of the old part of downtown New Brunswick, far from the center, or Centre, where Moose's wife worked. The latter was Disneyland clean with almost–Rodeo Drive kinds of high-end shops and restaurants. The former was where she had been earlier in the day on Harbor Street. Where the dead buildings were . . . where people started fires for nefarious reasons.

Like if they wanted to, oh, say, get rid of some office equipment that maybe they didn't want anyone else to see or find?

"That's great. Hey, Moose?" She hit print and her wireless Brother started chattering on the corner of her desk. "I'm actually working right now. Was there something you needed?"

"Oh, that's right. You're a fire inspector. How's that going?"

"Today was my first day." *And it was rocky, thanks, Moose.* "What can I do for you?"

"Hey, is Don Marshall your boss?"

"Yes, he is."

"Did you know that he used to play college ball for Syracuse—"

"Why was it that you called, Moose?" As the connection went quiet, her heart beat a little faster. "Moose?"

"Yeah." The long, slow exhale did not inspire confidence. "Listen . . . it's about Danny."

Her heart outright pounded. "Is he dead?"

"Oh, no. Nothing like that." There was another pause. "I mean, not right now. At least as far as I know and I left him about fifteen minutes ago. But, yeah, he . . . he's not doing real good. He needs someone who can really talk to him. Make him see what he's doing to himself."

She wanted to ask what exactly that was, but she knew. Or at least could guess.

"Hello? Anne?"

She focused at her prosthesis. And thought of Don Marshall so appropriately handing her her ass.

Danny was a complication. Big time. And she had a new job, more recovery to work on, and . . .

She wanted to see him too much for comfort.

"Don't take this the wrong way." She cleared her throat. "But I can't get involved, Moose. I'm out of that life with you all now. I actually don't know why you called me."

"No one else has a shot at reaching him, Anne. And you owe him. You know *exactly* why I called you."

Ten minutes later, Anne got in her car. Then she hopped back out, jogged up to her front door, and checked to make sure she had locked things. She had, but she tried the door again, feeling the resistance of the dead bolt. It was nearly impossible not to do that a third time.

Forcing herself to walk back to the Subaru, she told herself she knew what this was. Knew exactly why she was obsessing and what to do to counteract the black hole of not-rational she was falling into: The only solution was to keep going, no matter how panicky she felt. Ever since the fire, her brain had had these triggered-by-stress glitches, almost as if the anxiety she'd felt while trapped had been so great that it had destroyed some of the normal neuropathways in her brain. Now, if something made her feel uneasy? She tripped and fell into repetitive action as opposed to introspection and processing, the external expression of the disquiet getting twisted into an illusion that, if she could just be absolutely certain she had done something correctly, everything would be all right.

It made sense, but it was also bullshit, and she was getting tired of pulling herself out of the tailspin.

The good news was that she had all of this to mull over on her way across town. Which was better than wondering what the hell Danny Maguire was going to do when she knocked on his door.

As it turned out, he didn't do anything.

He and his three roommates had lived on the bottom floor of the same powder blue forties-era duplex in Pleasant Heights since they'd graduated from UMass New Brunie. From what she'd heard, the landlady lived upstairs and was Jack's mother's first cousin or something.

Anne had only been to the place a couple of times. Once for a Fourth of July party and then for Moose and Deandra's engagement shitshow, as it had been called: Generally speaking, if you couldn't civilly make it through the announcement of your intention to get married, it probably was a good indication you shouldn't be aisling it. But whatever.

Walking up onto the shallow front porch with its side-by-side pair of storm doors and matched set of mailboxes, Anne tugged the sleeve of her fleece down over her prosthesis and knocked with her right set of knuckles. When there was no answer, she gave it another shot, the little chain up top rustling against the cheap metal frame.

There was no doorbell and no reason for a peep hole. Two firefighters, and a pair of SWAT guys didn't need to worry who might be trying to get into their place.

Taking out her phone, she dialed Danny's number. She wasn't sure exactly when she had memorized the digits, but they were in her head like the address of her childhood home, the date of her father's death, and all the New Brunswick fire station numbers.

No answer.

Propping that storm door open with her hip, she tried the doorknob and found it locked. After banging some more, this time on solid wood, she stepped back and looked up. Like that was going to do anything.

With a curse, she descended the five steps and crossed the shallow lawn, hooking up with the asphalt drive that led down to the detached garage. There were no lights on in his place, but a couple of windows down, the blue flicker of a TV was a subtle strobe in the darkness.

As she went along, her footfalls seemed extra loud, the shuffle and crunch through the fallen leaves the kind of thing that should surely wake up the entire neighborhood. Around back, Danny's rear door was sheltered by the set of stairs that led up to the second floor, and she was glad the cheap fixture overhead was out. She didn't want to shine a bright light on any of this.

No storm door here, so she knocked on the jamb and then cupped her hands and leaned in to see through the glass window. The kitchen was a bomb zone, dirty dishes in the sink, empty beer bottles on all the counters, crushed packs of cigarettes lying around randomly like the wrecked cars of a demolition derby.

She knocked again and then tried the knob, expecting it to be locked and for her to be free to go—

The door opened so easily, it was as if the apartment had joined the list of people trying to turn her into a savior. Damn it.

"Danny?" When there was no answer, she stepped over the threshold. "Danny, come on . . . wake up, wouldja?"

The sitting room was through the kitchen and down the hall some, the last space before you got to the block of bedrooms and the pair of baths. And as she walked forward, the flickering light of the TV cast shadows on the floor, making her think of the guiding beacon of the afterlife.

What if he really was dead?

She paused and called out, "Danny?"

When there was no response, she cursed and kept going. Heart pounding, palm sweating, she halted in the archway of the parlor. The sound of soft snoring made her go weak with relief.

Danny Maguire was alive but seriously out of it, collapsed on the couch with nothing but a pair of black boxer briefs covering him. His head was propped up on the heavy arm he'd cocked over his shoulder, and his hard-muscled body was stretched out in a sprawl that was so sexual she had to look away and catch her breath again.

God, she'd forgotten how many tattoos he had.

Her eyes had to return, and she flushed. His chest was enormous, the pads of his pecs developed and maintained by the demands of his work, and his ribbed stomach was the anti-Moose, all six-pack and then some. Then there were his hip bones and his . . .

Shaking herself, she checked out his tats. The ink he had gotten over the years wasn't the result of some metrosexual, hipster grand plan. It was a layering of meaningful events, all of them losses: Danny carried the department's dead all over himself, the birth and death dates, the nicknames, even portraits, on occasion, of those who had been lost forming a map of mourning in his skin that was as beautiful as it was tragic.

Where would you have put me? she wondered.

"Anne?"

As he spoke her name, she swung her stare northward, away from the waistband of his black Hanes.

"Danny."

He blinked a couple of times and lifted his head. "Am I dreaming?"

His voice was a husky whisper, and she knew it was hoarse from drinking, from getting into that fight at Timeout with that rich kid, from trading punches with Vic Rizzo. Moose had given her the run-down. And now that Danny was awake and staring at her, she could see the bruising on the side of his face. He was going to have a black eye tomorrow.

"You don't look so good," she said. "No offense."

Danny groaned as he sat up, and she ignored the cracking sound that was either his back or his shoulder. Or maybe both. And then she had to look at the TV as he rubbed his short black hair—because otherwise she wouldn't have been able to take her eyes off the way his biceps bulged.

When he reached for a pack of Marlboros, she shook her head. "Are you serious?"

"What." He put one of the cancer sticks between his teeth. "And I suppose you won't get my lighter for me, will you."

"I absolutely will not. I'm not your maid, and you were just treated for smoke inhalation, for godsakes."

"So which one of those little old ladies called you to come over here?"

As he got to his feet, she turned away and needed a place to go, so she wandered down the hall toward the bedrooms. It seemed weird to look into two of the four spaces and see nothing but dust bunnies and forgotten hangers. Then again, Moose had moved in with Deandra and Mick was in rehab out of state—the addiction kind, not the phys-ical. The third bedroom, Jack's, housed little more than a stripped bed and a bureau that looked as if it were throwing up the shirts and pants that were in its drawers. The final crib was Danny's, and she merely glanced in as she pivoted around for the return trip—

Anne stopped. He was leaning against the hallway wall like James Dean, that cigarette lit between his fingers.

His eyes were hooded as he stared at her, and she wanted to tell him to put some damn clothes on—except that seemed like an admission that she was noticing his body.

"I've lost two and a half of my roommates as you can see." He motioned to the vacant rooms with his free hand. "They're dropping like flies, I tell ya."

"Times change." She crossed her arms over her chest. "Your face is busted up."

"Vic needs to lose your number."

"Moose was the one who called me."

"Him, too, then."

"What are you doing, Danny." She nodded into his trainwreck of a room. "I mean, look at this place."

There was laundry on the floor—in two piles that she guessed meant one was clean and the other dirty. The bed was a shambles of sheets and blankets with a bald pillow at the headboard. And the window's curtain had bought the farm, the rod hanging cockeyed, a blanket nailed in place so he didn't flash the neighbors.

"I don't spend a lot of time in there," he muttered before taking a drag.

She bent down and picked up a flimsy piece of lace. "At least you're not alone, though."

He shrugged. "I might as well be."

"Oh, come on." Anne let the lingerie dangle. "What was wrong with her? Given the cup size here, I'm thinking her anatomy was just fine."

Danny was quiet for a while. Then in a low voice, he said, "She wasn't you. That was the trouble."

I n the charged silence, Anne decided she hadn't heard that right. Nope. She most certainly hadn't heard that.

"Enough with the bullcrap." She dropped the Victoria's Secret and wiped her hand on her hip. "Moose is worried about you. A lot of people are worried about you."

Danny shrugged. "No reason to be."

"You got into a fistfight."

"No, I didn't. I choked the bastard after he insulted Josefina. So I didn't actually punch him."

"I'm talking about Vic. You hit one of us—I mean, you. You hit another firefighter—"

"He was in my way—"

"—because he wouldn't let you kill someone when you'd had six beers in sixty minutes."

"I'm sober."

"Not when you were strangling him. And if by some miracle your liver was able to process all that alcohol load by now, then you need to follow Mick's example and go inpatient." She shook her head. "Seriously, what the hell are you doing to yourself. You risked your life today at that fire. You blew off procedure—"

"Moose *really* needs to forget he knows you."

"—and endangered yourself—"

"This coming from you?"

"—and nearly didn't get out of there alive. All for a kid's homework." She put her palm up. "And don't give me that holier-than-thou about how important it was for her. That's an excuse. If you're looking to commit suicide, do your department a favor and just put a bullet in your head or hang yourself from the ceiling. But don't do it on the job where every single man or woman on-site will feel like it's their fault. That is not fair to them. It's just not."

There was a tense pause. And then his eyes dropped to her prosthesis.

As they lingered on the model of her hand, she shook her head. "Don't you dare. Don't you for a second use what happened to me as a justification for self-destructing. You do *not* get to do that."

"You expect me to feel good about cutting your fucking arm off?"

"It was my wrist and hand, for one thing. And what I expect is for you not to pretend like it happened to you." She held up the elephant in the room. "I have to live with this. I lost my career. I am having to reinvent myself. You, on the other *hand*, still have your life, your job, your friends, and your calling. You've got everything you had the moment you jumped into that stairwell. Nothing has changed for you."

Danny straightened and walked toward her, his body filling the distance between the corridor's walls. As he stopped in front of her, he swept his hard stare over her face. "I was buried under a thousand pounds of debris. I lost part of my colon, all of my spleen, and a quarter of my liver. Not as dramatic as a hand, granted, but as long as you're bringing that kind of crap up, let's be accurate. And how about you not tell me how I'm supposed to feel? Thanks for giving me the suicide tip, though. I'll put it in my back pocket for later."

The memory of him in that ICU room made her nauseous. "I'm not suggesting you weren't hurt."

"Oh, I guess I misunderstood the nothing-has-changed-for-you part. Sounded to me like you think it's been a party on my end. But yeah, I got that wrong. Clearly." He leaned forward. "It's not like I single-handedly maimed one of the best firefighters this city had and then spent three months trying to walk again. It's not like I was stuck in the belly of the beast with you. It's not like you and I were both surrounded by that fucking monster that's been picking off members of our department one by one, year by year—"

"Shut up."

As he recoiled, Anne took a step forward and lifted her chin. She was tall for a woman, but he still managed to dwarf her by a good six inches and more than a hundred pounds. Not that that his size advantage mattered when she was standing up for herself.

"You don't get it." She shook her head. "Fire isn't a beast. It isn't evil. It's not an animal that prowls around and takes revenge for all of its buddies we've killed with our charged lines. Jesus Christ, Danny." She motioned to his tattoos. "You're taking everything too personally—"

"*What did you just say.*"

"You heard me."

"I—" He looked to the ceiling. "Wait, actually, this is a relief. Because the fact that you just told me I shouldn't care about my friends and my family being killed in the line of duty means this is a fucked-up dream—"

"You're wrong—"

He yelled over her. "—and I'm about to wake up hungover and *pissed off that I have to go to work!*"

Anne stared up at him and wished like hell she could give him the realizations that had come to her over the previous months of suffering and change. But you couldn't do that. People had to find their own evolution. Or not.

"You got it all wrong, Danny. Fire is like cancer. It doesn't care what it kills. We mean nothing to it because it's not alive. You're not battling a beast. There's no monster there. It's exactly the same as a rogue set of cells that wipes out a young girl or an old man, a rich person or somebody who's poor. My father, your brother, and Sol all died from doing a job. Not because fire stalked them and took them down." She raised her prosthesis. "This happened to me because of my *job*. And I had to decide whether or not I was going let random circumstance, in a risk pool I was well aware of swimming in, ruin my life or not. I wasn't a target. I wasn't singled out. It was a danger I accepted, and I got hurt, and everyone who's been injured or killed made the same calculation and just happened to come up short. I'm not saying you shouldn't mourn the people we've both lost. What I'm telling you is . . . don't let that fire we went into willingly a year ago kill you by default. You made it out alive, don't give that blessing up."

She waited for him to respond.

And the longer he was silent, the sadder she became. "I don't want this for either of us, Danny. And I am sorry, I am so . . . sorry . . . that I fucked up and you came to get me, and things went bad. I never wanted to put anyone in that position, but certainly not you."

After a moment, he said, "Why am I different?"

"Do you really want me to answer that?"

"Yes."

"Well . . . to be honest, it's because of what you're doing to yourself right now. I worried this was how it would go in the aftermath."

"Oh, so you think I'm a pussy," he muttered. "Thanks."

"The strong do not wallow. They don't drink themselves into a stupor, they don't fuck around at their work, they don't throw punches at their friends. They move forward. You did what you had to do to me. What I *told* you to do to me. And instead of moving on from that, you're using it as an excuse to self-destruct."

His face became remote, a mask settling into place. And then he took a draw on the cigarette, exhaling over his shoulder.

"So that's why you came, huh." He refocused on her. "To make this little speech. Pretend that you're in a movie and laying down a monologue that magically turns the damaged idiot around on a oner. That's Hollywood, sweetheart. Not real life."

Crossing her arms, she searched his face and saw nothing she could work with in his hard expression. "I was hoping this would go better."

His eyes focused on her lips, and a sudden shift in the air had her taking a step back. But not because she was scared of him. No, for another reason.

Anne pushed her hair out of her face and tried to regroup. "I should leave."

"Finished talking at me?" His voice grew even deeper. "And that's that?"

"I only wanted to help."

"Why."

She glared at him. "You weren't going to leave me to die in that fire. And I don't want to leave you to kill yourself after it. It's really that simple—"

"I'm not so sure it is, Anne."

"What?"

"Why don't you want me to die now?"

Anne started to walk around him. "Let's talk when you're sober—"

He snagged a hold on her upper arm and pulled her back. "I'm sober enough. Answer the question, Anne. You seem to know everything else on the planet. What's one more pronouncement from on high? If you don't take things personally because you're so above everything, why do you care whether I live or die now?"

"I don't want any of us to be killed!"

"Why?" He put his face in hers. "I thought it wasn't personal? Oh, wait . . . maybe it's not all random risk, Anne. Do you think maybe you don't want me to self-destruct because you might feel a little responsible if I do? That you're worried you might wonder after the fact about whether you could have done something more, something better, something different? Do you think it's because you might possibly spend night after night after night staring at the ceiling, replaying, again and again, every single second you were here with me now, looking for opportunities or openings that maybe you hadn't seen in the moment—and then also praying that you don't find any? Because if you do, and there was an action you could have taken, you just might be at fault?" He released her abruptly. "But nah, that can't be it. Right? Because if a tragedy like me killing myself happened, you would just dust yourself off and skip away, light and free as a child. Off into the sunset, perfectly sound mentally because it was just a risk pool. Tra-la-*fucking*-la."

As her head started to pound, she rubbed the back of her neck. "You need to go to that psych eval, and not just to keep your job."

Danny threw his arms up. "Moose *totally* needs to shut his mouth."

"There's more going on here than I, or anybody else, can deal with."

He jabbed a finger right into her face. "Don't you pity me."

"Then don't give me a reason to." She looked at his body from head to toe. "And you're wrong. I wasn't the best firefighter in the city. That's you, Danny. Everyone knows it. You're the best we've got, and we need you. We need you healthy and strong on all levels. So fine, if you can't put this into perspective, and you don't want to see reality for what it is, then stay in your paradigm—and protect people from that beast you fight. Stay alive yourself so you can save others. I don't really care what the rhetoric is or what vocabulary you put on it. What I care about is the result—which is you still on this planet with a fire hose in your hand."

Abruptly, her eyes stung and she had to blink quick and look away. She was *not* going to cry in front of him—

The palms that cradled her face and turned her back to him were calloused yet gentle.

"Let me go," she said hoarsely.

But he wasn't holding her. Not really. She could have broken away at any second, and he would have dropped his hands.

"Anne . . ." His voice cracked. "Oh, God, Anne . . ."

The following morning, at eight a.m., Anne called Dr. Delgado at the vet clinic. As she waited for the receptionist to answer, she drummed her fingers on her kitchen countertop. Took a sip of her coffee. Tucked in the back of her blouse—

"Metro Vet, how may I help you?"

"Oh, yes, hi." She cleared her throat. "This is Anne Ashburn calling about the—"

"The rescue you brought in? The gray pit?"

"Ah, yes. I'd like to—"

"We just gave him over to the New Brunie pound. So you don't have to worry about any more charges to your card—"

"Wait, what? You gave him to the city shelter? I thought you were going to try to adopt him out?"

"We really couldn't keep him here. His injuries were not life-threatening, and we are not in a position to—"

"Hold on, stop." Anne reminded herself that yelling was not going to help. "Who can I call there? I mean, who can I phone to—never mind. Thanks, bye."

As she hung up, she couldn't breathe, and went for her keys. But then she stopped herself. The rehab social workers had warned her not to make any big life-altering plans in the first twelve months following her injuries—and with her working all day at a new job, how was she going to take care of a—

"Screw that," she said out loud. "That's my damn dog."

Traffic was horrible as she tried to get across town, and no matter how many red lights she ran or bypasses she took, it was clear she was in trouble for time if she wanted to make it to work by nine.

When she pulled into the city shelter's parking lot, she was one of only three cars, and as soon as she got out, she heard the muffled barking.

She jogged to the front door, only to find it locked.

Knocking. Lots of knocking.

Eventually, a tired-looking middle-aged woman with a travel mug appeared on the other side of the glass door. "We're not open 'til nine—"

"My dog is here," Anne said loudly. "I need to get him now. I have to go to work."

"I'm sorry, I can't let you in. It's policy and—"

"Debbie?"

The woman leaned in. "Anne . . . ?"

The door got opened in a flash and a strong pair of arms shot around her. "Oh, my God, I haven't seen you forever."

Anne closed her eyes and tried to keep her voice level. "I know, right?"

Debbie Fazio pushed her back. "How are you. And I mean that really. Not socially."

"I'm okay. How's Sal?"

"He's good. He's Sal, you know the drill. Working overtime at the 508."

Sal Fazio was a veteran firefighter, a good man, and almost at re-
tirement. He and Debbie had three kids, and Anne had met the family
at department functions.

"So you got a dog?" Debbie said. "After you . . ."

As the woman tripped over words and avoided looking at the
prosthesis, Anne wanted to hug her again and tell her it was all right
to feel awkward. Instead, she nodded. "Yes, I got a dog. I mean, I
found him on the streets yesterday and the vets couldn't keep him and
I've decided to— I'm babbling. I just, can I have him?"

"So he didn't have an owner?"

"He was feral."

"What vet did he come from?" Debbie motioned for her to come
in. Then she relocked the front door and indicated for Anne to follow
her. "Oh—wait, we have a delivery coming in. It's being processed."

They went behind the registration desk and entered a concrete
kennel area that stretched out behind the administration section of
the facility. Anne looked at the first couple of dogs, and then found
that she had to focus on the bald floor or she got teary. It helped that
everything was clean, and the animals perky, but all she could think
about was how they had come to be here. And what would happen if
they didn't get chosen.

"Hey, Bobby, where did those three dogs come in this morning?"

Anne glanced up at a young guy dressed in a green janitor's uniform. He had dreadlocks and a calm smile. "I brought 'em in and
they're in B down at the end."

"Great. Thanks." Debbie hung a left and opened the door to another kennel run. "We have four different buildings."

"I don't—I gotta be honest, I don't know how you do this job."

"We save so many. I love to see the families come in with the kids.
It's not always easy, but we do good work—we ease suffering, stop cru-

elty, and give joy every day. You have to focus on the happy if you're going to keep going, you know?"

"Ah, yes . . . yes, I do."

Debbie started down another run. "Okay, here we are. Over here."

At the far end of the sixty or so kennels, Debbie stopped. "One of these three?"

The first two dogs were the wrong size, so she turned to the last and—

The gray mix was all the way back in the cage again, his tail tucked in tight, his head hanging low, his eyes unfocused. But then he looked up and seemed surprised.

Anne went over and lowered herself onto her knees. Curling her fingers through the chain links, she checked his carefully sutured and bandaged wounds and measured the swelling of that ear. "Hi."

That tail wagged, just at the tip. And then the animal shuffled over slowly and sniffed at her fingers. Licked at her.

"Looks like he knows who his mom is," Debbie said.

———————

"Okay." Anne glanced across at her passenger seat. "Here's the plan, Soot."

As the light ahead turned red, she hit the brakes. "We're going to go up the back stairs and I need you to keep a low profile. You can hang out behind my desk in my office and I'll take you out on the regular. Debbie told me the guy who picked you up said you are not a biter, and I'm going to ask you to keep that up."

Looking in the rearview, she thanked Sal's wife in her head again for all the things that filled the back seat. The woman had lent her a collapsible crate that was big enough for Soot to be comfortable in, and provided a stack of old but clean towels, as well as a bowl for water.

There was also a halter and leash, and Soot was sporting a plain red nylon collar with his brand-new license and rabies-vaccine tags on it.

"So what do you think? We good?"

Soot's caramel eyes looked around, checking out the passing cars and the shops as they went along. He was calm, and she told herself he somehow knew that he was safe with her. Whether that was true, she had no idea.

When she pulled into the parking lot of the Fire and Safety Building, she went around back. She was ten minutes late already, but she was going to add to that injury. Soot was patient as she put his halter on, and he let her lift him out of the seat and down onto the pavement.

He wasn't necessarily big, but he was dense even though he was thin.

"Okay, let's go potty." What the hell was she doing? "Come on, let's go onto the grass."

Soot didn't move, which made sense. Because he didn't friggin' speak English. What he did do, however, was limp along with her when she walked onto the mowed strip of faded lawn. He didn't seem to like the halter and he shook his head a lot, as if either his ear were bothering him or he hated the leash.

But he did squat and pee.

Anne felt triumph like she had won the Nobel Peace Prize.

Sneaking him into the building and up to her office with the towels, the crate and the bowl was a thing, though. They used the rear stairs—slowly, because Soot was tentative about it all—and then she was trying to rush him down the carpeted hall of her floor, passing enough open doors to make her feel like she was on a Broadway stage. But they made it.

Closing them in, she quickly set up the crate behind her L-shaped desk and padded the base with all those towels. As her hands lingered on the soft bed of towels, she thought of all the animals that had come into contact with the terry cloths of various colors. She prayed all of them had found homes like Soot had, even as she knew that wasn't the case.

When things were set up, she eased back on her heels. Soot was watching her in that way he did, his big, exhausted eyes on her. "Come in here, boy. This is where you have to be."

When he didn't move, she reached in and patted the towels. "Come on."

Nope. No go.

Another Fiber One did the trick. She got the bar out of her purse, fed him a little, and put the rest on the nest she'd made.

Soot walked in, ate slowly . . . and curled into a ball facing out at her. As she stared at him, she had an absurd worry that he might not like her over time. Saviors were one thing. Friends? That was a choice—

Abruptly, her conversation with Danny from the night before barged in and took over—as it had been doing since pretty much the second she'd stepped back from his almost-kiss and beat feet out his front door.

It had been a while since she'd watched the sunrise. Not since the rehab hospital. But, yup, this morning's had been peach and pink and magnificent.

"You're going to be okay in there. And I'll take you with me if I leave."

He laid his head down and stared at her.

As she went to close the crate door, she stopped and took off the jacket that matched her slacks. It wasn't anything fancy, just a knock-off she'd gotten at TJ Maxx when she'd had to find at least one week's worth of office clothes at a dead run. But it smelled like her, and maybe that would help them bond? Or something?

"God, what am I doing," she muttered as she wadded the thing up and put it in the crate. "I've never even had a house plant—"

The knock on her door was sharp, and she quickly stood up. Tucking in her blouse, she smoothed her hair and tried to look professional. Damn it, she should have put on that lip gloss.

"Yes?"

Don Marshall stuck his head in and muttered, "I didn't know it was Bring Your Dog to Work Day."

17

Moose was fucking late. Of course.

As Danny stopped his truck in front of a dilapidated old house with a *Jumanji* yard, he yanked the parking brake and made sure the gear shift was in first before he canned the engine. Getting out, he rubbed his wet hair and jacked up his work pants.

Twenty minutes, two cigarettes, and three voicemails later, he was still killing time.

To keep himself from cursing, he stared at the structure and was reminded of his own farm. As with what he had saddled himself with, this place was two stories of vacated-long-ago, the roof holier than the Christmas season, the dormers more broken glass than window, the siding worn to paint chips and bare wood from countless winter blizzards, spring gales, summer thunderstorms, and fall winds. Maybe the property had once had a lawn, but now a meadow on its seasonal last gasp was a scruffy base for the vines that grew Charles Addams–style all over everything.

The nearest neighbor was a quarter of a mile away.

Walking forward, he high-stepped through the tall grass and weeds until he crossed over onto a broad, freshly mowed ring around the house and its collapsing porch. As he mounted the three steps, he stayed on the nail pattern on the left so his weight was supported by the stairs' undercarriage.

Beside the off-kilter front door, there was an official document stapled to the jamb, proclaiming that the structure was going to be used by the fire department on this date, and that trespassing was prohibited.

Hinges creaked as he opened the way in, and inside, everything was all haunted house, cobwebs hanging from darkened corners, dirty windows filtering light that seemed more portent than illumination, rotting places in the floors and ceilings creating pockmarks, open wounds, sores.

Danny walked throughout the first floor to make sure there were no people and no wild animals anywhere. It was a short trip. Upstairs, he went more slowly because there was a lot longer distance to fall through courtesy of a bad floorboard. He checked closets, inspecting the odd lonely hanger. He ducked into bedrooms, reviewing the shells of bedposts and bureaus. He stepped into baths that had claw-footed tubs with cracked porcelain and broken mirrors over stained sinks.

The attic on the third floor was all bat guano, water stains, and leaves that had come in through the holes in the roof.

As he went back downstairs, his sinuses were pissed from the mold and dust, his ribs sore from that messy rescue the day before, and his head pounding from the alcohol and the no-sleep he'd pulled during the night hours. And yes, he refused to see any parallels between the state of his life and the condition the old house was in.

Nope.

There was no connection between the two.

Off in the distance, he heard a low growl. "'Bout fucking time."

As he went out the front door, Moose's bumblebee-yellow Charger was stopping behind his truck, and the guy unfurled his heft from the driver's side with a glower.

"You got a helluva nerve."

"Good morning to you, sunshine." Danny put his cig out on the tread of his work boot. "What took you so long. You're late."

Moose stomped over and did not come up onto the shallow porch. He looked tired with those bags under his eyes, and his hair was messy like it had taken a page from his beard's book and was trying the disorderly routine out at a higher elevation. New Brunie FD shirt was tighter around the middle, looser than it had been on the shoulders, testament to brawn turning into paunch—oh, and naturally, his heavy khakis had the faded stains of motor oil all over them.

"You're not supposed to be here," the guy said.

"You've never done a training exercise by yourself."

"You're suspended."

"Do you have the accelerant?"

"Don't change the subject."

As Danny thought about Anne showing up in the middle of the night, that anger of his came back. "Fine, how's Deandra. She ask about me lately?"

Moose went still. "No, she hasn't. And don't be an asshole."

"Sorry. I thought I was being polite. You wanna talk about your car instead?"

"Don't get pissy with me about Anne, okay? That shit's on you—"

"You should *never* have called her." Danny went down the steps, ignoring that follow-the-nails rule. "She's got more than enough on her plate. She doesn't need to worry about me or anybody else."

"Come on, Danny. What am I supposed to do, huh? There's talk about you and not just at the station. Jack's worried about you, too—"

"I'll tell you what to do. Live your own life. If you can stand it."

"What's that supposed to mean?"

"You know exactly what I mean."

Even though Moose had inches and pounds—note: horizontal inches—on him, the other man looked away.

"You think you're paying me back for Deandra?" Danny stepped up even closer. "Because she called me the other night?"

As Moose seemed surprised, Danny wanted to curse himself. He really didn't need to bring up the guy's wife-mare—and besides, Moose was just a good man in a bad situation. It was his Mrs. that was the problem.

"I told you," Danny muttered, "she's no good. I warned you—"

Moose's head ripped back around. "You always got to win, don't you."

"You're the only one who's competing here. I've never given a shit about her."

"That's your problem, Danny. You don't care about anyone or anything."

"Spare me the moral superiority when it comes to women. Not only do I know too much about you, I've covered for you too many times. All I care about is keeping Anne out of this. Do you understand me. No more phone calls to her."

Ever since the two of them had met in Economics 101 freshman year at UMass New Brunie, there had been a keep-up element to Moose, a foster-kid leftover that dragged down the adult, a fault line under the thick bluster and big-man facade. And that was why Danny knew that this was the last time they were going to have to talk about the Anne issue.

"I don't want you calling her ever again," he repeated. "Not about me. Are we clear?"

After a moment, Moose looked away. "Yeah. Fine."

"Good, now, you want a cig?" Danny asked. "I just opened this pack."

As he held out the Marlboros, he knew Moose was going to take one. And the guy did, but not before he made Danny wait there for a while.

Danny shared his Bic. "So we gonna light this place on fire or what."

"Chief's not going to let you work this drill."

"He'll get over it."

Right on cue, Tom Ashburn's SUV pulled up behind the truck and the Charger, and Anne's brother got out of it like he was prepared to hop into an octagon and break someone's head.

Oooooor maybe he won't get over it, Danny thought.

———————

"I can explain," Anne said as she got to her feet. "I, ah . . ."

Don came in and walked around the desk. As he looked down, Soot shrunk back inside the crate, ducking his head and letting out a soft growl—which might have been threatening if the dog hadn't been shaking like a leaf.

"Poor kid," Don murmured. "Poor damn thing."

"Look, I didn't mean for this to happen. This morning. I mean." She cleared her throat. "What I'm trying to say is that I called the vet to check on him, but they'd let him go to the city pound and I was worried he was going to be put down. I had to go on the way here or risk—"

"What's his name?"

"Soot. You know, 'cuz he's gray."

Don backed away. "So about those emails you sent last night."

Anne looked at the dog. Looked at her boss.

Don's face was utterly composed. And when she seemed confused, he raised an eyebrow. "The three emails you sent. At ten p.m.? Or were you sleep-typing."

"Right." She pushed her hair back. "So, ah, yes, you have to agree that there's a pattern. Six fires in the last two years. All in that same zip code with an unusual amount of office equipment at the scenes. It's an arson cluster."

"Or it's a bunch of abandoned buildings in a bad area of the city known for drug deals and gang territory disputes. I'm not sure we need to call *60 Minutes* yet," he said dryly.

"Did you read my report?"

"Twice. While I was on the StairMaster this morning."

"There was too much plastic noted in three of the reports on those other scenes."

"So?"

"If the buildings were abandoned, what's all that office equipment doing in them?" She shrugged. "Looters are not picky and very thorough. They take everything that isn't nailed down, but in half of those sites, there is forensic evidence suggesting things like cell phones and computers were in those buildings. Why?"

"Previous use. Recent abandonment."

She shook her head. "The blaze I was in last November? There were old cubicles and office stuff on the first floor, granted. But when the collapse happened, I remember getting hit with a laptop from above—and it was a MacBook. I didn't think anything of it at the time. I'm beginning to wonder, though, given what I observed yesterday at that scene—especially in light of the debris noted on those other reports. What if someone's using these fires as a way of disposing of goods? Or the information in the computers? Or for some other reason."

Don shrugged. "You hear hooves, don't think zebras. But keep digging."

"I intend to."

Her boss turned away. "Departmental meeting in an hour."

Anne hustled around the desk. "Wait, I'm sorry, I have to be clear here. I'm not fired for bringing him in? I mean, Soot?"

"I just told you about a departmental meeting. You think I'd can you in front of the whole team?"

"Well, it might be a good way to reinforce—or establish—a no-dogs policy."

Don looked over her shoulder, in Soot's direction. "If it were a cat, it'd be different. I don't like cats."

"So . . . I can keep bringing him? During this adjustment period."

"Do you always push the limits?"

"Yes, as a matter of fact, I do."

Don crossed his arms and stared off into the hall, his lips flattening, but not because he was angry. He was trying not to smile. "You are going to drive me nuts. But you stay on task, I'll turn a blind eye to the damn dog, deal?"

Anne started to smile. "Have you ever watched *The Office*?"

"Why?"

"No reason." She glanced at Soot and gave him a thumbs-up. "Thanks."

On the way home from work, Anne stopped by Petco. She wanted to take Soot in with her, but she didn't know how he would react to the stimulation and it was a very cool day, so she left him alone in her car. Inside the store, she was quick as she could be, grabbing dog food, treats, a seat belt restraint for him, a dog bed, and a second crate for her home. When she came out, she half expected to have a fire engine by her old Subaru, one of the teams breaking the windows of her Outback to free the dog as he went crazy and chewed everything to shreds.

Nope.

As she came up to the car, she found him curled in her seat, and he lifted his head and wagged at her. "Good boy!"

She picked up a salad on the way home, from the Greens-R-We drive-in, and she talked to Soot the whole time, telling him about the departmental meeting, her investigation, that cluster. And also the fact that her mother had called and left a message about something or another.

Pulling into her driveway, she—

Slammed on the brakes. As Soot did a quick scramble so he didn't hit the dash, she cursed. Danny Maguire was sitting on her front stoop, his black hair and his big body bathed in the setting sun's orange rays and taking up every inch of concrete step there was. He was smoking, but he pinched the ash off the tip of the cigarette and put the butt into his jeans as he got to his feet.

"Shit," she muttered as she put the car in park.

Getting out, she shut the door so Soot didn't get any ideas about eating the guy.

"Hey." Danny came across her lawn. "You need help carrying stuff in?"

"What are you doing here?"

"I came to apologize. For last night."

"Which part?" She shook her head. "Never mind. Apology accepted, now if you don't mind, I'm going to go inside—"

"You got a dog?" As he leaned in, Soot sank back against the seat and Danny nodded. "He's a rescue. Good deal. What's his name?"

Anne looked away to the clear blue autumn sky. Him asking about her dog, carrying pet supplies in, walking through her house, felt all wrong. Like they were entering a time warp through day-to-day normalcy . . . a time warp that tried to pretend Everything Hadn't Happened.

"Danny, we're not doing this."

"Let him out so we can be properly introduced."

"He doesn't like strangers. Especially men."

"He'll like me."

"Your ego can be exhausting." When Danny just stood there, like he was prepared to wait until Christmas, she shrugged. "Fine. He bites you, it's on you."

She opened the door and took the leash. "Come on, Soot. Let's get you into the back so you can meet your yard."

Anne gave a tug, and the dog resisted, his caramel eyes on Danny. "Don't worry about him. He's not going to hurt you. Come on."

Soot's head tilted to the side and then he skulked across the seat. As he jumped onto the ground, she turned to Danny and—

Danny wasn't standing behind her. He was on the grass, flat on his back, his arms stretched out, his feet crossed at the ankles, his eyes closed.

"What are you doing?"

When he didn't speak or move, Soot sniffed the air. Took a step forward. And another. Danny stayed perfectly still except for breathing, his big chest inhaling and exhaling slowly.

He stayed just like that as Soot closed in, the dog's weight as far back into his butt as he could make it, his tail a flagpole of alarm.

"It's okay, buddy," Danny murmured with his lids still down. "Take your time."

Soot sniffed a hand first. Reared back. Sniffed the arm. Sniffed the chest. Sniffed the face.

Danny slowly opened his eyes. "I'm a friend of your mom's. It's good to meet you."

Soot and Danny stared at each other for what felt like an hour. And then the dog curled into a sit, his skinny body leaning against Danny's torso. It was only then that a hand lifted and gently stroked the animal's flank.

"See? I told you he'd like me."

Anne crossed her arms over her chest and glared at the pair of them. She'd had to offer bribes of Fiber One, FFS. But for Danny? Soot gave it up for free.

Men.

"So," Danny said, "you got any dinner plans?"

Anne opened her mouth. Closed it. And somehow ended up muttering, "Just leftover pizza and a salad."

"Perfect. I'm starved."

There was a long moment of quiet, and then somehow, for reasons she didn't want to look too closely at, she took him into her house, into her kitchen, over to her table. And after she had reheated the pizza, she sat down across from Danny with her salad.

"So what are you working on?" Danny said between bites of the pepperoni-and-onion.

She tried out the salad and decided it tasted like cardboard. "You know what a fire investigator does."

"How's it going?"

"Okay."

"Your salad good?"

She put her fork down. "Danny, this is—"

He wiped his mouth with a paper towel. "Look . . . I just wanted to see you when I was sober. Last night, I was outta my mind, and not making any sense. And I would have called first, but you'd've told me not to come over."

"So you just showed up. Have you ever waited for an invitation in your life, Danny?"

"Not any more often than you have, Anne."

"I hate when you smile like that," she muttered as she poked at her lettuce some more. "And can we just stipulate that you're sorry about almost kissing me—"

"I'm not sorry about that." When she looked up at him, his lids lowered. "I'd be lying if I told you otherwise."

Instantly, she was back in that dark, messy apartment of his, standing face-to-face with him, her name a hoarse sound leaving his lips. Right before his mouth dropped toward hers.

Arousal came hard and fast to her body, and she shifted in her chair. "So I'm working on a fire just like ours, actually. I mean, our last one. You know."

Danny sat back and crossed his legs, ankle to knee. Then he peeled off a piece of crust and offered it to Soot, who had curled up on his new bed. After a moment, the dog hobbled over and took it as gently as an English nobleman, whispering back to his bed and chewing it down on a oner.

"He's so quiet," Anne said. "And mild-mannered."

"That's a good dog, right here. You lucked out. Both of you." Danny's shoulders eased up. "So what about this fire you're on. Which one is it?"

"Warehouse downtown."

"The one on Harbor Street? From two days ago?"

"Yes, that's it. Same vintage structure as the one we were—well, you know. Anyway, there are some similarities between the two. And get this, there have been others. I'm wondering if there's a connection."

"Lot of crazies in that area. Sometimes they burn shit for fun."

"True." She put some lettuce in her mouth.

"Is it safe for you to be down there? Do you go in a pair or something?"

"I have a handgun. I'm licensed to carry concealed."

"Good girl."

"Woman." She chewed. "Not girl."

"Sorry." He smiled a little. "So can we go back to the elephant in the room?"

"Did Moose come into my house and I somehow missed him?"

Danny frowned and then laughed. "I already talked to him. He's not going to bother you anymore."

"This mean you're going to turn over a new leaf and stop acting like an idiot on the job? Great. I feel this is a really good decision on your part. And I'm *so* glad you're cutting down on the drinking and putting Uber in your contacts—"

"Can you ever really forgive me?"

Anne lowered her fork. God, with Danny, she kept falling into these holes of emotion, the floor of her logical side giving way and leaving her at feelings' mercy.

"No offense," she said, "but I'm not the one who has to do that."

"Did I cut some other person's arm off?"

She lifted her prosthesis. "This is not that big a deal."

"The hell it isn't."

Anne studied his face and resented the shit out of the guilt she saw there. Abruptly, she put her fork down. "How much time do you have?"

"When? Now? I have no plans."

"I'll be right back."

Sitting at Anne's kitchen table, Danny listened to her move around upstairs. She was walking right above him, her footsteps purposeful and quick. Then again, when was the last time she had meandered about anything?

"More pizza crust?" he asked the dog.

Soot got himself up and came over, accepting the final length of crust with the softest mouth this side of a Labrador.

"Listen up, my man." The dog went back to his red-and-black bed and re-settled, looking across the way as he chewed. "I need you to watch over her, okay? She's tough and she's smart, but she lives here alone."

Well . . . at least from what he understood she lived alone. And he didn't want to think of the alternative. Had she dated anyone since their fire?

Shit, the idea any other man had been with her made him want to do pull-ups and sit-ups until he threw up.

You know, to make sure he was yolk'er. Or more yolked. Or the yolk-iest.

Which was pathetic.

"Okay, let's go."

He looked up. Anne was in leggings and a fleece, with a duffel hanging off her shoulder—and he couldn't help but eye her strong, muscular thighs. He had had them around his hips only once, but that was all it had taken for him to never, ever forget what it felt like to be with her.

"Where are we going?" he asked.

Not that he gave a shit. She could have been taking him to get his eyebrows waxed off and his toenails painted and he'd be in.

"You'll find out."

She snagged a dog biscuit and led Soot into his crate—which she had refused to let Danny help set up. "You be a good boy. I'll leave the TV on for you."

"Music is better." When she glanced over her shoulder, Danny shook his head. "If an ad or a show has a dog in it, it can be a trigger for him. Especially if he's enclosed and can't run."

"Since when did you learn about dogs?"

"Just picked things up from Jack. They work with the canine unit a lot."

On her way out of the kitchen, she turned the radio on to the local PBS station. And as the dulcet sounds of the BBC World Service murmured from the little speaker, he followed her lead through the front door and over to her car.

Fifteen minutes later, they were pulling into the parking lot of Mounteria, a wall-climbing place he knew well—and hell, he'd liked the trip so much, he wished it had taken longer. It felt good to sit so close to her, to have excuses—as they talked about nothing—to study her profile, to smell her laundry detergent, to listen to the cadence of her voice.

"Am I going on the wall with you?" he murmured.

"That's up to you."

"I think I'll enjoy the view from below."

As they got out, she glared across the hood of her Subaru at him. "That is not the purpose of this."

"Can I mention it's a side benefit?"

She swung her duffel into place on her shoulder. "Then I'll tell you to not look at my ass."

Okay, so he needed to stay quiet on that subject. 'Cuz he shouldn't make promises he couldn't keep.

The sky was getting dark as they walked through the packed parking lot toward the lit entrance. Mounteria had walls for every skill and age, as well as a juice bar, babysitting, and instruction, so there tended to be two kinds of vehicles outside: minivans that carried kids and roof-racked SUVs that carried serious climbers.

Beside him, Anne was all business and he felt as though he needed to catch up even though he was walking right beside her. Then again, Anne had always been like that: Out in front even when they were in the same place, and he supposed that part of her appeal was the fact that he always felt like he was chasing her. Other women? They tried to rope him in, chain him down, get him to sit, stay, roll over. Not his

Anne. She was too busy living her own life to worry about what the hell he was up to.

God, she was amazing. He just wished . . . fuck, he didn't know what he wished for.

As they walked in, the two guys behind the registration counter looked up and went *Cheers* on her.

"Anne!"

"Yo, Anne."

They were younger, bearded, and in their stringer shirts, they were sporting all kinds of lean muscle. Which naturally made him think about all kinds of throwing stars he didn't own yet.

Too bad you couldn't get that shit on Amazon Prime.

Narrowing his eyes, Danny marched up to the counter and stood higher on his spine so he looked even bigger than he was. "I'm with her."

"He's my guest," she said as she offered her card for swiping. "Can he just watch?"

"Sure, Anne."

"Anything for you."

Danny's caveman wanted to reach across the granite counter and do a little swiping of his own, but he overrode that impulse and continued on through the turnstile, entering a cavernous space that echoed with chatter from the adults and squeaks from the kids. People strung on harnesses were crabbing up verticals, clawing and toe-stretching to hold themselves to multi-height'd blue, green, red, and yellow tilted panels.

Anne went over to the black climb that was the only one with no traffic on it. Then again, the bitch started on the floor and quickly curved back on itself so that you were hanging upside down in mid-air, only your grips and your strength keeping you from peeling free and falling to the mats flat on your ass.

She was going to climb that? he thought. Holy . . . shit.

While he hung back and tried not to tell her to stop being crazy, she put her duffel down on a bench and took off her fleece. In her sports bra and her Lululemon, she was like a fitness model, and he saw that her prosthesis was a passive cosmetic restoration, a static sculpted hand and wrist that attached below her elbow and was held in place by a roll of flesh-colored fabric and plastic. With deft efficiency, she removed that and attached a base that locked in both at the elbow and the shoulder. It was an entire bionic arm, and he respected the fact that it was black and neon green, totally mechanical, and really badass. The end of it was blunt, and she screwed in a curved, fin-like terminal.

"Sit," she ordered him.

Danny went over and lowered himself onto a bench, rubbing sweaty palms on the knees of his jeans. When that didn't go far enough, he had to take off his windbreaker and wipe his brow. If asked, he couldn't have explained why he was stressing.

And then he didn't have anything to worry about.

Anne moved like a dancer, all lithe, energetic strength, and she didn't climb up onto the overhang. She fucking leapt from the mats, jumping up and catching herself. With a swing of her lower body, she gripped with her climbing shoes and proceeded to spider from hold to hold, her torso tight to the wall's face, her fin and her real hand working beautifully.

No hesitation. No missteps, slips, recalibration.

No safety halter, either. Which he was very sure was in violation of Mounteria's rules, but no one stopped her.

A lot of people stopped to watch, however. Within moments, folks gathered around, murmuring, pointing.

She went higher and higher, until she was on the ceiling four stories up. She had barely broken a sweat and her pace never changed as she continued across the ceiling over his head.

Her back was ribboned with muscle fibers, her legs and her calves knotted with strength, her shoulders and upper arms carved. He might have joked about ogling her, but when it came down to it, sex was the last thing on his mind as he played witness to her extraordinary . . . everything.

"Mom? I want to be like her."

He glanced over at a mother-daughter pair who had come to play witness. The girl must have been about ten or twelve, and she was in pink-and-black climbing gear, her eyes wide, her hands on her hips.

"You can absolutely do that," the mom said, "if you work hard enough."

After a moment, Danny cleared his throat. "And if you got the guts," he added hoarsely.

19

Anne was not into showing off. If there was one thing she'd learned as a firefighter, it was that people who wanted to make big impressions got corrections from Murphy's law that inevitably hurt. But if Danny was going to carry around some mantle of guilt, he'd better get a clearer picture of how "badly off" she was.

Dropping back down to the mats, she clapped her palm on her leggings to get the chalk off and turned to—

A circle of people had gathered where she'd been climbing, and their expressions showed a kind of awe that made her wish she hadn't jumped on the wall. And then there was Danny. He was sitting on a bench, his elbows on his knees, his heavy arms cranked with tension like he'd expected her to crash and burn.

He was all she could see, his eyes so intense they took ahold of her.

A tall male body with a bearded face stepped in front of her. "Another great climb, Anne."

Shaking herself, she smiled at Chris, the front desk attendant. "Thanks."

"You know you gotta use a harness, though, right?"

Shit. See? "That was my bad call. It won't happen again."

He put a hand on her shoulder. "We know you got it, it's the other people we worry about. Plus, insurance."

"Yeah."

Danny came up and loomed over Chris like he wanted to underscore that he had a good fifty pounds and four inches of height on the other guy.

And yes, the whole world could see that I'm-a-tough-guy black eye, Anne thought.

Predictably, Chris retracted his hand like an ADT alarm had gone off on her. "So, okay. Yup."

Then he frowned over at the wall where two young guns looked like they were ready to do something stupid. As he walked over to them, Anne was ready to leave. She'd meant to cut the conversation about disability off, and she'd done that. Time to close this door between her and Danny and move along.

Putting her prosthesis up, she pegged him with a stare. "Stop thinking of me as broken or not whole. Put that bullshit down and walk away. It's not doing you any good, and it's insulting to me." When his eyes refused to focus on her fin, she put the thing into his face. "Look at it. Go on, it's not going to hurt you, and it's not going anywhere."

The flush that ran into his cheeks could have meant a lot of things, but she wasn't going to parcel the emotions out. That was his job.

"Your climb was impressive," he said. "For anyone."

"You've got to look at it."

His frown made him seem taller. "I actually don't. Your point's been made, and I appreciate what you're capable of. But you can't legislate where I'm at. It is what it is."

"If I'm the basis for you destroying your life, you're damn straight I can rearrange your thinking. Because it's wrong—"

A chorus of loud talk brought her head around. One of those kids had mounted the wall and was throwing grips out at a fast clip—and Chris was pissed.

Anne refocused. "You need to let me and the past go. Just like I have."

"Well, aren't you self-evolved—and I don't know that I believe you. You're saying you're glad you're not on the crew anymore? That you're psyched you aren't coming to work at the firehouse? That you don't miss our life?" He shook his head like he was rattling his thoughts back into order. "That life, I mean."

"What's my option? Drink myself into a stupor? Get into fist-fights? Screw random people I don't care about because it's a distraction from facing reality? How about I take up smoking and—"

"I'm allowed to cope in a different way than you do."

"Coping? Is that what it's called? I thought the technical term was more like 'implosion.'" As someone gasped behind her, she ignored the sound. "And honestly, I do not understand why—excuse me. Will you *please* look at me when we're talking?"

His stare swung back to her. "First of all, I'll do what I want with my eyes. And second, I'm a little distracted by *that*."

When he pointed over her shoulder, Anne cranked her head around. Up on the ceiling, that teeenage climber was hanging upside down by four points of contact, his hands clawed around two grips, his feet braced against a pair of others. His thigh muscles were vibrating, his forearms shaking. Drops of sweat fell to the mats that were a good twenty feet below him, their soft impacts ringing out in the silence of the crowd, a metronome marking the time that was running out for him.

The kid was in good shape, for sure, well muscled and lean. But he'd let enthusiasm get ahead of his skills and strength, and now he was freaked out and stuck. Without a safety harness on.

Chris was talking to him. "Just stay where you are, my man. We're coming for you."

Anne ran across. "Let me take a harness up to him—"

"Chilli's on it." Chris dropped his voice. "I told him to stop. But he mounted the wall before I could—"

The kid's foot fell free and the crowd gasped. Chilli, the other receptionist, was going as fast as he could, stepping into his own harness and buckling himself in. Good luck, Anne thought. Even if he moved like the wind, things were degrading too fast overhead and this was going to get bad. Time to get her phone—

"I'm already calling it in to EMS." Danny put his cell up to his ear. "He's going to hit hard."

"Hang on, my man!" Chris called out.

The fifteen or so people let out another gasp as, sure enough, the guy lost his other foothold and swung free, all Spidey between two 'scrapers without the web. God, those hands. They were getting more slippery because of the sweat, and with all that weight hanging off them?

Anne went over to the crowd and held her arms out wide. "Let's back up, folks. Way back."

She put herself in front of a young girl, who had to be about twelve or so. "Hey, I love that shirt."

The girl looked down. "I, ah . . . it's my camp."

"I went to Camp Hill, too." Those eyes returned to the ceiling, but Anne took a side step so she was once again in the way. "What cabin were you in?"

"It says it right here."

Just as the girl glanced at her shirt and pointed to the name, there was a collective cry, followed by a hard hit.

Anne looked at the girl's mother and said in a low voice, "Take her into the locker room, right now."

That snapping sound? Had been at least one, maybe two, tibiae breaking.

Danny ended the call into emergency services just as the show-off lost his grip and fell in precisely the wrong position. Well, wrong assuming the kid didn't enjoy the fireworks that came with a pair of compound fractures: He went straight down to the mats, knees locked as if he were going into a pool, arms pinwheeling. Like that was going to help.

The landing would have been a solid ten—if this were the *Jackass* Olympics and Steve-O was a judge. Instead, it was a fundraiser for an orthopedic surgeon, the left leg sustaining a compound fracture that sent the broken bone out through the skin of the shin.

As Anne held the crowd back, Danny front-and-centered with the climber, now patient, taking one of those writhing hands in a strong grip. Junior was sporting the T-shirt of one of the local Catholic private schools, and between the Proactiv complexion and the clear issues with risk assessment, it was obvious they were in minor territory.

Not that people who had reached or surpassed the age of consent couldn't be morons, too.

Kettle. Black.

"Stay still," Danny said. "Help's coming."

"Is it broken? Is my leg—"

The kid lifted his head to look down his body, but Danny cut that bright idea off at the pass. Adding a visual to the pain was not going to help considering the lower part of that leg looked like a human anatomy exam.

"Stop moving, buddy." Danny pushed those shoulders back to the mat. "I want you to relax and take some deep breaths. What's your name?"

"David. Dave Richmond."

"Hey, Dave, I'm Danny. I'm a trained medic—how old are you?"

"Eighteen."

"Are you allergic to anything?"

"N-n-n-no. Aw, man, my mom's going to kill me."

"Any underlying medical conditions?" Other than a garden-variety case of testosterone-linked stupids. "Anything I need to know about?"

"No—what's wrong with my leg? I can't feel anything."

Probably shock, but spinal injuries could be sneaky, and until there was a rule-out, they couldn't take anything for granted.

"Just lie still, 'kay? How can we reach your mom?"

Anne came over and knelt down. "How we doing?"

For a split second, Danny was back in the past, the two of them out on an emergency call, bent over a patient, assessing vitals, calling in status to the ER, going on transport. She was always his partner—

Had been. *Had* been his partner.

And yeah, it was fucked up to get all nostalgic about him and Anne dealing with pain and suffering and injury, but he missed that connection. That day-to-day contact. That sense that he didn't have to say things to her; she just knew.

Because her brain and his worked the same way.

"Dave's doing great." In a low voice, Danny added, "Little shocky."

"Looks it. Who's coming on the call?"

"We are."

Anne's face got tight, but she hid that quick by addressing the climber's friend, who was all nervous off to the side. "Can you get his ID for us? From whatever locker he was using?"

The blond-haired kid looked at the break and swallowed as if he were in conversation with his gag reflex. "Yeah. Is he—is he in trouble? I told him not to do that."

"We just want to take care of him. So if you could get his wallet and phone, it would be a huge help."

The friend walked off, and Anne got up and spoke to the two receptionists. Frick and Frack, the bearded nonconforming conformists, were as agitated as the Instagram set could get about anything other than the inhuman atrocity of almond milk instead of soy in their matcha lattes.

Or maybe he was just being unfair as he read into their vaguely annoyed expressions.

Probably.

Distant sirens grew louder and louder, and then flashing red lights penetrated Mounteria's glass front, strobing the injured kid's panicked face. And then the friend was back with the wallet.

Danny took it, flipped the thing open, and cursed. "You're seventeen, not eighteen, Dave."

"I'm almost eighteen."

"The law doesn't count 'almosts.' So how about we get a parent on the phone? We're going to need to get consent for treatment."

"Your mom's gonna be so pissed," the friend muttered.

Dave shook his head. "Can't we just take me to the hospital—"

Danny cut that shit off, his patience running out. "No. Let's get Mom or Dad on the horn. Now."

20

When members of the 499 arrived with a stretcher, Anne stepped back and needed a distraction so she chatted up Chris again. It turned out Dave of the broken leg was a serial PITA who hadn't been properly checked in, and both receptionists were finished with his act.

"You've done the best you could," she told him. "It's going to be fine."

As she spoke, she was mostly talking to herself. Moose, Danny's old roommate, was at the head of the stretcher and Emilio Chavez was on the back end, the pair advancing through the open space with purpose. Both men were dressed in working uniforms, the shirts with the fire-service crest on the pec and the navy blue pants, what Anne used to wear every day and night.

The men faltered when they saw her. And again when Danny stood up.

Then Moose snapped out of it. "Hey, you two. What have we got here?"

Danny looked at her. She looked at Danny.

"Compound—"

"Fell from the ceiling—"

"—fracture due to—"

"—resulting in a compound—"

"—unrestrained fall."

"—fracture."

As they shut up at the same time, she forced herself not to look away. "David is a minor, and his mother is on the way."

Moose gave her a smile and then it was all about the patient, he and Chavez following a protocol that Anne knew only too well. In New Brunswick, the fire service also functioned as paramedics and EMTs, and she ran through each assessment step in her head.

I can still do this, she thought. *I can still do my job.*

But even as the conviction hit her, it was a useless revelation, a lantern without a wick. This kind of a run was only part of it. Sure, a person on the fire service needed to be able to handle a kid with a broken leg in a non-confrontational, non-emergent environment like this. But they also dragged charged lines up stairs, punched through drywall with axes, pulled downed colleagues out of hot spots.

Danny moved over to her, his head tilting as he watched the IV line get set. "How you doing?"

The words were so quiet, she almost missed them, and she was reminded of the way he'd always spoken to her on the job. Private, even in public.

Anne opened her mouth to I'm-fine him, but didn't follow through on the impulse. She wasn't sure why she couldn't speak the lie—and had no intention of looking too closely at the way the perfectly appropriate deflection dried up in her throat.

After Dave was on a board with a cervical collar around his neck and his lower leg stabilized, Moose and Chavez got him up on the stretcher. Mom arrived just as they were strapping him down, and she was in full scramble, hair a mess, her coat flapping, her purse clapping against her leg as she ran to her son.

"What the hell is wrong with you, David!"

Danny muttered, "Not the first time she's been in this situation."

"Yeah." Anne went over and got her duffel. "Let's go."

This show-off session had been a colossal mistake, and the fact that it was ending with her on the sidelines as Moose and Emilio did the job she'd had to leave behind? She'd been right. God did not like the prideful, and although she had wanted to prove to Danny she was a-okay, she had to cop to some ego being involved.

As Moose interceded with Mom and brought the woman up to date, Emilio hesitated and then came over. He nodded at Danny, but it was a cursory hello—because hey, those two were going to see each other on next rotation.

"How are you, Anne?"

Chavez had always been a good guy, and the gentle way he looked at her was everything she remembered about him. He was also still the tall, dark, and handsome firefighter hero who belonged in a centerfold calendar of men in turnout bottoms holding long hoses—and yet he'd never been her type. Nope, back in the day, she'd never managed to look past Danny Maguire.

What was the question?

"I'm good." She smiled brightly, and then hit the dimmer switch so she didn't come across as desperate. "I'm great."

After the collapse in that warehouse fire, Emilio had come by the rehab hospital once, and the resolute way he'd focused on her face and not her arm had made her rush through the visit. He'd seemed relieved at the excuse she'd given him to leave, and she hadn't faulted him. As he'd stood awkwardly next to her hospital bed, no doubt he'd been glad that he hadn't been hurt—and he was decent enough of a guy to feel bad about that understandable relief.

"How's you?' she asked. Because she had to.

"Ah, great. I'm great. Yeah, thanks."

He smiled, but then lost the expression. When he resolutely put the lift back on his lips, she wanted to tell him not to bother.

Anne rubbed her sweaty palm on the seat of her leggings again. "I'm glad. That's good."

"Yeah, it's . . . it's good." He glanced over his shoulder. "Looks like we're moving. Good to see you, Anne—later, Dannyboy."

"Great to see you," she said too loudly. "Really great."

Chris came over. "I didn't know you're friends with the EMT guys."

"I'm not. I mean, I was. I used to be—" She shook her head. "Listen, I've got to say it again. I feel really badly about all this. I shouldn't have been showboating."

"That kid's been trouble since he joined. At least now we have an excuse to cancel his membership. And he signed the standard release, so hopefully we won't get sued."

Danny stepped in. "If you need us to make statements, you know where to find us."

"You have *my* number," she corrected. "Let me know if I can help. I feel responsible."

Chris smiled. "You're the best, Anne. Chilli and I appreciate you."

"Nice to meet you," Danny said as he barged in and stuck his hand out like it was a sword pointed at the other man's gut.

There was an awkward pause before Chris shook what was put out there, and then Anne headed for the door before Danny broke the poor guy over his knee and threw the two halves into the street.

Outside, it was dark as midnight, and Moose was closing up the rear of the ambulance. The flashing red bubbler on the cab took her back to the job again, the rhythmic pulses of light so familiar and yet so foreign, now.

Sadness, insidious and castrating, stole her breath.

"So," Moose said as he looked back and forth between them.

His smile was slow and suggested Danny was going to get a boat-load of shit back at the firehouse. And all she knew was that if Maguire tried to put his arm around her shoulder or insinuate anything, he was going to learn firsthand what it was like to be in her situation.

'Cuz she'd rip his damn limb off.

"Don't you have a patient to take care of," Danny muttered.

Moose shrugged. "Chavez is taking a medical history."

"Which can be done in transit."

"Mom asked us to wait so she could bring her car around. She wants to follow."

Anne was tempted to walk off, but then Danny wouldn't have a ride, and no doubt that would come up in conversation.

"So." Moose rocked on the heels of his boots. "Nice weather we're having—"

Danny glanced at her. "Come on, let's go."

Damn it.

"Hey," Moose said, "we should do dinner this Saturday. Come to our place—Deandra is taking a cooking class and she loves to show off."

As a tense silence bloomed like a bad smell, Anne threw some words out to fill the void. "I thought she was going to be a hair-dresser."

"Well, that's just the first tier of her lifestyle business. She wants to be into hair, makeup, skin care, fashion, home decor, healthy eating. She's going all the way. I'm very proud of my wife."

When the guy gave Danny a look, Anne lost her patience—and was rescued by Mom tooling up in a minivan that had led a very hard life. The thing had a ding on the front bumper, scratches down the side, and a side-view mirror that was hanging by its proverbial optic nerve.

Made you wonder whether the apple didn't fall far from the tree—either that or maybe it just stole the car keys a lot.

Moose clapped his hands. "Gotta go! See you Saturday—Anne, I'll give Deandra your number so she can text you with instructions."

Instructions? And how the hell did she yell out, *Please don't*, without being offensive? The last person she wanted to get to know better was that wife of his. She'd been through the wedding from hell, and that had been more than enough contact.

The ambulance left sweet diesel fumes in its wake as Moose piloted it off in the direction of the University of New Brunswick Hospital, the beaten-up minivan a sad-sack wind sock following behind.

Anne looked at Danny. "I'm not going to have dinner with them. Or you. It's not appropriate."

"Not worth the time, is more like it. These two are a mess."

They stepped off the curb at the same moment, and the fact that they fell into stride together as they headed for her car was the kind of thing she deliberately messed up with a hop and a skip. The good news was that as they got in, he seemed uncharacteristically quiet.

At least he wasn't spewing a bunch of it'll-be-great rhetoric about the never-happening, in-Moose's-dreams Saturday dinner from hell.

Out on the road, as Anne went through a series of stoplights and bunch of turns that she could do in her sleep, she found her palm getting sweaty again. Matter of fact, her body felt like it was under a heat lamp. As she came up to a red light, she peeled her fleece off over her head and tossed it into the back.

"How did you get to my house?" she asked. "I didn't see your car."

"I walked."

She glanced over. "Five miles?"

"I needed to clear my head." As his hand dipped into his windbreaker, he cursed and took it back out. "Yes, I know. No smoking in your car."

"Absolutely not."

"Already said I know," he shot back.

At the next light, she noted the way his knee was bouncing up and down like the left half of him was running a hypothetical sprint.

Just as when they'd fallen into step across the parking lot, she knew how he was feeling. Her heart was beating about as fast as that foot of his was tapping in that wheel well, and she wasn't stupid. They were both rattled, the past and present colliding and leaving shattered pieces of "normal," "forever," and "never going to happen to me" in the street.

That was the thing about life. Habit and routine made things feel permanent, but that was all an illusion based on the very flimsy foundation of repetition. Change and chaos was a far better bet to put your faith in.

At least you would never be surprised when things went tits up.

"I'll take you home then," she announced.

"I can walk."

"I know you can."

"It's fine—"

"It's cold—"

"Thanks, *Mom*."

Anne locked her molars. It was either that, or this—whatever it was—was going to escalate into a whole lot of yelling over nothing.

And meanwhile, the pressure was still building. In her. In him. Until she was damn sure they were within two psi of blowing the safety glass out of her Subaru's doors and windshield.

When she got to his house, she pulled into the short drive, went around back, and hit the brakes. She could tell he was rank pissed at her reroute, but guess what. She didn't care.

She wanted him angry at her.

It was safer that way: Somewhere along the ride to his apartment, frustration and pain had kindled into energy of a different kind. Heat of a different kind. Urgency . . . of a dangerous kind.

Abruptly, the confines of the car's interior shrunk down on her. On them.

"Put the car in park," Danny said in a gruff voice.

Nope, she thought. Not a good call. Reverse was the gear she wanted.

But her hand had other ideas, not just moving the gear shift into place but turning the engine off. In the sudden silence, she was aware of breathing heavily, and she parted her lips to get some more oxygen into her lungs.

"We are not doing this." Her voice was too low. And not in terms of volume. "I am not doing this."

"You sure about that." Danny turned to her. "So tell me to get the fuck out of your car—"

"Get the fuck out of my car."

Except only a part of her meant it—and Danny, who was an idiot savant when it came to emotions, knew that. The bastard *knew* it.

Losing her temper and her mind, Anne reached for him, clapping her hand on the side of his neck and yanking him to her mouth. And because she could always rely on Danny Maguire not doing the right thing, he didn't hesitate.

He kissed the ever-living shit out of her, his lips grinding on hers, his tongue penetrating her with such an erotic dominance that she was instantly reminded of why he'd given her the sex of her life the one time she'd been with him.

When they finally came up for air, his hooded eyes were a mirror she didn't want to look into. She did not need confirmation that all her heavy-handed, holier-than-thou rhetoric was about to get haymakered in favor of Danny's first-choice coping mechanism.

Namely, meaningless sex.

"Are you going to make me ask," he said. "Because I will."

Damn it, there were all kinds of reasons not to do this.

Too bad each and every one of them was in a foreign language.

"I don't want to talk," she said as she grabbed her keys and got out of her car.

And what do you know, as Danny came prowling around to her, he didn't seem to be interested in conversation, either.

21

No talking. As Danny followed Anne to his back door, she was obviously determined not to think too much about this, and that was fine with him. He wasn't into talking. He wanted in that woman right now. The delay taking down her pants and fucking off his button fly was going to test the limits of his patience.

Once they were inside his crappy kitchen, it was on again, their bodies colliding in the darkness, his hands rough, her nails digging into his windbreaker. Backing her up to the counter by the sink, he popped her off the floor and jerked her knees apart.

He didn't want this to happen in his bedroom, and not because the place was a mess. He had done a number of women in there, and even though the first thing Anne was going to do was convince herself this didn't mean shit, he was not confusing her with those one-night stands.

This was different.

When Anne braced herself up, he hooked the waistband of her leggings and stripped them off. Then he was running his hands up those smooth muscles of her thighs. She was in great physical shape, nothing like those soft, augmented types he'd been picking up at Timeout, but he wouldn't have cared what her body was like.

This was *Anne*.

"I used a condom. With the others," he said as he looked her straight in the eye. "Every one, each time."

When she closed her eyes, he figured he'd blown it, but he wanted her to know. And the truth was, in the last ten months, he'd practiced safe sex not because he gave a shit about himself, but because he had hoped, prayed, for this moment with her.

He had taken care of himself for her.

"Just kiss me," she muttered.

And that was the last thing they said to each other. Beneath his roving hands, she arched, bringing her breasts against his chest. Closer, he wanted to be closer to her, but he also wanted to slow down because he needed to remember every second of this.

When her hand fumbled at his fly, he was on it, tearing the buttons apart, his cock doing the rest of the job.

Anne tilted her hips and took a hold on him, the sensation of her hand on his shaft was enough to make him groan. It was awkward, though, their two bodies not quite right at counter height—so he solved the problem by cupping her ass and holding her up.

It was better than he remembered. The fit. The slick, hot squeeze. The smell of her shampoo, her hair in his face, her grip on his shoulders strong and sure.

He walked them through to the sitting room, letting his stride do the pumping and the rhythm. And then there was a brief parting as he laid her down.

That didn't last.

Danny was on top of her in a heartbeat, hooking his forearm under her knee and cranking her leg up, his erection going back in

on a rush. He didn't hold back, his pelvis punching in tight and re-
treating, her body absorbing the pounding, her breath harsh and
hoarse.

He refused to orgasm. Even though his body had been on the
brink the instant he'd entered her, he was holding off. But it was getting tough. He was starting to shake, the temptation to let himself go
becoming a painful denial.

Anne solved his problem. With a gasp, she threw her head back,
and that was when he stilled. He wanted to feel her come for him, and
he closed his eyes concentrating on the way her sex gripped him. And
then he was off on his own ride, his hips rocking into her, locking in,
his release the kind of thing that made his head spin.

So good.

Too good.

Damn it.

As Anne felt Danny pump into her, she knew what that meant.
Also knew that he was the kind of man who wasn't done even after he
finished.

Opening her eyes, she stared at the ceiling of his sitting room and
decided she was way too old for the kind of college hookup this was:
guy's apartment, on the sofa, reckless and regretful.

Or at least that was what she was telling herself this was.

Danny lifted his head. Just as she was about to tell him she had to
go, he started moving again, deep inside, slower this time. The thrusts
were hell and heaven combined, and there was a challenge in his eyes,
like he knew she was going to try to downplay how amazing the
sex was.

Which would have been easy to do if it didn't feel so right.

Too bad the sensations were the only thing that made any sense.

Closing her lids, she fell back into the abyss, her body taking over, her brain taking a seat in the waiting room. God knew there was going to be plenty of time to ruminate over the stupids she was rocking. For the moment, she might as well just feel him.

And God knew there was so much of Danny to feel.

He was big and heavy, and all that mass and weight was part of the appeal. Built as she was, Anne didn't feel dainty very often—and that little-girl-needing-rescue stuff wasn't something she was interested in anyway. But there was something erotic about being under a man with the size and power of Danny—

From out of nowhere, an image of them in the fire together came to her and she vividly recalled their eyes meeting through their air masks, the fire roiling across the ceiling, the danger and isolation so real.

I love you.

As the words ricocheted around her head, she pushed at his shoulders, but it was too late. She was orgasming again, the release taking over everything. Tears, unexpected and unwelcomed, pricked her eyes and she blinked to clear them.

Danny's tremendous body churned above hers, and a panic that he might see her cry took her out of the sex, trapping her inside her head.

The truth was, he mattered too much to her just like she mattered too much to him. And this erotic collision was a recipe for disaster . . . that was somehow totally inevitable.

When he finally went still, she was breathing hard, but not from exertion. And she decided to count to twenty before she tried to get out from under him in the hopes she didn't look as frantic as she was.

She made it to fourteen. "I have to go."

Danny's head dropped into her shoulder. "Okay. Yeah. Sure."

Just as she was about to push at his shoulders, he moved back. And still she scrambled out from his body, barely giving him time to stand.

As soon as she was on the vertical, she was reminded that there had been no condom and she moved quickly to the bathroom, shutting herself in. There was a roll of toilet paper on the sink counter and she unraveled some around her fin, wadded it up, and tucked it between her thighs.

Out in the hall, she walked stiffly into the kitchen. She'd worn a thong with her leggings and put that on quick to hold things in place. She felt better when she was fully dressed, and it was only then that she went back to the sitting room.

She would rather have left without saying a word.

Then again, she had expected him to come out. And the fact that he didn't made her uneasy, although that was just part of the long list of things she didn't want to examine too closely.

Standing in the archway, she looked at him. He was where she'd left him, sitting on the sofa, his hair a mess. He'd done his jeans back up, thank God.

She remembered walking in on him the night before, those tattoos out on display for an audience he had not anticipated.

"I know," he said roughly. "You don't have to repeat it."

"What."

"Just one night. Only once." He exhaled as if he were smoking, except there was nothing lit in his hand, no haze in the air. "You said that the last time we had sex, remember?"

Anne felt like she should apologize, but come on. They were two consenting adults, and he was right. That was exactly what she was going to tell him.

"I'm glad we're on the same page."

His laugh was sharp. "Yeah."

Anne turned away. "Take care of yourself."

She headed for the door, expecting to be called back at any moment. But he let her go—and as she stepped out into the cold, she told herself that was what she wanted.

"And it is, damn it," she muttered as she got into her Subaru.

Behind the wheel, she sat and stared out the windshield. A pain behind her sternum had her do an internal myocardial infarction inventory, but there was no nausea, left-arm pain, or dizziness. So she wasn't having a heart attack.

She just hurt in a place that had been silent for a very long time. But that didn't change anything. What had just happened between them was rooted in the past, in ten months ago, in a fire that had long ago been extinguished, not even the embers burning.

It had been . . . a physical release of all that emotion stirred up by the rescue call for that kid.

With no further implications than that.

Starting the car and putting it in reverse, she found poetic justice in pulling out of his driveway backward—as if she could unmake the decision to go into that dark apartment with Danny. She didn't remember the trip home. One second she was K-turning in front of the duplex. The next, she was parking at her house.

Letting herself inside, she was so glad she had Soot to look after. Otherwise, she was liable to pace around and clean something that was already clean.

Soot stood up in his crate as she came in, his bony tail rattling the links.

"Hey, big man." Crouching down, she let him out. "How about a piddle?"

She expected him to go immediately to the back door. Instead, he took his big head and rubbed it on her hand, her torso, the outside of her leg. Putting her arm around him, she gave him the space to circle. And circle. And circle.

Under her palm, his short fur was smooth and warm, and she loved the feel of him pushing into her.

"I'm glad to see you, too," she said hoarsely.

c h a p t e r

22

M id-morning the following day, Anne left the office and went downtown to the registry of deeds. Parking between a Chevy Equinox and a truck that had rusted lace around its wheel wells, she got out and walked up to a building that was right out of the seventies: Floor after floor of individual windows were covered by a superfluous lattice of grungy concrete that was about as attractive as those plaid suits with the huge lapels had been.

If it hadn't been for the set of steps, she would have had no clue where the entrance was.

As she walked into a lobby that was as well-appointed as a Greyhound terminal, she could smell old mold and ancient nicotine. Then again, the fake wood paneling had no doubt been an original installation and the stuff was porous when it came to scents, a jealous guard of dubious treasure.

The registry was on the first floor, and she pushed open a heavy door marked with the city seal and block roman lettering that was flaking off. On the far side, she got a load of the fry-station equivalent of civil servants. The two receptionists, a man and a woman, were seated behind a partition that was like a bank's, with cutouts to pass papers through and twin computers—and the pair of them looked as if they were along the lines of that not-really-oak paneling: Mr. and Mrs. Anachronism were both in their sixties, with polyester uniforms and the same hair style of a perm pushed back off the face and sprayed into place.

Anne went over to the woman. Because girl power.

"Hi, I'd like to do a records search." She smiled to seem warm. Nice. Non-threatening. "It's on six parcels of property downtown? I have the addresses, but when I tried to get a log-in online, I was denied."

"Did you call the help line?"

The phone started to ring, and the man next door picked up after three, no, four . . . wait, five rings. "Hello. Help line."

Anne glanced at him as he doodled on a pad. Then she looked back at the woman. "Well, it sounds like those calls get answered here."

"Did you call the help line?"

Is this like a video game where you have to get to the next level? Anne wondered.

"Yes, I did. And I was told to come down here."

The receptionist over on the phone said in a bored voice, "You'll have to come down here and get one issued. Our server is down."

"So that's why I'm here," Anne said. "Except if your server's not working, how will being here help me to get a log-in?"

The woman took a piece of paper off a stack and slid it across the counter. "Fill this out."

Anne glanced down. "Can I just go through a physical search?"

"Fine." The form was retracted and an old-fashioned ledger was pushed across at her. "Sign in. And I'll need to see your driver's license."

After filling in her name and address, Anne flashed her ID, and the receptionist hit a buzzer that released a locked gate over on the right.

"Here's the map," the woman drawled. "We're here for questions."

But I'd have to fill out a form, right? Anne thought. *Or call your buddy.*

With a nod, she took the piece of paper and walked through. Guess she went down the hall?

Some three doors later, she found what she was after. The deed room was lit bright as an OR and had a tall ceiling that was useless, as the rows of metal file cabinets only went up to chin height. There was a long desk with three computers on it, but she didn't have a log-in sorted, natch. Besides, she preferred to do things by hand—

Between one blink and the next, she got an image of her fingers clawing into Danny's shoulder as he churned on top of her.

Exhaustion, a parting gift from her night of no sleep, bear-hugged her. But she'd already spent enough time trying to force what she'd done into any kind of rational framework. At least Danny hadn't tried to call or text. She needed space.

On that theory, she should move to Canada.

Right, time to look at the map and go on the hunt.

A number of desks with chairs were in the middle of the room, and she claimed one by putting her bag and her coat on it. As she got out her notes, she thought of her new boss's pep talk. Someone had died in at least two of those old warehouse fires. And hell, she had been permanently changed.

So there were crimes to solve here.

There was still something worth fighting to protect. And in this case, it was justice.

"Sorry I'm running a little late."

As Danny got up from a sofa that was too soft, he put his hand out to a fifty-year-old woman with thick gray hair and a shapeless brown dress that reminded him of the tarp he had over the chopped wood out at the farm.

"It's okay," he said.

Her limpid, concerned eyes made him want to go Warner Bros. cartoon through a wall.

"Daniel Maguire." She smiled as they shook. "That's a good Irish name."

"Yeah."

"I'm Irish, too. Dr. Laurie McAuliffe. Won't you come in?"

Not if I had a choice. "Sure."

The office beyond was pretty much what he expected, a lot of earthen tones and more Wonder Bread furniture, some sort of ornamental water thingy in the corner making I'm-a-fountain noises.

"Where do you want me to sit?" he said.

"Anywhere you like."

Danny surveyed the choices—two-seater couch, armchair, armchair, rocker—and wondered whether this was the first of the tests to determine whether he was keeping his job or not. As he couldn't guess what it was assessing, he went with the closest armchair.

Lowering himself down, he was not surprised she took the rocker. Given the pad on the little table next to it, it seemed like it was her normal perch.

"So, do you want to talk about why you're here?"

No. "I have to do this to keep my job. How long does the test take?"

"Test?"

"Yeah, I have to pass a test, right?"

The woman smiled again. "Not really."

"Don't lie to me."

As her eyes narrowed, he got his first inkling that maybe things weren't as loosey-goosey, touchy-feely as he'd thought. "That's not a lie. My job is to evaluate your mental and emotional state, but I do not do that by giving you a bunch of fill-in-the-blanks."

"You've read my personnel file, right?"

"Yes. I have. It's right over there."

He glanced across at a desk he'd missed when he'd come in. There was a stack of books on the blotter, a mug with the Harvard crest, and a thick manila folder right in the center.

Danny shrugged. "So you know everything I'd tell you anyway. Why don't we save time and agree I've got your version of PTSD. Then we can put together a therapy plan, that I won't ultimately follow, and be on our merry ways."

"Why don't you tell me what's in that folder?"

Danny leveled a stare at the woman. "Mother committed suicide when I was twelve. Father was a drunk. Brother died at a scene a couple of years ago. Lost a fellow firefighter a little while later. And then . . . yeah."

"And then what."

He shifted his eyes to the water feature. Given that it didn't have a cord running into a socket, he guessed it was battery operated. Or, knowing the inevitable politics of people like Dr. McAuliffe, solar powered. 'Cuz global warming—or climate change. Or whatever they were calling it these days.

"Danny? And then what."

"There was an accident at work, and whatever, no one died."

Danny thought about Anne the night before, fully dressed but for her leggings, staring at the ceiling while he orgasmed into her. He could still feel the hard contour of her black and green prosthesis, moving across his lower back.

She had gotten off, too. He'd been sure of it. But he wasn't fooling himself. She'd used him like a dildo, and he'd let her do that again a thousand times if she wanted to.

"Tell me about that accident," the doctor prompted.

"You read the file."

"I know the facts, not how you feel about them."

Danny shrugged. "I was thrilled that I cut Anne Ashburn's hand off. Absolutely the highlight of my career, something I'll look back on with pride and satisfaction for decades to come. My only disappointment is that I didn't get some kind of commemorative plaque down at the stationhouse for it. How's that?"

The woman's stare narrowed again. "You do realize that if you ever want to go into another fire again that I'm going to have to sign off on it? There is a pass or fail on this, even without any pen or paper. So you're incented to be candid as opposed to belligerent. Assuming you do want to go back to work."

Sitting forward, Danny pegged her with hard eyes. "This is bullshit. Twenty years ago, firefighters didn't have to sit through—"

"This psychology crap? I can guess where you're going with this tantrum, and in the interest of saving time—which seems to be an imperative for you—I would say that what is bullshit to you is a field of discipline that I've got a PhD in and will spend the rest of my life further researching, participating in, and advocating for. So if you're looking to persuade me that there isn't value in what I do, you're pushing water uphill. You're also not changing the reality that I am the gatekeeper of the hurdle you need to get over if you want to ever hold a charged line again."

"So what if I just lie to you and tell you what you want to hear."

"You don't know what I want to hear." The woman smiled again. "So how about we start with Anne Ashburn. Tell me what happened ten months ago."

Danny crossed his arms over his chest. And then dropped them because of the whole tantrum thing.

"Believe it or not," Dr. McAuliffe murmured, "I want you to get back to work. I really do. It may not feel like it, but I'm here to help you. We have the same goals, you and I."

He thought back to Anne showing up and finding him passed out on his couch the night before last. She'd thrown a lot at him, but she'd had a point. She was the one dealing with a permanent injury. He was just being a little bitch, trying to light the world on fire because he was angry at himself.

"I'm in love with her," he said gruffly. "Anne, that is. And that should pretty much tell you what you need to know."

23

Anne was back at her office, packing up for the day, when a
sharp knock got her attention. "Yes?"

Don walked in. Her boss had his suit jacket off, and the
sleeves of his business shirt rolled up. His tie was red and the city's sig-
nature anchor was on repeat.

He looked like he was on the twelfth hour of a ten-hour shift. "We
need to talk."

"Yup, I got you something."

As she leaned down under her desk, he muttered, "Is it Advil?"

Straightening, she held out a pink plastic bag. "Surprise."

"You mind telling me why Charles Ripkin is on my phone."

"Here, I'll open it for you." She took out a wrapped-up object.
"Unless you want to do the honors?"

"He's threatening to go to the mayor and complain."

She shrugged. "On what grounds?"

"He said you demanded a meeting with him, wanted to see proof
of insurance, were harassing his executive assistant. What the hell are
you doing?"

Probably not a good time to remind Don about his pursuit-of-justice pep talk, she thought.

Anne unwrapped the white mug and turned the thing around so the black lettering faced him. "Ta-da!"

Don took the gift. "'World's Greatest Boss'?"

"You're my Michael Scott. Just without the, you know, stupid stuff."

"I'm thinking about firing you again, FYI."

"But it's for a much better reason, right? Now you're frustrated that I'm taking the job too seriously, so this is improvement."

Don's lids dropped to half-mast. "You are my punishment for sins in an earlier life."

"More like virtues. Anyway, I went down to the registry of deeds this morning."

"So I can expect a call from them as well? The private sector always moves faster than we in government do, which explains why Ripkin got to me first about you."

"Ripkin Development has purchased three of the six warehouse sites in the last twenty-four months. You don't think there's a connection?"

"He's buying cheap real estate to develop. That's what developers do. Hence the title of his company. And nothing devalues even depressed sites more than a good fire."

"He bought those warehouses before the fires."

Don frowned. "So what are you suggesting. The structures weren't worth much. I mean, you want to make some money doing insurance fraud, you torch a mansion to the ground. Not a dilapidated warehouse."

"What if you wanted to clear the land and not have to pay for it?

You burn what's on it, cash in the insurance policy, use the proceeds to clear what's left in terms of debris—which is considerably less than even the rotted shells that were there first. It pays for itself—not that bad a strategy."

"You could get away with it once. But you try that two or three times and it's like an engraved invitation for fraud charges."

"What if you had different insurance companies. The properties are all owned by different entities. It wasn't until I went on a wild-goose chase through layers of incorporators that I discovered Ripkin owns them. He's covering his tracks about a lot of things."

There was a long silence. And then Don shut her door. "Listen, about Ripkin."

"Do not tell me I can't go talk to him. I reject completely the notion that rich people should be granted special privileges. He's no different than any other witness or interested party."

"I agree."

"But . . ."

"You recall that fire at Ripkin's oceanfront estate. It was about, what, just over a year ago?"

"I responded with the four-nine-nine to it."

"I remember from the report." There was another pause. "I put a really good investigator on the scene, a guy named Bob Burlington. He was doing a thorough job."

"You'd accept nothing less from a subordinate."

"But he didn't finish the investigation because his body washed up on shore in the bay about three weeks into the case."

Anne frowned. "Now that you mention it, I read something about that in the paper. And there was talk at the station. He had a heart attack though, didn't he?"

"I don't think we're ever going to know the truth. His boat was found first by a trawler, and there was no evidence of foul play. His remains turned up a day later, and they had been chewed on. The medical examiner stated that the probable cause of death was an MI, which given Bob's affinity for fried food and no exercise made sense. The manner, however, was undetermined."

From what Anne understood about determinations of death in Massachusetts, the Commonwealth's medical examiner and his or her office assessed the remains and assigned a cause that could be anything from a disease process like cancer, cardiovascular problems, or an infection, to trauma to the body like an internal bleed from a gunshot wound or blunt force from someone getting hit with something. The manner was then assigned to one of four categories: natural, accident, homicide, or suicide. If the medical examiner could not place the cause within those criteria, then it was ruled "undetermined."

In Bob Burlington's case, you had to wonder if he'd had a heart attack on his boat and fallen overboard because of it—or whether someone had thrown him off the vessel and he'd died trying to swim to shore.

Except if you were trying to kill somebody, you wouldn't take a chance on the guy's ticker quitting halfway to land, would you.

Maybe he was strangled first.

"So an autopsy was performed?" she asked.

"It was. But again, because of damage to the remains, it was impossible to rule out trauma—or state it had conclusively taken place."

"And you think Ripkin was involved in the death?"

"I don't know, but I am very clear that I feel a responsibility to all you guys not to put you in harm's way. So be very careful with that man. I won't stop you from going up there because you've laid out a valid investigatory rationale for talking to him. But I do think Bob's death was suspicious, and I'm not about to bury another agent on my watch."

"What happened to the investigation afterward?"

"It was closed by another agent of ours, and the question I still ask myself is what did Bob know that he didn't get to document officially before he died."

"Fair enough. I'll watch myself."

"Good." Don lifted the mug up and looked inside. Checked out the handle. "I'm a coffee drinker, you know."

"I didn't. I might've guessed from the bagel, but I don't like to take things for granted."

"You sure about that?" He looked around the desk. "How's the dog."

"Great. He's a good boy." Soot offered a wag, like he knew he was being discussed. "I'm really glad he's with me."

Her boss took his mug back over to the door. "If Ripkin gives you any problems, I'll get you a warrant. I'd love to bring him down. And if you need someone to watch the dog during business hours, I'll let him out. Long as he doesn't bite me." Don opened her door. "Oh, and we're getting some bad storms later. Be careful on your drive home."

———————

God, Tom hated rubber chicken dinners. And suits. And ties.

As he walked out of the howling wind and hail and into the Grand Canyon–sized lobby of the downtown Marriott, he was already planning his exit and the immediate removal of the navy blue straitjacket and red hangman's noose that were not just cramping his style, but making him scratch.

As he was childless, he didn't have the sick-kid/nanny-issue/sitter's-a-no-show option.

But he always had the firehouse-emergency card in his back pocket.

The registration tables were mobbed, folks lining up for their Hello, My Name Is badges. He skipped that nonsense. He never wore a name tag. For one, he'd been in the paper enough that his identity spoke for itself, but more than that, he wasn't going to encourage approaches, casual conversations, or the airing of issues. Especially after the Anne thing.

God, the first month after she'd been hurt had been ridiculous, all kinds of acquaintances and hangers-on coming at him with various levels of sincerity. Like his family business was any of theirs.

"Chief, over here."

Brent Mathison, the president of IAFF Local 5690, waved from the base of the escalators. The guy was dressed in a navy blue suit and a red tie, his union pin on his lapel, his military haircut making him look like the security detail for a dignitary.

People called out Tom's name as he went across the patterned carpet, and he nodded at the various political wonks, society types, and media whores.

He put his palm out to Brent, and they did the shake and slap. "Just so you know, I plan on having an urgent stationhouse call in thirty-five minutes."

"Shocker." Brent straightened his tie. "So Graham Perry came and found me. The mayor wants to see us."

"Now? What about her dog and pony show to the masses."

"It's the cocktail hour. There's time. Come on, the greenroom is over here."

Tom fell into step with the other guy. "Why do I get the feeling I'm being set up?"

"Because you're paranoid."

Tom nodded at a pair of lobbyists, but didn't slow down as they started to roundabout. "Tell me something, how old are you?"

"Excuse me?"

"How old?"

"Thirty-five."

They entered a carpeted hallway that was nothing but brass-plaqued double doors and poster ads for theater shows, high-end restaurants, and jewelers. The air smelled like steak, which suggested the hotel had ventilation issues, and he wondered when its management had last done a fire drill for the staff.

Brent looked over. "Why'd you ask me my age?"

"Because you look a little old to be this naive."

"I don't know what your problem with Catherine is—"

"Oh, so now we're on a first-name basis with her, are we. What's next? Netflix and chill?"

"—a good mayor, a better person, and she gets us. Her father was a firefighter."

Tom shook his head. "Politicians do one thing with reliability and that's look out for themselves. You're going to learn this the hard way, but that evolution is not my problem."

"You don't know her." Brent stopped in front of something called the Salisbury Room. "And you're too young to be this cynical."

"We'll see about that."

Brent opened the way in, and talk about standing room only. There were a good fifty people crammed in around a boardroom table long enough to bowl on, everyone talking loud enough so they could be heard over the very din they were creating.

"There you are." The mayor's right-hand guy came over, porcelain caps flashing as he smiled and put his palm out. "Thanks for stopping by, Chief."

Graham Perry was the kind of sharp, useless, egoist-in-a-Brooks-Brothers-suit who made Tom want to one-eighty in the opposite direction. He'd had to deal with them all his life, these Ivy League golden boys with their Greco-Roman playbooks, all kinds of *Et tu, Brute?* pole marks on their asses. If this was who the mayor thought she needed at her side? She was either a bad judge of character, or she shared Perry's opinion that people would fall for a faker.

Brent cleared his throat and elbowed Tom in the ribs. But he was not shaking that greasy hand.

Perry retracted the offending item and smiled some more. "Well. We just wanted you to know how much we appreciate your department's support in this election."

"I haven't given it to you."

As Perry looked at Brent, there was an awkward pause.

"Are you kidding me," Tom muttered. "Seriously, did you—"

The warm bodies in the room parted like the Red Sea and he knew without a proper look that there was only one person who could get that kind of effect.

Mayor Catherine Mahoney was wearing red, the dress totally modest, the body it was covering absolutely not. Tom kept his eyes on her face, but his peripheral vision filled in all kinds of details about her that he really could have done without.

He wasn't going to be Brent, damn it.

"Tom," she said in her smooth voice, "I'm glad you came. Thank you so much for your support. It's going to make a big difference in the election. Barring is going to be a tough opponent."

"I didn't give you anything." He turned to Brent. "I thought I made myself clear. I'm not endorsing anyone."

The flush that rode up the guy's face made Tom want to bitch-slap him.

Perry spoke up. "Mayor Mahoney is very pro-union, and I don't know if you're aware of this, but her father—"

"Was a firefighter," Tom muttered. "Yeah, I've heard. What you two don't mention is that it was for six months on a volunteer basis to build his application for B-school. I doubt those skills held up much over the last thirty years that he's run Mahoney Technologies. Now if the bunch of you will excuse me, I'm going back to work. It's clear you don't need me."

He hit the door and strode off, his molars locked, his throat loaded with all kinds of fuck-you-Brent. Unbelievable. The guy had a hard-on for that woman and was willing to sell the futures of three hundred New Brunswick firefighters down the river just to get into that red dress—

"Tom!"

As a female voice called out his name, he cursed and almost kept going, but he wanted to yell at someone—and clearly, Mayor Mahoney was willing to put a target around her neck. Turning around, he tried not to notice how those long legs of hers were eating up the carpet between them.

"I gather that was a surprise." As she halted in front of him, he was surprised to find she was tall enough to meet him right in the eye. "It was my understanding that Brent had discussed the endorsement with you."

Her security detail discreetly parked it about fifteen feet away, the man with the earpiece and the hidden gun staring off into the otherwise empty corridor.

"Oh, we talked about it." Tom crossed his arms over chest. "I didn't agree with the endorsement."

Hazel eyes. She had hazel eyes that matched her brunette hair. The latter was shoulder length and curled at the bottom. Not a lot of makeup; the lipstick neutral; the lashes real, not fake. She smelled like clean air for some reason.

"I'd welcome the opportunity to change your mind."

"Is this the part where you remind me your father's a firefighter?"

"No, it's where I tell you that if Barring gets this job, he's going to shrink your workforce by ten percent to fund a new arena. He wants his NBA team, no matter what it does to this city."

"People have been talking about that for a decade."

"Barring will do it. On the backs of the firefighters, the cops, and teachers."

"Fearmongering."

"What's your email address?"

"You can find it on the website."

"You don't have a card?"

"What are you going to send me?"

"The truth. And then maybe you and I can meet and talk."

Tom narrowed his stare and wondered just exactly what they would do at the "meeting." It wasn't ego that made him look for signs she was propositioning him: He was not ugly. He had a little positional power in the city. And it wouldn't be the first time an elected official had headed down a dirty road for reelection.

How far had she gone with Brent?

"I'm a straight shooter," she maintained. "There are good reasons to support me. I've only had nine months to do this job. I want four years so I can really make a difference."

"Look, I don't know you—"

"I want to change that."

"—and I don't need to know you. My department has been struggling for a decade. As we are chronically under-funded, we spend half our downtime repairing our equipment, our pay base is lower than

the national average for a city of this size, and our facilities are in desperate need of renovation. And you're going to stand in front of me
and maintain you can magically change all that? Bullshit. I've been in
the service for the last fifteen years and every single politician has said
that and done nothing. I never put any faith in elect-me rhetoric—and
as for the four years you want? When Greenfield died, your father
paid the Metro Council to get you elected to finish out his term. You
are a rich girl playing with the city I happen to give a shit about, so
please don't tell me about how well suited you are for this position or
how much you want to change things."

"You've got me wrong. I am different."

"The other politicians—who had a leg up on you when it comes to
relevant experience—all said that, too. And pardon me for not taking
you seriously. It's not like your father wants to make you mayor so he
can get tax breaks for that new division he wants to set up down by
the wharf."

"My father is not involved with my campaign—"

"I'm not going to argue with you, and I'm going to save you valu-
able suck-up time because there are a couple hundred people here
waiting for you to kiss their asses. You've got our union endorsement
from its president. Take it, add it to your campaign materials, and go
about your business. Just like I'll go about mine."

"Give me a chance. That's all I'm asking."

Tom looked into her eyes and did not like what he felt. At all.
"You've got what you wanted. Leave me out of this shitshow."

"I'm going to win you over."

His eyes went up and down her. "I'm not interested in any of your
attributes, professional or otherwise. If Brent wants to lock the union
in, that's up to him as its president and I won't stand in his way. He is
going to be held accountable, however, and this is a lesson he's only

going to have to learn once. Now if you don't mind, I'm going to stay focused on my job."

Tom walked off, confident that not only would she let him go, she wouldn't send him anything.

He was almost through the lobby and out the revolving doors when his phone went off. As he checked who was calling, he gritted his teeth and let it go to voicemail.

In his current mood, he couldn't deal with his mother. He just didn't have the patience for her telling him that it was raining and there was thunder and he needed to drive carefully and to call her when he was home and off the roads.

Like he was sixteen with a learner's permit.

Outside, the storms were whipping sheets of rain around and bending treetops, and the weather suited his mood. Jogging through the fury, he was jumping into his SUV when his cell went off again.

It felt good to slam the door shut.

His mother was largely a flincher and a worrier, and it was times like this that he understood Anne shutting the door on the drama. But his sister's boundary setting meant he got the full, undiluted brunt of the anxiety.

Taking out the phone, he—

Frowning, he accepted a call from Captain Baker. "Chip. What's up."

"Emilio Chavez OD'd a half hour ago. He was found by Remy La-Salle and taken by ambulance to University. I thought you'd want to know."

Tom closed his eyes. "Shit."

As Danny ran through the rain to the entrance of University
Hospital's ER, he knew where he was going before the receptionist and the triage nurses pointed him toward the "Staff
Only" door next to the check-in area. A buzzing noise sounded out as
he got in range, and when he punched the bar, the heavy steel panel
swung free.

On the other side, he strode to the patient bays. He didn't need to
ask where Chavez was. Moose and the others were standing in a cluster about halfway down, and as he came up to them, the grim expressions on those faces were too familiar.

"How we doing?" he asked Moose.

The big man nodded off to the side, and Danny went with him,
stepping away from the crew.

"They Narcan'd him." Moose lowered his voice. "LaSalle found a
needle with heroin residue in it and disappeared the evidence. They're
telling everyone it was a reaction to prescription meds, but that's a lie."

Remy LaSalle was a police officer and a good guy. Looked like the
department was going to owe him. "Any other paraphernalia?"

"They didn't look very hard, if you know what I mean."

"How'd LaSalle know to go there?" Danny patted around for his cigarettes, but then stopped himself because lighting up was a no-go. "Did someone call him?"

"They were going to play some pickup ball."

"If that was the plan, why'd Chavez be doing H?"

"I don't know. LaSalle said Chavez called him like an hour before and told him to come by, the door would be open. LaSalle didn't think much of it until he got there, and . . . yeah, he was just off duty, so he had the Narcan with him because he came in a squad car that had a dose in the trunk. If it hadn't been for that coincidence, we'd be making funeral arrangements right now."

"Where's Chavez's mom? She on her way?"

"Yeah. I called her."

Danny looked at the closed door of the treatment room. There was a break in the interior curtains that had been pulled for privacy, and he could see a sliver of Chavez's pale face and closed eyes. His body was so big and muscular, it made the hospital bed seem like something a child would put in a dollhouse.

"Did you call the chief?" he asked.

"Captain Baker did."

"Is he coming?"

"Yeah, so you might want to leave, right now."

"I'm allowed to be here."

"Suit yourself."

Danny put his hands on his hips and debated the odds of an argument between him and Tom. The timing and place were bad, yet the alchemy for ugly was ripe. On that note: "Are we allowed to go in and see him?"

"They said it was okay. But nobody's . . . well, you know. We've stayed out here. What do we say?"

Danny waded his way through his crew, then he knocked on the glass and didn't wait for an invite. He went into the room and made sure the door shut behind him.

Chavez didn't open his eyes. "Danny."

That voice was nothing but a croak, and Danny did a quick scan of the monitors. Blood pressure was low, pulse low, oxygen sats down.

"How'd you know?" Danny crossed to the bed. "Mind reading again?"

"You smell like a pack of Marlboros."

"Stop with the compliments. Mind if I pull up a chair?"

"Whatever you like." Chavez turned his head, lifted his lids, and seemed to struggle to focus. "And I could do with a cigarette."

"I'd give you one if it wouldn't get us both kicked out of here."

"I should have told LaSalle two hours."

Danny parked it close and rubbed his face. He'd been debating how real to get and Chavez had answered that one. "So you planned this?"

"Maybe. And don't pretend you haven't considered it every now and again."

"I won't deny it." Especially after John Thomas had been killed. "I mean, who hasn't."

Chavez exhaled. "This is why I can talk to you. Everyone else would preach at me and then call the psych ward."

"Don't get ahead of yourself. I am preparing a very stirring rendition of the you've-got-so-much-to-live-for speech."

"Spare me."

Danny linked his hands and stared down at them. "How many times have you tried before now. And don't lie."

"Never." Chavez put a heavy hand to his heart. "I swear."

"So what did it? Seeing Anne?"

That dark head moved side to side on the pillow. "No. I was glad she's doing good, you know? I mean, I didn't want her to get hurt, but you saved her—"

"So why'd you try to off yourself?"

"You don't want to talk about your woman, huh."

"She's not mine."

As they fell silent, the soft beeping of the machines filled the void.

"I got the HIV, Danny."

Danny tried to catch his reaction before his expression changed. But the shock must have showed because the other man looked away.

"You can't tell anyone. No one else knows."

Danny cleared his throat. "It's not a death sentence anymore. You have to know that—"

"I went to my annual physical for the department and they took a blood sample. I forgot all about it." Chavez's stare drifted to the far corner of the treatment bay. "But they called three days ago."

"This doesn't mean you can't do your job."

"It's not just about work. It's about . . . someone. I can't tell her that I can't be with her now. It's losing her that I can't deal with. I figured a good dose of H would do the trick, and I was right, or I would have been if I'd just told LaSalle to come a little later. Fucker is always on time."

"Jesus, Chavez."

"I worried that someone else would find me. You know . . . someone who might be upset."

Danny thought back to Timeout's best waitress. "How'd you get it, Emilio? Do you even know—hell, am I allowed to ask that?"

The guy put both hands up to his face. "I shared steroid needles at my neighborhood gym about six months ago. I shouldn't have. It was fucking stupid. I mean, I'm a goddamn EMT. But it's all guys I've known since high school, and it was only one cycle. Besides, compared to doing IV drugs, the risk was so low. Until it wasn't."

Everyone on the fire service needed to be in shape, and yeah, sure, some of the guys juiced to get bigger. It was what it was; Danny had never judged. And now, in a quick rush of paranoia, he thought about what he had done in the gym. No 'roids or hormone shots, for sure. And thank God he'd been religious about condoms, especially during the last ten months when he'd been making some questionable choices.

Except he'd be a fool not to recognize that here but for the grace of God went he.

Chavez shut his eyes so tight, his lips curled off his teeth as if he were in pain. "I don't want this, Danny. I can't handle this."

"Yeah, you can." Except even as he said the words, he was worried he was lying. "You can. You just need to . . . figure out a plan."

"I'll be fine," Chavez said bleakly.

"How about I go get Josefina—"

"No fucking way, Danny." Chavez looked over. "She can't . . . no, she can't ever know. I mean, we're not even together yet."

"She's going to find out what happened—I mean, about all this ER shit. She's going to hear you were admitted from someone else. You don't have to talk about the HIV now, but you could at least . . . I don't know, tell her that you made a mistake. With the overdose."

It was the only thing Danny could think of to suggest. Because shit, sometimes, the woman you loved was the sole reason you stayed on the planet.

He knew that firsthand.

"If you love her," Danny said, "and I know you do—'cuz I've seen the way you look at her—you don't want her hearing you tried to kill yourself from someone else. People are aware you guys are getting close. Even if Remy is leading with the reaction-to-prescription-drug line, you never know what else could be said."

HIPAA was great for patient privacy in hospitals. But New Brunswick was a very small town when it came to gossip.

"I'll bring her over." Danny put up a hand. "Again, you don't have to go into the HIV thing right now, but at least you could see her and remember why you're going to want to see her again."

"There's no future for us."

"You keep saying that, but you don't know if that's true."

"Why would anyone want to be with someone who's infected."

"Do you honestly think that every person who's positive is living alone in a dark corner like a fucking leper in the Middle Ages? Really? Seriously?"

As they got quiet again, the monitor keeping track of Chavez's heart rate measured a steady beat with a steady beeping, and Danny supposed he should be reassured by how even everything was. But he worried that was just temporary. Undoubtedly, Chavez would reassure whoever needed the platitudes that it had been a garden-variety OD, and he would agree to go to a drug-awareness program. Except that would just be to get out of here.

They sat there for what felt like an hour, but was probably only ten minutes.

"I guess I should go." Danny got up. "Your mom's on the way."

"She needs to stop worrying about me."

"Then quit giving her reasons to."

Chavez cursed. "Look, if Josefina were to come here, I don't know what I'd say. I mean, it's way early for us. Or was. She has no reason to get involved with me."

"Don't make your mind up about that. Lemme bring her over. Come on, Chavez. She's a good woman, that's the reason you love her.

You don't have to talk it all out right now, but at least let her know you're okay firsthand before she hears something from a customer at Timeout."

There was another long pause. "Okay."

"You're gonna be all right."

When Chavez looked away, Danny wondered whether he was doing the right thing. But if you had to have something to live for, it might as well be love, right?

"I'll be back in about twenty minutes. Don't go anywhere."

Chavez rolled his eyes. "Like they're letting me out of here anytime soon."

Outside, anxious faces stared at Danny like they were trying to read the future in his expression. But he couldn't give them what they were after. Hell, even if he could, he doubted any of them would like the prognostication.

"I gotta have a smoke. I'll be back."

Leaving the crew behind, he went past the nursing station and exited into the ambulance bay. There were a couple of guys he knew standing out of the rain with their rigs, so he went away from them while still staying under the overhang. As he took out his cigarettes and lit one, he was violating the hospital "No Smoke Zone" rule and told himself not to feel bad about it.

Didn't work.

After three deep inhales, he stabbed the thing out just as a set of headlights flashed when an SUV pulled into the restricted area. He didn't pay any attention to the who and what of it, but then a man with salt-and-pepper gray hair was walking over to him.

Anne Ashburn's brother was the last person he wanted to see. That was the way shit was rolling down his hill lately, though.

"Chief," he muttered. "Here to see Chavez?"

"Captain Baker called me. How's he doing?"

Danny crossed his arms over his chest. It was unwritten policy that members of the crew didn't comment on questions like that. At least not truthfully. The response that was expected, and the one he knew he should give was: *He's fine. He'll come through. He can't wait to get back on a ladder.*

The words refused to come out of his mouth. He just kept seeing Chavez in that bed.

There was no looking at the chief as he spoke. "He's suicidal. He's going to lie to get out of here, and in a matter of weeks, I'm fucking terrified that we're going to be in dress blues next to his weeping mother."

Tom's recoil told him more than he needed to know about what he'd just done. But it was what it was. He was willing to keep Chavez's secret about the HIV, but that was as far as it went for him.

"I'm not saying this because I'm under psych review myself." He turned back to the chief. "I'm tired. I'm fucking tired of getting eaten alive by shit I can't get out of my head. And if Chavez kills himself because I didn't say something? I don't have room for that. I can't carry that. My arms are full."

Hell of a mic drop: He'd triggered a mandatory suspension and review of a man who was a terrific firefighter and an even better human being. It was the worst betrayal.

Danny had just put the poor bastard on the very path he himself was walking.

But he was done adding wrongs to his conscience.

Anne headed for UMass New Brunswick's ER the second Moose texted her, grabbing her keys and going out into the rain so fast, she forgot to put Soot in his crate. Halfway across town, she realized her mistake, so if she came home to ruined sofa cushions and shredded running shoes, it was on her.

The University's hospital campus was like a small city, the cluster of buildings ringed by a grass verge that had glowing signs with directions to all the different departments, clinics, and services. The emergency room was around to the side, and as a trained EMT who had served on the 499's rescue squad, she was very familiar with the place.

It was also where she had been brought for treatment for her arm.

She had very spotty memories of that trip in the ambulance. The assessment of her injury. Her transfer to an inpatient room.

All she'd been focused on was whether Danny had made it out alive.

As she pulled into the parking lot for visitors, her wipers slapped back and forth, offering clear glimpses of the lineups of cars that did not last long. When she parked and got out, she pulled the hood of her windbreaker up and shoved her hands into her pockets.

Just as she started off for the glowing entrance, a tall figure came out from the ambulance area.

She recognized who it was immediately.

Changing trajectory, she headed for Danny, and he seemed to know it was her because he stopped.

"Hey," he said gruffly as she came up to him.

"Moose got in touch with me."

"He does that, doesn't he."

He hadn't bothered to shave, his face rough with stubble, and his windbreaker was wrinkled, as if it had been wadded up somewhere. But his jeans were clean and he smelled like soap even in the rain.

He didn't seem to notice the latter, even as it dripped off his nose and hair.

"What the hell happened?" she asked.

"Moose didn't say?"

"No, he just texted that Emilio was going to be admitted for observation. Was it a fire?" Danny shook his head and she frowned. "So he was in an accident?"

"No."

"Oh . . . God."

"I gotta go."

"Where?" she asked before she could stop herself.

"I'm doing a favor for Chavez."

Danny said a quick good-bye and walked away. And Anne told herself to stay put.

She lasted two heartbeats with that before she jumped forward to catch up with him. "I want to help."

Danny didn't slow down. Didn't look at her. He just kept striding through the storm. "What?"

"Emilio." The wind changed direction and blew her off-balance. "I want to help you with the favor."

"It's nothing I can't handle myself."

She grabbed his arm. "Danny."

He stopped and stared over her head. "I don't need your help, okay."

"Please, this is about Emilio. Not us."

"Right. Sorry. I forgot we're supposed to put our head in the sand and pretend there's nothing going on—and spare me the there-isn'ts. Everything is about us. Your fucking arm, my shit. It's all about us, Anne. And yeah, sure, you're more mentally advanced, or whatever you want to call it, than I am. But out of the two of us, I'm the only one who sees clearly."

She put her hands on her hips. "This is about Chavez—"

Danny threw up his hands and walked off into the storm muttering to himself.

Anne ran after him. "What does Emilio need?"

Lightning flashed overhead, the strobing reminding her of being on a scene, and as the answering thunder rolled through the night sky, rain got into her eyes, making them burn. As they came up to Danny's truck, she expected him to just get in and drive away. But of course, he refused to follow any pattern of behavior.

He stopped again, put his hands on his hips, and stared down at her. "What'll you give me."

Anne blinked and pulled her hood further forward. "Excuse me?"

"I want something." He didn't seem to notice it was pouring or that gale force gusts were tackling them from all sides or that they were having to shout over the storm. "And no, not sex, for fuck's sake. But quid pro quo."

"Are you even serious?" She pointed back at the ER, and on cue, more lightning flashed. "There's a man in there fighting for his life."

Danny shrugged, his face slick and reflective of the hospital's security lamps. "I have something you want. So gimme something I want and I'll let you help."

"You are an asshole."

"I know." He tilted his head and adopted an expression like he was doing long division in his head. "Let's see . . . I need help out at the farm clearing brush. Could be another opportunity for you to prove you're perfectly fine—plus, if we have to call an ambulance out there, it won't be the four-nine-nine who responds, so there's that. Or . . . even better, you could promise me that you'll come to Moose's Saturday night—"

"Fine. I'll go to that dinner with you," she snapped.

"See." He started to smile. "So easy. Now get in my truck. We're heading to Timeout to find Josefina."

Anne was talking to herself as she went around and got in. As her feet squished in her soaked running shoes and a trickle of water snuck past the open collar of her Patagonia jacket, she was cursing him.

Sending Danny a glare, she didn't care that she was getting his truck cab all wet. Then again, he didn't seem worried about that, either.

"I could just be lying," she said. "About going to Moose's."

As he started the engine, he looked over at her. "You aren't. You never flake on something you promise. So are we bringing red or white wine as a hostess-warming gift?"

25

"So how's work going?"

As Danny spoke up, Anne was not in the mood. The inside of his truck smelled like his aftershave and the remnants of his Marlboros, and she resented the fact that she enjoyed his scent in her nose.

"You really want to pretend this is social?" she muttered.

"Oh, no. By all means, let's talk about Chavez trying to commit suicide."

She looked out her side window and could see little through the sheets of rain. "How about we don't say anything."

"Nah. And fine, I'll start. I went to see a shrink today."

Anne whipped her head around so fast, she didn't have time to hide the reaction. "You did? How'd it go?"

And so help her God, if he played another round of tit-for-tat, she was going to punch him somewhere that would show. Although on that theory, that black eye of his hadn't faded yet, so at least one piece of prime real estate was already taken.

"You mind if I light up? I'll crack a window."

"You shouldn't need the crutch."

"Fine, I'll wait until we're parked."

"Just open a damn window. And I hope you get wet."

"Er."

"What?"

"Wet-er. I am already wet."

As he let in some fresh, cold air, he turned on the heater, and the warmth blowing on her feet felt good. And he waited until they hit a red light before getting his cigarette on, his exhale aimed away from her.

"I tried to get out of the appointment." He glanced over. "This should not be a surprise."

"It isn't."

"She was smarter than I thought she'd be. I'm not going to get cleared, of course, which also proves she's a real professional."

Anne was aware of a piercing disappointment. But come on, like she'd really expected him to sit on a couch for fifty minutes and undergo some existential transformation for a hundred and fifty bucks? There were no easy fixes in life. Especially not after the kinds of things he'd been through.

"I expected more of a response from you," he said.

"I'm glad you went."

"Can I ask you something?" He looked across the seat again. "And I'm serious about this."

She rearranged herself into exactly the same position. Then pulled her seat belt away from her chest and brought it back in. "Okay."

"When you were in the rehab hospital, you had to see a shrink, right?"

"It was part of my treatment, sure." She frowned. "Didn't you have to see one?"

"I was supposed to, but—"

"You got out of it."

"—I got out of it."

"Of course you did." Anne shook her head. "And?"

"Did they help you?"

Anne thought back to the three awkward meetings she'd had with a well-meaning, tender-hearted, twenty-four-year-old who'd been fresh out of a master's program and wholly unequipped to deal with anything outside of theory. Anne had answered the questions posed to her with honesty, but she couldn't really say she'd gotten anything from the sessions. Maybe it had been the pain meds. Maybe her mood. Maybe it was the therapist's inexperience.

"Well?" Danny glanced over. "What happened?"

"I don't know how to answer that."

"So it wasn't helpful." He frowned. "But what was? Seriously, Anne, how did you pull yourself back up to normal?"

His expression was so intense, she knew he was dead serious, and that earnest searching was a surprise that opened her up.

"It wasn't the therapist at the hospital. Not that she wasn't well intended . . . we just didn't connect, I guess." She focused on her prosthesis as it sat on her thigh, a sculpture of what had been lost. "They can be helpful, though."

"You're saying that because you want me to keep going."

"Yup."

"So again, what was it for you?"

Anne turned the prosthesis over and looked at her "palm." Then she pulled up the sleeve of her windbreaker and followed the carbon fiber length that plugged into what was left of her lower arm.

"I got an infection," she heard herself say. "It was about a week after I got out of the rehab hospital. I'll never forget waking up in my bed and feeling this terrible fatigue, like I was coming down with the flu. The end of my stump didn't hurt—well, that's not true. I had phantom pain, and I assumed that any discomfort was all part of the damaged-nerve thing. So I just kept going, but then I popped a fever, and when they did a wound check, they found the beginnings of the infection. My skin was so red, it was like it was made of blood. Things went downhill fast. They took samples to target the antibiotic, put me on broad spectrums at first, then they ratcheted it up. It was a race and we did not win for a while. I developed these bright red lymphangitis streaks, and shortly after that, I went septic. I just crashed. That was when I was readmitted."

She was aware she was giving him factual particulars instead of other things that were much more personal: It was like she was reporting the stats of a patient, and that distance was the only reason she could get through the story.

She'd never talked about it before.

Anne glanced out the front windshield. "It's green."

"What?"

"The light is green. We can go."

Danny seemed to shake himself. "Oh. Yeah."

As he hit the gas, she wanted to stop talking—and told herself she didn't because she wanted to help him. Inspire him. This was about proving to Danny there was another way.

It was *not* connecting with him on a personal level.

Or sharing her story because it was something she probably needed to get off her chest.

Crap.

"You must have been scared," he murmured.

"It was touch and go." She told herself not to go too deep. "But your brain gets fuzzy so you can't think clearly."

"I didn't know it got that bad."

"I was very lucky. It wasn't MRSA. The intravenous clindamycin saved me." Her heart tripped and then pounded, as if the memories were an intruder trying to get back into her body. "Anyway, you wanted to know what turned me around."

She fell silent as she tried to find the right words. Somehow, this felt more intimate than the sex they'd had. "So the night of the fire and the first day after, I was all 'I'm going to beat this' and 'nothing is going to stop me.' And pretty much I kept that up until I was released and I went home. Something about being around my things, my house, my routine made it real in a way that it hadn't in the hospital. That was when . . ."

"When it hit you."

"Yeah." She refused to speak of the sleepless nights, the toxic depression, the distortion of her anger and fear. "I got into a tailspin—'life is over,' that kind of thing. But then suddenly I was back in the hospital and it was not at all apparent that I was going to make it."

Anne glanced over at him. "When you were little, did you ever picture your funeral?"

"No. God, never."

"Well, I did. Like out of A Christmas Story when Ralphie was blind? I'd pretend I was in my coffin and people were coming to pay last respects and weeping over the loss of me. It was usually in response to a punishment I thought was unfair." She shrugged. "So there I was, an adult, on the verge of dying . . . and all that actually happened. I stared up out of the death spiral I was in and saw all these faces looking down at me. Everyone so upset . . ."

An image of her mother, that hair all done, the makeup perfect, stung. Even when that woman's daughter had been close to dying, she'd had to be sure to look presentable.

"Tom came." She frowned. "He sat in a chair in the corner of my ICU room almost the entire time. I figured he was waiting for me to rally so he could tell me again how irresponsible I'd been."

"Like the infection was your fault? Come on."

"More like my getting stuck in that hot spot in the first place." She shook her head. "Anyway, at the worst point, I had a dream that my father appeared from out of nowhere. He stood at the side of the bed and he told me that it wasn't my time. That I had to fight because I was his daughter and that's what men in the family did."

Danny's head swung around. "Holy shit, he came to you."

"No, I don't believe in ghosts. I think my subconscious coughed that up out of the fever and the drugs I was on because I'd spent my whole life trying to make up for the fact that I was born a girl. It's inherent in my personality inventory. But it worked—so clearly my brain pulled the right lever for motivation. I decided that I had to fight and I couldn't let anything stop me. Not the loss of my hand or my job or . . . yeah, anything."

Up ahead, Timeout's sign glowed red and gold, a beacon on the down-market street.

She couldn't remember when she'd been in there last. But she knew which pool table tilted left, and how the stall in the middle of the ladies' room had the toilet that ran, and what to order: Fries, yes. Burger, yes. Never the fish, because even though they were on the ocean, the place only served frozen cod.

So many nights she'd gone there with the crew, one of the few women in the boys' club and proud of that fact.

It was a lifetime ago. And she missed it. But then she deliberately thought of Soot's dear face.

"I think people who survive need to get to an aha moment," she said quietly, "where the fog lifts and you realize there are things worth living for and goals worth pursuing. Even if they're different than what motivated you before."

────────────

As Danny parallel-parked in front of the bar, he knew who he wanted to live for. Too bad Anne wasn't looking for a pedestal to stand on for the rest of their lives.

He glanced over as he killed the engine. "I had no idea that things got so rough for you. I mean, beyond the . . . you know."

"You had your own things to worry about." She turned to get out of the truck. "So when did Emilio and Josefina start seeing each other?"

He reached out and put his hand on her arm. When he felt something hard and cylindrical, he pulled his palm back.

"It won't bite." She put her prosthesis up. "I promise you."

"I'm sorry."

Anne shook her head sharply, the conversational equivalent of shutting a door. "Come on, let's find Josefina."

She left him with no choice but to hurry his ass and catch up to her, and as they entered Timeout, they shook the rain off like a pair of dogs. The bar was not all that crowded, and Josefina was an easy spot across the field of tables. She was taking orders from a six-top of police officers, and as they nodded in Danny's direction, she glanced over her shoulder.

And froze. As her face paled, she said something to the cops and came over.

"What is it?"

They always knew, Danny thought. The loved ones always knew when there was bad news.

"Emilio's in the hospital," Danny said in a low voice. "He was taken in about an hour ago."

"How bad is he hurt?" The woman put a hand to her mouth. "Is he . . ."

"He asked us to come find you. He's going to pull through."

Josefina spoke some quick Spanish and made the sign of the cross over the front of her black-and-white pseudo-referee uniform. "Thank the Lord. I tell him to be careful on that job—too many hurt. Too many!"

Danny stayed quiet on the whys of everything, and felt so badly for Emilio. This was going to be a hard road. "He wants to see you."

"Let me ask someone to cover for me," the woman said. "My manager, she understands. She is married to an ambulance. EMT, I mean."

"Do you need a ride over?" Anne asked.

"Yes, I take the bus here."

Danny swung his keys in his hand. "We'll wait for you."

As Josefina headed for the back, he stared at Anne. She was looking around the place as if she'd never seen it before, and he wondered whether that was a good or a bad thing for her. She seemed to want to leave everything behind. Him included.

Then she faced him. "Moose told me your fight here the other night was with some yachtsmen because they insulted her."

"They were being disrespectful. They got less than what they deserved."

"You always were protective."

He pictured someone doing Anne a wrong. "I still am."

There was a pause. "I really don't think I should go to Moose's dinner on Saturday."

"There will be other people there." Or at least, there would be when he told the guy he better damn well invite half of town. "It won't just be us. And I'll make sure folks know that it's not a case of 'us.' Besides, you're missed."

"I'm not a member of the crew anymore."

"We do hang around with outsiders, you know. Particularly ones with a good sense of humor."

"I'm sorry. I just can't. It's not appropriate and you know it."

"Worried you might want to have sex with me again?" Danny didn't bother hiding the bitterness in his voice. "We both enjoyed it."

"No." Her jaw tightened. "I'm not worried about anything."

Liar, he thought.

"Suit yourself." He nodded toward the exit. "I'll go start the truck. It's cold as ice tonight."

Outside, he took advantage of a break in the downpour and lit up, even though the cig got soggy fast on the short walk to the truck. As he got in, his phone went off. When he took it out and saw the text, he cursed.

Great. The chief wanted to see him first thing in the morning.

Looked like he was getting fired sooner rather than later.

c h a p t e r

26

Anne didn't want to be rude. Except by the time Danny pulled the truck into the ER's parking lot, she had a pounding head-ache and a knot in her stomach that might have been hunger but felt like a bowel obstruction.

The fact that she'd ended up sitting between the two of them was a big part of her problem. The entire trip back, which lasted all of ten minutes but seemed like twenty-five years, she'd had Danny's leg bumping against her own. Just like old times in the engines.

Not what she wanted to be reminded of, especially after what they'd done at his apartment.

Danny found a parking spot right by the ER's entrance, and Jose-fina fumbled her purse as she got out, dumping everything all over the pavement. Anne immediately dropped down to help the woman gather keys and wallet, Tampax and makeup bag.

"Listen, I'm going to let Danny take you in." Anne passed over a Kleenex pack. "There are a lot of people here already for Emilio."

"Thank you for coming and getting me."

Anne looked away from those teary brown eyes. "No problem.

Take care of him." Straightening, she looked over the truck's hood at Danny. "I have to go."

His eyes were in shadow, and that was just as well. She didn't want to see what was in them.

As she waved and headed for her Subaru, she felt like she was dumping the whole situation on him—and that was not perception; it was fact. But she was a distant relative to all of this now, and she needed to respect the boundaries.

Back in her own vehicle, she got turned around and ended up exiting through the entry, which was a commentary on the night, wasn't it. But at least she was free of the drama.

She was just going to go home, check and see if there was anything chewed up, and then go to bed early.

Or at least that was the plan.

When she came up to her little house and saw a familiar car parked in front of her walkway, she hit the brakes. And then debated on whether she could just drive on by.

Her mother.

Pulling into her driveway, Anne got out and went on the approach. As she came up to the ten-year-old Honda Civic, the window went down—and she realized she hadn't actually set eyes on her mom for months.

Nancy Janice Fitzgerald Ashburn did not look her sixty years. She'd never been a smoker or a drinker, had stayed out of the sun and followed a "regime"—whatever that was. So even without plastic surgery, her pale Irish skin was still fair and largely unwrinkled, the powder and foundation light, the lashes curled and darkened, the lipstick a perfect shade of pink for that complexion. And of course, the hair was done. She colored it to cover the grays, but not in a brassy way: Ginger streaks through the auburn, everything cut well so it framed her face and brushed her shoulders.

"I was going to call you," Anne lied.

"I am so sorry to bother you, but I can't reach your brother."

"What's going on?"

"Do you want to get out of the storm?"

"No, I'm fine." Anne looked up and got a raindrop directly in her eyeball. As she squinted and rubbed away the sting, she was frustrated with the whole world. "Do you need something?"

"You know that big maple tree in the backyard? The one you and your brother swung on—"

"Yes. I know."

"Half of it broke off in the wind and landed on the house." As Anne exhaled with exhaustion, her mother hurried through her speech. "The nice man behind me tried to put tarping up, but there's terrible leaking in your father's and my bedroom, and then downstairs. I'm looking for a place to stay—and I promise, I tried to reach your brother. He must be busy."

What Anne wanted to say was that Nancy Janice should try Tom again. Try him a thousand times. But she wasn't going to turn her mother out into a storm, for godsakes.

"Ah, let me go check my house. I've . . . ah, I've got a dog and I need to make sure he's secured before you come in. I'm still not sure how he does with strangers."

"You got a dog? You should have told me." The hurt that flared in that face went through Anne's chest like a spear. "But it's all right. I've been telling you for a year to get a pet. This is really good."

"Stay here."

Anne jogged over to her front door and punched in her code. Inside, she glanced around, expecting to see the sofa shredded. Nope. Proceeding into the kitchen, she found the trash bin was where she'd left it, no garbage strewn about. But he also wasn't in his crate.

Dear Lord, her mother was going to spend the night.

As she wondered how this had happened, she was very cognizant that in most families, that was commonplace—parents staying with their children.

But their family hadn't been normal. It had only looked that way from the outside, the hero firefighter, the perfect homemaker, and a little boy and girl to boot. Real nuclear stuff until you scratched the surface, particularly when it came to Tom, Sr.

And that was also Nancy Janice's problem. The woman was only surface, no substance.

Whatever, though. She could make it through one night with her mother.

After Anne finished with the first floor, she got paranoid. What if Soot had snuck out somehow? With a surge of anxiety, she all but ran upstairs. Flipping on the hall light, she—

As she looked through the open door of her bedroom, she saw her dog curled up on her bed, his nose tucked under her pillow as if he wanted her scent with him in her absence.

"Hi, Mr. Man," she said softly.

He startled and lifted his head, sleepy eyes blinking. Then that bony tail of his thumped on the comforter.

Anne went across and stretched out with him, putting her face against his and breathing deep. In response, Soot nuzzled her, and she marveled at the connection they had. It felt as though they'd been together all her life.

Pulling back, she stared at him. "I need you to do me a favor and not eat my mother, 'kay? She's only going to be here until the morning, and she's . . . well, I think she'd taste like a marshmallow Peep, anyway. Way too sweet. Not your kind of entrée."

Soot was a perfect gentleman, and Nancy Janice fell in love with him. Then again, her mother's very nature was fall-in-love. Everything in her life was "perfect" and "beautiful" and "wonderful."

Her glass was not just half full. It was overflowing with rose-scented denial. And Anne refused to see her intolerance of the woman as some kind of moral failing.

They had nothing in common and had never been close—hell, maybe that was why Anne had felt so betrayed when she'd learned what kind of man her father really was. Tom, Sr., had passed before she'd found out the truth. And before her wake-up call, she had been prepared to live up to his memory for the rest of her days, to follow the example of bravery and charisma he had seemed to set.

Instead, the curtain had been pulled back on his true character and that had left her without any kind of connection to her family. Her brother had already been living his own life at that point and going into the Academy, and as for Nancy Janice? Anne had barely made it through a childhood of being forced to wear dresses and ringlet curls and patent leather shoes.

She'd been waaaaaaay done with being pigeonholed into a feminine standard she didn't care about by a woman she did not respect.

"Everything is so neat." Nancy Janice stood up from petting the dog. "So tidy."

"You make that sound like a bad thing." Anne dropped her mother's fifty-pound overnight bag at the foot of the stairs. "I have to take him out. Come on, Soot."

"It's not a bad thing." Her mother followed the way to the back porch. "It's just so spare."

"I don't see the need to clutter my space with crap from the Home Shopping Network."

The way her mother sighed told her that the message had been received as it had been intended: That house Anne and her brother had grown up in had been crammed full of knickknacks, fads, and cutesy "moments."

Nothing like being raised in an infomercial ecosystem.

"Out you go, Soot." She opened the door and stood to the side. "Go on. G'head."

Soot stood in between the jambs and eyed the sky with suspicion.

"You want me to go out with you?" *Please make me go out with you.* "Here, we'll go together."

"I'll make tea," her mother said. "Where's your kettle?"

"I don't have one. I use K-Cups. And I still don't drink tea."

"What's a K-Cup?"

"Don't worry about it. Help yourself."

"I don't drink coffee."

"Come on, Soot."

Thankfully, the dog decided to commit to a visit to the backyard, and Anne took the opportunity to breathe deep and brace herself for the return. When they came back in, her mother had set out two mugs and was boiling water in a pan.

"Don't worry, Annie-Banannie, I brought plenty of Celestial Seasonings for the both of us."

Annie-Banannie. God, she had hated that nickname her entire life.

As she stayed quiet, the smile her mother sent over her shoulder was cheerful in a determined kind of way. "It's for nighttime. For rest."

Anne grabbed a dish towel and bent down, taking each of Soot's paws in turn, wiping off the mud. "I told you. I don't drink tea."

"Oh. Well, I could make you a coffee? I could—"

"No. Thank you. I don't need anything."

"Oh. All right."

Anne lowered her head. "I'll sit with you."

"Oh, I would love that. I've missed you."

Yeah, wow, she'd forgotten how three-quarters of Nancy Janice's statements started with "Oh"—as if she were constantly shocked by conversation, in spite of the fact that she was a chatter. Then again, she'd been a seen-and-not-heard wife to a flamboyant force of nature. It probably was still a surprise, even after all these years, that anybody listened to her.

It wasn't Anne's job to step into that void, however. And giving her mother an opening to speak was like setting off an entire can of Febreze in an enclosed space—and then thinking you could keep the flower-fresh stench from your nose by batting the air away from your face.

Anne sat down at her table and told herself she needed to ask what the woman had been up to, but she wasn't sure she could feign interest in Pilates, bridge, and senior center volunteering.

Especially as she thought about Emilio in that hospital bed, and Danny struggling to find his way, and the people who had died in those warehouse fires down by the wharf.

See, this was the problem. There was a vast, un-crossable distance between what her mother worried over and what Anne had on her plate. It was Kleenex to surgical gauze. Sandals to steel-toed work boots. An off-key hum to a scream for help.

Her mother took a green-and-white box out of her corgi-themed purse and put a tea bag in each mug. Then she poured the hot water from the pan and brought her solution to insomnia over.

As she put the tea in front of Anne, her pale eyes were like those of a dog begging to be let in from the cold.

"Just in case you change your mind," she said softly.

I won't, Anne wanted to holler. *For godsakes, is this the reason Dad cheated on you?*

c h a p t e r

27

The following morning, Danny pulled his truck into the parking area behind the 617 stationhouse and checked his phone. He was fifteen minutes early, but not because he'd planned it that way and set some kind of an alarm.

You needed to be able to sleep to worry about alarms. And anything even remotely REM-related had been a nonissue for him.

Lighting a cigarette, he cracked his window and blew a stream of smoke out. Following the storms, the September sun was back out with a vengeance, the bright sky and utter lack of clouds making him think of someone starting an organic diet after a McDonald's binge.

He blinked gritty eyes. Drank some coffee. Smoked some more.

Five minutes 'til nine, he doused the butt in his cold Dunkin' and got out. The chief's shiny new stationhouse had a dedicated administrative entrance, so at least he didn't have to enter through the bays and face the crew—who'd all know why he was here.

Anne's brother was going to love this meeting.

And hey, at least his last act as a firefighter was going to be making someone's day.

Danny pulled open the glass door and stepped into a waiting

room as fancy as any you'd find in a lawyer's office downtown: leather couches, coffee table, flat-screen TV, even a throw rug that picked up on the gray-and-blue color frickin' scheme.

Nice to know that Ripkin's people saw to everything. Not just the donation and the building, but the goddamn curtains and the furniture.

It even smelled nice.

Given how executive-ish everything was, he always expected some assistant to come out and demand his ID and fingerprints before he could get in to see the big man.

Nope. He just walked over to the fishbowl: The chief's office was three sides of see-through, and the man was sitting at an old beat-up desk that was buried in paperwork, the phone in danger of falling off the far edge, a dead plant wilted on shelves that were mostly empty.

Ashburn was like an isolated contaminant in all the otherwise perfectly orderly and new.

Tom looked up. "Come on in."

Or something to that effect. The office was soundproof.

Danny pushed his way inside. "Morning."

"Sit down."

Why bother. He wasn't going to be in here long. But Danny followed the order, parking it in a creaky wooden chair.

He crossed his arms over his chest. "So this was quick."

Anne's brother eased back and steepled his fingertips like he was a school principal with a delinquent. The man looked exhausted, dark circles under his eyes adding age to his face, that salt-and-pepper hair pulling an assist on the almost-fifty vibe. The poor bastard was only in his mid-thirties, though.

"Dr. McAuliffe got back to me yesterday."

"Where do I sign?"

"What?"

Danny sat forward and motioned over all the paperwork. "On my release papers. I already know I wasn't on service long enough to vest my pension, but I want my COBRA."

The chief didn't respond. Then again, no doubt this was like a good meal, something to be savored.

"I want you back on shift. But you're on probation."

Danny shook his head to reset his ears. "What?"

"You heard me. Because of Emilio being out, I've shuffled the crew at four-nine-nine around, and you need to work today's shift out, off tomorrow and Sunday."

The chief picked up a piece of paper, his eyes scanning back and forth. Then he looked up. "Why are you still here? You're late for roll call at the four-nine-nine."

Danny was aware of a shaft of anxiety hitting him in the chest. "I don't get it."

"I think I'm being clear enough."

"Why aren't you firing me?"

"You really want to argue this point?"

Danny shook his head again. "I'm confused."

"That's because you think it's personal between you and me. It's not. The therapist's report stated that she felt you were suffering from severe trauma and undiagnosed depression. She's advocating for a three-month suspension and mandatory follow-up. She also believes you have a problem with alcohol and is recommending that you address this."

"So why are you putting me back on shift."

"If I waited for a clean bill of mental health for all my firefighters, I'd have engines with no engineers, lines with no one to hold them, and ladders with nobody to climb."

Danny clasped his hands together because he had a case of the shakes he didn't want to share. "Thank you."

The chief's eyes went back and forth on the paper, but in the same position as he read whatever line he was on over and over again. After a moment, he said gruffly, "Payback. We're equal now."

"I wasn't aware we had a debt to discharge." That was a lie. There was Anne. "A recent one, at any rate."

"Chavez." Tom glanced up. "If you hadn't said anything, I wouldn't have . . . anyway. Yeah."

In the back of his mind, Danny did the math on switching one unstable man for another, but he was not going to fight the chief. Something was finally breaking his way.

"But there's a condition."

Here it comes. "Which is."

"Not one violation of any procedure or policy. Everything will be by the book, and yes, I'm putting this in your personnel file. I am not fucking around. I will fire you and to hell with the personnel shortage if you fuck anything up."

Hard to argue with that standard, Danny thought.

"Go on to the four-nine-nine then." Tom got to his feet. "And shake my hand. So we both know we have an agreement."

Boston traffic was a thing.

As Anne passed another marker on I-93, she checked the clock on the dash of her municipal sedan. She'd called Ripkin's office first thing and informed them she would be arriving at nine sharp. She wasn't going to make it by that time, they'd said they didn't expect the big man in until nine thirty.

New Brunswick had its share of tall buildings, but it was JV next to the pros when compared to Beantown's glass-and-steel forestland. The fact that Ripkin owned an entire skyscraper was testament to his wealth, and she had to admit she was impressed.

But at this rate, she was going to be a hundred before she got anywhere near the place.

The lanes of the highway were congested, making her think of clogged arteries, and sump lines that were full of silt, and gutters that had yet to be cleaned of autumn leaves. She also thought of all the lives in all of the cars, the details, the timelines, the beginnings, middles, and ends. In this respect, every morning and every evening, in every major city across the globe, biographies gathered on the asphalt, books lined up one to another as if on a shelf, the pages at once anonymous within the collection and totally personal between the covers, in each automobile.

Humanity was a galaxy, countless, unfathomable, too vast to comprehend.

Not that she'd ever wanted to be God.

When she finally pulled into the Ripkin Building's underground parking garage, it was 9:20. She got her ticket, found a slot on the third of the six levels, and was not surprised to learn that Ripkin's office was all the way up on the skyscraper's top floor, a king surveying the world he had conquered.

When she stepped off the elevator, there was no question which way to go: Down to the right, a wall of glass bearing the Ripkin Development logo cordoned off a reception area that had been built around an enormous crystal sculpture depicting the letter *R*.

Anne entered and went over to the black granite desk. The attractive blonde was like any other piece of art, dressed in black, her hair slicked back into a bun that gave Anne a headache just looking at it.

"I'm Inspector Ashburn," she said. "I'm here to see Mr. Ripkin."

Flashes of Bud Fox showing up at Gordon Gekko's office and getting put on the back burner for hours made her think of her boss. Thank God Don was on Soot duty for however long this took.

"But of course. He's expecting you."

But of course? When was the last time she'd heard that expression? She wasn't going to argue with the access, however.

"Please come this way."

The blonde didn't so much stand up as levitate, and as she led the way down a long gray hall, Anne wondered whether she was a fembot or something. She moved like her bones were wire and she had ball bearings for joints.

Utterly bizarre, Anne thought as she looked around at all the closed doors: She didn't hear any phones ringing. There were no voices. Nobody else striding the corridors.

"Mind if I ask you something?" she said.

The blonde glanced over. "As you wish."

As I wish? Is this an Alfred Hitchcock movie? "Is this Ripkin Development headquarters?"

"Ripkin Development takes up the top ten floors. This floor is solely for Mr. Ripkin."

"An entire floor. Wow."

"Mr. Ripkin is a very busy man."

"Well, I would think he would be with all the buildings he owns."

"You are very lucky Mr. Ripkin decided to see you. Ordinarily, he is booked months in advance."

"Arson should be a priority. Especially when it happens on property you own."

"Mr. Ripkin is not worried about meeting with you."

Okay, Bob Vance, Vance Refrigeration. "I didn't catch your name?"

If she said Phyllis, Anne was going to believe for sure God existed.

"Persephone." The future Stepford wife stopped in front of a pair of dove-gray doors that were tall as a waterfall. "Please wait here. I will announce you to Mr. Ripkin."

As she was left to her own devices, Anne wondered if Mr. Ripkin was sleeping with good ol' Persephone/Phyllis. It was a fair bet that was a yes. Loyalty like that either had to be bought with a good wage, or it had to be seduced with the promise of a good lifestyle. Besides, hadn't the original Mrs. Ripkin died a few years back?

The doors opened again. "Mr. Ripkin will see you now."

As the woman stood to one side, Anne entered a room she knew she was never going to forget. The ceilings were even higher than the entry doors, and the square footage was nearly that of a hotel lobby. Everything was covered in gray marble, great sheets of the stone covering the walls and the floor. No rugs, no paintings, just windows on three sides, and three or four sitting areas with a couple of conference tables.

Framed against a view out to the vast ocean, "Mr. Ripkin" was seated behind a vast desk that was uncluttered by even a phone. The man was seventy, but he looked sixty, no doubt the result of some very expensive, very subtle plastic surgery. His hair was snow white and thick as a snow drift, and his expression of calm professionalism reminded her of a hockey goalie's mask.

He was protecting a lot behind that composure, making sure no one pucked him in the face.

Anne instantly mistrusted him, and she thought about that stationhouse the man had bought the department.

"Inspector Ashburn." Voice was even, the townie in the vowels mostly brushed out, like stain from a cloth. "How nice of you to come."

As if he'd issued an invitation? "Thanks for seeing me."

"Perhaps we'll sit over here. Would you care for coffee? Tea?"

"No, thank you."

He issued a curt nod and she knew without looking over her shoulder that Persephone was going to vanish sure as a shadow chased away by the light. And as they proceeded over to some silk-covered chairs, Anne was aware that her hand was beginning to sweat.

"You will sit here," he announced as he pointed to a seat that appeared to be no different from any other.

Yeah, except for the wire that was running out the back and into the floor. And she would have chosen another, but she was willing to bet that whatever he had had installed in the thing was the same in all of the others . . . except for the one he picked.

As Anne sat, she wondered what was being monitored in her body. How much was being recorded. There were ways now that people could measure the slightest deviations in skin temperature, weight shift, breathing.

She sat on the very edge of the cushion. "So about those warehouse fires."

The man smiled slowly, and it was only then that she realized his eyes were the color of his decor, the color of dangerous fog on the sea.

"Won't you sit back and relax, Inspector Ashburn. We aren't in any kind of hurry."

Anne glanced at the double doors she'd entered through. "My boss is expecting me back in the office ASAP."

"He'll wait."

28

As the engine's brakes squealed and Company 17 pulled up to an apartment building with a second-story burn, Danny hopped down to the pavement and went for the lines in the back.

"Dannyboy, you're on clear first." Captain Baker nodded at Moose. "You, too."

"Roger that."

He and Moose got their tanks and masks on and then went for some additional equipment, pulling up the panels. As the lineup of axes and tools was revealed, Moose palmed two long handles and turned to Danny.

The sight of the axes made Danny sweat underneath his turnouts. "I'ma take the adz."

"Why? We need axes to get through doors—oh. Sorry."

Don't dwell on it. Just keep going.

Danny grabbed a hickory-handled length that had a fifteen-inch steel blade on one end and looked forward to using it to pry open doors. Besides, one axe was enough. They didn't both need one.

As they jogged over to the front door of the apartment building, he kept going with the list of reasons why there was a strategic imperative for him not to have an axe.

Residents were funneling out of the entrance, some still in bathrobes even though it was by now eleven thirty in the morning. Most were elderly and he anticipated a lot of cats. Meanwhile, the building's alarm system was going off, the shrill ringing hurting his ears. And the smell of smoke was heavy in the air.

This is a hot one, he thought. He could tell by the scent.

An old guy with Albert Einstein hair and a robe that looked like it had come out of Archie Bunker's closet stopped in front of Danny.

"I told her that kid was going to kill her. Be careful—I don't know if he's got a gun."

"Who?"

"Her grandson. Bad news. Been with her for the last three weeks. Has someone called the cops?"

"You better get moving." Danny nodded to the slow-up the guy was causing. "We'll handle everything."

"Righto."

As the man kept going, Danny hit his communicator. "Two-fiver-eight-seven, over." When he was acknowledged, he said, "We may have domestic situation. Confirm NBPD arrival, over."

Captain Baker replied, "ETA three to four minutes. Over."

"Two-fiver-eight-seven, over and out."

He and Moose hit the second-floor landing and peeled off from the traffic on the stairs. One look to the far end, and Danny's warning bells went off: There were eight doors down the hall, four on each side, and all but one were open or cracked, the residents in a rush to get out—or adhering to a not-uncommon building protocol requiring that everything be accessible during evacs.

The lone standout? The only one that was closed? Was where the smoke was.

"I think we should wait for the badges to get here," Danny said. "I got a bad feeling about this."

"Are you kidding me? Don't be paranoid."

They started down the well-trod carpet, the chemical sting in the air irritating the nose and back of the throat. The smoke curling out of the affected apartment, both from around the door and on the outside of the building, made Danny run through the critical analysis quick: volume, velocity, density, and color.

Volume was sizable, suggesting a hot fire in a limited, poorly ventilated area: There was a layer of smoke up along the ceiling in the corridor that was thickening, and through the window at the end of the hall, he could see great dark clouds billowing from the apartment into the open air. Velocity was bad news, the smoke choppy and spastic, another sign of poor ventilation and a warning that an autoignition flashover was likely. Density was trouble as well; the smoke was like a solid, laden with airborne fuel solids, aerosols, and gases, all of which were ready to party. Finally, the color was the worst. Black meant high toxicity, and so the likelihood anyone was alive in there was very low.

A few breaths of that kind of "air" and a person loses consciousness, with death to follow in a matter of minutes.

Danny hit his communicator. "Two-five-eight-seven, over." When the acknowledgement came, he stated, "We have black smoke in a chop on the second floor. Closed door. We need this vented and cooled right fucking now or this corner of the building is going to go H-bomb. Over."

Captain Baker responded. "Can you open the door?"

"Not advisable—"

"Yup," Moose interrupted on the line. "I'm doing it now."

Danny grabbed the sleeve of the guy's turnout. "Anybody in there is already dead."

"Maybe not. We have to try."

Captain Baker's voice came over the connection. "Get in there. The ladder is in position and we are venting."

There was a distant crash of glass, and instantly the volume of smoke dropped, the pressure released.

"We need to wait for that temp to cool," Danny said.

"Don't be a pussy."

Moose marched over to the door, positioning himself off to one side. Taking the heel of the axe, he banged on the thing. "Fire and Rescue. Open your door." When there was no response, Moose pulled a repeat. "Open up or we're coming in."

Through the window at the hall's terminal, Danny saw the ladder shift position. They were breaking more windows, giving the fire a chance to lose heat and stabilize.

Moose tried the knob and, finding it locked, yelled, "We're coming in!"

He swung his axe in a fat circle, and Danny had to look away from that sharp blade biting into the smooth surface of the door. A couple of good hits and Moose punched his fist in, feeling for the release.

"Sonofabitch. Deadbolt with no key."

Danny put his mask on. "I'll shoulder."

Moose stepped back to secure his own air source as Danny threw his weight into the panels. The wood, weakened by incineration, splintered, and a wave of heat and smoke knocked him back. Crouching down, he triggered his head lamp and entered. Daylight didn't mean shit with the air so thick with soot and contaminants, and he proceeded in a crab-walk through the interior, visualizing burned furniture, blackened walls, rugs that were nothing but stains on the floor.

Everything was still combusting, even the lowered temperature still hot enough to consume all manner of wood, plastic, and metal.

He found the first body in the hall.

It was lying with the arms and legs outstretched, as if the person had been running for the door when an explosion or other force knocked them off their feet. Impossible to tell whether they were face-up or facedown, male or female, clothed or naked. All the hair and any clothing had been burned off, and the charring of the skin and meat over the skeleton was so extensive, there were no discernible features.

"Two-five-eight-seven. We have one deceased in the hall off living room. Proceeding further, over."

"Two-five-eight-seven, prepare for water."

"Roger. Over."

The hoses were opened from the ladders, gallons and gallons of H_2O arching in through the windows that had been broken. Smoke flared, white now from evaporation.

The first charred door he opened revealed a crappy bathroom that had been spared some of the damage, the plastic shower curtain melted like modern art on the edge of the tub, the walls glazed and sweating, the color scheme of pale blue and yellow dulled but extant.

The next door was probably going to be a bedroom—

As Danny opened the way in, he couldn't process what he was looking at. Walls were stained with something, the pink-flowered paper marked with . . . brown handprints? That was when he saw, through the haze, a body spread-eagled on the bed. The wrists and ankles had been tied to the posts and there was a red gag in the mouth.

No movement.

Then again, the older woman appeared to have been gutted like a deer. Very recently.

Danny spoke into his communicator. "Second victim, bedroom. This is a murder scene."

He forgot to ID himself, but he didn't care. He went over. The old woman was staring through sightless eyes in terror at the ceiling overhead. Her loose skin was like folds of pale felt pooling under her arm pits, at her neck, on either side of her bony thighs.

He wanted to cover her up. Find a sheet or a blanket and give her some dignity. He couldn't risk compromising any evidence, however.

"What the fuck." Moose came in and stood next to him. "So that's what was cooking when the fire started."

Y ou know, I like unusual women."

As Charles Ripkin spoke, his eyes focused on Anne's pros-thesis. "Tell me, how did you lose your arm?"

He already knew the answer, she thought. He had to have re-searched her.

"I think we need to stay on topic. Let's talk about those fires in your warehouses."

"Did it hurt?" The man smiled. "I've always wondered what it would be like to be deformed."

"I understand these buildings are all held by various LLCs. I'm cu-rious why you didn't put them in the name of Ripkin Development."

"Do you feel ugly now? You know, as a woman. Now that you're not whole anymore."

"I'm also curious why they're insured by different companies. If it's to spread the risk, I guess you were smart, given those fires."

"Not to get too personal, but when you're with a lover, do you hide the stump? Keep it under a pillow, a sleeve, a fold of sheet? So they don't see it. Get distracted. Lose the mood."

"Because it's quite a concentration of arson in that area. Six fires in just a few years."

His left eyebrow twitched. "Are you ashamed now? Of yourself. Do you miss who you used to be?"

"Yet no one has been charged. I realize that an argument could be made that it's just been derelicts, but if that were true, that area of the city has been run-down for decades. Why in the last two years is all of this happening?"

"Once a firefighter. Now a pencil pusher. You are your own cliché, you realize."

"Do you have any explanation?"

"Of course I do. It's a bit obvious to have to paint a picture to a smart girl like you, but since you asked—you lose your arm, and now you're an also-ran with an unsatisfied yearning to get back to work. The problem is, you can't do the work you want anymore because you can't pass the physical tests you used to ace. You're stir-crazy, searching for purpose, and this itch that cannot be scratched no matter how many forms you fill out or investigations you do is driving you insane. So your brain is finding connections that do not exist, which is what women do, and all of that mental storm got you in your little gray municipal sedan and drove you all the way up to the big city." The man sat forward. "I permitted you this one get-together because I feel sorry for you. I have a daughter for whom I care very much, and she, too, had a fire ruin her. She was once very pretty. Now she looks like a monster. But you people saved her life and that's why I gave you that new stationhouse. I am very pro-firefighter, very supportive of your previous profession."

"So you have no comment."

"I just gave you plenty."

"You didn't explain anything, but I'm not going to argue with you."

"Good." The man stood up. "Now, if you'll excuse me, I have to go on about my day. As I said, I have indulged you with this visit because I feel sorry for you, but anything past this I will regard as harassment. There are consequences to things, as you have learned firsthand. Let's both make sure you don't lose anything else, shall we?"

Anne got to her feet. "I'm going to do my job, Mr. Ripkin. If you're hiding anything, it's going to come out. You need to be prepared."

"I always think it's wise to take our own advice."

"I'll be in touch."

"We'll see about that. Oh, before you go, how's your mother?"

"Excuse me?"

"Nancy Janice. She lives alone, doesn't she? In that house on Crandall Avenue. A tree fell on it from the storms, didn't it."

Anne froze and her stomach knotted up. She thought about Bob Burlington, the arson investigator whose body had washed ashore in the bay, and also her boss's warning. But she was not going to be bullied.

"Mr. Ripkin, I am very sure this act of yours works with most of the people you come in contact with, and I congratulate you on the cultivation of such a successful intimidation tool." She put her hand up. "Wait, before you tell me that I need to take you seriously, I'd like to show you something."

She took her cell phone out and turned the screen around to him. "I've recorded this entire conversation and every two minutes this handy app has sent a file to my boss, Don Marshall."

"That is not admissible as evidence," Ripkin said in a bored tone.

"You're right. But Don believes you had Bob Burlington murdered because he investigated the fire at your mansion. So if anything happens to me, my family, or anyone close to me, I've got that little comment of yours about my mother's house on lock—" As her phone vibrated, she smiled and pointed at the screen. "Oh, look. It's just sent another file—watch what happens next." A text notification came through. "And here's Don, confirming receipt."

"No one can do anything with it. You gave me no notice you were recording this."

She pointed to the chair she'd been in. "Don't pretend you don't have your own monitoring here. Guess we're even."

The double doors opened and the animatron with the great legs waited in between the jambs like a Doberman pinscher.

Anne walked across and then looked over her shoulder. "One more thing. I'd rather have a plastic hand and a clear conscience than be an OCD-ridden Cialis candidate with hair plugs and murder in his background. I can change jobs and enjoy the satisfaction of helping to put sociopathic criminals like you behind bars. Your future, on the other hand, is going to involve more male pattern baldness as well as the joy of sharing a communal shower with all kinds of people who you will view as beneath you. Oh, and as for the erectile dysfunction, I'm just guessing at that because only a guy who can't get it up would try to play the 'you're lesser as a woman' bullshit with someone like me—hey, look." She indicated her phone's screen again. "Another file got sent. I think I'll make a best-of CD and send it to the local CBS affiliate—no, wait, you're so excited about being in the big city, CNN is even better 'cuz it's national. Have a good day, Mr. Ripkin."

Anne left the office and did not look back. As she went down the corridor, her legs were like rubber and she wanted to wipe the sheen of sweat off her forehead—but she resisted the latter because she didn't want to seem weak.

Behind her, the executive assistant's footfalls were sharp as curses.

As Anne came up to the glass wall that fronted the reception area, she was glad when she could push it open and get the hell out of there.

At the elevators, she used her prosthetic hand to push the down button.

Her real one was shaking too badly.

By the time she re-emerged into the parking garage, she was light-headed from adrenaline and fear, and as she went over to her car, she looked up. Pods containing security cameras were set into the ceiling at regular intervals, and she was willing to bet every property that Rip-kin owned was the same.

A man who watched everything like this? No accidents happened on his land without his knowledge.

Approaching her municipal sedan, she half expected her tires to be slashed, and she gave into paranoia, covering her hand with the sleeve of her jacket as she touched the handle to open her door. She didn't take a deep breath until she was driving out onto the street and merging into traffic. When she was back on I-93 and heading for New Brunswick, she called her boss.

Don picked up on the first ring. "That sonofabitch."

"You're right. He's capable of anything."

"Are you okay?"

"Yeah, I'm fine. Did you like my speech at the end?"

"Outstanding, I couldn't have said it better myself. The recording was a great idea of yours. Good job, Anne."

A bloom of professional pride warmed up her chest. "Thanks, boss."

"Drive safe. And watch out for anyone suspicious around you."

"Will do. How's my dog?"

"He's in my office. I told him we'd have lunch at the deli—you're coming with us."

"Great. I should be back in about an hour."

"Just be careful."

As she ended the call, she took a deep breath and felt echoes of what it had been like to battle a fire, the rush of fight-or-flight as she faced off at a blaze with a charged hose in her hand, the mental and physical challenge, the conquering of fear, the triumph at the end.

The smile that hit her face came from a very deep part of her, a part that she had resigned to leave behind.

It was affirming to find purpose—and, to use Danny's monster analogy, something to slay.

On that note, she tried to remember what had happened to Ripkin's daughter.

The young woman had been at Ripkin's shore house by the New Brunie yacht club when the fire had broken out. It had been off-season, October, and she'd been there alone. She had been found badly burned on the third floor, having run upstairs, as opposed to outside, to get away from the fire that had started in the first-floor parlor. At the time, the blaze had been ascribed to a faulty gas line that fed the hearth in question, with a resulting explosion ripping through the old home. No internal sprinkler system—the mansion had been updated to include a car wash and a movie theater, but for fire safety, all it had had was the most basic of alarms.

Anne remembered what the daughter had looked like, being taken out on a stretcher, sheets of skin melting off her as she was put in the back of an ambulance. It was callous, but once the crew had returned to the stationhouse, Anne hadn't thought about it again.

Just one more in a long series of alarms that had gone off that night. That week. That month.

Why had Constance Ripkin gone up instead of out?

When Danny had first come in as a probie fresh out of the academy, Allen Gould, a since-retired lieutenant, had taken him aside and told him that, sooner or later, every fireman went on a dead-baby run.

Horrible way of putting it, but an accurate enough description for the phenomenon.

As Danny sat rear-facing in the engine on the way back to the stationhouse, he remembered the morbid curiosity and shameful excitement he'd felt at the prospect. He couldn't wait to get into the grit and the grime, see the underbelly, lift up the rock of inhuman ugliness and check out the twisted, gnawing worms beneath.

The dead-baby run was the incident that stained your brain, like the first glimpse, out of the corner of your eye, of a woman who had been sexually tortured, doused in lighter fluid, and lit like charcoal for a grill with a match.

He could still remember how she'd smelled like barbequed meat.

And after six years, he still didn't order ribs in restaurants because of her.

Veterans of the fire service usually had only one. That was because if you had more than one that stuck with you, followed you around like a ghost, became the nightmare your subconscious fed you when you were stressed, you got out of the job.

You either learned to process and let go of what you saw, or you were not cut out for a long-term career.

Danny had always prided himself on his ability to triumph over all manner of gore and depravity. He had held people as they'd bled out, pulled the bodies of children out of crawl spaces and out from under beds, done CPR and lost that fight . . . hell, he'd broken down the door to a messy room just as a seventeen-year-old kid on the bed had put a shotgun to his own face and blown his brains out all over the Shaun White poster above his headboard.

It wasn't that Danny didn't remember all of those incidents. But on the rare occasion he recalled them, they were a black-and-white foreign movie with subtitles projected onto a tiny screen—all of the frame-by-frame with none of the immediacy.

That was how it had to be. Otherwise, you'd crack.

"—some fucked-up shit." Moose shook his head. "I mean, that old lady got tore the fuck up."

Duff shrugged. "Just made me hungry. Any chance we can get goulash for lunch?"

"You are some kind of Hannibal Lecter," Doc muttered from up in front.

Moose stared at Duff. "How can you say that after you saw Betty White lookin' like that?"

Danny stared out the window. They were passing by a stretch of strip malls, the boutiques, hair salons, and cafés all locally owned and struggling. The sun was out and people were walking in small groups. What day of the week was it? Friday?

Guess so.

"—ain't that right?"

When Moose knocked Danny in the thigh, he realized the statement had been made to him. "Sorry?"

"You and me are making lunch when we get back."

"Yeah. Sure."

"Come on," Duff spoke up. "How do you guys not want goulash?"

Danny returned to the view outside. As they rumbled along, the smoky postnasal drip down the back of his throat made him nauseous.

Just focus on the here and now, he told himself. *And you'll forget everything else. That's how it's always worked.*

A t the end of the day, Tom got into his SUV and told himself that he did not just put a clean shirt on and tuck it into a pair of khakis. He also did not get out his best set of Merrells from the back of the closet, the ones that he was still breaking in. And he most certainly hadn't shaved a second time.

Yeah, clearly all of that had been done by an alien who had taken his body over for a temporary, earthly visit.

He was pulling away from the stationhouse when his cell phone went off, and when he saw who it was, he cursed but answered it anyway. "Look, I told you I was working on getting the tree removed. I thought we could get over there today, but we were slammed."

For godsakes, he'd been dealing with an apartment fire started when a man with schizophrenia carved up his grandmother and tried to eat her intestines for lunch.

"I'll make sure it happens tomorrow," he told his sister, "and yes, before you ask, I've already arranged for two of the boys from the six-one-seven to patch the roof. I'm on it. You won't have to put up with Mom for more than another twenty-four hours—"

Anne jumped in. "She can stay as long as she likes."

And speaking of aliens, who the hell are you and what have you done with my sister.

"I thought you were desperate to have her out of there."

"Listen, Tom, do you remember the fire at the Ripkin estate. About a year ago."

"Yeah. Of course." He took a left and headed to the better side of town. "What about it?"

"So, I've been reviewing the file over here. No charges were ever filed."

"Gas line malfunctioned. Backed up into the house. When she lit the fireplace, everything ignited." He hesitated to mention Anne had been at the scene and surely recalled all that. "Why?"

"So I'm working the warehouse fires."

"Which ones? Down by the wharf?"

"Yes. And I went to see Charles Ripkin up in Boston today."

"How'd you manage that? From what I've heard, the man's office is like a fortress."

Her voice got dry. "Funny how if you mention you're an arson investigator, doors open."

"I gotta remember this."

He braked at a red light and watched two young women pass in front of his SUV. They both looked at him, did a double take, and stared like they were sizing him up for a fuck.

Ah, yes, the younger generation with their high standards and fine-tuned morals at work. And if he had any sex drive at all, maybe he'd reroute from this stupid meeting and go pick the two of them up in a bar.

Instead, he might as well have been checking out a pair of bicycles.

There was something very, very wrong with him.

"Hello?" his sister said.

"Sorry." He hit the gas as the light changed. "What were you saying?"

"I never got to sweep the house. As soon as the fire was out on the first and second floors, we got called onto another alarm. The six-one-seven closed the scene and you were the Incident Commander."

"Yeah. So?"

"Did you guys find anything that wasn't in the official arson report?"

"Are you accusing me of withholding evidence?"

"No. I'm asking because the investigator from my office died before he finished his job on the scene, and I'm worried that information was lost."

"Oh . . . shit, that's right. I remember something about the guy dying. Lemme think, I mean, you saw it all yourself: old house, daughter was a mess, Charles Ripkin shows up the next day and does a presser on how he owes the department an unbelievable debt. A month later, he sends a crew to break ground on the new six-one-seven. Daughter, Kristina, survived, but was scarred."

"Constance was her name." There was a pause. "It just doesn't add up. Why'd she make her way to the attic? While she was on fire?"

"She panicked. Instead of dropping and rolling, she ran and ended up in the elevator. She told us later she thought that was where a fire extinguisher was. She flailed around, pushed a bunch of buttons, fell out upstairs. She was found half in and half out of the open doors of the thing."

"That makes no sense."

"It's what she told police happened. Why would she lie?"

"I don't know. I want to find out, though."

"Anne, you're not a homicide detective, and the case is closed. Oh, and there was a fire extinguisher in the elevator, mounted under the button panel."

"Really?"

"Yeah."

"So why didn't she use it on herself?"

"I guess she collapsed. I don't know." There was a silence. "Hey, before you go. What's up with you and Mom? You can't wait to get rid of her most times and won't even talk to her on the phone—and now she's staying with you, all open-ended?"

Up ahead, the Canterbury Inn's lit-up exterior looked like an ad for autumn in New England, the maples on either side just beginning to turn red, the colonial's yellow clapboards, white trim, and black shutters as traditional as they were attractive.

"She's fine," Anne muttered. "It's whatever."

As Tom pulled into the lane that went back to the parking area, he was aware of a loosening in him, his breath entering his chest and exhaling with greater ease. How long had he been suffocating? he wondered.

Okay, that was a question he'd do well not to dwell on.

"Thank you," he heard himself say. "Thank you for . . . being with her. She loves you a lot and has never understood why you hate her so much."

———————

Anne was pulling into her driveway as she ended the call with her brother, and as she tossed her cell into her bag, she glanced back at Soot.

"You ready for dinner?"

The dog wagged his tail and chuffed, which was something he was starting to do. After a couple of days of food and antibiotics, his personality was beginning to emerge. Turned out he was a talker, ready to respond with a vocalization whenever he was addressed. He'd also started dreaming, his paws twitching and muzzle working when he was at rest.

He was also sleeping with her now, apparently. After she'd found him in her bed the night before, she'd tried to crate him when she and her mom had gone upstairs. He'd stared at her with such tragedy in his eyes that she'd brought him to her room . . . and woken up with him curled in against her in the morning.

It had been the first good night's sleep she'd gotten since before she'd lost her hand.

Too bad she was not going to enjoy one again anytime soon. Thank you, Ripkin.

Hooking Soot to his leash, she went up to her front door and—

Her mother opened things before she could unlock them, and the woman was ever perfect, ever smiling. The scent of meatloaf, home-cooked and prepared with a mother's love, made Anne want to think up something she absolutely had to do—on the other side of town.

"You're home!"

Charles Ripkin's shark eyes came to mind. "Yes. Hi. Um, hello."

As she stepped in, she stopped and looked around. "What the hell have you done?"

Her mother closed the door. "Well, I thought things would work better this way. The flow was blocked by your sofa, that chair was going to fade in the sun, and I bought you that new coffee table."

"Where is my old one?"

"I put it down in the cellar. It wasn't right."

Anne shut her lids and started to count to ten. When that got her nowhere, she decided to shoot for a thousand. "Mother. You can't just take over here. This is my house, my things, and I don't care about 'flow,' okay? Cut it out."

"But it's better this way."

The words came out before Anne could catch them: "Your better and my better are not the same. Just like you and I have absolutely nothing in common and never will."

Her mother clasped her hands together. "I am sorry. I just . . . I thought you would like it."

"Didn't it occur to you that I put the furniture where it was because I wanted it there? And stop trying to please me. You're only making me mad."

"You're so like your father."

"I am *not* like him at all. But whatever, that's a compliment compared to being like you."

"Anne!"

She let Soot off the lead and put her purse down. "You are the most passive-aggressive person I've ever been around, yet you crumble when it counts. You always have."

Cue the tears. "I've only ever tried to love you. I know that you don't . . . respect me because you think I'm just a housewife. But I'm proud of you, I always have been, and I've been worried about you." That high-pitched voice with the Watertown accent, cracked. "When you were in the hospital, recovering, I just wanted to—"

"Rearranging my furniture is not the way to work out your issues about my injury." Anne forced herself to dial back on her anger. "My hand is not your problem."

"But I would like it to be. I want to be your mother, Anne. Even though you've only ever seen me as your father's wife."

Anne laughed harshly. "I don't see you as that, either."

"How can you say such cruel things?"

Crossing her arms over her chest, she looked around her little house and realized this confrontation, which had been coming for years, was the reason she hadn't wanted to be with her mother. There were things you couldn't take back, words that were daggers, glares that left marks.

But courtesy of Ripkin, she couldn't have her mother leave. As much as she would have preferred to have the woman anywhere else, she knew Nancy Janice was safe here. The house had a good security system and great locks. Plus Anne was just down the hall if anyone broke in.

Lowering her head, she decided she needed food and Motrin. "I apologize. I'm sorry."

She didn't mean it. But people had levers to be pulled in certain circumstances and her end goal was to have her mother safe until she figured this Ripkin thing out.

At least she knew the woman was safe here.

"I am, too," her mother said sadly.

Striding into the Canterbury Inn's lobby, Tom felt the floorboards under the deep red carpeting bend beneath his weight, the shifting causing creaks to rise up each time he put a foot down. Everything was brass-chandelier, old-school New England, lithographs of American revolutionaries on the walls, grandfather clocks in the corners, simple moldings on the low ceiling.

He half expected a lobster in colonial dress to be behind the front desk.

Wrong. It was a brunette in a uniform.

As she looked up at him, he gave her a wave and pointed in the direction of the dining room. She nodded and went back to whatever she was doing.

Probably refreshing her memory on the Boston Tea Party. Paul Revere. Faneuil Hall.

None of which was in New Brunswick, all of which the city had commandeered as part of its tourist trade, like a little brother mugging his older sibling's stuff.

The dining room was red and navy blue, all patriotic, the tables set far apart, the place more than three-quarters full of the white-hair-

and-dental-implant set. Autumn always brought the leaf peepers, bus-loads of over-seventies riding the highways through the colorful season so they could return home with Vermont maple syrup, fake ivory carvings from Maine, and miniature laminated maps of the Freedom Trail from Massachusetts.

"May I help you?" the hostess asked from behind her stand.

"I'm here to meet—"

"There you are!" Graham Perry came out of nowhere like a grem-lin. "We're in a private room."

In any other circumstances, Tom would have been pissed that he had to deal with the guy. But he would have taken anyone as a chaper-one for this, including Mr. Hi-how're-ya.

"I'm not staying long," Tom said. "And why the hell are we meeting in a private room. I thought campaigns like to save money."

"We're building a coalition."

"And you can't do this at a Howard Johnson's?"

"They don't exist anymore. And no, we can't."

Perry opened a door, and yup, it was another boardroom setup, but this time Tom was looking at a whole bunch of aftermath, the seats turned away from the table, bound reports open and cockeyed, mint wrappers and half-empty Snapple and Poland Spring bottles next to glasses with melting ice in them. A portable screen and pro-jector were in place, and a laser pointer that had been left on was beaming across at the side wall, a red eye focused on nothing of im-port.

"The mayor must have gone to the bathroom. Hold on."

Perry shuffled to the exit and Tom felt like following the trend. In-stead, he sauntered over and checked out one of the reports.

"Warehouse District Repurposing Proposal" was the title, and he smiled. Flipping through the pages, he saw Ripkin Development's name all over the place.

"Thanks for coming to see me."

Tom looked up at Mayor Mahoney. Navy blue dress tonight, same figure, same hair, same scent. God, he wished he weren't attracted to her.

"Warehouse wharf development, huh." He tossed the report on the table. "Big plans. Expensive plans—what were you saying about firefighters and teachers?"

"We need businesses to thrive in this city."

"I thought we weren't allowed to talk about your father."

She almost caught the frown before it hit her face. Almost. Her problem was that he'd seen it so many times, that expression that reflected the internal thought: *Wow, you really are the asshole people say you are.*

"It's not about my father."

"So is it about Charles Ripkin? I see his name all over that."

"He's a potential major investor."

"Who owns a lot of property down there."

"Which is why we have to get him involved." The mayor shook her head. "But that's not why you're here."

Tom became very aware that Perry had not returned to the room. And that the doors were closed.

He put his palms up and took a step back. "Oh, no you don't. I did not come here to get hit on."

"What?" The frown returned. "Are you suggesting I would—are you serious?"

"Don't pretend that it doesn't happen. And you've made it clear you'll do anything to get re-elected."

Mayor Mahoney's jaw clenched, and he found it interesting that she was forcing control over her emotions—because it suggested there might be some heat underneath all that composure. Then again, he'd just accused her of using sex to get an endorsement, sooooooooo . . .

"I would like to make this very clear," she bit out. "I asked you here to discuss my plans for addressing the city employee pension deficit so that you can have some confidence that your firefighters will get what they deserve when they retire. I was also going to ask for your help with on-the-job injury compensation. There are some best-practice models out of LA and Chicago that we might be able to use. What I most certainly was *not* offering was any part of me."

Mirroring her pose, he crossed his arms, too. "I guess I misread you," he muttered in a bored tone.

"You know, you've got a problem, Chief Ashburn."

"Do I."

"You have a reputation around town for being inflexible and closed-minded. No one can argue how you take charge of and oversee the department and its equipment and facilities, but you are very difficult to get along with and people are forced to work around you."

"You know, it's strange. I thought my job *was* to run the fire department for the city, including its equipment and facilities."

"It is."

"So I'm knockin' it out of the park."

"Not really. Compared to national standards, you have among the highest levels of personnel dissatisfaction and burnout. Your men and women feel disempowered to make changes in procedures, they're frustrated by a lack of support from management, and they're worried about their futures. You are the head of a very unstable unit, Chief."

"What the hell are you talking about? You don't know anything about my people."

"You don't think your union is on the pulse of its membership? And willing to share that information with me?"

Brent, you fucker, he thought.

"What I see," he ground out, "is a group of people fighting fires with equipment that is aging in facilities that need renovation, and your buddy Ripkin's 'donation' was more a showpiece for his name than a gift designed to help my department. Before you harp on me about a bunch of intangibles, maybe you should look at our resources."

"Personnel are your resources. And they're hurting. Your people need support—"

"Don't talk to me about what I need."

"If I don't, no one else will."

"Why, because you're so special? Don't believe everything your daddy tells you."

"No," she snapped, "it's because I'm *your* boss. I'm the mayor of this town and that means you work for me, you answer to me—and I will have no trouble firing you if you don't realign your attitude and realize *you* are part of a very serious problem in this city's fire service."

In the silence that followed, Tom knew he had to leave before he said something he regretted.

Leaning in, he said in a low voice, "Stay out of my business."

"Do you hear yourself? I tell you you've got a problem in the department and your only response is about you. You're not even open to hearing the issues or considering your own behavior. All you want to do is get territorial and shut off the noise. That's not a leader, Tom. That's a despot."

"Don't call me by my first name. I'm Chief Ashburn to you. And when I watch Barring whip your ass on election night, please picture me smiling from ear to ear, will you? It'll add to my satisfaction."

On that happy little note, he left the boardroom. As Perry came out of nowhere again and started to run after him, Tom nearly grabbed the guy by the throat and threw him across the lobby.

"Not now, Perry."

"But I just want to put a bug in your—"

Tom wheeled around. "Stay away from me. Or you will not like what happens next."

Apparently, the guy had basic survival skills in addition to all his ambition because he backed the fuck off like he had a gun pointed at him.

Smart. Real smart.

32

On Saturday morning, Anne walked up to a three-story apartment building that had about thirty units. On the second floor, its brick exterior was stained with black streaks and plywood panels had been nailed over a line of windows that had been broken. A tree close to the corner had sustained loss, its gumdrop shape given a heat shear on one side.

The crime scene investigators were on-site, two of their boxy vehicles parked in front, and there were a couple of marked NBPD cars behind them. Television crews from the local stations were parked across the way, a uniformed cop staring at the primped-and-prettied reporters and the casually dressed cameramen like he expected them to try to get into the place.

The media's interest had been intense. Details of the murder of one of the building's residents, supposedly by her grandson, and the subsequent fire that had started in the kitchen, were so sensational that the crime had been sucked into the vortex of the twenty-four-hour news cycle, clickbait to be served up as the Internet's newest fast-food meal.

She'd already seen two memes featuring something cooking in a cast-iron pan.

Grandma. It's what's for dinner.

Grandma. The other white meat.

Bastards.

After flashing her ID to the uni at the door, she went up four flights of stairs, and the nuances of the fading smell of a contents fire confirmed on an olfactory basis that they were indeed some twenty-four hours out: The acrid stench had dissipated some, but it was still strong enough that she could catch the plastic high notes.

As she closed in on the apartment in question, there was a walk-of-shame element to the aftermath, the excitement gone, the frenzy over, nothing but water and smoke damage left as artifacts of the emergency. These residuals were concentrated down at the end of the hall, where some NBPD yellow caution tape ran on a diagonal to cordon off the scene's door.

As she approached, she had her ID out, but the cop on the business side of the tape just held the length up so she could duck under.

"Gloves and booties are here," he said.

"Thanks."

Stepping over to a box of nitrile gloves and a larger container of shoe covers, she got herself ready to enter. Don had assigned her a support role on the case, the primary investigator having already been over during the night as soon as the fire was extinguished. Residents and the firefighters had been interviewed then, and a preliminary report filed. She was on origin and cause, but, as a probie, also required to do a start-to-finish on the investigation as training.

As she pushed open the door with her gloved hand, voices, soft but insistent, murmured deeper inside the apartment.

Initializing her recorder, she spoke into her iPhone. "Upon entrance, there is extensive evidence of a high-temperature contents fire in the living area . . ."

Following investigative protocol, she continued to describe what she saw as she proceeded forward into a short hallway, stopping at a marker indicating where the first body was found. Continuing on, she noted the fire's characteristics and prevalence, its spread outward from the kitchen, its—

Anne stopped as she looked through an open doorway and into a bedroom that had been spared. Of the burn, at least. The violence that had occurred within its four walls more than made up for the lack of fire damage, and the pair of crime scene investigators working by the bed didn't look out of place in the slightest.

She'd read both the preliminary investigation report and the log from the 499, and was prepared, but the bloodstained sheets were still a pause-maker. All she could think of was Danny opening the door in the blaze and seeing a relatively smoke-less room with a gutted seventy-nine-year-old woman tied by her extremities to the bed.

Must have stopped him in his tracks, too.

One of the crime scene team glanced up from where he was taking samples from the pillows. "Anne? How're ya? Timmy Houlihan, Jack's second cousin. We met last year at Fourth of July."

"Oh, yes." She lifted her gloved hand. "Hey."

"Messy, huh," he said as he indicated the stained bedsheets. "Horrible. This here's Teresa La Favreau."

Anne nodded at the woman who was bagging something on the floor. "This has been all over the news."

"Kid had a history. Went off his meds. Tragedy."

"Awful. I guess the residents all warned her?"

"Yeah, well, it wasn't just him. Some jewelry, engraved with her name and birth date, showed up late last night in the west end at a pawnshop. The guy who brought the stuff in smelled like a fire and had soot all over him, and he took off before we could get there." The man indicated around the tidy, modestly furnished room. "We've got good prints and some hair samples, along with the images from the shop. We're going to find whoever it is."

Anne focused on some framed photographs of a young man that were sitting on the bureau. "Well, I'll just head down into the kitchen and do my part."

"Good to see you."

"You, too, Timmy."

As Anne kept going, she talked into her phone, noting the evidence of intensifying heat in the hall, the Sheetrock eaten away, the studs in walls and the joists overhead showing signs of intense charring. Here, closer to the source, the fire had transitioned from contents to structure.

After taking samples and photographs, she began to construct a sequence of events. Photographs posted by the grandson on social media, since taken down and now used as evidence, detailed that he had been cooking his grandmother's internal organs on the stove top. They hadn't been selfies, however, which suggested they'd been taken by the second man. And then something had happened.

An argument? Or the plan all along?

According to the preliminary report, residents above the apartment and on the same floor stated there had been a big explosion, and the fire had been fast and violent, something that required a secondary, sustainable ignition source.

Dousing someone in lighter fluid would not get that effect. And tampering with a gas line? That would blow the whole apartment building up. In her training, she had read cases where entire houses were destroyed, with the debris scattered two hundred yards away in a circle.

No, that was too much power.

Instinct told her this was a gasoline blow. The problem was, with a fire as hot as this one had been? So much evidence was destroyed. But that would explain the explosion people had heard: Pawn-store suspect uses gasoline to get the grandson on fire after they murder the grandmother and leaves. Grandson careens around the kitchen, trying to put himself out. Lights things on fire like drapes, rugs, tablecloths, hand towels. Heat begins to build. He transitions down the hall. Meanwhile, the remaining gasoline in an enclosed can, stored somewhere in the kitchen where it shouldn't have been, gets hot. Pressure builds and cannot be contained.

Gasoline in liquid form won't catch fire below temperatures of 500 degrees. The vapors are the danger. And if you have it in a storage container that ruptures from heat expansion, and add sufficient air and ignition, you're looking at a bomb because that vapor goes everywhere.

Residents heard the smoke alarms first. Had anyone smelled any gas? Because maybe that suspect decided to try to cover his tracks and doused things around the kitchen with the accelerant. But that wouldn't account for the explosion—so there had to have been some gas left in a container in the hot zone.

And what about the evidence in the bedroom. If the guy had been thinking properly, he would have lit that room on fire, too.

Then again, considering what he and his friend had been doing at the stove, "properly" was not a word to associate with his mental processes.

As she voice-recorded notes and took other photographs for her own reference, she just kept thinking . . . what the hell had Danny thought as he'd walked through here?

He was like a shadow, following tight on her heels.

And that was when Moose's wife, Deandra, called her cell phone.

———————

Anne didn't get back home until five. Investigating Ripkin Development had left her with some backlog work, and then there was the report to file on the apartment fire.

Plus, her mother.

The idea of spending an entire Saturday with the woman had been enough to take Anne's work ethic, already strong, to juicehead levels. It wasn't that her mother was totally awful—and that was part of the problem. If Nancy Janice had been rude, cantankerous, angry; then Anne's avoidance would be justified. Instead, she was stuck with the reality that she was being a little unfair, especially after she'd let loose in anger the previous evening.

"Come on, Soot," she said as she hooked the lead on his collar. "Time to check out your backyard again."

She'd crated him at her office for the three hours she'd been over at the apartment site, and then they'd enjoyed a nice long walk to a coffee shop for lunch. After all that exercise, he'd curled up at her feet for the rest of the afternoon.

Bracing herself, she let them both in. "Mom?"

When there was no answer, she went through and let Soot out. She found a note, written in her mother's flowery flourish, on the kitchen table.

Okay, so Nancy Janice was due back at six after an afternoon of bridge. Which meant Anne had an hour to decompress.

After feeding Soot, she went upstairs and started the shower. It felt good to take her prosthesis off. Even better to get under the hot water.

She was squeezing shampoo on the top of her head, which was what you did when you only had one palm and had to use it for dispensing, when she looked down and focused on her stump. The taper from her elbow down to the blunt end was pronounced due to muscle atrophy and the flesh was still mottled and angry from that infection even after nine months had passed.

Ripkin's smug voice wormed into her ear, taunting her even as she told herself it shouldn't.

But the truth was, there might have been more than one reason she hadn't wanted to get all the way naked with Danny. And she hated that Ripkin, that shit, had tapped the nerve even as she'd denied it to his face. He'd been wrong about one aspect, though. It wasn't a female thing to feel less than whole if you lost a limb. It was a human thing. She'd been in that rehab hospital with men who had been in motorcycle and farming accidents, even one guy who'd had some bad luck with a chain saw.

They had been just as scared as she'd been, not only about how to work through life and job issues, but with who they were. What they had become. And physical attractiveness was part of that.

Telling herself she was just fine, she finished her suds-and-rinse routine and stepped out. As she was drying off, she glanced at her naked body in the mirror—and couldn't remember the last time she had really looked at herself.

It wasn't going to start tonight, she knew that much.

Dressed in jeans and a fleece, she went downstairs and checked the clock on the microwave. Twenty-three minutes left of peace.

On that note, if she could get dinner organized, that would cut down on conversation. Opening the refrigerator door, she—

"Oh . . . God."

Everything had been reorganized in there, the shelves moved up or down to accommodate a new arrangement of milk cartons and juice bottles and leftover containers. Shutting the thing, she went over to her cupboards on a hunch.

Yup. Her plates were—okay, all the way across the room now. Spices were also in a different location. Silverware had been put in plastic slides in a drawer that had previously been for hardware.

Great. How could she possibly have known that setting the don't-touch-my-stuff boundary required an asterisk that included cupboards, closets, and drawers?

As her temper mounted up and got ready to ride the range, she knew she had to leave for a while. And there was only one option.

Talk about the lesser of two evils.

After putting Soot in his crate, she scribbled a quick note on the other side of what her mom had written on, and then she set the security alarm and was out of the house like she'd stolen something.

The evening was going so well. Really.

33

Moose and Deandra's ranch was halfway to Danny's farm, located in a not-quite-rural, but definitely not suburban, zip code that had the houses spaced on overgrown lots of ten and twelve acres. It went without saying that the couple was not going to last here. This was Moose's dream, what with the privacy and the space for his car-restoration equipment—but a nightmare for Deandra's urban, upwardly mobile streak.

Danny knew Moose had bought the place without telling her, a *Surprise, honey!* that had been meant to show the woman he could afford big things. When she'd lost her shit, his response had been to lease a closeout BMW 3 Series for her.

The second the oh-goody glow wore off that car, Moose was going to have a tiger by the tail, but that was his problem, not anybody else's. Bad timing, though. Almost all firemen supplemented their income with second jobs in things like roofing or construction, and with the bad winter weather coming on, Moose was going to be forced to take on security work around the holidays to pay for keeping his wife in a good mood.

The guy hated walking warehouses alone, not because he was scared but because he needed constant stimulation.

Again, not Danny's problem.

The road into the property was gravel, which had to be another negative in Deandra's eyes, and as the curve rounded and the house was revealed, Danny laughed. A townie who was determined to elevate her status was going to see the otherwise perfectly nice ranch as a noose around her throat.

No Subaru parked off to the side on the mowed grass with the other trucks. But he hadn't expected Anne to change her mind and come.

Parking himself next to Duff, he got out and tucked his shirt in. It was a brand-new button-down flannel, the kind of thing his boys wouldn't notice and smack his ass about, but that he'd chosen in case Anne showed. And anyway, his mother had always said he should wear blues and grays because they brought out the color in his eyes.

Too bad the thing was green and black. But it did have a pinstripe of gray in between the—

Okay, he needed to quit the pathetic shit.

Walking over to the front door, he found things were open, a screen keeping out what few bugs were left from the first hard frost the week before. He banged on the loose jamb and let himself in.

Holy . . . wow.

Even he, a confirmed bachelor with no fashion or decorating sense, knew the black and white furniture wasn't appropriate—and not just because it was oversized, the bulky forms conceived for rooms that were three, four, five times the size of the single-story's eight-by-twelves. The real problem was that everything was a cheap imitation: plastic made to look like leather, Plexiglas that didn't fool the eye, and stretches of almost-chrome, like Deandra was trying to convince people that she was living in a Manhattan penthouse and working for a modern art gallery—instead of cooling her jets out here in the country and answering phones and taking messages at a second-tier spa and salon in New Brunie.

The knockoffs were striving rather than achievement. Which, on the theory that people's houses reflected their identities, put paid to the couple.

And then there was the "art." Christ, if he had to look at one more saccharine picture of her at their wedding from hell in a fake silver frame, he was going to hurl. The things were hung all over the walls and propped up on side tables, a shrine to the seven hours in Deandra's life when she had been the princess, the winner of the beauty crown, the head of the line.

Did Moose ever notice that he had been cropped out of 90 percent of the photographs?

"Is that you, Danny?" the bride called out from the kitchen.

"Yeah. Hey, Deandra."

He walked through to the back. The lady of the house was at the stove, a pair of pink hot pants upholstering her ass, her silver lamé blouse so tight the only more revealing option would have been body paint.

As she turned around, he realized she'd gotten breast implants. And from the way she arched her back and pushed those bags of saline out at him, it was clear she wanted him to notice.

"Long time, no see." She smiled, showing off caps. "Can I make you a drink?"

"Where's Moose."

"Out back. Where else would he be. It's not like all of his friends are coming over and he's expecting me to do all of the work by myself. Hey, why don't you help me in here? I've got lasagna made with gluten-free noodles, and gluten-free bread, and I was just cutting up organic vegetables. You could toss my salad."

Her hair was lighter by a couple of shades, and he wondered, if this trend kept up, whether she'd have a triple-H chest and Daenerys Targaryen's coloring by Easter. And he knew exactly what she was playing at.

Danny shook his head. "I'm not good in the kitchen. Sorry."

Deandra's heavily lashed lids lowered, her smoky eye going down right stinky. "Anne's not coming, you know. I spoke with her this afternoon."

Ah, yes, all the charm I remember so fondly, he thought.

"She's really busy." He turned for the back door. "Let us know when the food's on."

If it had been anybody else, he would have stayed and helped because it was rude to have only one person cooking for five or six. But considering it was Deandra? He was going to follow Moose's example.

Opening the slider, he stepped out into the unseasonably warm night. The back porch was half-finished, the planks stopping partway across the frame—and the project was going nowhere until after the winter, Danny was willing to bet.

Ah, yes, the sprawl was starting.

The back acreage was all cleared meadow circled by a ring of forest, and Moose was starting to fill it with crap. The two-car garage had been turned into a workshop and there was a commercial dumpster, a transport box trailer, two rusted-out cars, and half a dozen drums full of God only knew what metastasizing outward.

No doubt the guy was going to gradually fill the field to the property's tree line with that kind of stuff.

Danny got to walking, closing in on the glow of the lights as Bruce Springsteen's "The River" got louder.

"Dannyboy!" Moose's voice boomed from the garage. "My man!"

The guy ducked out from under a raised, rusted-out Shelby Mustang that was about as structurally complete as his porch and far, far older than he was. With a Bud in one hand and a wrench in the other, grease was his middle name: the stuff was on his UMass T-shirt and his old Levi's, and his work boots were black from gunk.

Danny clapped palms with him, nodded at Duff and Duff's cousin T.J., and gave Deshaun a bear hug. And he was surprised, in a good way, to see Jack, his supposed roommate.

"Where you been, asshole?" Danny gave Jack at hard embrace. "I keep thinking I hear you coming in at night, but nope."

"At least I'm still paying rent."

"Good point."

"Beer?" When Danny nodded, Jack went over to the red-and-white cooler. "Coors Light?"

"You remembered. I'm touched." As the longneck came flying at him, he caught it and cracked the thing open. "How's your sister?"

Everyone got quiet, and Danny wanted to curse. Some things were best not asked about. On that note, he was hoping no one else brought up Anne.

"She's the same. You know . . . the same."

"I'm sorry." He took a swig and looked at the car carcass. It had been blue once, and the engine as well as all four tires had been removed and were off in the corner. "So, Moose, what's this mess?"

"Mess? Can you not see the potential?" The guy banged on the steel frame. "Come on, she's a '66 Shelby GT350, bitch—one of the first two hundred and fifty-two that were '65 Mustang K-Code Fastbacks before Shelby American converted them."

"Jesus Christ, Moose, how'd you get a hold of her?"

"I bought her out of Ohio and just shipped her in today. She's gonna be gorgeous."

"After a lotta plastic surgery."

"All women want that," Moose muttered.

No, not all, Danny thought as he pictured Anne on that climbing wall. Some recognized they were perfect just the way God made 'em.

"So lemme help," Danny said. "I like getting my hands dirty."

As Anne parked her Subaru at the end of the lineup in Moose and Deandra's front yard, there was only one truck that she saw. Getting out, she took a minute to pull up her jeans and make like she was checking out the property: good bit of cleared acreage surrounded by a loose fringe of trees and underbrush, a.k.a. Mother Nature's version of a chain-link fence.

Wow, nice cars, she thought as she headed for the front walkway.

Moose's eyesore of a Charger was next to a brand-new BMW. Wedding present? she wondered. Then what was the house—the honeymoon?

Knocking on the screen door, she waited. When there was no answer, she backed up and went around to the rear. It turned out to be a good guess. In the gloaming, the lights in the open garage were intensifying and illuminating a classic male-bonding scene: dudes with beers around a car on a lift.

Of course Bruce is playing, what else would be? she thought.

And then it was a case of double takes on the part of the menfolk. Jack and Moose saw her first. Deshaun, second. Duff and T.J., his cousin, third. Danny had his head shoved into some part of the undercarriage, and it wasn't until he stuck his hand out and no tool smacked into his palm that he glanced out from under and saw her.

His face showed no reaction. His eyes went up and down her body.

"Hi," she said to everybody. "Sorry to crash, but I decided to change my mind."

"This is great!" Moose said. "Come here, lemme hug ya."

She got wrapped in a big embrace, and then she was greeting the others, starting with Danny's old roommate, Jack. The SWAT team leader was as military-looking as ever, his dark hair buzzed so tight on the sides you could see his scalp, the top like a trimmed hedge. He was wearing an NBPD T-shirt that stretched over his heavy, tattooed arms and camos on the bottom. Even his treaded shoes looked like the kind you could climb Mount Kilimanjaro with.

"Jack, I haven't seen you in forever." As she hugged him, it was like trying to throw her arms around a house. "How you doing?"

"Same ol', same ol'." The guy forced a smile. "Everything's great."

So his sister had fallen off the wagon again. Poor man. He was more determined than that woman was to keep her alive and on track—and that was the root of his problem.

"Duff," she said. "T.J., God, it's been a while, too."

And then there was Danny.

He was back under the car again, his torso and legs emerging from the bottom like he'd mutated into the Transformers' old grandpa.

"Hey, Danny," she said. Back in the old days, whenever she'd been around the crew with him, she'd called him Dannyboy. But you could only do that if you were a member of the club and that was not her anymore.

"Can you hand me the five-eighths wrench?" he said.

"Yeah, sure."

She went over to the beat-up built-in table, and of course, Moose's tools were as organized as he was, everything in piles that made no sense. She weeded through, found what she was looking for, and went back over to the Shelby Mustang Fastback.

"Here."

Danny's dirty hand stuck out from under, and man, she liked the looks of a calloused male palm. There was something erotic about the strength, the utility, the competence for practical things.

The speculation about how it would feel across her naked skin.

She gave him the tool, but before she could get out of range, he said, "I need another hand in here."

As he looked out at her, his eyes were not flirtatious. They were factual, and she ignored a flush of pride that came with being asked to help him.

"Yeah, sure."

Under the car, she was able to stand up all the way, and she inspected the automotive anatomy. They were stripping everything so that the rusted undercarriage and crappy floor pan could be cleaned with a wire wheel and drill, then resealed to form a stable, healthy foundation for the restored car. Danny was having trouble removing one of the corroded brackets.

"Here," he said. "You hold, I torque."

"Not going to work." She leaned out from under the car. "Moose, you got a spot welder? We'll be here 'til next week with this. Cutting it is the right call."

"Yeah." The guy nodded toward the table. "It's there somewhere."

"I'll get it," Danny said. "Hold this just in case?"

"Sure."

Anne braced her hand where his had been, and when he shuffled out, their bodies brushed. Sexual attraction, fickle, subversive, and unwelcome, rippled through her.

Don't get all hot and bothered, she told herself. *This is only an excuse to get out of the house and nothing more.*

D eandra was actually not a bad cook, Danny decided. It was her ingredients that were for shit.

Okay, fine, maybe it was a case of both a crappy chef and weird components.

As he sat with a plate on his lap in the living room, he picked around the sweaty mess of lasagna with his fork . . . separating the "noodles" from the watery sauce and the cheese that somehow managed to be crumbly even after it had melted.

Across the way, Anne was in an armchair, and everyone else was in the kitchen at the table. Deandra had insisted that people eat inside even though it was one of the last warm nights of the year. Then again, Danny had the feeling she was showing off her furniture—which was why she'd insisted Anne and he go in here.

Jack entered with a second plateful and sat down next to Danny. "Man. What a meal."

"Do not tell me you like this stuff?"

"Oh, no. I'm just starved. The 'man' was for what's doing in there." Anne's head nodded in that direction. "Awkward?"

"You could fry an egg on Deandra's forehead, and meanwhile

Moose is hammering beer, Deshaun has his coat on like he's already out the door, and Duff and T.J. look like they want to kill themselves."

Danny kept his wince to himself on that one. "I don't get why Moose puts up with it."

"Have you seen the way she's built?" Jack glanced at Anne. "No offense."

"None taken." Anne smiled. "And she was not built like that at the wedding."

"Too right." Jack methodically took forkfuls and put them in his mouth, chewing only once before the swallow like he was on *Fear Factor*. "So what are you working on at Fire and Safety, Anne? I like arson investigation. It's fun."

Anne laughed. "Only you would put it like that."

Danny gave up on eating and set his plate down on the coffee table. At this point, he was hankering for a cigarette, but there was no way he was giving Jack a chance to sweet-talk his Anne.

Not that Anne was his. And not that Jack was sweet.

Anne started to talk about the warehouse fires she was investigating, and Danny watched everything about her under the guise of paying attention to what she was saying. He didn't hear a word. He watched her lips move. Her breathing. The way she fiddled with the thumb of her prosthesis.

Her legs as they crossed and uncrossed.

All he could think of was getting inside of her again. It wasn't right and it wasn't fair and he didn't care. Except this time, he wanted her totally naked. And like, not on his couch for a quickie that she was determined to pretend hadn't happened.

He wanted memorable that lasted a lifetime.

From out of the corner of his eye, he saw someone lingering just outside the room.

Deandra was in the shadows, and she was staring at him in the same way he'd been looking at Anne.

The funny thing about Jack was that he was so easy to talk to.

Anne had to force herself to stop speaking. "Anyway, yeah, so I went up and saw Ripkin and he was bizarre."

"What do you mean 'bizarre'?" Jack asked.

Even though she'd been addressing the man, Danny was the one she was really aware of, and given the intense way he was looking at her, she decided it was best not to go into too many specifics. Especially about the threat against her mother.

Danny was liable to do something stupid. Like go up to Ripkin's office and throw the bastard out of a window: One thing you could be sure of when it came to Danny Maguire? He stood up against what was wrong, no matter what it cost him.

"Ripkin's used to getting his way," she said. "He's a successful businessman, and I think he believes the world and everyone in it is his for the taking. But it was nothing I couldn't handle."

"Did he come on to you?" Danny asked in a low voice.

"Not in the slightest." Anne shrugged. "He just did a lot of posturing, none of which impressed me."

Jack put his clean plate down—which made him worthy of a medal, as far as she was concerned. The lasagna had been like an MRE.

"You know, I have a case you might be interested in." The guy sat back on the enormous white couch that was big as a river barge. "You talked about finding a lot of office equipment in those fires? Well, we served an arrest warrant on a guy with previous offenses and gun felonies, and found an entire room full of cords, chargers, and parts of monitors and computers—as if he'd been storing a Best Buy's worth of phones and PCs there, but had to move them quick. He was obviously a black market dealer, and the timing is interesting, is all. I mean you're talking about office equipment in these fires—and he's been up on so many charges over the past two years that I wonder if he didn't burn evidence a number of times."

Anne was unaware of having sat up straight until she nearly slipped off the slick cushion. "I want to talk to him. And see the case file."

"You got it." Jack took out his phone. "Come to our HQ Monday morning. I'll show you everything, and then you can work your channels to interrogate him."

"That's great. Thanks, Jack."

"My pleasure. I'll text you tomorrow after I get it all set up."

Danny got to his feet. "Hey, Anne, come help me with that pan out in the garage? I think we can get it out if we work together."

"Sure. No problem."

As she followed him into the kitchen with her plate, she felt like she was walking into a brick wall. The vibe was tense at the table, Duff and T.J. playing eyeball ping-pong, Deandra sitting with her arms crossed over her chest, Moose cracking open another beer. Deshaun was getting up with that coat of his on.

"We going back out?" Moose said with all the hope and anticipation of someone about to be called up from the DMV line.

"There's dessert, you know," Deandra said. "But fine. It's not like you ate anything."

"I've got to go," Deshaun interjected. "Thanks for dinner."

Duff stood up and T.J. was a split second behind. "We've got to head out, too. Sorry. But we're on shift tomorrow, which was why we weren't drinking."

"Aw come on, you guys can stay a little longer." Moose looked back and forth between them. "You got to stay. It's frickin' eight o'clock."

But there was no stopping the tide, and Anne was glad to be on the forefront of the evac, even if she was arguably heading deeper into Moose and Deandra's territory instead of away from it.

She and Danny were quiet as they walked back to the garage, and as she entered its cool confines, he stayed by the open bay and lit a cigarette with his Bic. The sun had long since set, and it was dark out, but the lighting from the rafters shone down on him, making him seem even bigger.

As he exhaled over his shoulder, she went across to Moose's tool zoo. Working through the tangle, she started to make piles of screwdrivers, wrenches, vises.

"You're a huge help, you know. With the car."

She looked over at him. "It feels good to be doing something with my hands. Hand."

"Yeah."

"Deandra is a god-awful cook."

"Moose could stand to lose some pounds."

"He'll be lucky if that's the only thing she takes off of him." Anne shook her head. "I knew they were making a mistake at that wedding. I just didn't expect it to get this bad this soon."

"It's their bed. They gotta lie in it." He turned his cigarette around and stared at the lit tip. "Listen, I got a favor to ask you."

"What's that?"

"Talking about hands and all. I could use an extra set out at the farm tomorrow. I don't have many good working days left on the property, and I could finish what I started if I had another hauler for the debris, another person on the saw."

Anne followed his example and inspected the star-shaped tip of a Phillips-head. The idea of being outdoors, conquering a tangle of brush, having something with an easy start and finish, was exactly what she needed. But Danny was always a complication.

"I'd really appreciate it," he said.

She thought of her mother. For Nancy Janice, Sundays were church, lunch with her girlfriends, and usually a movie and tea. Lots of people, places, busy, busy. There was a chance that she might feel compelled to stay home to be polite, though.

"Can I bring Soot?" Anne asked abruptly.

35

To Vic Rizzo, fall Sundays were sacred, and not because he was religious. He was as lapsed a Catholic as a man could be, much to his mother's disgust and heartbreak. No, if he was lucky enough to get the Lord's day off rotation, he worshipped at the altar of ESPN, prepared to do nothing but veg in front of the TV and work the remote around college and pro ball games.

Seeing no one. Talking to no one.

Just sitting on the ratty couch across from his concave-screened paradise, breaking only to re-beer and re-chip.

His apartment was a one-bedroom, one-bath in a converted triplex just five blocks down from the 617. He was on the middle floor, over an old couple who had the ground level, and the seventy-two-year-old owner who was on the top. It was a quiet place, and he helped everyone take their garbage to the curb, and shoveled snow, and fixed all manner of minor problems around the building.

He kept his more . . . hardcore . . . pursuits well away from his home. Then again, he didn't want his identity or his address known.

That was why he always wore masks.

With a groan, he lowered himself down on Old Faithful and extended his stiff leg out onto the beat-to-shit coffee table. Turning on the TV, he was ready to watch the LSU/Bama game from the day before that he'd DVR'd and then transition to the Pats game—

The knock on his door was loud, a single pounder that clearly came courtesy of a big set of knuckles.

Putting the recording on pause, Vic reached under the cushion next to him and palmed his nine. "Who is it."

Not a question. More like a warning.

"It's your boss."

"Tom?" Vic released his hold on the gun and sat up. "What the hell?"

He groaned as he got to his feet, although that was a function of not just his bad shoulder and the sore leg, but because his vibe was being ruined.

When he opened the door, he frowned. Chief Ashburn looked like he'd been pulled through a thorn bush backward, his face weary and drawn, his mouth a tight line—as if he didn't want to be here any more than Vic wanted to welcome anybody into his crib.

"What the fuck happened to you?" Vic demanded.

"You got a second."

"For what?"

"I need to talk to someone."

Vic stepped back. "I'm not a good listener, I give shitty advice, and I have all the compassion of a hunting knife, but sure, by all means, let me be your therapist."

The chief brushed by him. "You got a real way with charm, Rizzo."

"Call me Hallmark." He shut the door. "I'm a giver like that."

Tom looked around. "I see you used the same decorator we did back at the old stationhouse. Cheap meets fraternity. Good call."

"No reason to mess with perfection." Vic limped back across to the couch. "Have a seat with me."

Tom parked it on the sofa, then got back up and took the gun out from under the pillow. "Your security system got a registration?"

"Nope." Vic extended his legs once more. "And no serial numbers, either. You gonna write me up."

"Nah." The chief handed the weapon over. "Paperwork bores me. Just don't shoot anybody while I'm here."

"Roger that." Vic tucked the gun under where he was sitting. "Let me guess, this is about Damnit. What's he done now? Is Chuckie P. quitting? Or did the asshole pick on Wedgie again?"

Tom focused on the TV. "This the Pats game from yesterday?"

"Don't tell me who wins."

"I didn't see it, either."

As the chief fell silent, Vic hit Play because the quiet was grating. "So what's on your mind."

It was much better with the chatter of the commentators, the distraction making whatever was going on less intense.

Kinda.

"I need your assessment of the department," Tom said in a low voice. "Like, how we're functioning both within our units and as a cohesive whole."

A commercial for Buffalo Wild Wings came on and made Vic hungry.

"I think we're good," he said. "I mean, we do fine."

Tom glanced over. "How do you think I am at my job as chief. That's what I'm really asking you."

Vic didn't bother to hide his surprise. Probably couldn't have anyway. "In what way?"

"How I handle personnel issues. People. Problems."

See, this was why he liked to spend his Sundays by himself, Rizzo thought. No, wait, that didn't go far enough. This was why he liked to be alone, period.

"What do you want me to say?" he muttered. "You're great."

"Don't throw bullshit."

Vic rubbed his face and wished he had a drink. But it was a little early for beers.

And as the chief waited for a real answer, he knew there was only one way out of this conversation.

"The guys all look up to you." Vic put his hand into his chief's face. "You asked me what I think so I'm going to tell you. You are respected greatly. You're a natural leader. I mean, come on, you're responsible for the biggest bunch of crackpot adrenaline junkies on the planet, and you manage to keep us all alive and focused and mostly in line."

"Do you think people feel like they can't come to me with their shit?"

"Yeah, I do. But you can't be friends with people you manage, and you want to try to keep Damnit on an even keel without screaming at him? Unless you're hitting that idiot upside the head with a frying pan, I don't think you're gonna get far."

"But maybe there's another way." Tom rubbed his eyes like he had a migraine. "I don't know. I don't fucking know."

"Where's this coming from?"

"I had a come-to-Jesus meeting with the mayor."

"A one-on-one with Mahoney?" An image of the tall, authoritative woman came to mind. "She's something else."

"She served my ass to me on a plate."

"That's hot." As Tom shot a look over, Vic shrugged. "What. It's the truth."

"She's an elected official."

"So I'm not allowed to notice her as a woman?"

"No. You're not."

Ahhhh, so it's like that, Vic thought with a smirk.

"Lemme get this straight, Chief," he said. "You have one conversation with Mahoney and now you're thinking we've got to wipe each other's asses or some shit? Come on. We're firemen, not in community theater. Besides, do you want to get into the ins and outs of disputes over parking spaces, shit left in the refrigerators, and who used whose towel in the shower? Hell no. And 'scuse me for mentioning this, but remember last year, when you gave up yelling for Lent? You lasted three days and had to go to confession because you called Damnit a cunt loud enough for his dead grandmother to hear it in her grave." He looked over at the guy. "You got a bad history with impulse control, Chief. But what you do *not* have is a problem doing your job well—or a problem with helping the rest of us stay on track."

The chief exhaled a curse. "We got a lot alcoholics in the departments. People with serious problems, Vic. You know this."

"That's on them. Not you."

"I'm not so sure of that right now."

"Look, you're fine. We're fine. Everything is cool. And if you bring in therapy dogs to the next stationhouse meeting, I will laugh at you. Then probably play with them. I love dogs. Dogs are awesome. Can we have dogs?"

Tom smiled a little. "Anne just got one."

"Really? I always did like your sister." Vic put his palm up again. "No, not like that. Jesus, and people think I'm a perv."

"You *are* a perv."

Vic started to grin as he thought about what he had lined up later in the week. "Yeah, I am."

"You got any beer?"

As the Pats kicked off, Vic nodded toward his kitchen. "Help yourself. And bring one back for the host."

The chief groaned as he got up, and Vic knew exactly how the guy felt. "Oh, and you're buying lunch, Chief."

Tom glanced over his shoulder. "How'd you know I'm staying?"

Vic stared up at his boss for a moment. The guy really did look worn out, and Vic had to wonder if maybe Sheila, the ex-wife, hadn't hit him up about something. But there was no asking about that. Wives and girlfriends were not even on the list of acceptable guy talk.

Exes? No fucking way.

Vic shrugged. "I can just tell you're here for a while—and it's cool. As long as you stop talking and keep bringing me cold Buds, you're welcome on my couch. And I want pizza from Antonio's, pepperoni with the thin crust. I'd like a large. Oh, and they'll bring more beer if you tip them well, too."

He expected a hard comeback. Instead, the chief just nodded and went for the kitchen. "Good deal."

36

The following morning was classic New England in the autumn, the sky a bright, endless blue, a clear sea flipped on its head, the sun so intense, it turned the world to chrome. As Anne traveled away from houses and neighborhoods, shopping centers and office buildings, she felt a calm come to her. Forty minutes later, she was almost to Danny's farmhouse.

"You ready for the country?" she asked.

Soot had his head out the window and was looking around at the trees and the fields. He was wagging to himself, his tail going back and forth.

The lane she was looking for came just around a tight corner, and Anne had to double back after turning around in the middle of a straightaway. Rolling meadows intersected by low stone walls and vibrant trees made it impossible not to fall in love with the area—and then she came up to the farm.

Not what she had expected.

The buttercup-yellow Victorian was set back on its land at the top of a little rise. The closer she got to it, the more she saw the age in its flaking paint and sagging front porch, but that didn't matter. With some work and some time, it was going to be a haven away from the stress of Danny's job—

It was the perfect place to bring up a family.

The errant thought pierced her heart, a javelin of deduction. She didn't have time to think about it, though, because as she rolled to a stop, Danny opened the front door.

"Hey," he called over.

"Hey," she said as she turned off her engine. "Nice place."

"Glad you made it."

Going around and letting Soot out, she wondered if she should hook his lead, but then he just stuck by her, trotting along as she went across to the three steps up onto the porch.

Danny was in work clothes, old jeans hanging low on his hips, scruff on his jawline, a muscle shirt giving some of his tattoos airtime. Scratches that were partially healed marked his forearms, evidence of the work he'd been doing.

"This is . . ." She motioned at the house. "Amazing."

His smile was that of a boy who'd been told he got the answer right in school. The teenager with hard-to-get concert tickets. The grown man who had something special and shared it with someone who mattered.

"How much acreage do you have?" she asked.

Danny's knees cracked as he got down on his haunches to greet Soot—who welcomed him like a close friend, well missed.

"Fifty." Danny put his face right into the dog's. "I missed you, boy. How's tricks. You ready to mark my property?"

"But where's the mess?" Anne tried to keep the suspicion out of her voice. "I mean, everything looks great here."

As she motioned to the mowed grass around the house, Danny rose and thumbed over his shoulder. "Wait for it. But first, lemme show you inside." He held the door open for her. "I've got running water and electricity, but other than that, this is a work in progress."

He wasn't kidding. Every window was hung with shredded drapes, and what little of the glass showed was layered with such dust that you couldn't see out of them. The floorboards were scuffed, and the wall-paper throughout was so old and faded, it was hard to tell what its original colors had been. Finally, the kitchen was a discordant seventies-era harvest gold and pea green mess, the appliances all throwbacks out of a Sears catalogue from the Jimmy Carter years.

But God, the potential.

All of the woodwork in the halls and rooms was incredible, the molding heavy on the ceilings, around the fireplaces and up the stair-case. There were also no stains anywhere, which suggested the roof and the plumbing were sound, and the doors were all plumb.

Upstairs there were three little bedrooms, and just one bathroom for all to share—but holy crap, that claw-foot tub.

It was deep enough to qualify as a lap pool, and she could just imagine what being in all that water would feel like.

"So who'd you buy this from?" she said as they went back to the first floor.

Soot was leading the charge, his nails clipping down the bare, creaking steps in hops.

"It hasn't been lived in in forever. It was in a trust and the woman who had the life estate survived for a decade in a nursing home. I look at it as a long-term project. I shouldn't have bought it, but sometimes you just do things."

"You must have purchased it after . . . the fire."

"When I got out of the rehab hospital, I needed something to do."

"I get that."

"So you wanna meet the problem?"

"Sure."

Danny took her out the kitchen's back door, and that was when she got a load of what he was talking about. The bank or whoever had been looking after the property had only paid attention to the front. Everything behind the house was a tangled mess—or had been. He'd obviously been hard at work, piles of brambles, vines, and saplings grouped here and there around an old barn, an icehouse, and then a storage building.

As Soot wandered over to a bush and did his business, she shook her head. "We are going to need more than just a day."

When she realized what she'd said, she shook her head. "You're going to need that, I mean."

It wasn't until Danny saw Anne step up onto the porch that he realized he'd bought the house for her.

In some crazy, delusional part of his mind, he'd seen the thing advertised in the back of the *New Brunswick Post* one Sunday and decided to take it on. He'd had to stretch to make the money work, but it was amazing what he'd saved living in that shit hole apartment with the boys.

"Where are the saws?" Anne asked.

"In the barn, come on."

The sunshine was warm on his face and the air was cool on his bare arms. And having Anne at his side paled even the splendor of the morning.

Sliding back the barn door, he spooked a couple of swallows from the rafters.

"Here's what I got." He showed her the array he'd laid out on two rough boards suspended between a pair of sawhorses. "Choose your weapon."

He was not surprised as she went right for one of the chain saws, picking the heavy weight up with her right hand and steadying it with her prosthesis. As she moved it around, he could tell she was testing out how she would handle things, making sure she could retain control before she cranked the power on.

"I brought a couple of different prostheses options," she murmured as she braced her legs and took the static blade through the air. "But I think this will work fine."

I love you, he thought.

Instead of speaking his mind, he grabbed the other chain saw and gave her ear protection. "You ready?"

She nodded as she put in her bright orange plugs. Then frowned. "I'm wondering if I shouldn't secure Soot with his whizzer lead. What if he spooks?"

"Believe it or not, it's all fenced in. See the gate over there? Well, the gate under those bushes."

She looked in the direction he pointed, and he got to enjoy the way the sunshine streaming into the barn, hazy with fine dust, bathed her in golden light.

Danny cleared his throat. "I walked the line this morning soon as I got here because you said you were bringing him. It's a wire fence, but it's sound and he can't get over it or through it. Also, no barbs, so he won't get hurt."

She glanced down at the dog. "You hear that? You can roam. Don't worry about the noise."

They walked out and agreed to concentrate on the northern edge of the acreage. Taking posts about fifteen feet apart, they got the chains going, and then it was a high-pitched whine duet. He checked on her a couple of times and then just worked along with her, him heading to the left, her to the right, the distance between them growing as the debris they created multiplied.

Soot was the perfect supervisor. He picked a shady spot by the barn, lying on the cool grass, but he did not put his head down. He watched them the whole time, as if he were ready to intercede if whatever protocol he was measuring them against was violated.

Phase two was hauling, and Anne took off her navy blue fleece for that, her Under Armour shirt contouring her torso. She worked without slowing, her body honed by exercise, her focus so total, he wondered what she was working through in her head. And then it was back to the saws. And more with the hauling.

They broke for lunch, eating the subs he'd gotten on the way in and talking about nothing in particular. And then it was four in the afternoon.

She cut her engine first and wiped her forehead on the back of her hand.

He knew it was getting late, as the sun was fading and their work was adding up—and he wanted her to stay the night even though all he had was an air mattress upstairs that smelled like a latex glove and no food.

Anne surveyed the wide swath they'd cut, the thin stumps now poking out of the dirt, the stubble of the earth.

"We got more done than I thought."

"Still plenty left." Then he added, "Not that I'm saying we have to keep going."

"Good. Because I'll be the first to admit, my shoulders and arms are shot."

All Danny could do was stare at her. Her lips were moving, and it was clear she was talking, but emotion had jammed up his brain.

"Danny. I asked you a question."

"Huh?"

"Why are you staring at me like that?"

He looked away. "You know why."

She cleared her throat. "I, ah . . . I guess it's time to go."

"Yeah. You better head out."

They took the chain saws back to the barn and removed their work gloves. He'd gotten a burn on the back of his neck, and it felt good to get the plugs out of his ears. Soot came over and sniffed around, but he largely stuck with Anne, and Danny liked that.

A woman alone in that house of hers? It was good to know she had somebody looking out for her with those kinds of teeth.

Not that the dog seemed aggressive at all. Then again, nothing was threatening his mom.

"Are you staying here tonight?" Anne asked as they went into the house.

Danny cracked another water bottle and gave Soot a refresher in his collapsible bowl. "Maybe. But I don't know, I'm on shift tomorrow morning, and the commute is bad at rush hour coming into the city."

"Yeah." She focused on the ceiling. "I get it."

As she continued to stare up there, he wondered if she'd seen a leak or something.

Then he did the math. "Yes. You can get in my tub. And I'll give you all the privacy you want."

37

As Anne went upstairs, she felt her body in a new way, and not just because she'd been doing hard physical labor all afternoon. Soot was by her side, although when they got to the top, he seemed conflicted given that there was someone he cared about on the first floor as well.

She was also very aware Danny was downstairs in the kitchen, drinking water from a bottle by the sink.

"You can lay down here," she murmured, leaning down to pat the floor at the head of the steps. "That way you can monitor everyone."

He took the advice and curled up in a ball, his head lowering as he seemed to keep one eye on her and the other on the front door downstairs.

The bathroom was aglow in warm afternoon light, the fine dust swirling in the diffused, filtered sunshine in a lazy way as if the air were water with a gentle current. As she went over and cranked the faucets, she half expected to have to call Danny because things didn't work.

And she was disappointed when she didn't have to.

Water, clear and soon warm, cascaded into the deep basin, the rush explosive, the pressure old-school, when things like conservation hadn't been on anyone's radar. Bending over, she swished things around to rinse off the bottom and sides, but someone had either used it recently or cleaned it because it wasn't that dirty.

Turning the water off, she swished everything toward the drain so she could start fresh. And as she pictured herself naked and sinking in under the level . . .

Ripkin's nasty voice went rugby on her mind, barging in, all elbows and hard knocks.

The sound of something heavy coming up the stairs brought her head around. Through the open door, she saw Danny hesitate before making the turn around the banister.

He stopped. "I heard the water go off. Is something wrong?"

His eyes were hooded, his body tense.

Straightening, she couldn't help but stare at his hips as Ripkin's subversion got louder and louder.

"No," she said as she turned the water on again. "Everything is fine."

Before she could think too much, she took the bottom of her shirt and pulled it up and over her head. Tight as it was, her breasts bounced free as she hadn't worn a bra, and then she went for her work pants. The thick fabric and heavy-duty zipper went easy and then she was stripping off everything, her panties included.

Danny's eyes were hot on her skin and his body responded, his erection thickening up quick.

She paused as she went to remove her prosthesis. Fear rose up even as she told herself this wasn't a reveal. This wasn't . . . anything different than any other part of her.

The lie didn't stick. Her heart pounded as she released her static appendage and removed the sock. It took all her self-control not to put her arm behind her back, and she had to hang her head.

All of this was stupid, of course. If you looked for validation from other people, by definition they could take that away if they chose. The safest path, as always, was to be your own rock, your own harbor, your own shelter.

Am I okay? should only ever be answered by the person asking that question.

The trouble was, if you had to make the inquiry, by definition you didn't know. And after all these months of battling her way back from the fire, solving problems, healing her body, finding her way . . . she hadn't thought much about what the loss of her hand meant to her as a woman.

Maybe she'd deliberately not considered it.

But that which she had avoided, Ripkin had ferreted out and exposed, a new wound that required tending to.

And the truth was, there was only one person she could do this with, show this part of herself to. Regardless of all the stay-aways she put between them . . . she couldn't imagine getting over this hurdle with anybody else.

Danny had all kinds of weaknesses and bad news sides to him, but one thing he had never done was let her down when it counted.

God, she felt like they were back in that hot spot together, flames all around, death prowling. Just the two of them, with only their resources, their ability to work together to rely on. And like in that crucial moment, she needed him to help save her. As much as she wanted to rely on herself, she couldn't do this alone.

Am I still whole?

Danny's eyes watered.

As he looked at the beautiful woman before him, her lowered

head and the awkward way she held her arm off to the side gouged into his chest.

But at least what she was looking for from him was something that was easy to give.

Walking forward, he went to the tub and turned off the water. Then he put trembling hands on her shoulders and slowly drew them down her upper arms. She stiffened as he got to her elbows, but she did not pull away.

He waited until her eyes swung up to his own. "Thank you."

"For what?" she breathed.

By way of answer, he dropped his head and began to kiss her. When he felt her mouth finally relax against his, he moved her arms up to his shoulders, stroking them.

Her body was lithe strength, everything smooth under his palms as he drew her against himself. He loved the feel of her hips, the dip in the small of her back . . . her ass, so tight as it filled his hands. Most of all, he loved the trust she was putting in him.

Breaking the contact at their mouths, he pulled the tie out of her hair and fanned the brunette rush around her shoulders. Then he traced her features with his fingertips, her cheeks, her nose, her mouth, her chin. The column of her throat was a path he followed to the wings of her cheekbones . . . and then he went lower, teasing her nipples with a soft touch, first on one and then the other.

Anne began to breathe harder, her front teeth biting into her lower lip.

Farther down, still. To her belly . . .

Lower. To her sex.

She gasped as he slipped his hand between her legs, and he took over from there, wrapping an arm around her and bending her back so he supported her weight. As he kissed her again, he stroked at her wet core, so slippery, so hot.

"Anne," he whispered against her lips.

"Yes . . . ?"

"Do you want to know how I feel when I see you like this? Do you want to know what looking at you does to me? What my dreams at night are like and my fantasies during the day?"

There was the faintest trace of fear in her stare as she looked up at him.

When she finally nodded, he put his mouth back on hers, licked his way inside of her . . . and made her come so hard she gasped his name, her hand clawing into his shoulder.

Sometimes, it was best to show, not tell.

As she cried out, he held her and kissed her and told her he loved her in his head. And when she was finished, he picked her up and lowered her into the warm water. She went lax against the back of the tub, her body loosening under the undulating waves, her lids lowering as she relaxed.

"Don't you need a bath, too?" she asked.

Say. No. More.

If not for the fact that Danny had nothing else to wear, he would have torn his fucking clothes off. Instead, he bitched internally at the two minutes it took to whip off his muscle shirt, kick off his boots, and lose his pants.

As he joined her, water splashed out onto the floor, but he didn't care. He was going to redo the wooden boards up here anyway. Maybe the ceiling down below, too, now.

He wouldn't have cared if he'd had to raze the entire damn house.

Cupping water in his palms, he brought it to her shoulders, letting the warmth flow over her. He did the same with her sternum, the level licking at her nipples, leaving them a glistening wet that nearly had him orgasming. He carried more to her upper arm, her elbow . . .

The place where he had cut her.

When he went to touch what was left of her forearm, he wondered if she would stop him. She didn't. She just watched him take the blunt end into his hands.

His eyes teared up again as he re-lived bringing that axe down on a part of her precious body and doing all that damage. Hell, he could see the remnants of the infection's ravages, the skin across the end bumpy and discolored.

"It doesn't hurt," she said quietly.

Well, it was agony for him.

Drawing her arm up, he kissed the inside of her elbow, where the blue veins ran down, and stroked her skin with his thumb. Then he went lower with his lips as he cradled her limb in his hands.

"It must have been torture," he said hoarsely. He had been through pain, but losing a spleen, what did that matter? At least when he'd been hurting, he'd known that when he came back from that stretch of agony, he was going to be himself again.

Physically, that was. Mentally, he hadn't been right—although how much of a change was that really?

"I don't remember much of the infection," she murmured. "But it's true what they say about phantom limb pain. It's terrible. I could feel my fingers and my palm, even though they weren't there."

Strange, but the same could be said for him back at the station-house when he'd returned. He'd seen Anne at every turn: in the break room, the bunk room, on the engines and the ladders. He'd heard her voice, caught the scent of her shampoo.

And yet she had not been there, and it had been painful every time reality had come crashing back to him, reminding him that she was gone.

"Sometimes I still can."

It took him a moment to catch up with what she was saying. "Does it wake you at night?"

"Yes."

He knew how that went. It was why he drank so much. The alcohol helped him get through the dark hours when his brain insisted on running through that series of events around her amputation like somewhere, in those memories, there was the treasure he searched for.

Forgiveness.

"Kiss me," she said.

He would have given her the world. That all she wanted was something he would have begged her for was more than he deserved.

They ended up with her straddling him, her thighs split around his hips, the tub big enough to accommodate them both. Sitting her up straight, he took one of her nipples into his mouth and held her core against him through the warm water. As she arched, he entered her and they each groaned.

Anne rode him slow, and as he leaned back into the curve and cupped her breasts, he had never seen a woman so captivating, the fading light making her glow.

Or maybe that was her soul.

Before he got lost in the orgasming, he said, "I need to tell you something you're not going to want to hear."

She stopped. "What."

Brushing some of her wet hair back, he picked the lesser of two not-so-hots. "I don't want this to be the last time."

On Monday, Anne dropped Soot off with Don at the office and proceeded over to SWAT headquarters.

Having been born and bred in New Brunswick, and then having worked on the fire service, she knew every nook and cranny of the city. Still, it took her three tries to find the sprawling, unmarked building located out by the airport. Talk about hiding in plain sight. With all the airplane hangars, UPS storage facilities, and shipping businesses, the SWAT team's base seemed like just one more metal-sided, flat-roofed, nothing-special.

As she pulled up, an unmarked door opened and Jack gave her a wave. "Park over there."

"Got it."

She eased the muni sedan off the asphalt and set it parallel to the facility.

"Thanks for having me out here," she said as she walked over to Danny's roommate.

"No problem." Jack gave her a quick hug, and then welcomed her into an open bay that was so big it should have had its own zip code. There were thirty or so marked, unmarked, personal, and armored vehicles lined up, along with all manner of four-by-fours and ancillaries. The ammo room was a locked cage in the far corner, the weapons mounted on pegs in rows, everything from assault rifles to shotguns to handguns registered and accounted for, in addition to whatever the officers had on their bodies at the time.

"Check out our new BEAR." Jack played Vanna White in front of an armored troop transporter. "Her name is Shirley. We also call her Big Momma."

"She is beautiful."

"I love a woman who can appreciate fine equipment." He led the way over to a coded door. "Come on in, I've got everything up on the computer."

The conferencing space was a lecture hall with two dozen tables set up facing a dais and a screen. Off to one side, a dozen men of Jack's physical description were clustered in groups over laptops, and there was both an electronic board and a dry-erase with all kinds of staffing notes and tables on them. Framed photographs of teams from different eras were mounted around a blacked-out American flag, and a glass display shelf had a lineup of badges memorializing officers killed on the job.

All of the men and two women looked up as Anne entered, their eyes making a quick and professional assessment before returning to their work.

"We're over here." Jack took her over to a laptop. "So meet Ollie Popper."

Anne sat down in an office chair. "Tell me that is not his given name."

"It's what he's known by. Works for him, don't it."

The mug shot showed a twenty-ish Caucasian with long dark hair, bulging eyes, and the pockmarked skin of a meth user.

"Cute, huh. Bet his mother loves him, though." Jack changed images. "And here is his collection."

"Holy . . . shit." She moved closer to the screen. "That's . . ."

"Got a bad case of sticky fingers, don't he."

The rooms that had been photographed appeared to be standard eight-by-twelves, with nine-foot ceilings and different window configurations—and they were all crammed with so much office equipment, it looked like Ollie was running a return center for telephones, computers, laptops, and projectors.

"Where does he get it all?" She shook her head. "This is crazy."

"We think he's got crews working for him across the state. The third parties execute the petty theft, breaking into cars and lifting things from public places, and he gives them a cut when he sells the shit."

"But who's buying from him?"

"Ever heard of this thing called eBay? And there are other sites."

"That's a lot of work, though. I mean, he'd have to post each one, right?"

"We're thinking he sells 'em bulk. The detectives are getting warrants to access his online accounts."

Anne sat back. "So how would it work with respect to the warehouse fires? Like, he pops a warrant for something else."

"And then he's got a problem." Jack hit another button, and an image of the same room she'd been looking at came up showing the space mostly empty. "He has to get rid of the evidence before the cops come to serve him or search his premises. He's familiar with those empty warehouses down by the wharf because he sells drugs and does drugs, and that area is good for his clientele."

"He takes the stuff down there."

"Picks a building."

"And lights it up?" She looked at Jack. "That seems like an inefficient solution to his problems."

"What's the alternative? Burying the shit in his backyard?" Jack sat back as well, his heavy shoulders shifting under his SWAT T-shirt. "Here's the thing. The fucker is smart. He doesn't want to kill anybody because that's a rap that's hard to beat, so those buildings are a fairly good bet for being vacant. Plus, who's watching them? And what better way of making sure he can't get tied to anything when all that plastic melts and destroys serial numbers and hard drives. Untraceable is his friend."

"Does he have a fire background?"

"How much background do you need? Gasoline is everywhere. Toss a match and run."

She thought of the apartment fire she went to on Saturday. "True. But how the hell did he get all of it moved?"

"You think you can't buy cheap labor with drugs? Means, motive, and opportunity."

"But it's pretty circumstantial."

She was aware she was fighting the logic. Then again, she wanted to nail Ripkin. That bastard had made it personal when he'd brought up her mother and her arm.

"I'm going to arrange to go and talk to Ollie."

"Good deal." Jack frowned. "There's something you need to know, though. We think Ollie's got friends in low places."

"Isn't that a country-and-western song?"

"My favorite, as a matter of fact. But in this case, I'm talking about the mob. We just can't figure out exactly who else he's been working with."

"Good to know. I'll expect delays and obstruction."

"You need to be careful, too. Ollie as an independent contractor on the black market is one thing. Backed by the mob? He's going to have resources and people looking out for his interests, if you know what I mean."

"I'll be careful. Thanks, Jack."

Like most of the fire stations in New Brunswick—except for Chief Ashburn's fancy present from Charles Ripkin—the 499 had been built for its purpose in the early 1900s. Made of brick that was given a fresh coat of red every five or six years, it had three bays for the engines and the ladders, a shorter addition for the ambulance, and bunks and bathrooms on the second floor. The kitchen and eating/hang-time space was in the back on the first level, and there was also an office for the captain.

Danny was in the galley, surveying the cupboard contents. After check-in, Moose had taken up res on the sofa in front of the TV, Deshaun, Duff, and T.J. were lifting weights in the bay, and the other six men on duty were scattered throughout the stationhouse, cleaning equipment, checking the engines, restocking the ambulance.

Against his better judgment, Danny had volunteered for cook duty, even though he'd caught shit from everyone about it. But he couldn't sit around without doing something between out-calls, and pumping iron with the boys was not an option thanks to him and Anne having worked on his farmhouse's backyard all day yesterday.

Uninspired, he went over and opened the fridge. As he became threatened at the sight of the eggs and the milk, the leftovers and the blocks of cheese, he was confronted with the fact that even after all these years in the stationhouse, he still had few cooking skills. And he gave Duff a hard time?

Closing the icebox's door, he decided to go out the back and have a cigarette while he considered his options. There were ten guys on shift today, and he had about two and a half hours, barring an alarm or training drill, to get this figured out.

When in doubt, he could do sandwiches. There were enough cold cuts and lettuce in the fridge. Fresh jar of mayo in the cupboard. Chips, too. For dessert, he could give them ice cream.

Looked like he had it sorted, after all.

"Where you going?" Moose said from the sofa. "You don't want to miss this. The mother-in-law is in denial and Phil's about to serve her a whole lot of reality."

Moose loved Dr. Phil. Then again, he was probably looking for tips on how to handle his wife.

"I'ma go out back for a sec."

"You need to stop smoking."

"Give up your beer first, then we'll talk."

"Fuck you," Moose replied genially.

The back door opened out to the parking area, which was fully fenced in, the crew's personal trucks parked against the chain link. No sun today. Colder.

As he lit up, he leaned back against the bricks and propped the sole of his boot on the side of the building.

When his phone went off, he nearly dropped the cig into his undershorts as he fished it out of his pants pocket. Was it Anne—

Frowning, he nearly let the call go into voicemail. "Yeah."

There was a pause. "Is that any way to speak to me?"

"Deandra, what the hell are you doing on my phone?"

"I wanted to talk to you." There was a rustle. "I wanted to hear your voice."

"You gotta stop this."

"Why."

"Because you're married to Moose." He took a drag. "Come on, Deandra."

"I told you I wanted it to be you."

"It never will be. And I'm not answering anymore, 'kay? We're done with this bullshit—"

"Why, because you're with Anne?"

"No, because you're not my type."

"I used to be." That voice dropped into the phone-sex-operator octave. "You know you liked it with me. You know you want me, Danny—"

Moose put his head out the door. "Yo, Captain Baker wants us to review Friday's apartment fire."

"Coming."

Deandra cut in. "*I* can make you come. You remember, Danny?"

As Moose ducked back into the stationhouse, Danny had really fucking had it with the two of them. "Don't call me anymore. If you do, I'll have to tell your husband."

"Tell him. I don't give a fuck. I'm tired of that house out in the sticks, I'm tired of him, this whole thing was a fucking mistake."

"Then fix your own damn mess, I got more than enough of my own to work on."

"She's never going to be with you, Danny." That cruel edge he knew so well sharpened the corners on all those consonants. "Anne's never going to want you the way I do. She knows the truth about you and it turns her off."

"Says the woman with fake tits. Forgive me if I don't look to you for opinions on authenticity. Don't call me again or you won't like where it takes you."

"Two can play at that game."

"I've got less to lose than you do, sweetheart."

As he hung up, he banged his head back against the building. Deandra was a road that he should never have gone down. Their hook up had been a classic across-the-bar kind of thing. Danny had been sure that he didn't have a chance with Anne, and he'd taken up on the offer Deandra had so emphatically presented to him.

As far as he'd been concerned, it had been a one-nighter, an over-and-done-with-the-sun. Deandra had disagreed with that assessment and had come by the apartment at all hours of the day and night. Seeing a lady in distress, Moose had stepped into the void, first as counselor, then as a willing piece of gym equipment that the woman had ridden to much vocalizing effect.

Danny hadn't bothered to point out what seemed obvious to everyone but Moose. Then again, the guy had needed a "win." After he'd had a rough time in the foster care system, he'd barely graduated from college, had failed at SWAT, and compared to Danny, Jack, and Mick, had always been the Michael Anthony instead of the Eddie Van Halen or David Lee Roth. The George Harrison rather than the John or Paul.

The store brand, not the name brand.

Deandra had taken things way further than anyone had expected, all the way to that walk down the aisle. And now that she was trapped with Moose, she was thrashing in the net she'd thrown over herself. Talk about knowing the truth, though. She wasn't the type to jump ship until she had another landing pad, so these phone calls were attempts to set up her exit strategy. When it didn't work, she was going to move on to someone else.

Which was how she'd wound up with Moose in the first place.

The call Anne had been waiting for didn't come in until she was packing up to leave her office at the end of the day.

The male voice on the other end of her desk phone was brisk and efficient. "I'm calling from traffic enforcement. You're seeking access to camera feeds down at the wharf?"

She sat back down in her chair. "Yes. I have the dates—do you want me to send them to you?"

"We've got a form I can email you? It takes two weeks to process."

"Two weeks?" She looked over at Soot, who was curled up in his crate. "Is there any way to get it faster?"

"That's for a subpoena."

"I'm working six fires, and there were at least two deaths. I'm really trying to get through all this."

"How far do your dates go back?"

"A while."

"We don't keep footage very long. Only thirty days."

And it takes two weeks to get the access? What the hell? "Okay, well, I'd appreciate it if you'd email me the form. I'll get the ball rolling with you, then see if there are some other angles I can get to."

"Listen, the form tells you to send it back to the open inbox, but shoot it back to me. I'll see what I can do."

"Thank you. That'd be great."

Hanging up, she'd been hoping there was another way, but it looked like she was going to have to go with option two: hardball.

Getting to her feet, she grabbed a folder she had prepared during lunch. "I'll be right back, Soot. And then we're going home."

The Arson Investigation and Fire Inspection Division of the City of New Brunswick took up one floor of the Fire and Safety Building with its dwindling number of inspectors and their support staff working out of a rabbit warren of little spaces with more doors than windows. Don had a corner office, but it was not luxurious, what with its two-sided view of the parking lot.

As she knocked on the jamb, he looked up from his computer. "Now what." But he eased back and took his "World's Greatest Boss" mug with him. "You look like you're on the warpath."

"I need your help."

"Wait. I want to be prepared." He opened a drawer and took out a bottle of Motrin. After taking two, he muttered, "Let's do this."

She handed him the folder across his desk and then took a step back while he read.

Her boss went through the paperwork twice. Then looked up at her. "You want a warrant for Ripkin's security cameras on those buildings."

Anne paced around, unable to stand still. "I'm surprised the previous investigators on the first five fires haven't already. No offense, but I think they were writing the scenes off because of the warehouses' location and their lack of intrinsic value. We need to see who was going in and out of those buildings because if the Ollie Popper theory is right, he had a sizable amount of evidence to move around. There would be a vehicle that would pull up to the site and someone would transfer the goods and set the fire. Maybe we could make a positive ID."

She sat down in one of the two vacant chairs opposite Don and remembered the wired seat Ripkin had made her sit in while they'd spoken in his office. "But I've also been thinking about something else. Ripkin Development is a huge corporation, and I have a feeling the guy's paranoid about security and monitoring. So maybe Ripkin could be the one disappearing hard drives and laptops. There is no way to completely wipe out memory from computers, unless you melt them."

Don closed the folder. "You're focused on Ripkin."

"And Ollie."

"Mostly Ripkin. Be careful about seeking information to confirm your hypothesis." Taking a pen, he signed the bottom of the form. "But I like your diligence, Ashburn."

"Thanks, boss. I'm going to send this over to the court right now."

When she got back to her own office, her cell phone was ringing and she caught the call right before it went into voicemail. "Tom?"

Great, her brother only called her when something was wrong.

"Hello?" she prompted when there was no response.

"Can you meet me over at Mom and Dad's now?"

Anne frowned. "Your voice sounds weird. Are you okay?"

"Just meet me over there, all right?"

"Yeah. Sure—gimme ten. I'm still at the office."

Maybe the renovations needed to repair the tree damage were much more than he'd thought? Or . . . she couldn't think what else it could be.

"Is Mom going to be there?" she asked.

"No, just you and me."

As Anne turned onto her childhood street, she looked around at the houses and was surprised to find that her current neighborhood was almost identical. Why hadn't she noticed before? Then again, when was the last time she'd been down here?

A couple of years.

And why wouldn't she live similarly? Her father had bought the family's house on the same salary, adjusted for inflation, that she was earning now. Sure, she didn't have a wife and two kids—but he hadn't started out like that and her mom had contributed a kindergarten teacher's assistant salary to the household income in the beginning.

Jesus . . . it was still pale blue.

The two-story had been built in the late sixties, and the siding had been white back then. But her mother hadn't wanted to lose the opportunity to "pretty" it up. So that blue had been born and thrived, despite the fact that it turned the place into an Easter egg that no one wanted to pick up.

Anne parked the Subaru in the driveway, behind her brother's SUV. "Soot, I'll just be a few minutes. You already went out, so you'll be okay. Bark if you need me."

There was no sun out, and the temperature was at fifty, so he'd be fine, but she cracked all the windows anyway.

As she got out, she looked up at the second floor. Her parents' room had been on the right, hers on the left, her brother's in the rear. In the middle, there was the bathroom she and Tom had shared. Downstairs, there was a bay that anchored the living room and then the kitchen and the family room opened to the porch and the backyard.

The bushes were all clipped precisely. The walkway was free of weeds. The lawn was trimmed like it was a rug.

Going up to the front door, she propped the storm door open with her hip and fiddled with her key chain, her fingers sifting through to find the right one. It had seemed odd to have the key with her, especially as it was a symbol of everything that had been lost: Her father no longer the hero she had thought he was, her mother a weak person she couldn't understand.

God, it still smelled the same. Her mom loved scented candles, the sweeter and more flowery the better, and as a result, the house was like a Yankee Candle store, all cloying gardenias and lilies.

She was going to be smelling the stuff for like an hour after she left.

"Tom?" She closed the door behind herself. "Where are you?"

The living room was not arranged the same, the furniture she was familiar with having been moved around into different corners and straightaways. The drapes had been changed, too. Now they were peach. Rug was new as well.

Guess Nancy Janice didn't just work on other people's houses.

"Tom?"

When there was a soft answer, she went through into the kitchen and expected an addition to have been blown out the back or something. Nope. Decorator lust had not inspired a renovation of the dated, pickled pine cabinets or the white Stormtrooper appliances.

Didn't her mother know everything was gray and stainless now?

Then again, the house was a blue only her mom seemed to appreciate, so fads, based on the opinions of others, might not hold much weight. Anne had never bothered to ask how it all worked for the woman, and she wasn't about to start now.

The door to the back porch was slightly ajar, but she checked out the internal damage to the family room's flat roof first. The tree had been removed, and there was fresh Sheetrock on the ceiling, as well as a new window set into a freshly mounted, unpainted jamb.

Nice work, and she wondered who over at the 617 had done it. Probably Vic. He was the carpenter of the bunch.

There would be no charge for the labor. The NBFD took care of the widows and orphans of its firefighters. Her mom had never had to call plumbers, roofers, electricians, or woodworkers; someone was always ready to help from the extended blue family.

Stepping out onto the porch, she found her brother sitting in a lawn chair by the grill, his hands linked in his lap, his knees out to the sides, his eyes trained on the square of dying grass and yet totally unfocused. His NBFD T-shirt had flecks of sawdust on it—so did his navy blue work pants. And his boots were smudged with drying mud.

Behind him, the outside of the house showed where the repair had been made, the bald wood and feathered-in siding like a scar in mid-healing.

"Guess you did the fix."

As she spoke, he jerked as if she'd surprised him. But he didn't look over. "Yeah."

Frowning, she went across and sat next to him. For no particular reason, she noted that the pair of lawn chairs, along with the lounger and the two little tables, were going to have to be taken in for the winter. The grill would be stored in the garage. The swing across the way would stay.

Just as it had always been, the rotation of the outdoor furniture set tracking the seasons and measuring the years. Until its utility was lost and it required replacing.

It was the same with people, she decided, the older generations passing as new ones were born, the cycle repeating.

She looked at her brother. His icy blue eyes scared her. So did his stillness. "Is Mom sick? Are you?"

"What?" He finally glanced at her. "What are you talking about?"

"You need to just tell me. I've never seen you like this."

"Do you find me . . ." He cleared his throat. "Am I hard to deal with? You know, about . . . anything?"

Anne's brows shot up, and she momentarily blanked. Of all the things she had ever expected Tom to say, that was not it.

Not even close.

As Tom put the question out there, he knew Anne's answer by the way she straightened and stared at him like she'd temporarily forgotten the English language. And then there was a silence that suggested she was trying to find an appropriate way to answer.

Trying to tread carefully.

Which was reply enough, wasn't it.

"I'll take that as a yes," he muttered.

God, he was tired, and not just because he hadn't slept since Mayor Mahoney had tuned up her size-whatever stiletto and kicked him in the can: He was exhausted on a molecular level.

"Where is this coming from, Tom?"

"Just wondering, you know. Just . . . thinking."

As the silence stretched out, he waited. His sister never shied away from conflict, so she was going to reply. Eventually.

"You can be a challenge," she said after a while. "You've got your own way of doing things and it tends to supersede everything and everyone else around you."

"I've got to keep people safe. There are lives in danger every day on the job, and if I don't make sure things are done correctly—"

She put her palm up to stop him. "Hey, if you didn't want my opinion, you shouldn't have asked for it."

"Sorry." He scrubbed his face with his dirty hand, and his eyes stung from the sawdust on his palm. Shit, he had to change the subject here. "The house is fine for Mom to move back in, by the way."

"So I see."

"You must be relieved."

"I guess."

Now he was the surprised one. "You don't actually want her to stay with you, do you?"

"Not really. But I want her safe above all. That's what I worry about."

"She's not a geriatric who's a slip-and-fall risk. She can move back in tonight."

"Is the security system fully functional?"

"Not yet. They need to come and put contacts on the new window."

"Then she'll stay with me until that happens."

Off in the distance, a dog barked and the neighbor on the right came home from work, parking their Kia in their garage. He hoped they didn't see through the bushes that there were people out here and decide to come over and talk about the tree falling.

"Are you okay?" Anne asked. "I'm worried about you. You're too quiet."

"Nah, I'm fine. It's no problem. Nothing I can't handle."

"Okay." There was another pause. "You sure you don't want to keep talking?"

"Yup."

In the back of his mind, he was aware that they were following standard compartmentalizing procedure, and as he thought about Emilio in that hospital bed, and Danny going rogue-crazy, and Chuckie P's drinking problem, he felt compelled to open the normally closed door of stoic privacy.

Not as it pertained to his own life, though. No, no, not tonight, motherfuckers.

"Can you please tell me why you hate Mom so much?" he asked. And before Anne could shoot him down, he shook his head. "I just want to understand. I'm not asking to try to change your mind or where you're at or to judge you. I just don't get it. Maybe if I did, I could stop bugging you about her."

As Anne's eyes drifted over to the grill to avoid his own, he shrugged. "And if you don't want to tell me, that's fine, that's your business."

The way she looked back at him in downright shock made him think about the mayor's diatribe on his failings as a manager. Fuck. He really had a problem, didn't he.

Anne took a deep breath, as if she were bracing herself to lift a car off the ground. "Do you remember, two days after the funeral, when you and Uncle Aaron went on that biking trip? The one Dad was supposed to go on with you."

There was only one "funeral" in this context. And he hated the memories he had of that day: the hundreds of firefighters in dress uniform, walking behind an engine bearing his father's draped coffin; his mother twitchy in her black outfit; him, just graduated from college and ready to enter the Academy in the fall.

Anne . . . refusing to cry, even though she'd only been thirteen at the time.

Funny, he hadn't thought about it until now, but he'd considered her lack of emotion to be disrespectful. And he'd resented her because of it since that day.

He brought himself back to the present. "We were raising money for the benevolence fund on that bike ride." Images of him and their father's best friend, "Uncle" Aaron, pedaling like hell through Connecticut reminded him of how they'd both had anger to work out on those ribbons of asphalt through the countryside. "We made like fifteen hundred bucks for them."

"I stayed behind."

"You wanted to go."

"I was a girl, I wasn't allowed." As anger tightened his sister's features, he realized he'd rarely seen her without that expression hovering close by, a driver waiting to take the wheel. "You were supposed to be home the next night."

"We decided to hang at the campground."

"Yeah."

There was a long pause. "So?"

"A woman showed up at the house the next afternoon. She was young. Pretty, for a townie. She was frantic, so Mom invited her inside. When I heard the voices, I tiptoed down the stairs and listened out of sight. The girl was pregnant. She said it was Dad's."

A cold shaft went down Tom's spine. "What are you— who the hell was she?"

"She was his girlfriend. That's what she told Mom."

Tom blinked like he'd been slapped. "Jesus . . . Christ. What did Mom do?"

"She wasn't surprised."

"Excuse me?"

Anne shrugged and leaned back in the lawn chair. "I gathered this wasn't the first time it had happened. That a woman showed up at the house, I mean. I also got the feeling that the girl had been banking on a very different outcome than carrying the baby of a dead fireman. She was looking for money. For an abortion. She'd just turned twenty."

Tom stared at his sister, looking for signs that this had been blown out of proportion, improperly extrapolated, falsely reported.

"I'd spent my life trying to impress that man," she said. "And he knocks up a nineteen-year-old? And then Mom . . . she gave the girl the money. She didn't even seem upset. It was like paying off a yardman for godsakes. I didn't sleep all night. I just kind of was done with them both at that point. Mom, I'd never had anything in common with, anyway. She was always pushing me into these frilly, flowery dresses, and trying to get me to go to dance class. I'd been sick of her for a while, but after that? I just lost all respect for the woman. Like, seriously, what kind of doormat do you have to be to get betrayed to that extent and just take it? Yell! Throw things! Stand up for yourself. Leave the bastard, especially if it happened before. But don't roll over like you don't have a voice in your own life. It's as if she were just cleaning up one more mess for him—how the *hell* could she live with herself?"

Nineteen? Tom thought. *Nineteen.*

As he did the math, he figured his father had been even older than he was now. The thought of a relationship like that made his stomach roll.

"And when it came to Dad?" Anne shook her head. "I just refused to buy into the lie anymore. He was supposed to be this hero down at the station, this stand-up guy who rescued people and saved pets by running into burning buildings. Come to find out, he was a philanderer who liked girls barely out of high school. All I'd ever wanted to be was him, and suddenly, I had nothing to live up to, nothing to be proud of. Those two people brought me into this world. I guess I owe them a debt for that. But I don't like either, and wouldn't choose to associate with them otherwise." She cursed. "At the end of the day, he fucked a teenager and she enabled him, and it wasn't the first time. And that's too ugly for me to bother trying to rationalize."

Tom opened his mouth. Closed it. Tried again to speak . . . and failed.

"You had no idea, huh," his sister said quietly.

He just shook his head. "Is it wrong to say . . . I liked the hero image better?"

"No, it's honest."

"Do you know who the girl was?"

"No, I'd never seen her before. And as far as I'm aware, she never came back." Anne rubbed the back of her neck like it was full of tension. "How many others were there, you know? I mean, you don't just start there. That girl was the culmination of a pattern of bad decisions and behavior."

Images of their father, tall and strong, in turnouts at the station came to him. Like Anne, Tom had molded a life on living up to those memories, and the fact that the man had been killed early had turned those recollections into legend.

Taken the man and made him a god.

But the Bible had a point about not worshipping false idols, didn't it.

———

When Anne finally left her parents' house, she was nervous abandoning her brother on that porch. He was too still, too composed, for the bomb she'd just dropped on his head.

Pent-up anger had finally made her speak frankly, and as she got into her car, she wondered whether she'd done the right thing in staying quiet all this time. Didn't that make her as bad as her mother, who'd covered up things? Looking at it like that, she should have told Tom long ago.

Then again, when would she have had the chance to talk to him about it all? Tom was just as she was, locked behind a fence of barbed wire when it came to things of a personal nature.

At least, she'd finally done the right thing. Pulled back the curtain. Cut the shit. Spoken the truth.

So why did she feel so goddamn awful?

Driving through familiar streets, she got caught up in the past, remembering a childhood spent running after her brother and being left out of things because she was a girl. She had always ended up sidelined with her mother, relegated to cheerleader instead of participant because of something she couldn't change and hadn't volunteered for.

And her mom had been perfectly fine with all that, content to raise a daughter in her image of pretty possession instead of equal partner.

Anne had to guess that to do it any other way would have shined too much light on how fucking lame Nancy Janice's own existence was.

And we wouldn't want to do that, especially not when there was furniture to move around and clothes to pick out.

As for her father's funeral, that somber display of firefighters coming out to honor one of their dead was the last afternoon Anne had been proud to be an Ashburn. After the service at St. Mary's, she and her mom and Tom had gotten in a Lincoln Town Car and proceeded to the Catholic cemetery where the family plot was.

Tom had been remote. Anne had been determined not to cry like a girl. And Nancy Janice had only cared about everyone having a Certs so their breath was fresh.

Like hygiene and the impression made on others was the only thing that mattered.

It had been a spring day, cold and bracing, the wind eating through coats and chilling ears and noses in spite of the sun in the sky. After disembarking from the limo with her minty-fresh breath, Anne had stood in her black dress, next to her mother in a black dress, by her brother in a black suit, in front of the black hole of the freshly dug grave. The fire engine bearing her father's coffin had been the one he had crewed on, and it had been draped in black bunting.

The firemen escorting it had all had tears in their eyes.

But Anne hadn't. Even as the men had shifted her father off that engine's top deck and carried him over to the grave that was waiting for him, even as the little girl inside of her had wept and been lost, she had refused to break with the decorum that was all around her.

She had searched for women on the service. Been relieved to find four or five in the two hundred or so in uniform—because that meant that she had a shot.

Tom had eventually cried. Not her, though. Not even as the priest in the black vestments had read from the Bible as her father, her hero, the head of their family, had been lowered into the greedy earth.

And the next day that pregnant girl had shown up at the house.

She had stayed about an hour. Anne had tiptoed back to her room when the conversation had come to an end, the cost of $582 given, the question of a check answered, her mother heading to the kitchen for her purse.

The windows by Anne's bed had looked out on the front yard, and the crappy car parked across from the house had been one she'd never seen in the neighborhood before.

The girl had left and walked over to it. She'd put the check in the pocket of her jeans as she'd gotten in, and as she'd pivoted, Anne had seen her face. If it had been a put-on, then she'd been a terrific actress: she'd been crying so hard, it had been a wonder she could drive, her face contorted into a mask of pain and suffering.

No, Anne thought. It hadn't been a lie.

Coming back to the present, she saw where she had driven to and cursed. "Shit."

It was the 499 stationhouse. Somehow, in her distraction, her hand and feet had taken her here.

Then again, it had been her father's house, too.

Putting the Subaru in park, Anne sat back and stared across the road. The old red fire station was framed by the gray sky, its windows clean, its sidewalk swept free of fallen leaves, its bay doors down.

They were probably on a call. Even though it was cool, going on cold, the doors were always open for the fresh air if they were on-site.

The past returned, sure as if it were a passenger getting into her car with her.

By the time Tom had returned from that bike ride after the funeral, Anne had hated both of their parents. And in the decade and a half that followed, all of her emotions had gotten locked into that one-note of righteous anger.

Except . . . now that she considered everything, she worried that the truth might be more complex.

Hazy memories of things she hadn't thought about in years bubbled up. She remembered her father coming home after long shifts, changing and leaving immediately for Timeout—even as her mother's face had fallen in disappointment. She recalled with clarity Nancy Janice planting a patch of flowers in the backyard and her father making a wisecrack about wasting lawn space.

But worse, she re-lived what it was like to hear her father's booming voice rattling the closed door of her parents' bedroom as he yelled at his wife about what had been cooked, cleaned, purchased, or given away. Big Tom had been a product of the military, and as such, nothing in the house could ever be out of his control. And if an errant pair of shoes had been taken off by the back door and left there? It had never been the kid's fault.

It had been Nancy Janice's.

Looking back on it now, the dominance her father had exerted over everything at the house, even as he'd rarely been home, seemed like just an excuse to yell at the wife. A way of justifying the release of anger and frustration that built up as the result of him doing a brutally hard and dangerous job.

God, Anne thought. Put like that, what else had she expected her mom to turn into?

Maybe the adaptive behavior of being a doormat wasn't a critical character flaw.

Maybe . . . it had been survival.

Help me . . . I can't . . . breathe . . ."

Danny leaned down and put his face through the side window of the T-boned car. The older woman behind the wheel was in her late sixties, and there was blood in her gray hair from where her head had struck the inside of her door on impact.

"I'm getting you out, don't you worry. What's your name?"

"Silvia. My granddaughter—"

Danny nodded. "We got her out of her car seat. She's just fine. Let's get you free."

The accident had taken place in the middle of a four-lane intersection. The woman had been traveling westbound on the green light when some eastbound hotshot had blown through his red turning arrow and hit her so hard, it'd pushed her car all the way off the asphalt and onto the shoulder.

"I can't . . . breathe . . ."

"There's gonna be some noise. Stay with me, Silvia."

Bringing the hydraulic splitter up, he crammed the twin wedges into the hinged seam of the door and engaged the power. The squeaking and squealing rang in his ears as the tool separated the busted steel panel from the body of the car so that he could yank it free and expose the victim.

Paramedic team members ran forward and began their assessment as Danny tossed the useless hunk of door out of the way. The aggressor's car had likewise cue-balled off into the weeds, and its driver was standing off to the side with airbag powder all over his black shirt, his face swollen and red.

Made you want to go over and finish that nose job with your fist.

Danny refocused on Silvia. Her mouth was open, and she was wincing and gasping. Given what kind of shape her door was in, she probably had broken a rib or two and had a pleural effusion due to a pneumothorax or hemothorax. Or both. But the good news was that head wound looked mostly superficial even though it was bleeding.

She was going to live.

At least . . . he thought she was going to live. What if she had underlying conditions? What if it was a blood clot in her lungs instead?

Or a myocardial infarc?

As the last of the light bled out of the sky, and the headlights of the rerouted traffic flashed in his eyes, his heart started to pound and he looked toward one of the ambulances. In the glow from the bay's illumination, the four-year-old granddaughter was screaming her head off as strangers with scary-looking medical things came at her.

She was terrified about her grandmother and for herself. All because some prick was in a hurry.

How many times had he seen this, innocent lives interrupted by assholes who thought their shit was more important than the traffic laws.

"Danny?"

As his name came over to him on the motor oil–scented air, he turned and was blinded by the strobe lights of police cars. When all he saw standing in front of him was a tall broad shape in turnouts and a helmet, reality bent and twisted, no longer something linear, but a convolution that doubled back on itself.

"John Thomas?" he breathed as he saw his dead twin brother before him.

"What the fuck?" Moose stepped closer. "What the hell are you talking about, Danny?"

"Sorry." He shook himself. "Nothing. What's up?"

Moose pointed to a flatbed truck that Danny hadn't noticed having arrrived on scene. "I thought you might appreciate not getting run over as that thing backs up. 'Cuz you don't seem to have seen it."

As the reverse lights came on and the towing vehicle started coming toward Silvia's wreck, Danny got with the program, picking up the door he'd taken off like he'd meant to do that all along. Man, it was alarming to note how much had progressed at the scene since he'd checked out. The other damaged car had been removed, Duff was putting sand down over the oil leaks under the light, and the police squad cars were getting ready to release the rerouted traffic.

On the ride back to the stationhouse, he stared out the engine's lowered window. The others were talking about the Patriots game that was coming up, and Duff was saying he needed to get laid, and Moose was talking about his Charger, and Doc was behind the wheel, humming.

Danny tracked all of it to reassure himself that he was actually on the planet and that his brain was still capable of keeping up with reality.

As they approached the firehouse, he didn't know how he was going to make it through the rest of the shift—

The Subaru parked across from the bays had to be another figment of his imagination. But just in case it wasn't, he jumped out as soon as Doc stopped the engine to back it in.

"Where you going?" Moose hollered.

Danny let his walking answer the question. And as he came over to the Outback, he was relieved when Anne put her window down.

Her eyes were sad as they looked at him. "I shouldn't be here."

"Yeah," he said. "You should."

———————

The bays of the stationhouse still smelled the same—like baked bread, fresh engine oil, and lemon air freshener.

Anne had never expected to walk into them again, and somehow, having Soot by her side on his leash made everything easier. Guess comfort dogs worked.

She stopped between the engine and the ladder truck and looked up at the old-school pole that they didn't use anymore. The hole at the top, which was in the center of the bunk room, had been paneled over.

But her father had gone down it during his time.

"You want dinner?" Danny asked quietly. "We got plenty."

She leveled her head and stared at him. "You have bags under your eyes. You're exhausted."

"I think there's even leftover roast beef. It was too rare last night. I could cook it again for you."

"What kind of call were you out on?"

"Car accident. Two injuries in the sedan obeying the traffic laws. The asshole who was speeding and cut the red light walked away just fucking fine."

"That sucks."

Off in the distance, familiar voices echoed into the tall ceiling. Moose. Duff. Deshaun. None of them knew she'd come in. All of them had watched as Danny had jogged across the street to her car.

Abruptly, she frowned.

"Hey, do you remember those pictures we used to have over there?" She nodded toward the workout equipment. "Where'd they go?"

"When we had a bathroom leak, it ruined the wall."

"Did they get killed?" As if they were mortal. "I mean, were they thrown out?"

"Nope. They're upstairs in the hall. We figured they'd be safer. You want to go up there and see 'em?"

"Yes, I do. But will you take me? I mean, now that I don't work here anymore and I'm not on the crew—"

"You're always welcome. Anywhere."

She waited for him to take the lead, and as they walked over to the old steps to the second floor, she gave the boys who were around the incident command center a little wave.

God, she felt like she was sneaking around and had just gotten caught.

"Hey, Anne," Moose called out. "You staying for dinner?"

"Nah, I'll leave the eating up to you."

"Is that your dog?"

"Yup."

Before she could get tangled into a conversation, Danny stopped at the base of the stairs and motioned the way up. As she ascended, the steps still creaked the same, the narrow walls like entering a chute.

The second floor was still beadboard that had been painted a million times, and the bathroom with the shower stalls still had that frosted-glass entry door.

The twenty or so framed pictures had been hung down the hall, the sizes and frames different, some of the images in color and some in black and white. She instantly recognized her father in the five he was in.

God, he and Tom looked so alike. And somehow their father had managed to be the center of every picture he was in. But he'd been like that. The fulcrum around which things revolved, the leader who only appeared to be phlegmatic about his role. In reality, she knew he must have taken that identity and its preservation very seriously.

If adulation had been currency, then Tom Sr. had been rich through his own design. As long as you didn't count what he'd done to his wife.

"He was larger than life," Danny said quietly. "Your father was the standard everyone lived up to."

Anne looked down at her prosthesis and wondered about the nature of anger. She wouldn't have identified herself as a hostile person, just someone who was direct and got what she wanted and needed out of situations.

Refocusing on the images of her father, standing so proud and tall among others of his generation of firefighters, she reflected on how pissed off she had been about everything—and for how long.

She also thought about that fire that had changed her life, and her determination to send Emilio up those stairs. Then she pictured him in the emergency room after his suicide attempt, alive by a stroke of luck and nothing else.

She didn't mean to turn to Danny and reach for him, but she did.

As his arms came around her, she stared at all the pictures, and not just the ones that her father was in.

"He saved a lot of lives, you know," Danny murmured.

He ruined a lot of them, too, she thought.

42

The next morning, Anne woke up at six a.m. Or, rather, she got out of bed at that time. She hadn't done a lot of sleeping. After getting dressed, she went downstairs to the kitchen with Soot. While he went out to do his business, she opened her cupboards.

Instead of viewing her mother's rearrangement as an intrusion, she looked at the order that had been made: the canned goods had been grouped together by whether they held soup or vegetables. The crackers were by the soups. The boxes of pasta were next to the sauce jars.

She opened the drawers under the countertops. Her silverware was next to the dishwasher—which would make the latter easier to empty. The plates had likewise been relocated above the dishwasher for the same reason. Pot holders were by the stove instead of across the way next to the refrigerator.

Closing everything up, she stepped back. Then she let Soot back in, sat at the table, and stared out to her living room. The sofa was now on the far wall—so you didn't need to walk around it to enter the kitchen. The armchair was by the fireplace and the lamp on its table had been pulled in tight.

If you wanted to read a book or do needlepoint, the illumination would come over your shoulder.

Perfectly.

Anne was still sitting there when her mom came downstairs. As Nancy Janice rounded the corner, she stopped. Her face was made up. Her hair was done. But she was still in her nightclothes, the matching gown and bathrobe pink with yellow flowers. She even had slippers that coordinated with the color scheme.

Her pleasant expression, which was so ubiquitous it seemed like an actual feature—like the woman's nose or chin—was lost instantly.

"Good morning, Anne."

As Nancy Janice entered the kitchen, the actual number of steps she took was small. The distance she traveled was greater than miles. And Anne noted the lines in that face. The slight stoop to the shoulders. The gray hairs coming in at the temples as that auburn hair color grew out.

Time was passing, leaving its mark, taking its taxes and penalties in the form of fading beauty and function.

Anne thought of those pictures in that hallway at the stationhouse. And then of her father's funeral. And finally of the childhood house that had been a place to start off from for her and her brother . . . but which had been, for their parents, a goal reached.

"I didn't touch anything else." Her mom put out her hands. "I swear, Anne."

Sunlight glinted off the gold wedding band on her mother's left ring finger.

"Can I ask you something?" Anne said in a low voice.

Nancy Janice came over and sat down. "Anything. Please."

As if there had been a wait of years for such an approach.

"Why do you still wear that ring?"

Her mother stiffened, those eyes dropping away. And then she put her hand under the table, out of sight.

"Why, Mom?" Anne shook her head, aware she was asking about so much more than only the band. "Why."

Just as she became convinced there'd be no reply, Nancy Janice said, "Marriage is a private affair between two people, consecrated by the church."

"If you have children, it's not just about two people anymore."

"Your father was a good man. An imperfect but good man."

"I know what he did, Mom. I'll spare you saying it out loud. But I know."

The crumbling that occurred was on the inside. Even as the outward composure was retained, it was but the facade of a building, the walls and ceilings of which had fallen from their nails and screws.

Her mother's voice was weak when she finally spoke. "All I have ever done was try to make things better than they were. For you. For your brother. I have done what I could to . . . make things work. There were no resources for me. I didn't graduate high school when I got married. He didn't want me to get a job. I have no skills. Without his pension now? I don't know where I would go. Where I would be. What I would do."

Anne looked past her mother to the rearranged living room. To the armchair with its perfectly placed lamp.

"I am nothing," her mother whispered. "That's what he always told me. I am . . . nothing."

As Anne's eyes filled with tears at the defeat in those sad words, she stood up and went around her little table, getting down on her knees. Wrapping her arms around her mother, she realized it was the first time they had hugged in . . . forever.

"Oh, God, Mom," Anne said hoarsely. "God . . ."

Damn him, she thought to herself.

They stayed that way for the longest time, her mother crying softly, Soot padding over and sitting as close as he could to Anne.

When she finally eased back, she took her mother's hands in her own—both the one that was of flesh and the other of molded plastic.

"I am so sorry you were hurt, Anne," her mother said as she stared down at where they linked. "I am so sorry. It has killed me to know . . . you were hurt."

"It's amazing what you can live through," Anne murmured, "and come out stronger on the other side."

Putting her mother's left palm on her prosthesis, Anne took that wedding band between her fingertips and slowly pulled it off. She wanted to toss the fucking thing across the room. Instead, she placed it on her table and then reached up and dried her mother's tears.

"Time to let old lives go, Mom." As her mother stared at the ring, her eyes were exhausted, and Anne knew how that felt. "Old lives and old dreams that were really nightmares. Strength only exists if it is tested, and I promise you, you are stronger than you know."

"I have never been strong." Those eyes closed so hard, her lips peeled off her teeth. "And that's why you hate me. Because you know I'm not like you—"

"Yes, you are." Anne smiled through her own tears. "I'm your daughter so half of me is you. If I can resurrect myself, so can you."

Her mom's eyes opened once more. "I wanted so desperately to have something in common with you, but I was always so glad you were not like me. You're the strongest person I know."

"Let's shoot for two in this family, 'kay?" Anne squeezed her mom's hand. "We can do it. Together."

43

The following day, Anne went down to the municipal court and county jail complex, arriving a good twenty minutes before she was supposed to see Ollie Popper, real name Douglas Contare. After going through a metal detector and getting wanded by a deputy, she was given very precise directions to the northwest corner of the maze of concrete and glass. Talk about your foot traffic. There were hundreds of people milling around the mall-sized facility. Some were in professional dress. Others were harried and scrambling. And there were cops and sheriff's deputies everywhere.

When she got to the jail entrance, she had to wait to get buzzed through, and then she was checking in at a bulletproof window. After that, things moved fast, and she was shown into a long thin room cut in half by thick Plexiglas. Private cubbies were created by partitions on both sides, and there were chairs and two handsets for conversation between prisoners and people who were visiting.

Left alone while they got Ollie, she debated taking a seat, but decided to wait until the guy was brought in.

Five minutes later, a door opened behind her. Another deputy, different than the one who'd brought her in, entered.

"Are you here for Contare?" the woman asked.

"Yes?"

"Sorry, wrong place. His lawyer is waiting in an interrogation room for you guys."

Anne frowned. "You mean his public defender?"

"No, his attorney showed up just now. Said Ollie could talk to you only if he's in the room."

The re-routing was good news as it gave her a little time to adjust her approach. Preparation for interviewing witnesses or interrogating suspects was critical: Before you sat down with anyone as part of an investigation, you needed to know what you were going after, what the goal was. You also had to have your facts straight and be prepared to retain your composure no matter what direction things went in.

A lawyer was a surprise. Especially when they showed up at the last minute.

The room she was taken into was as she expected. No windows, a table and four chairs that were bolted into the floor, and a video monitoring camera mounted up in the far corner. There was also sound-proofing on the walls and fluorescent lights on the low ceiling. Standard-issue.

The silver-haired lawyer in a silk suit that stood up was not. "Ms. Ashburn? How are you. Sterling Broward."

No reason to correct him on the "Ms." even though her proper title was Inspector. "Mr. Boward, nice to meet you."

"Broward," he corrected.

"Of course," she said with a smooth smile. "Shall we bring your client in?"

"Just so you and I are clear, none of this is under oath and it is my intention to keep the focus tight."

"Your client is a person of interest, not a suspect."

"Exactly."

After Broward gave the deputy the go-ahead to get Ollie, Anne sat down and the attorney joined her in taking a chair.

"Don't you want to get your notepad out?" he said.

"No. Do you?"

The lawyer sat forward, linking hands that had buffed nails together. His expression was one of great kindness and benevolence. "I'm just trying to help you do your job."

His "little girl" tack on was implied in the tone. And as Anne regarded the man, she couldn't wait until the inevitable passage of time ushered this older generation of males off the planet and to their royal reward—rather like a pantry was cleaned of things that were past their "best by" dates: Their condescending attitude's shelf life was up, and it was time for their act to go into the trash.

When she just stared him straight in the eye, he raised his brows, and she dubbed in his internal monologue on the hairy-arm-pitted feminist who was too much of a man-hater to accept some kind advice from someone who knew better and was looking out for her.

"You know," he said, "I've heard you were difficult to deal with."

"My job is not to make people feel comfortable."

"I think you'll find you attract more bees with honey than vinegar."

Anne sat forward and mimicked his pose. "How long have you been working for Charles Ripkin?"

The change in the man was subtle but instantaneous, those brows lowering by a millimeter. "My client is Donald Contare."

"Douglas. His name is Douglas." She leaned farther forward. "And right now, I'm wondering how a two-bit drug dealer and addict like Ollie Popper can afford a lawyer with your kind of wardrobe. Mystery, isn't it. Guess Ollie's been saving his pennies from all that office equipment he's been burning up in Ripkin's warehouses."

"Those isolated fires have nothing to do with Ripkin Development."

"Boy, that denial seems to just roll off your tongue. I'll bet you find yourself saying stuff like that a lot, huh."

The door to the interrogation room unlatched and opened, and Ollie was smaller in person than he'd seemed in those mug shots. He was only about five feet six, and he couldn't have weighed more than a buck forty, buck fifty tops. Also his eyes were not manic anymore, whatever he'd been on during his arrests having been metabolized.

The shackles were a surprise. He didn't seem dangerous.

When he saw Broward, he froze, the sheriff behind him bumping into him. Ollie recovered quickly. "Hey. Wassup."

His voice was fried, the rasp a result of inhaling hot contaminants.

His attorney made nice, shaking hands and doing that double-clasp thing with his palms, the equivalent of a politician's I-really-care-about-you.

"I told you I was coming," Broward said. "You know what this is about."

"Yeah. Sure. I get it."

Ollie focused on Anne, not that that involved much more than his eyes passing over her. He seemed more concerned with Broward as he sat down, and he tried to move the bolted chair away from the other man.

Anne cleared her throat and took her ID out of her suit jacket pocket. "I'm Inspector Ashburn. I'd like to ask you a few questions about some fires down on the wharf."

"I don't know nothing about no fires."

"Okay. Well, maybe you'll indulge me as I describe a couple of the incidents anyway. There have been six of them in the last two years, and the reason I wanted to talk to you is because of the excess office equipment found at the sites."

"I don't know nothing about office equipment."

"That's funny, because I've seen pictures of the three apartments you're leasing right now. And there were rooms full of old laptops, desktops, and phones in them."

"No, there ain't."

"I've seen the photographs."

"They empty now—"

Broward interjected. "We are off topic. This is about the fires down by the wharf, isn't that right. In those abandoned warehouses."

"I don't know nothing."

Anne looked back and forth between the two of them. "Ollie, I'd like to give you some dates and ask you where you were on them."

"I don't remember where I was."

"I haven't given you a date."

"I don't remember."

"Where were you last—"

"I don't remember."

Anne was not surprised when, after she listed each of the six dates, the response was the same. She even asked him what his addresses were and got his party line. She was going to inquire where he'd left his brain, but the problem wasn't his gray matter.

Although it had certainly taken a beating courtesy of his drug use.

Anne smiled. "Well, I'm just going to assume I know where you stand with regard to working with Ripkin Development—"

"I don't remember."

"So you don't deny you're working with them. You just can't recall when it started." She got up. "That's all I need to know—"

Broward jumped in sharply. "My client has not responded in the affirmative to that question or any others pertaining to Ripkin Development. In fact, he has denied such an allegation."

"When did that happen?" Anne asked. "Wait, I don't think he has. Let's give him a chance, shall we?"

She cupped her ear and leaned in. "Come on, Ollie, say the words. And then maybe when they kill you and throw your body off a trawler and into the ocean, they might not drag out the murder part."

That got Broward out of his chair—and good thing it was bolted to the floor or he would have knocked it through the wall behind him. "You are out of line."

"It's a statement of opinion."

"By a city investigator in their official capacity."

"Now you're remembering I'm an investigator, huh. I'll make note of that. When I get my pad." She shook her head at Ollie. "Don't take the plea, Doug. Considering the people you're dealing with, you're safer here behind bars than you are out on the street."

c h a p t e r

44

As Anne stood in front of her stove at home, dinner was making itself. Which was why she'd picked up a box of fettuccini, a flat of chicken breasts, and some broccoli after she'd left the office for the day. She'd already had a jar of alfredo sauce in her rearranged cupboards—something that, if her mom hadn't worked her magic, she might not have known.

It seemed strange not to have her mother under the same roof even though it hadn't been a long stay. But Nancy Janice had gone back to her own house after ADT came and put a contact on that new window.

Almost seven.

When her cell phone started to ring, she hoped it wasn't Danny cancelling, but told herself that if it was, she'd have leftovers for two nights and that didn't suck.

"Hello?" She frowned when there was nothing but a whirring sound. "Hello?"

There was a click and then silence over the connection. Frowning, she went into her call log. Unknown Caller appeared at the top of the Recents page.

Heavy pounding on the front door brought her head around, and Soot jumped up from his spot by the back door, his ears flattening as he growled.

"Anne?" More knocking. "Open up."

"Danny?" She jogged over and unlocked things. "What's—oh, shit. What happened to my car?"

When she went to go out, he caught her by the shoulders and shoved her back into the house. "You're not going out there—"

"My windshield's broken. I want to know what the hell happened—"

He pushed his way inside and shut the door. "I think it was shot at." He put his phone to his ear. "Neither one of us is going out there—Jack? Hey, I got a problem. Can you get someone over here to Anne's on the QT? Right now."

Back in the kitchen, the pasta water overflowed with a hiss and she went to turn the heat down. As soon as she got to the stove, her phone went off, but this time it was with a text.

The message had been sent from WatchingAnne@gmail.com:

Boiling over. Better watch.

She glanced over her shoulder to the glass panels where her office was. Then she looked out the window over the sink. Night had fallen, and she didn't have any of the security lights on, so she couldn't see anything.

Or, rather, what illumination was thrown from her neighbors' houses was so spotty, there were plenty shadows for someone to hide in.

"What's on your phone."

As Danny spoke in a flat voice, she focused on him for the first time. He'd taken a shower and his hair was still wet, his NBFD navy blue hoodie adding heft to his shoulders.

"This." She turned the screen to him. "Can we trace it?"

He leaned in and read the message. "Probably not. There are all kinds of apps and websites both for iOS and Androids which allow people to be anonymous for shit like this. All you have to do is sign up with any random Gmail account and you're good to go. And if they're smart enough to do it from a burner phone as an extra level of protection? Those burners are untraceable if you buy them with cash, and God knows they're available at everywhere from Walmart to Target. The cops deal with these things all the time with harassers and it frustrates the fuck out of them."

That Unknown Caller had to be the same person, she thought. "Is Jack coming now?"

"Yeah. Let's close all the drapes in your house."

Moving quickly, they worked together, pulling halves together, dropping venetian blinds, closing shutters. When they were done, they returned to the kitchen and she tried to make like things were fine.

"Dinner's ruined." She took the overdone fettuccini noodles off the stove. "I think these have lost all their structural integrity."

Danny didn't buy the distraction. He just stood with his boots planted and his brows in a caveman half-mast that suggested his frontal lobe was arguing with his brainstem's base urge to go after whoever it was.

"Maybe you're wrong about my car window."

"I'm not." He shook his head. "I heard the impact."

"The shot, you mean?"

"No, they used a suppressor. I heard the bullet hit the front windshield." He jabbed his finger at the phone. "What is going on."

"I don't know."

"Yeah, you do. What are you working on now? Those fires down at the wharf, right?"

Anne cursed. It looked as though Ollie wasn't the only one who needed to heed a warning about who they were dealing with.

Oh, man, it was good to have friends who were members of SWAT, Anne thought thirty minutes later.

Jack came with two friends who were trained killers just like him. And they didn't announce their arrival. They simply showed up at the back door, a trio of black-draped wraiths who moved in silence and were covered with weapons.

As Anne let them in, she had to take a step way back to accommodate their sizes, and Soot immediately started growling in earnest, something she'd never seen or heard him do. Then again, the SWAT guys had ski masks pulled down over their faces, only their badges IDing them as law enforcement.

"Sorry," Jack said as he took his off. "Don't mean to scare your dog."

Anne went over and sat with Soot as the other guys likewise revealed themselves. "Did you see anyone?"

"No." Jack took something out of his pocket with gloved hands. "We found this in your car, though. It was lodged in the inside jamb of your trunk."

The lead slug was small, but that didn't mean a thing considering how fast it could go when it was shot out of a frickin' gun.

"She's getting harassed on her phone." Danny nodded at her. "Show them."

Anne tossed the phone over. "The code's four-nine-nine-nine. I got a call from a blocked number right before it happened. I didn't check first when I answered because I thought it was Danny. All I heard was whirring on the other end."

"Did you meet with Ollie today?" Jack asked.

"Yes. And he had a lawyer with him. Sterling Broward."

"I thought he just had a public defender. That's what I saw listed on his case."

"Broward identified himself as the attorney. I looked into him when I got back to my office, and he does a lot of work for Ripkin Development. He keeps a very low profile, and doesn't appear to have a background in criminal defense."

Danny looked over. "I never liked Ripkin. Never. That fire at his house on the ocean was always bad news in my opinion. And he was creepy as fuck at the opening of the new firehouse two years ago."

"Let's get this incident logged in," Jack said. "And we'll have—"

Anne took her phone back. "I don't want Ripkin to think I'm scared."

"You just had a bullet put through your fucking window," Danny snapped. "Next time it could be your head."

Jack nodded. "I gotta back my boy up here. Brave is just this side of stupid sometimes."

Anne shrugged. "Fine, put in a report if you want. Take that lead slug to the lab. Come back during daylight hours and see if there are footprints. Try and find out who called me and sent me the text. But I will bet that it all goes nowhere. If this is Ripkin, he would hire a professional to scare me and they will leave nothing behind."

There was some arguing at that point. And then she enjoyed a lecture by Jack and his SWAT boys about staying safe—after which they left, disappearing into the darkness to whatever vehicle they had ghosted into the neighborhood in.

"I'm spending the night," Danny announced before the door was even closed behind them.

Anne crossed her arms over her chest. She was about to say no when she saw Soot staring up at her, his eyes worried, like he sensed danger.

"Okay."

"Good."

"I have to take him out, and then we can see if the chicken is edible—"

Ding!

As her phone went off, she felt a spike of adrenaline. But it could be anyone, really. Right?

It was a text from that Gmail account: *Left you present out in backyard.*

"Shit," she whispered.

Danny grabbed the phone and then marched to the back door. "Stay here."

"Are you out of your fucking mind."

Before she could stop him, he ripped open the—

When he didn't move, her throat closed up. "What is it?"

Leaning over her desk, he took a pen out of the mug she stored them in and crouched down. When he turned back to her, there was a gun hanging upside down off the Bic, speared through the trigger circle.

"Guess this is what they used," he muttered grimly. "And it looks like we're calling Jack back over here."

Her phone went off again with another text.

"Read that out loud," Danny demanded.

Anne had to clear her throat. "'Stop now and I go away. Your choice what happens next.'"

Anne must have fallen asleep upstairs in her bed because she came awake in the midst of an explosive blur of movement. Her brain, used to dealing with accident scenes, caught up quick with what was going on: Danny, who had been naked in between the sheets with her, had jumped out from under the covers with such force that he hit the wall across the way.

"Danny! Are you shot!"

Even though the drapes were unruffled and the windows were intact and the security system wasn't going off, somehow it was as if a bullet had hit him in the gut.

In the nightlight's glow, he was clutching his stomach like it had been struck.

Scrambling over to him, she pushed his hands out of the way—

Nothing but clean, unmarred skin. Yet he was staring down at himself in horror, his face contorted from pain.

"Danny?" When there was no response, she tugged at his arm. "Come over here and sit down."

His eyes, wide and white rimmed, struggled to focus. "Anne?"

"I think it was a bad dream. Come back to bed."

He followed her as a child would and stretched out on the messy sheets. Trailing her fingertips over the tattoos across his torso, she double-checked that her assessment was correct. But he wasn't injured.

"I think it was a nightmare," she murmured as she slid in next to him and pulled the covers back into place.

Danny put his hands up to his face, his biceps thickening, his heavy chest rising and falling a number of times like he was trying to reel in his brain.

"Do you want to tell me what it was?" she asked softly.

She wasn't surprised when he shook his head. Night terrors were not uncommon in first responders, although she had never known him to have them before. Then again, when had she ever slept in the same bed with him?

Not that there had been much "sleeping" going on tonight. After an anxious, anemic dinner of chicken, broccoli, and the entire half gallon of chocolate chocolate-chip ice cream she'd bought as a dessert, they'd put Soot in his crate and made no pretenses about what was going to happen the second they got upstairs.

Three times: Once in the shower. Once on the rug by the bed. Once in the bed.

As she put her arm around him, she hoped to ground him in reality. "It's okay."

She said that even though she didn't know if that was true. She just wanted him to come back from where he had been.

"Yeah." His voice was rough. "I'm all right. It wasn't me."

With a surge, he turned to her and kissed her urgently, bringing her against him, his warm hands traveling over her skin, delving between her thighs. As their mouths ground against each other's, his hips surged, his erection hot and hard against her leg. Rolling over, she pulled him on top of her as his lips kissed their way down her neck to her collarbone. Lower. To her nipples, which he sucked as he stroked her sex.

"Anne . . . I need you."

Raking her nails down his back, she arched against him. "I need you, too."

He pushed his way between her legs and all but impaled her, his sex driving into her own and pumping like he was possessed. The headboard banged so hard against the wall, she was glad she didn't live in an apartment, and as he shoved the pillows out of the way, one of them knocked some stuff off her bedside table.

Not that she cared.

She had things she didn't want to think about, too. Things like that bullet, and Ripkin, and fires she was fighting even though their flames were out. But as Danny pounded into her and she linked her legs around his hips, nothing else registered. It was just the pleasure and the heat, the rising tide of pleasure that wiped out everything but him.

She was dimly aware of him shifting, and then his hand was between them, his talented fingers going right for the top of her core. He knew exactly what she wanted and how to touch her—and the orgasm that shot through her was so violent, it was as if she hadn't had sex in years.

Danny took things from there, his rhythm going back to haywire until he locked in against her and kicked deep inside of her.

And then all was still except for them breathing.

As he dropped his head into her hair, he mumbled something.

"What?"

"Must be heavy. Me. I."

Except when he went to roll off her, she shook her head. "I like the way you feel."

Over his big shoulder, she measured the light bleeding around the edges of the drapes. Dawn had arrived, the new day and all that BS. But she wanted to stay in the cocoon of her bedroom forever, just the two of them.

Sweeping her hand down his back, she felt the muscles that fanned out from his spine, the smooth skin, the heat from his flesh. It felt good to not hurry, and with the security system on, she knew if anyone tried to get in, they'd hear about it. Also, Soot was downstairs in his crate, and going by the way he'd greeted the SWAT guys before he was properly introduced, the dog was an equally good alarm.

If Danny kept staying over night, she was going to have to bring the dog back up. Maybe she could put him in the bathroom.

Wrapping her arms around the vital man who was still inside of her, she put her face into Danny's neck, his hair brushing her forehead, the shadow of his beard on her cheek. For some reason, she became acutely aware that her blunted arm was against his rib cage, and she thought about how he didn't treat it as any different from any other part of her: He welcomed the contact, cherished it, craved it.

The way he treated her partial arm was better than any list of words he could have spoken to tell her he still found her beautiful, desirable . . . whole, even though she was missing a part. And though it scared her to admit it, this time here, with him, had healed her, even though she had no more open wounds.

Acceptance was a balm to that raw place she had refused to acknowledge.

Closing her eyes against sudden tears, she held onto him. "Danny . . ."

"Yes?"

I love you. "Thank you," she breathed.

He pulled back a little. "For staying the night? Are you kidding me, I wouldn't leave you here by yourself to deal with this. And whenever I'm off shift, you'll have me back."

"I would like that."

"Me, too."

His staying over wasn't even about her car window getting shot out. It was about so much more, a connection that had started the day she had walked into the 499 as a probie and looked up, way up, into the blue eyes of an Irish wild man. Sometime along the way, over the passage of days and weeks and months, he had become part of her life, part of her history.

She told herself that it was only through retrospection that things felt inevitable. She wasn't sure she believed that in her heart.

As the sun rose higher, it seemed as though they had been destined all along for each other.

And because of that, she decided to stop fighting it, fighting him . . . fighting the outcome that seemed to, no matter the particulars or the place, always bring them together.

Sometimes strength rested not in resistance, but in the release of arms against a foe of one's own creation.

L ater that morning, Tom was sitting back at his desk in the fishbowl, drumming his fingers on reports he was supposed to
read and sign off on, when someone came into the stationhouse.

Getting to his feet, he motioned for them to enter his office, and as
his sister opened the door, he was embarrassed that she might have
seen him staring off into space.

"Didn't know you were coming over." He nodded to the vacant
chair on the far side of things. "You need a seat?"

"Yes, thanks."

As Anne got settled, he studied her. "So Mom called me yesterday.
She said you two had talked."

It wasn't a surprise when her eyes ducked his own and instead
locked on all his disorganized paperwork. "I . . . ah, I might have been
really unfair about her. To her. I think she had to deal with some
things that I was unaware of. I also think our father might have been a
monster under all that I'm-a-hero shit, but you and I can argue about
that at a different time."

"I'm done arguing." When she looked up sharply, he put a hand out. "That sounds defensive, it isn't. I am literally, for myself, tired of arguing with everybody."

"Who are you and what have you done with my brother."

"You know, I could say the same thing about you with Mom."

"So we've both been taken over by aliens. Good to know—do we have to get new driver's licenses?"

Tom smiled a little. "Yeah. Maybe we do. So what's up? You need something?"

"I want to talk to you about Charles Ripkin."

Leaning back in his old wooden chair, he crossed his leg, ankle to knee. "Don't know the guy, really."

"When he talked to you about this building"—she motioned around his work space and all the bright-and-shiny beyond it—"was he . . . did you ever feel like he was trying to buy us off? The fire department, I mean."

"In exchange for what?"

"Whatever happened at his house with his daughter? Maybe those fires down at the warehouses?"

"No." Tom crossed his arms and told himself now was the time to stick to his new leaf. Namaste and all that shit. "What are you insinuating? That I took a bribe or something? What for, we didn't do anything wrong."

"I agree. I've read all of our incident reports. I just . . . a man like that doesn't do anything for a purpose that doesn't advance his self-interests, right? I mean, his reputation is what it is for a reason. He's ruthless and shady, and I've done extensive searches on him. Do you realize that this firehouse is the only philanthropic thing he's ever done?"

"That's not possible. All rich guys give to places. They get museum wings named after themselves, donate libraries and research centers."

"Ripkin hasn't. He gives to political candidates, but not non-profits."

Tom frowned. "What kind of politicians?"

"He's a registered Republican, but he donates across the spectrum."

"What about Mayor Mahoney. He give to her?"

"Yes. He's topped out for this election."

"What's that mean?"

"He's given Mahoney's campaign up to the legal limit. I can show you the report if you'd like?"

"Nah. Not a surprise." Tom shrugged, although whether that was to convince his sister or himself that he didn't care, he wasn't sure—and didn't want to dwell on it. "He's in deep with her on this wharf thing. I had a meeting with her the other night, and she and her lackey Perry had just met with Ripkin Development. Doing that area over is one of her election imperatives—or whatever they call them."

As Anne grew quiet, he sat forward. "What's going on."

"Just trying to figure this all out."

"Define 'this.' And before you tell me to mind my own business, I'd like to point out that in your entire professional career, you've never come to my office about anything. You must be here for a reason."

There was a period of silence, and then Anne looked him directly in the eye. "I think Ripkin tried to kill his own daughter and make it look like an accident. And I believe he gave this building to our department and played the grateful parent to support the appearance that the fire at his mansion was a terrible accident and we were the heroes. I also think we're screwed to try to implicate him. There's no statute of limitations on arson in the Commonwealth, but all the physical evidence is gone. There's nothing to reexamine."

"What do you mean? Like, at the site?"

"No, as in, at all. I went into our storage facility to get the evidence box and it was gone. There's the written report online, and a few photographs, but the actual samples and evidence have disappeared."

"Was there much in it?"

"I don't know. Samples were noted, but I don't know how thorough the listing is."

"Who was the investigator on your end?"

"Bob Burlington."

"Wait, didn't he die?"

"In a boating accident about three weeks into his investigation. His body washed up on shore in the bay. They said he'd had a heart attack, but the sharks got ahold of him so it was hard to know if he had any other pertinent injuries."

A ripple of unease teased the nape of Tom's neck. "What does this have to do with you, Sister."

As her eyes swung back to his, she shook her head. "Nothing? Why?"

"Remember when you used to sneak out of the house at night after Dad died? Mom would ask us at breakfast if we'd walked around after bedtime—and you'd have this exact same expression on your face."

Even though Danny had only had twenty-four hours off, he was back at the 499, and for once, it seemed like it was going to be a slow day. Then again, it wasn't freezing cold, so people hadn't gotten out their space heaters yet, and folks were no longer doing crazy stuff from the summer heat. Also, not a full moon, so bonus.

After running a drill on breathing apparatuses, he was doing laundry in the bay and thinking they needed a probie. And not just because if they had more crew members, they'd be able to get back to a more normal schedule—

"Oh, shit. Here we go." As Duff spoke up from the Nautilus machine, the guy pointed out to the street. "Moose not make the bed this morning?"

Deandra got out of her BMW and marched across toward the stationhouse, her Chanel tote bag banging against her hip, her stilettos clipping over the pavement, her now-red hair flouncing in her wake like a war flag.

"Wasn't she a blonde this past weekend?" Duff asked.

"I don't keep up with it." Danny hit the dryer button and started the tumbler. "I'll go get him."

"Is he even here? He was late."

"From fighting with her, no doubt."

After making sure the washer's spin cycle was still going, Danny went inside to the rec area. Moose was sitting on the sofa, legs crossed on the beat-up coffee table, hands linked on his beer gut.

"You got a visitor, my man."

The guy didn't look away from the *Dr. Phil* episode on the TV. "No, I don't. I told her not to come."

"She doesn't speak English when it comes to 'no.' Remember how much your wedding cost?"

Deandra marched right in and stopped short. "You are a fucking asshole." When Moose refused to acknowledge her, she went over and blocked his view of the television. "You canceled my credit card."

Moose tilted to the side. "Can you move."

"You know you fucking did—"

"No, I fucking *didn't*." The guy burst up to his feet. "You ever hear of a credit limit? Like, you spend the amount they're willing to float you and then you can't spend no more? They cut you off, Deandra."

"You did this."

"That bag did it." He jabbed a finger at what was hanging off her shoulder. "How much was that? Huh? Two thousand dollars? Three? What the fuck, Deandra."

"Stop saying my name like you're my father or some shit."

"Then be an adult and pay for your own crap."

"You told me that you would make it good. That if I married you, you'd make it good. And here we are, living out in the sticks, and I can't buy a Starbucks on the way to work because you—"

Danny stepped in between them. "Enough. You guys take this into the locker room if you have to, but you can't do this here, okay? The rest of us don't need—"

"He's a better fuck than you, Moose." Deandra smiled like a serial killer about to go to work. "He can make me come. You never have."

Danny put his palms up and backed away. "I'm out. This is not my problem—"

"He's been fucking me for the last month, Moose. And you know what I do, Moose, when you're on shift? I put my hand on my pussy and I think of him—"

Moose went for her like he was going to snap her head off her spine, and Danny played human shield, jumping forward and taking the hit.

"Calm down, Moose—"

Moose suddenly focused on him. "You fucked my wife!"

All that rage got channeled at Danny, those meaty hands locking on his throat and shoving him backward.

"I did not fuck her—"

"And I love when he does!" Deandra yelled. "He fucks me better than you ever will and I can't wait for him to—"

Danny grabbed Moose's thick wrists and tried to free the guy's brutal grip. "Shut up, Deandra!"

Duff and Doc came barreling in, and the two of them took hold of Moose's arms and pulled. But even they got nowhere, the four of them advancing to the pong table until Moose had Danny laid out on the playing surface.

"You are a fucking whore!" Moose spat. "You're a fucking—"

"I am not!" Deandra tossed back.

He's not talking to you, bitch, Danny thought. "Moose—I didn't fuck her!"

"Liar!" Red-faced and spitting, the man was trembling so badly his hair was flopping. "You fucked her—"

"Not since you got with her!" Holy shit, he couldn't breathe. "Not since—"

"Like anyone can believe you? You don't give a fuck who you hurt! It's all about you—"

Deshaun threw his arm around Moose's thick neck and took his wrist in his own hand. Yanking back on the chokehold, he pried the man free.

As Moose kicked and punched at thin air, Danny flopped flat, his arms rolling out to both sides as he brought his legs up to relieve the pressure on his spine. Taking deep breaths, he got his vision back from checkerboard-landia.

Captain Baker burst into the room. "What the hell is going on in here!"

"You are a gentleman and a scholar. This is amazing."

Anne put the receiver of her office phone between her ear and shoulder and went into her email, hitting refresh on her Outlook. When nothing came in, she hit it again. And a third time.

"Has the link come through?" her new buddy from the traffic office asked.

"Not yet—oh, here it is. And I got the log-in you set up for me. Thank you so much—I know you rushed this for me."

"No problem. Call me if you need any other files because I've had to limit your access to your scope of inquiry per regulations. Sorry we don't go back more than four weeks."

"This is going to be a big help. Thanks again."

Hanging up, she double-clicked the link, got to the log-in, and entered her ID and temporary password. The screen presented her with a table of video feeds marked with alphanumerical descriptors that matched the street addresses of the cameras around the most recent warehouse fire.

Opening the first one, she saw a black-and-white image of a dark street and a navigating panel at the bottom. Using the mouse, she ran time fast-forward starting at 12:01 a.m., watching what continued to be a mostly empty stretch of asphalt: only a couple of vagrants entered and left the camera field. Then the sun came up.

She stopped and took a map of the city out of her desk. Flattening it, she found where the camera was, orienting herself. Then she went back to the files and chose another location. According to the incident reports, the fire had started in the abandoned building sometime around nine thirty p.m.

Talk about watching paint dry.

Nothing changed but the shadows, the relentless shift of the sun broken up only by the occasional truck or car or ragged pedestrian. Night came at this angle. Now there was once again just the glow of the streetlight on the traffic-free corner. Nothing approached or entered the warehouse—until there was a sudden flash inside. Smoke. Then the fire engines and the rescue crew's ambulance arrived.

She switched to another camera after she reoriented herself again. Now she was checking out the road that went along the side, and the process started all over again, the monitoring beginning at 12:01 a.m. and going through dawn to the following nightfall. Then the fire.

And again with the street camera on the other side. Dark. Dark. Light. Midday. Late afternoon. Nightfall. Flash. Evidence of smoke. Fire trucks. Ambulance.

Nothing out of place. No one showing up with a truck full of office equipment.

"Shit."

Sitting back, she cracked her spine and rotated her shoulders. Soot was snoring softly in his crate, and it was almost lunchtime.

One more to go. Firing the last file up, she started the review again.

Frankly, it was amazing that there were any feeds at all given how deserted that part of town was. But the mayor's office had set up cameras throughout that zip code as part of an initiative to encourage businesses to move down there and invest in renovation projects. With the amount of crime in that area, there had been some pushback on safety, and in a rare moment of loosening purse strings, the former mayor, Greenfield, had stepped in and identified the deterent monitoring as a priority.

But of course, God only knew what Ripkin had kitted his properties out with. Not that she expected to see anything from that information demand anytime soon. Sterling Broward was going to pump the brakes—

"What? Wait, what was that?" she muttered to herself.

Leaning in to her monitor, she reversed the feed and initiated the file at a slow speed.

Three thirty-two a.m. Dark street. Dark street. Empty—

The box trailer and truck rolled past the camera and then bumped up over the curb and continued across the scruffy lawn. It stopped. Someone got out and rolled up a bay door in the warehouse's side wall, driving inside and closing themselves in.

Forty-six minutes later, at 4:18 a.m., the bay was re-opened, the truck came back out with its trailer, and then the driver shut everything up and drove off.

Unfortunately, the footage was so grainy, she couldn't catch any license plates or markings on the trailer or truck, and the individual who'd gone inside had been wearing a dark hoodie, so identifying them was going to be tough.

But it proved that someone had gone in there.

"Gotcha," she said with a smile.

As her cell phone started to ring, she absently shoved her hand into her purse and answered the call. "Hello?"

There was a pause. "Anne, it's Moose. We gotta talk."

Twenty minutes later, Anne was at Hereford Crossings, an outdoor shopping center that had cafés and locally owned restaurants along with stores that sold clothing for middle-aged women and shops that had pottery and handmade rugs in their windows.

It was the kind of place that her mother would have loved to check out, Anne thought as she walked along with the light crowd.

Moose was sitting on a bench in front of the Lunch Depot, his head lowered as he fiddled with something in his hands.

"Hey, Moose."

He looked up. "Hey, Anne. Thanks for coming."

But instead of getting up to go inside the restaurant, he just continued to run a thin gold necklace through his fingers.

"You ready to eat?" she asked.

When he shook his head, she sat down next to him and tried not to let her unease show. Not that he was looking at her.

"Danny's been fucking Deandra."

As he spoke the words, her first response was to laugh. That woman was nothing that Danny went for—

"She came to the stationhouse this morning. She said he was fucking her and he lied when he maintained they weren't."

With horrible clarity, she remembered going into Danny's room that first night she went to see him and finding that lingerie on the floor of his bedroom.

But we weren't together then, she told herself.

"Deandra said she couldn't wait until he fucked her again." Moose rubbed his face. "Look, I don't know what the status of your relationship is with him, but you've got to understand about the two of them. He slept with her right before our wedding."

Anne twisted so she could look right at the man. "What are you talking about?"

"He fucked her at the apartment. I found the two of them hooking up when I came back from the rehearsal dinner." He cursed. "I love her so much. She's all I've ever wanted—"

"Moose, I'm sorry but I'm not following." Or maybe it was more like she didn't want to hear it all. "What the hell are you talking about?"

"They were together having sex the night before we got married. It was after the rehearsal dinner. I wasn't supposed to see her until we met at the altar the next day. I was staying at the honeymoon suite downtown at the Hyatt, you know? 'Cuz that's where we were gonna be after the ceremony and reception for the wedding night. But I forgot my tux at the apartment."

Anne's heart started to beat hard. "So you went back for it?"

"Yup. Walked in and heard these noises. I thought the TV was on, but then a female voice sounded out loud and clear . . . I didn't turn the lights on. I just had this feeling. I went down the hall . . . I could smell her perfume. Her dress was on the floor outside his room. I went far enough to hear her say his name and I left."

A cold sweat broke out all over Anne's body, as she realized that, if what Moose was saying was true . . . Danny had fucked her the night after he'd done the bride-to-be. And the same thing must have been happening now that she had been hooking up with him again.

Safe sex my ass, she thought.

"Why did you marry her?" she blurted.

When what she really wanted to ask was, *Why did I fall for that bullshit?*

"I almost didn't. But she called me that morning in tears. She said she loved me. I never told her what I'd seen. All I cared about was that she wanted to marry me. She wanted to be with me—not him. She picked me—not him. Moose won over the great Danny Maguire. Finally."

Anne focused on Moose properly and got a good look at what was behind his hard partying, his linebacker persona, his brash frat-boy car freak: as he sat beside her, he was a slightly overweight, going-on-pudgy wannabe trying to keep up with the cool kids, the pick-me! instead of the leader, the wingman instead of the stud.

"I've tried to make her happy. I swear, Anne." His anxious eyes bored into her like he was giving testimony in court. "I did everything I could, but it's never enough. She's never happy—and it's because the truth is, I didn't win. She married me for the same reason I had to tell you about him. Danny's toxic for women. Deandra knew that he wouldn't ever settle down with her, and so I was second prize. You gotta know that he uses women, Anne. He's a bad guy."

Looking away, Anne seriously considered pivoting to the trash bin next to her and throwing up.

"Don't think you're different," Moose said. "I guess that's what I'm really saying. We all saw him flirt with you when you were on the crew. We used to have bets on how long it was going to take for him to fuck you because any woman he's ever wanted he's got. But you armed-length'd him, and that just kept him interested in you. He focused on you because he couldn't get you. And then there was the fire. Now, you're back and I don't know what you're doing with him for sure, but I have a feeling it's the same thing he's doing to my wife."

Anne opened her mouth. Closed it.

"I know he crashed at your place last night. You're telling me he slept on your couch?" Moose got up and stretched. "I can't go in that restaurant and eat. I want to vomit."

That makes two of us, she thought.

"When it came out at the stationhouse this morning, I nearly killed him," Moose said. "Well, first I nearly killed her. Then I went after him. I was told to take some time to collect myself, and after I did, I called you. I'm not telling you this to take something away from him or some shit. I'm fucking done with him. I just don't want you to be made a fool of like I've been. And I'm guessing by that expression on your face that you feel the way I do right now, like a sucker."

Anne glanced down to duck his stare, and as she looked at her prosthesis, she actually thought, for a split second, that this was much, much worse than losing her hand.

Because this meant she couldn't judge reality at all.

48

Three texts had come in throughout the day to Anne's phone. The first was a picture of her and Danny leaving her house in the morning with Soot—which as she looked at it again was the last thing she wanted to see for so many reasons. The second was three words: *I see you.* The third was a picture of her coming out of her brother's stationhouse.

All had been sent from that Gmail account.

And okay, fine, Danny had reached out, too, but she'd refused to acknowledge him.

Sitting back in her office chair, she looked out the window behind her desk. Darkness had fallen, and she didn't want to go down to the parking lot to her car. But at least Safelite had come and repaired the front windshield after she had driven the thing over here this morning. And it was the height of gallows humor, she supposed, to reassure herself that they could always come again.

If she got shot at a second time, for example.

But that wasn't the only thing she was thinking about—and it was a sad testament to the magnitude of Danny's snow job that, even in a situation where her life could be in danger, she was wasting any time on him.

When her phone rang, she jumped, but then she saw who it was. Answering it, she said, "Jack. I was just going to call you for an update—"

"Our good friend Ollie Popper killed himself in jail about an hour ago."

Anne sat forward. "He's dead?"

"They found him hanging in the shower from a loop made of bed sheet."

"Shit."

"Interestingly enough, the video monitoring camera had something put over it."

She frowned. "So it wasn't suicide?"

"Doesn't look like it in my opinion. They're going over the body with a fine-toothed comb, but I wouldn't be surprised if they found nothing. Danny's staying with you, right?"

"Ah, no. He's not."

"Oh, that's right, he's on shift."

She let that one stand. The last thing she needed was the SWAT team showing up as a character reference for a man they only knew in that macho brothers-in-arms way of first responders.

"You want me to come over with a couple of my boys?" Jack said.

An image of large, muscled, tattooed men in tactical gear sleeping like lions in a zoo on the floor of her living room almost made her smile.

"Nah, I'm okay. I'm not afraid."

"You get any more calls?"

"No."

"And how many texts," Jack said wryly.

God, the guy was like a bloodhound when it came to voice inflection changes. "Three. One was a picture of me leaving my brother's stationhouse."

"I don't like this, Anne."

"I'm going home with a bunch of work and I'm staying indoors with everything locked and the drapes drawn. I also live in a neighborhood full of people who can hear me scream."

"That didn't matter when your window got shot."

"They're just trying to scare me."

"Wonder if that's what Ollie Popper thought as they hung him up by the throat from a pipe. In a prison. With a hundred guards around."

So much for a slow day, Danny thought as he sat down with the crew for dinner: Four box alarms, two car crashes, a kid who got his head stuck between the iron bars of that fence over at the cemetery, and Moose losing his ever-loving mind. The only good news was that at least for once Danny hadn't been the one being a hothead and getting suspended.

It was early, though.

Taking out his phone, he checked to see if Anne had called him back. Texted him back. Anything, anything—nope.

Fuck.

Pushing his plate of reheated ribs and room-temperature slaw away, he pondered the effort involved in having a cigarette outside. Around the table, the other men were resolutely looking at their plates, the clinking of silverware the only sound in the room.

The last time they'd had a meal like this was after the Patriots lost to the Eagles in the Super Bowl.

He got up and took his plate to the trash, scraping off the food and putting the thing into the dishwasher. Then he left out the back door and lit up. The night was cold and he was just in his NBFD T-shirt and work pants, but he didn't feel a thing.

After trying Anne again, he decided, *Fuck it.*

Calling a number out of his contacts, he put the phone to his ear. "Jack. Wassup."

"My man. I just talked to your girl."

"Anne?" He frowned. "She answered her phone?"

"Yup. I had news to share. That suspect she questioned yesterday was found dead in the communal shower. I told her she needed to have you over at her house again tonight, but you're on shift."

"Yeah. On shift. Listen, could you do me a favor? Could you schedule some drive-bys of her house tonight?"

"I'm doing one better. Two of my boys who're off duty volunteered to stake out her house. They're each doing a four-hour shift, the first starting at ten."

Danny exhaled. "Thank you. That's awesome."

"We take care of our own, Dannyboy. And I told her to call me if she needs anything. I guess that asshole with the unknown number is still texting her."

"Yeah."

There was a pause. "I don't usually say this, Danny, but if there's any way you could talk to her about backing off Ripkin, it might be a good idea. This is not to say that she can't handle herself or that justice doesn't need to be served. But there are a lot of bodies around anything that threatens that asshole in his ivory tower in Boston. I don't want her to be the next one floating in the ocean or buried in a landfill."

"Neither do I."

After they hung up, he stared at the phone. And called her one more time. He didn't think she was going to answer—and she didn't.

As voicemail kicked in, he cleared his throat. "So I'm guessing by the fact that you'll talk to Jack and not me that Moose called you about the drama this morning between him and Deandra. I just want—look, it's got nothing to do with me. Deandra was just shooting her mouth off about shit because she was pissed off about money. I really hope you'll call me so we can talk things over. I love you, Anne. I wanted to tell you in person this morning, but I lost my nerve. I really . . . I love you and we were headed in a good direction. I want to keep going like that, for the rest of my life. Anyway, call me. Please."

Ending the connection, he stared at his phone until the lock screen came on. Then he looked at it some more.

When it stayed black, he didn't know what he expected—

Bullshit. He'd thought she'd listen to the message and call him back and tell him she loved him and agree that Moose was in a bad relationship with a bad woman and it was all just a misunderstanding.

Putting the cell phone back in his pocket, he smoked and thought of the nightmare that had woken him in Anne's bed.

It had been him back at that apartment where the old lady had been gutted. He had walked into the room, taken a look at the mutilated body, and started to throw up.

And then everything had morphed and he had been the one with hands and feet tied, screaming as a shadowy perpetrator had cut him open and removed his internal organs.

Pretty fucking horrific stuff. And yet that had been a party compared to what he was feeling right now, stuck at the stationhouse while what little glimpse of a good life he'd had dimmed and then disappeared into the night as if it had never existed.

He was going to fucking kill Moose.

49

Anne sat back on her sofa and closed her eyes. It was going on ten o'clock and she was surrounded by printouts of reports on those warehouse fires, the papers like the snow cover of winter, a December of documents on the floor, the coffee table, the cushions.

Except for where Soot was curled up next to her.

She had been going over the same information for the last two hours and nothing was sticking anymore. Good distraction, though. It had gotten her through the dead zone between dinner and bedtime.

"You want to go out one last time?"

Soot knew the cue and obligingly got off his spot. The jingle of his collar was a welcome accompaniment as they went to the back door and she turned off the security system with her remote.

Before she stepped outside, she took the nine-millimeter handgun she'd left on the corner of her desk with her.

The night was cold and dry, and the moon overhead was bright and clear. She took comfort that her neighbors were all home, their lights on, their bodies moving in and out of windows as the whole neighborhood settled for the rest of the evening.

Soot was efficient. No sniffing around. No investigating foreign scents on the wind or the bushes or the browning grass.

Which was another good sign as far as she was concerned. If anyone was or had been around, she had to believe he'd notice.

Back in the house. Back with the locked door. Back on with the alarm.

She kept the gun with her as she considered going upstairs to bed. In the end, she stayed downstairs. She felt like that way, if someone tried to get in, she'd hear them better.

As she resumed her seat on the sofa, Soot did the same, and she put her hand on his warm flank, stroking his short, smooth fur. When he let out a deep sigh of relaxation, she envied him.

Picking up a random incident report, she tried to get her brain to connect the dots that were refusing to be linked. She had Ripkin. She had Ollie-no-longer-Popper. And then she had whoever had showed up at that warehouse with the trailer—which might have been Ollie or might not have been.

"When was he arrested?" she said out loud.

Back into the paperwork to find the file on Ollie. Nope. Not him. He had been in police custody the night that most recent warehouse fire had been set.

Damn it, she wished she had CCTV for those other burns. The key was the identity of that unknown third person with the truck and trailer. If she could find out who it was, maybe she could make the tie from Ollie to Ripkin. Before the latter had whoever it had been killed, that was.

She thought about Bob Burlington being found in the ocean. Jesus, she did not want that to be her.

As her phone rang, she braced herself as she picked the thing up to see who it was. If that unknown caller was back—

It was Danny.

"Goddamn it."

She debated letting him go into voicemail again, but she wasn't some coward to run from the confrontation forever. And he was just going to keep calling until he got off shift and showed up on her doorstep at eight in the morning.

"Hello," she said.

"I didn't think you were going to answer."

"I'm busy."

There was a pause. "I left you a voicemail."

"I didn't listen to it."

"Did Moose get in touch with you?"

"Yes." She put the paperwork aside. "Listen, we're not going to do this, okay?"

"Do what."

"Pretend. I don't have time for it. Don't call me anymore, don't try to see me, and if you have a passing thought, some weeks or months from now that I might want to hear from you, I'm going ask you to re-play this conversation in your mind. I am *never* going to want to set eyes on you again."

"So you've made up your mind."

"There was nothing to make up."

She snagged the remote and turned on the TV across the room just so she could give herself a distraction from the drama.

"I didn't fuck Deandra."

"We all know that's not true—although it was a surprise to learn from her husband that you had her the night before she walked down the aisle with him. Guess you took what you wanted from her and told her to beat it. At least for the honeymoon."

"What the hell are you talking about?"

"I'm not going to go into it—"

"You better fucking explain yourself."

Anne sat up stick straight. "Excuse me? What did you just say? You think I have to explain *anything* to you? Forget what happened between the two of us, I'm just another heart and a hole you played with while you were at work. But Moose was your best friend, Danny. For a decade. And on the night of his rehearsal dinner, when he went back to get his tux, he saw you and Deandra in your bedroom at the apartment. Even if Deandra was lying at the stationhouse this morning, which I don't think she was, there was no hearsay involved with Moose seeing his future wife's dress on your goddamn floor."

"I didn't fuck her that evening," came the tight reply.

"Do you really expect me to believe that? Because I don't. And damn it, you were with me the next night!" She wanted to throw her phone she was so pissed, but she managed to calm herself down. "I have to admit that your success rate speaks for itself. You got me good. Two separate times. I'd give you a trophy, but in my current mood, I'd put it up your ass, and I am not going to jail for felony assault with this year's Best Lying Sack of Shit award."

"You got this all wrong."

"Do I? Gaslighting much?" She took a deep breath. "Here's the way I am going to view what happened between us. It was a movie that started as a comedy, segued awkwardly into a romance, and ended with Anthony Hopkins eating someone's liver with fava beans and a fucking Chianti. I sat through it, enjoyed a couple of parts, but overall, I'm giving it a bad score on Rotten Tomatoes because the narrative didn't ring true, the credible surprise was credible but no surprise at all, and the male lead was a one-dimensional sexual predator. Good-bye, Danny."

Anne ended the call, put her phone down, and crossed her arms over her chest. She did not expect Danny to ring again. And he didn't. Then again, the truth was out and there was nothing left for him to work with, no manipulations at his disposal, no wiggle room around reality. The thing with men like him—people like him—was they required instability and insecurity in their playing field.

Someone with both feet planted on the ground was not a good target.

She would never hear from him again. And he would, unfortunately, go on to find other women to consume, other marks to challenge himself with, other opportunities to exploit.

Just like her father.

Too bad scarlet letters were a thing of the past. She would have slapped one on him in a heartbeat with the *A* being for "ASSHOLE." But at least she was on the other side now. Man, he'd gotten her going, though.

Focusing on the TV, she saw Cher getting out of a boxy yellow cab, red shoes on her feet, a shimmering black coat catching the light as she walked toward a gleaming fountain. And there was Nicolas Cage, turning . . . turning . . .

Pain, unwelcomed and full of heartache, lanced through Anne's chest as she watched his face change when he saw his woman. And then they were talking in those wonderful New York accents:

"Hi."

"Hi."

"You look beautiful. Ya hair . . ."

"Yeah, I had it done."

Anne let her head fall back as they went into the opera house, stared up at the chandelier, proceeded into the cloakroom. Funny that a movie about a man who'd lost a hand was on. On that note, maybe she needed to try and date a Cher.

She nudged Soot. "See, this is where she sees her father out with the other woman. Or shall I say 'otha woman.'"

It was also the part where Ronny Cammareri tells Loretta, *It's been a long time since I've been to the opera.*

"He's not talking about the opera, Soot. And I feel you, Ronny. I totally feel you."

At this point, Anne felt like she'd actually never been to the opera. In her world, the Met was closed, the sopranos and the baritones, the orchestra and conductor all home with perpetual head colds.

Closing her eyes, she was lonely. And tired. And very sad.

Tomorrow was a new day, though. She was smarter than she'd been yesterday, and stronger than ever. And what she needed to do was figure out this Ripkin mess.

Danny Maguire was a thing in the past, nothing more than an ugly footnote in a life that was going to continue . . .

Disorientation struck as Anne opened her eyes. At first, she went for her gun because she heard the sound of bullets flying—but then she realized it was the movie on the TV, not anything inside or outside of her house.

Picking up her phone, she saw that it was almost seven a.m. Soot was on his back, paws curled in, snoring.

As soon as she got up, he was on his feet, and she turned off the alarm and let him out, standing watch. People were stirring in their houses, making coffee on the first floors, showering and dressing on the second.

She did the same.

When she came back downstairs, she poured herself a cup of java and realized she'd forgotten to take the phone up with her.

Bracing herself, she checked the thing, expecting to see a picture of herself with her hair a mess on the back porch as Soot piddled on his favorite spot by the corner of the house.

Nope. Nothing.

Which was relief of a temporary nature.

She was about to put the phone in her bag when she thought about Danny's stupid-ass voicemail. She hadn't even gone in to erase it, but on the theory of starting as one meant to go on, she opened the phone icon. The "Recents" screen popped up, and she was about to hit the voicemail icon with its red "1" on the lower right corner when something didn't make sense.

The list of calls started with Danny at the top. There was his name and "(4)" next to it, and the line was black because she'd answered the last call from him. Across from that, there was "Yesterday" in gray.

Then there was Jack. In black. With a gray "Yesterday."

And "World's Greatest Boss," which was how she had Don in her contacts. Black. With a gray "Yesterday."

And under that was "Unknown." In black. With a gray "Yesterday."

Scrolling down the list, she found the other "Unknown" caller. It was black from back when she'd answered the phone just before her window got shot out.

Except she hadn't answered two calls from an unknown number. Hitting the information button on the more recent one, she frowned. The time stamp was yesterday morning, and it showed a call lasting three minutes—

The world spun and she threw out a hand.

Moose. When he'd called her about Deandra and Danny. That was exactly the date and time when he had called her to ask to meet him at Hereford Crossings.

So was he the one who had shot her car window? Put the gun on her doorstep? Texted her and watched her?

Stumbling over to a chair, she sat down and stared at the details. Maybe there was another explanation . . .

She went through all her recents, all the way back to when he had first called her to go see Danny that night. There, the phone number in her contacts showed up with the entry that read "Moose."

So he had a regular phone and had gotten a burner to make sure he was anonymous when he threatened her? But what was his tie to Rip-kin and Ollie Popper, the warehouse fires and the office equipment—

"The box trailer. Shit. The fucking box trailer!"

Bursting up, she went to her sofa. She'd printed out a screenshot from the CCTV and it was here, somewhere—

When she found the piece of paper, she tried to see if the trailer was the same as the one Moose used for transporting his cars. She couldn't tell. There had to be a thousand of them in the city of New Brunswick.

With her heart pounding and her mind racing, there was a temptation to scream from the rooftops, to call Jack and send the SWAT team over there, to get a helicopter in the air. But she didn't want to put her foot in it.

And Moose was her friend.

Slow. Methodical. Let the situation reveal itself . . .

Besides, it made no sense. Why would Moose set fires in his own district to destroy electronics for Ripkin? The two of them had never met.

"Yes, they have," she said to herself as she fumbled with the phone.

When her call rang through, she could barely get the words out. "Tom? Tom! Listen, I need a favor—"

"What time is it?" her brother mumbled.

"In your office. On the shelf behind your desk. There's a picture—"

"Sis, you're talking too fast. What—"

"The picture. From the opening of the new stationhouse. The picture behind your desk. I need you to take a photograph of it and send it to me right now. Okay? Just take a picture of it and send it to my phone."

"Why?"

She thought about coming forward with everything. But this was not just her brother she was talking to; it was Moose's boss. What if she was wrong? All she had was "Unknown" caller—she didn't have the digits themselves. Jack was still working on that.

"I just need to see it. Please?"

"Sure, fine. Whatever. I'm upstairs in my bunk. Gimme five minutes."

After she hung up, she cradled her phone. Tom no doubt had heard about the blowup between Danny and Moose at the 499, and if she started talking like Moose was some kind of serial arsonist setting fires for a psychotic killer businessman, her brother was going to think she was nuts.

What she needed were facts. Proof.

Motive: Moose had, in the last year, somehow managed to fund a fancy wedding, a set of implants for Deandra, two expensive cars, a new house, and all that ugly furniture on a fireman's salary. Even if you assumed he was working as a roofer every second he was off shift? That was a couple hundred thousand dollars right there.

Ripkin could afford to pay well the people he had doing nasties for him.

Means: Moose was on the fire service. Fire service people did training runs in abandoned buildings where fires were set to burn in a controlled fashion. Back when she had been at the 499, he and Danny had always been the ones clearing sites and overseeing the training fires.

It wasn't that hard to imagine that he could set a controlled ignition by timer or remote device.

Opportunity: The box truck on the CCTV.

Assuming it was the one he owned.

"Come on, Tom . . . come on . . ."

From out of nowhere, an image came to her, coughed out of memories that she didn't like to dwell on.

It was from the fire, right after she had had her hand cut off. Danny had carried her to the collapsed wall that had presented an escape, and was pushing her through the hole, forcing her out . . .

Into Moose's waiting arms.

Anne went back to her mess of papers, flipping through reports, and tables, and photographs, and—

The incident report from the 499 was in standard format, listing the time of call to that warehouse, the address, the engines and ladders and ambulances that were sent . . . as well as the crew that was working that shift. And down at the bottom, marked with an asterisk was the name Robert Miller.

Moose had been med'd out that night due to a migraine.

Which was why, when he'd helped drag her out of the collapse, he'd been in civilian clothes, not turnouts.

How had he known to be there?

Her phone went off with a bing, and she opened the text from her brother. Calling the image up, she enlarged it, passing by the line of officers and Ripkin standing in front of a red ribbon at the bays of the new stationhouse.

And there it was. Off to the side.

Moose talking intently with a man in a slick suit with silver hair. Sterling Broward, Ripkin's fancy attorney.

Except how exactly had it worked? Ollie Popper had been running a multi-state fencing operation involving office equipment, and anytime things had gotten too hot for him with the police, he'd disappeared the evidence against him in fires that happened to be taking place in Ripkin's warehouses. Moose would know how to set a controlled burn and make sure the fire destroyed what it was suppose to. But that didn't necessarily mean he and Ollie were tied to Ripkin.

Just because Moose had clearly talked to Sterling Broward at a public event didn't mean the Ripkin connection was solid.

Her gut, however, told her something was there. That fire at Ripkin's mansion that had nearly killed his daughter? The arson investigator who had been killed in the boating accident? Ollie Popper, represented by Broward, dead in the shower before his case went any further?

Putting her phone facedown, she continued to think about it all, especially about what Don had gotten on her about before: Beware of information that only confirms your hypothesis.

And start with what you know for sure.

When it came to Moose, it was clear what she needed to do, and she went for her bag, her keys, and Soot's leash.

On the way out of her house, she made sure she had her gun with her. And her license to carry concealed.

nne hit the gas hard through the farmland. Moose had been on shift with Danny the day before, so if she hurried, she had a chance of getting a look at that box truck before the firefighter got home. And as for Deandra? Anne would just have to deal with the woman if she was on the property. If worst came to worst, she could pull the inspector badge out.

Except turned out no one was home.

She circled the property once before getting anywhere near the driveway, and was able to visualize the empty parking area in front of the ranch through the trees—as well as the mess that was all over the lawn.

Someone had moved out. Or been thrown out.

After a second pass around the acreage, she discovered a back way in. Given that she didn't know when anyone would get home, the approach was safer and she was able to get her car within a hundred yards of the garage.

And the box trailer.

"You stay here, Soot." She put his window down to make sure he had plenty of air. "I'll be right back."

Getting out, she had her gun front and center and her phone in the grip of her prosthesis as she jogged across the grass to the garage.

She froze as she back-flatted against the structure. When nothing happened, she shuffled along and stuck her head out around the corner.

The box trailer was big enough to fit a car in, with its roof and four walls enclosing its contents. The double doors in the back were shut and had a heavy lock on them.

Taking out her phone, she snapped a couple of pictures, and then went closer. She had to look inside of it, but how?

Moose's garage had been left open, and it was hard to tell for certain, but she had the impression someone had trashed the place—although given the mess he kept his tools in, who could be sure? Still, there had to be something she could use in there.

She found the axe propped up against the siding and picked the thing up. Given its weight and the fact that she was one-handed, she was not going to be able to control it well enough, so she put it back.

Only one way to do this.

Taking the safety off her gun, she returned to the trailer and leveled the muzzle at the lock. Making sure that there was nothing but woods on the far side of her trajectory, she started to pull the trigger.

In the back of her mind, she was aware that she was breaking the law. But this was kind of like telling Emilio to head to the second floor without her: Urgency over procedure.

Apologize, don't ask permission.

Get the fucking job done.

As the bullet exploded out of the barrel, the metal lock rang like a church bell and she lowered her weapon. Bingo. Worked like a charm. Opening one half of the doors, she took a deep breath.

Computers. Phones. Monitors. Laptops—

"Fucking hell, Anne. Now I gotta solve you like a goddamn problem."

Anne jerked around. Moose was staggering out of the house, his shirt stained with blood, a gash on his face, one foot trailing behind.

He looked tired. Frustrated. Exhausted. But mostly like a stranger wearing the mask and body of the friend and colleague she had once known and loved like family.

"Moose," she breathed. "What are you doing?"

The guy stopped and looked down at himself. "I crashed the Charger. It's somewhere in the woods. I was chasing Deandra off. And then I kept drinking."

"No, about this." She pointed to the trailer. "What are you doing with Ripkin?"

He threw up his hands—and that was when she saw the small black box in his right palm. "What was I supposed to do? I needed the money. Deandra is expensive. Was."

"Did you kill her?"

"What—no. I kicked her out. She's at her sister's. We're done." His bloodshot eyes finally focused properly. "But now, I gotta deal with you. I'm not going to jail, Anne. I can't. I hope you understand."

She took a step back and raised her gun at him. "Don't come near me."

"Is this where you arrest me?"

"You killed people. You put the lives of your own crew in danger. And you did it all while you were in turnouts."

"Don't get judgy with me, Anne," he bit out. "You're the sister of the fucking fire chief. Your life is all worked out. I got nothing. Nothing! My own parents didn't want me. I barely graduated from college. I couldn't make the SWAT team. Deandra didn't even want me, she wanted Danny!"

Her eyes flicked to what he had in his hand. The antenna gave it away—and she did the math quick.

Moving away from the trailer, she triangulated the distance to her car. "Look, Moose, I don't have to turn you in, okay? We can just forget—"

"No, I know you. I fought fires with you for how long? You're lying because you think I'm going to kill you and you're right. But I'm not going to pick you over me. Sorry."

The explosion in the trailer was instantaneous, triggered as he initiated some button on that remote, the force of the blast throwing her off her feet and carrying her some distance through the air. When she landed on her back, the breath was knocked out of her and the gun flipped free of her hand.

All she could do was stare up at the blue, cloudless sky, as she tried to get oxygen into her lungs.

Moose's face appeared above her own. "You know, I liked you, I really did." He brought up her gun. "And I'll do this quick and easy so you won't hurt—"

The gray flash came from out of nowhere, whatever it was moving so fast, it was just a blur.

But Soot knew what he was doing. He launched his attack at Moose's forearm, his impact swinging the gun away from Anne, the bullet discharging into the air. In response, Moose let out a curse and started punching the dog in the head.

Not that Soot noticed. Growling, snarling, his muscled body was as much a weapon as his teeth were, and he refused to let go as he thrashed.

"Leave my dog alone!"

Anne launched herself at Moose, going for his throat before she realized she didn't have two working hands. But she had a great intrinsic weapon, herself.

She took the hard fingers of her prosthesis and speared Moose in the eye.

He screamed and fell onto his back.

For a moment, she was convinced they had won. But then a boot came at her head and she couldn't duck in time. The heavy tread caught her right in the face, blood spooling out of her nose as she spun like a top.

And then there was a yelp and whimper from Soot.

52

Danny drove up to the front of Moose's cocksucking ranch and slammed the brakes on the truck so hard, he kicked up gravel. The bastard's yellow Charger wasn't around, but there were pink clothes and high-heeled shoes all over the front lawn. He knew Moose was home, however. Vic Rizzo from the 617 had texted everyone that after a drinking spell at Timeout, that muscle car had been found wrapped around a tree by two NBPD-ers and its inebriated driver had been returned to sender out here in the sticks.

Getting out, he—

The explosion was so violent, it rattled the windows on the house, and Danny ducked down to take cover as shrapnel dropped from the sky.

As a phone receiver hit him in the head, he cursed and jogged over to the front door. Going inside, he saw total chaos. Someone, most likely Moose, had taken a knife to the oversized black and white furniture, and there was stuffing and shredded pillows all over the place.

Every single one of the wedding pictures had been punched, bloody fist and palm prints marking the walls.

Danny ran through to the back. Outside, by the garage, Moose's box trailer was in flames, the curling smoke blowing toward the house and obscuring the view.

"Moose?" he called out.

Running toward the garage, he got smoke in his eyes and he coughed.

And then he saw the fight on the lawn behind the fire. Two people were rolling around on the ground. With something circling them.

Was the guy killing Deandra?

"Moose, stop! We weren't together, she's lying—"

Off at the tree line, parked at the head of a dirt lane about one hundred yards away, was Anne's Subaru.

What the hell?

Danny sidestepped the heat and the crackling flames that were coming out the back of the trailer. And as the smoke was blown in another direction, he got a clear view of something that made no sense: It was Anne and Moose who were fighting, and Soot was on the periphery, barking, snarling, limping badly like he'd been hurt.

Slow motion.

Everything went into slow motion: Moose flipping Anne on her back, Soot snapping at his hand as he pointed a gun in her face.

The most primitive and protective part of Danny's mind put the pieces together faster than his higher reasoning could organize proper thought. With every ounce of power he had, he surged forward at a dead run, and on his way, he picked up the first weapon he came to.

A long-handled axe that was leaning against the garage.

Just as Moose was about to pull the trigger, Danny skidded into place, swung the blade, and caught the would-be killer in the back of the head.

Moose stiffened in a full-body seizure, and Anne reacted with split-second reflexes. Even though she was bleeding from the nose, she twisted and caught the nine-millimeter, snatching it out of the man's control as he fell forward onto the ground.

Then she shoved herself free, scrambling out from under the now-limp deadweight that lay motionless, like a corpse.

Danny went so numb that he lost his bearings and released his hold on the handle, collapsing onto the ground . . . all the time staring at the axe as it held its own against gravity, sure as if he'd buried the blade in nothing but an oak stump.

"Soot!"

Shaking himself, he glanced at Anne. She was trembling as she kept the gun pointed at Moose and pulled her dog in against her, the animal licking at her, nuzzling, whimpering.

When she finally looked at Danny, he put his palms up into the air like she might shoot him, too.

Silence came over the scene and his brain tried to connect with a reality he didn't understand. Couldn't possibly grasp.

Anne seemed to be in a similar state of shock.

Why had his old roommate been trying to kill her?

"Are you okay?" he said roughly.

Her eyes, wide and glassy, locked on his face. "Danny . . . it was him. It was Moose. He lit the fires at those warehouses . . . and he was going to kill me."

Danny slowly lowered his hands. What the hell had Moose fallen into?

"He did it for the money," Anne mumbled. "That's where all the money came from, for the wedding, this house, that Shelby in the garage. He was disappearing evidence in those fires, but I wasn't able to connect him with Ripkin. I still don't know how Ripkin is involved."

Danny rubbed his face. "All I care about right now is that you're okay."

He leaned forward and took her hand. When she didn't pull away, he brought her up against him and squeezed his eyes shut briefly. Holding her tight, he looked over her shoulder at the body of his old friend.

The sadness was so deep he felt certain his heart was going to stop. He didn't know how a man he had lived with for years had turned so bad, but the one thing he was sure about was that Anne was alive.

Nothing else, even Moose, mattered more than that.

Easing back, he brushed some of the grass from her hair. "I need you to know I wasn't with Deandra the night before the wedding. Put a bullet in me now and send me to my twin brother, I will swear to that on my soul. She lied to Moose to make him mad, and she did it in front of the whole stationhouse, but it wasn't true. I wouldn't have done that to Moose. And I wouldn't have done that to you."

He let Anne stare into his eyes for as long as she needed to, all the while praying that the truth was something she could recognize in him.

After what felt like a lifetime, she whispered, "You saved my life again, Dannyboy."

"I will always be there for you." As her hand lifted up to touch his face, he captured it and pressed a kiss to her palm. "Always."

53

A nne sat on the back of the ambulance and held an ice pack to her nose. The bleeding had stopped, but she was worried it was broken. Every time she poked it, the middle made a crunching sound and that was not good news.

"—so that was when you decided to come out here and confront him?" the detective said to her.

Two more police vehicles came up to the scene and joined the four that were already parked in a circle around the ranch. The uniforms who got out were folks she remembered from her nights at Timeout, and absurdly she wanted to wave and say hello to them, like she was the hostess of this shit party.

"Anne?"

"Sorry." She refocused on the woman. "Yeah, I decided to come talk to him. It seemed like everything was adding up, but I needed to be sure. When I got here, I opened the back of the trailer"—edited to remove mention of her shooting the lock off—"and I saw the office equipment in there."

"What kind of office equipment?"

"Laptops. Computers. Phones. I'm guessing that Ripkin Development was either hiding things they wanted to destroy in Ollie Popper's extensive collection, or they have far more extensive dealings in the black market than law enforcement can even begin to contemplate."

"Okay, so then what happened?"

Her mouth started to move again, words leaving in a stream, and she guessed she was making sense. The detective was nodding and making notes.

But Anne had stopped listening to herself.

Danny came walking around the corner of the house, two uniforms with him, the three men talking intently. When he saw that she was looking at him, he stopped, like he wasn't sure whether he was welcome or not.

Soot, who had refused to leave her side, let out a chuff in greeting.

"That's all for right now," the detective said. "We'll let you get treated, but you'll have to make a formal statement."

"Anytime you want me at the station, I'll come down."

"Thanks, Inspector Ashburn. We appreciate your cooperation."

As she was left alone, Danny said something to the pair of cops and came over. "Hey. Nice nose job."

She took the ice pack off. "Do you think it's too much? I was just looking to get the bridge narrowed and the tip turned up a little."

"I think we need to wait until the swelling goes down."

"Yeah. Plastic surgery is like that."

"Can I say hi to your dog?"

Like they were strangers. "Of course. He loves you."

Danny got down on his haunches, that knee of his popping. As he put his face into Soot's, he said, "You okay there, boy? You were limping."

"I think Moose kicked him. But at least neither of us got shot."

As she regarded Danny, she measured every inch of him, from the way the sunlight flashed in his jet black hair, to those stupidly huge shoulders of his, to his hands. Those amazing, strong, blue-collar hands.

That had saved her life twice.

Because the truth was, she had been losing physical strength fast. And if Moose had pulled that trigger, he would have put a bullet in her head.

Tears flooded her eyes, so she closed them.

"Anne," Danny said in a broken voice.

There was a shuffle, and then he was sitting next to her on the lip of the ambulance. "Give us a minute," she heard him say to someone.

She sniffled herself back into order—or tried to. Jesus, her nose hurt.

"So in the rules of evidence," she said roughly, "the court allows deathbed confessions even if they're hearsay outside of that extenuating circumstance. You know, because people don't lie when they're just about to die."

"No, they don't."

"And following that theory, I'm thinking it's probably the same for people right after they kill their best friend." She closed her eyes. "Oh, God, did this just happen. I mean, really?"

A warm, calloused hand took hers. "Yes. To both, I mean."

"What?" Her head just couldn't seem to process anything. "I'm not thinking straight."

"I didn't lie, about Deandra." As Anne looked at him, he stared right back at her. "You don't have to be with me if you don't want to, but I need you to know the truth. I didn't lie about her. The night of the rehearsal dinner, it's true that she came on to me back at my apartment, but I turned her down. Moose might have seen her dress on the floor, but what he didn't catch was me frog-marching her out of the place and locking things up so she couldn't get back in. She wasn't for me. She never was. And I was never with her after they were married either."

When Anne took a deep breath, her ribs hurt and she grimaced. Which made her nose hurt more. But none of that mattered.

"I'm sorry," she said. "I'm so sorry. I just . . . I believed what was in front of me."

She fell into confirming her hypothesis, which had been that Danny was too good to be true.

"It's okay." He looked down at the ground. "It is what it is—"

"I love you."

His head turned back to her so fast, she heard his neck crack.

"Just figured I should tell you." Anne shrugged. "It's too little, too late, but—"

The kiss came out of nowhere, his mouth fusing with hers, and she was too shell-shocked to respond. At first. She got with the program quick, though.

When they finally parted, she couldn't get enough of staring into those blue eyes. "I'm sorry about Moose, too. I can't imagine what you're feeling right now."

He nodded as he brushed her hair back. "None of it seems real at all. Except for one thing."

"What's that?"

His face settled into hard lines. "If anyone tries to hurt you, I will come for them. And I will take care of the situation in any way I have to."

Anne's first instinct was to tell him she didn't need the help, but that was reflex, not reality. She wanted him in her life in all the ways that counted, and the knight-in-shining-armor stuff was part of that mix.

Provided he understood that she would do the same for him.

Reaching up, she smoothed his furrowed brows. "Guess what?"

"What?"

"Two can play at that game." She smiled a little. "I've got your back when you need it, too. I'm your partner, not a princess in a tower."

"And that, my fair lady, is why I love you."

He kissed her again, and she thought about all the emotions in the air between them: The hope, sadness, gratitude, anger, and confusion . . . even the fading terror. She had been through enough bad accident scenes and fires to know there would be a tail on all this. They would get through it together, though. What choice was there. You were either a survivor or casualty.

And they were survivors.

"Anne."

At the sound of her brother saying her name, they pulled apart. Tom was standing by the back of the ambulance, tall as always, autocratic as ever—with eyes that were tearing up.

Struck by even more emotion, Anne shifted off the steel bumper and went to him. There was an awkward moment, as they had never been huggers—

Her brother's heavy arms came around her and drew her against his big chest. Closing her eyes, she took a deep breath.

For a moment, the past and the present blended together, and she felt an echo of the way it had been for her as a child with her father, sheltered in the lee of something greater and stronger than herself. But then all that had gone away, the hero image replaced by a human with devastating flaws.

Which was why people needed to stand on their own two feet.

Pulling back, she looked up. The vulnerability in her brother's face was a shock. He'd never looked to her for grounding or support. He never looked to anyone for that.

"It's okay," she told him. "It's all okay. I promise."

He shuddered and dropped his head. "I can't lose you, Sister."

"You haven't. You won't." She smiled. "I'm an Ashburn."

Her brother's stare returned to her and he nodded gravely. "That you are. Through and through."

As they hugged again, Anne was aware of an uncoiling deep inside of her, that anger that had defined her for so long shattering like a mirror and dissipating. Growing up, all she had ever wanted was her father's respect.

It turned out that destiny gave her something even better, more worthwhile.

She had earned her big brother's.

In the periphery, Anne was aware of Danny sitting back and watching the pair of them, the smile on his face wide and approving.

When Tom reached out a palm toward him, Danny shook what was offered, a vow given and accepted on both sides: In the midst of chaos and death, a new family had been forged. One that was chosen as opposed to an accident of biology—and for that reason, more abiding and enduring.

O ne week later, Anne left her office on a long lunch break. Don was going to watch Soot, who had become the investigation team's mascot, and she had a feeling "watch" meant her boss was going to take the dog down the street to the deli and the two of them were going to share a turkey, cheese, and mayo foot-long and two bags of potato chips.

No wonder Soot also thought that man was the World's Greatest Boss.

The strip mall that was her destination was nothing she had been to before, although she had driven by it plenty of times, and she found a parking space easily enough. She was early and the noontime sun was still fairly warm, so she took a leisurely stroll past the stores.

The fallout around Moose's death was sad. His body was being buried, but not with departmental honors. How could it be? He had endangered the lives of his fellow firefighters. Committed arson. Tried to kill her.

The investigation into his crimes had expanded to include the FBI, given the interstate nature of Ollie Popper's black-market activity. An LG burner phone had been found inside Moose's house, and the calls to her cell had been in its outgoing log. An anonymous texting app, TextPort, was the only thing loaded onto it.

The money trail was cold. There had been just over five thousand dollars in cash in Moose's bedroom, but no clues so far on where it had come from. And as for Ripkin? That tie had not been exposed, but she still believed it was there. Moose's spending had far exceeded the random thousand here or there that someone like Ollie could pay somebody.

And that was why she truly believed it hadn't just been stolen office equipment in those fires. Ripkin was hiding secrets, although what kind, she didn't know and officially couldn't find out: She had filed her report on the most recent warehouse fire, and her amendments to the other five, but unless she was called into the Moose investigation, her role for her department was done.

Which was frustrating.

On top of that, she was worried about Danny. It was obvious that he was sad deep inside and keeping things to himself, and that concerned her. It might be the way things always had been, but that stoic, power-through mentality needed to change. It just wasn't healthy.

Everything else was great between them, though. He had moved into her house by attrition, every night heading over with another bunch of clothes, not that he had much. He'd also brought his fancy TV with him, and she had to admit it was a helluva improvement over her piece of crap.

He was letting that apartment go. An era over. The four men who had started out as fraternity brothers graduating on to adulthood.

Or the grave, in Moose's case.

Stopping in front of a dress shop, she tilted her head at what was in the window. Deandra had left town, quitting her job, packing up her stuff, and going off to God only knew where. She wasn't free, though. Not by a long shot. The authorities had questioned her and she was still on their list as a person of interest. It was pretty clear the woman might have had the motive, but there was no concrete evidence that she'd done anything criminal herself.

The investigation was ongoing, however.

"Anne!"

She turned and started to smile. "Hi, Mom. Thanks for coming."

As she met her mother halfway down the strip mall, she decided her brother was right. Their mom seemed much happier and lighter, in the last week.

Healing was good for people, wasn't it.

"You are not going to believe it," Nancy Janice announced, "but I sold two of my oil paintings at a gallery this morning! I can't stand it! Who would ever have thought anybody would want something I did?"

Anne hugged her mother and was surprised by how easy it was. "I'm proud of you."

"Me, too." Nancy Janice took Anne's hand. "Now, let's focus on you."

"Oh, God, this is a dumb idea."

"No, it is not. And I'll be with you the whole time. Come on, let's do this."

As they walked toward the hair salon together, Anne glanced over her shoulder. "And after we're done, I want to go to this other shop for a second. There's something I want your opinion on."

———

Danny could not frickin' sit down. On that note, he wished the waiting room was twelve times the size it was.

Back and forth. Back and forth. Back and—

The door opened and Dr. McAuliffe smiled at him. "Well, hello."

"Hi, Doc." He shoved his hands into the pockets of his jeans. "How're ya?"

"Good, very good. Come on back."

As she held the way open for him, he hesitated. But then he forced his feet to get moving.

"Thanks, Doc," he muttered as he went inside.

"Sit wherever you like. You remember the rules. There really aren't any."

He smiled because he felt like he had to and chose the sofa. "Yeah."

The doctor sat down, and he noted she was in another variation of what she'd had on at their previous meeting, although this time, there was some purple thrown in with the brown.

"So I was surprised to hear from you." She smiled gently. "But glad you called."

"Thanks for fitting me in."

"Of course."

He looked around, noting all the Purposely Calming details. Or maybe that was really her; maybe it wasn't all a calculation, but rather the expression of a compassionate soul at peace in the world and with her work.

"I guess I should explain why I'm here," he said.

"You can start, there. Sure."

Clearing his throat, he rubbed his thighs. "I, ah, I'm in love."

"Really! That's wonderful."

As he smiled, he ducked his eyes and blushed. Like an idiot. Like a schoolboy. Like someone confessing to his mother he was going out with a girl.

"She's amazing."

"I'll bet."

"She's a firefighter, too. Or was. Until she . . . well, it's Anne. You know, Anne Ashburn."

"Really." Dr. McAuliffe smiled some more. "That sounds like a beautiful relationship."

"I want it to be. She means so much to me, and I would do anything to protect her and make her happy." Abruptly, he focused directly on the doctor. "And that's why I'm here. I don't want to be what fucks it up. 'Scuse my French."

"No offense taken."

"I thought maybe you and me could talk about things that are up here." He tapped himself on the head. "Things that I can't unsee, things I can't undo, things I wish were different."

Like Moose.

Like Emilio, who was back at work and looking like road kill.

Like Sol, who they shouldn't have lost.

"I think that's a really good idea, Danny. Where do you want to start?"

He thought about the old lady on that bed in that burning apartment. The axe going into the back of Moose's head. Anne and her hand. Emilio in the hospital bed. Sol screaming, "Don't leave me, don't leave me," right before he was crushed by debris.

He thought of himself regaining consciousness at the bottom of the collapsed warehouse wall, his mask cracked, his body crushed, his breathing bad.

And then he thought of John Thomas.

"I want to talk about my twin brother."

"Okay. Tell me about him. Tell me all about him."

Danny had to blink his eyes as they started to burn. But then he smiled. "Oh, Jesus, he was an annoying little shit when we were growing up. He used to wait for me to fall asleep at night and then . . ."

I t seemed right that rain started to fall as Danny entered the cemetery. There was no gatehouse or visitor check-in because this was
the budget burial place, not the fancy old one on the other side of
the tracks with the monogrammed crypts and the statues of angels and
saints. Hitting the brakes on his truck, he checked the Kleenex box he'd
scribbled the directions on and then went left.

He'd been at Anne's when he'd gotten the call back, and the gray-
and-yellow tissue box had been the first writeable surface he'd
grabbed.

As he wound around the clusters of the dead, there were all kinds of
Irish Catholic names and Celtic cross markers, and he deliberately took
the long way to the section he was looking for. John Thomas was buried
in the northeast corner, along with their parents, and although he was
turning over a new leaf with Dr. McAuliffe, he wasn't ready to head over
there quite yet. He did think he'd bring Anne someday, though.

Seemed right to introduce her to the family. His parents had died
way before she'd come into his life, and John Thomas, per departmental policy, had not only been stationed at another firehouse, he'd died
the year before she'd joined the service. So he hadn't really known her.

They all would have loved her. Who wouldn't?

Rounding another corner, he eased off on the gas. Across a mowed lawn of browning grass, beneath a canopy of red and gold leaves, two groundskeepers were pulling a casket out of an unmarked van.

For a moment, he couldn't breathe.

Moose. God . . . what happened to you, Moose?

Danny's truck rolled onward, carried by a subtle slope in the lane that amplified the engine's idle. When he hit the brakes by the new gravesite, both of the men looked over at him.

He lifted his hand and got no response. The groundsmen just muscled the coffin over to a hole that obviously had been dug by the mini-dozer sitting off to the side, the union worker who'd operated it taking a break and smoking.

Danny reached for his own cigarettes and lit one. He'd sworn that he would stop, but the only thing going through his mind at the moment was, *Not today, motherfucker.*

Getting out, he approached the groundsmen. "Excuse me, but is—"

"You here for Robert Miller?" the one in front asked as the van drove off.

"Yes. Moose is—yeah, I'm here for him."

"You family?"

"I don't know." *Used to be,* he thought. *Kinda.* "Do I have to be?"

"We don't care," the other guy said.

They both grunted as they placed the casket on a mechanized platform that was going to lower it into the grave. As they straightened, they looked like brothers, both stocky and balding, Igors without the humps or the Mad Scientist bosses. Their dark green work uniforms were by the same maker that the firefighters used, their baseball caps bearing the bended-bough logo of the cemetery above the brim.

"You want a minute before we put him down in there?" the one on the left said.

They were identical twins, Danny thought as he looked back and forth at their weathered faces. Just like him and John Thomas.

"Yeah. If you don't mind."

"We gotta go dig another two holes anyway. Take your time."

One motioned to the Toro operator and the other started off on foot, and as the pair went away, he wondered if their names matched, too. Jim and Tim. Bob and Rodge. Fred and Ted.

Daniel Michael and John Thomas were an Irish rhyme, his mother had always said. Whatever that meant.

Danny took a drag and exhaled over his shoulder even though there was no one around to offend with secondhand smoke.

The coffin was simple, not one of those carved mahogany ones with brass rails and tufted satin interiors, and as sprinkles of rain dappled its black lid, they left glossy prints that were perfectly round. He wondered what Moose was wearing in there. Who had chosen the clothes. Whether the axe blade's damage had been repaired before the embalming had been done.

The hypothetical answers he considered and discarded were like the speculation about the twin groundskeepers, a way to give his brain a break from the reality that someone he had been close to for years, who he had thought of as a brother, who he had worked alongside . . . had been someone he hadn't really known.

He thought about Anne and her father. Just the other night she had talked about what had happened after Tom, Sr., had died, about the secret that had come out afterward. She had told him all about her

frustration with her mother, her anger at her father. The disillusion-
ment and disgust and betrayal.

A hero she had once put her faith into hadn't proven to be merely
human, but a bad man.

She would understand exactly how he was feeling about Moose,
and also how he was re-coloring previously positive memories with a
dark filter.

Moose had been the genial loser who'd struggled to keep up with
the big dogs, a good guy with a heart of gold who never quite made it,
but always managed to smile in the midst of his failures.

A Ralph Kramden, first of the frat house, and then later at the
apartment and the stationhouse.

The idea Moose could light fires that hurt people and accept
money from crooks . . . and try to kill someone, kill *Anne*, for fuck's
sake, meant that everything that had seemed true about him had to
have been a lie. Because the man Danny had known and lived with
would never have hurt anyone, much less one of their own.

He'd loved Anne.

Or . . . at least he'd seemed to act like it.

"Fuck," Danny said into the cool fall breeze.

The low growl of a motorcycle brought his head around and he
frowned. The black Harley he knew well, but he had not expected to
see it or its owner out and about for another three months.

As Mick Roth, his old roommate, killed the bike's engine and dis-
mounted, the guy removed his helmet and put it on the seat. His dark
hair had been recently cut and a tan dimmed the colorful tats that
wrapped around his throat. Blue jeans had holes in them. Leather
jacket was beat to shit.

Eyes were alert, but had black circles under them. "Surprised?"

"Yeah. But glad."

Mick strode over the cropped grass, sidestepping the gravestones. "So what's up, Dannyboy?"

The two embraced, and Danny held on hard. "What are you doing out of rehab? I thought you were supposed to be in Alabama another ninety days."

"Arizona."

"Sorry." They stepped back. "Did you walk out on the program?"

"Not exactly. I told them I'd come back after I saw you and made sure you're okay."

"I'm fine."

"Party line, huh." Mick looked around. "What the fuck are we doing here?"

"I don't know." As a blacked-out truck came over the rise, Danny shook his head. "And then there were three."

Jack parked his Ford behind the Harley and got out. He was in SWAT clothes, the black T-shirt with the crest on the pec and the camo pants accessorized by a couple of forties and a hunting knife holstered around his waist.

"You found it okay," he said to Mick.

"Yeah." They clapped palms. "Thanks, man."

And then the three of them just stood around the coffin, staring at the closed lid that had gathered enough rain so that the water dripped off its sides, tears that should have been shed, but could not fall in any other fashion. In the silence, a bird chirping in a golden-leaved tree was louder than it should have been. So was the beat of Danny's heart.

God, he could still remember meeting Moose during pledge week. The guy had been determined to out-drink anyone who challenged him, as if he'd recognized that consumption was his sole recommending feature for the fraternities. Jack, on the other hand, had been recruited for his game with the females. Danny, they'd wanted as a bouncer. And as for Mick?

The frats had been scared of what he might do if they turned him down.

"Someone should say something," Jack muttered.

"Yeah." Danny took a deep breath. "Shit."

"That about covers it," Mick said dryly.

Danny put his hand into the pocket of his pants and took out his Marlboros. After offering and lighting one for both of the other roommates, he put the mostly full pack and his Bic on the top of the coffin and then he hit the gear switch so that the casket lowered into the earth.

Each of them cast a handful of dirt into the grave.

As it turned out, the cigarette he finished smoking was the last one he ever had.

And he called Anne as soon as he was back in his truck and alone.

"Hello?" she answered. "Excited for tonight? I know I am."

He had to hit his wipers as he left the cemetery. "Yes," he said roughly. "I can't wait to see you."

"Are you okay?"

"I am now." Danny released a long slow exhale. "I just needed to hear your voice. Listen . . . I'm going to wanna talk about Moose."

There wasn't even a second of pause, and her voice was strong and steady. "Anytime. You can talk to me about anything at any time."

Just one more reason to love you, he thought as he drove on through the downpour.

At eight o'clock on the dot, Anne parallel-parked her Subaru on the busy street and sat back in the driver's seat. After a minute, she pulled the visor down and checked her face. As a set of headlights flared, she got a good look at herself.

With lipstick on.

Like, proper lipstick. Not a coat of gloss, but real, live L'Oréal stuff that had been applied after she'd used a lip liner.

Putting the visor back into place, she felt silly. But it was too late to change, and besides, the one thing she could guarantee about Danny Maguire was that he'd like her in whatever she was wearing. Well, actually, he preferred her naked—but considering they were in public, he would take whatever clothes she'd slapped on as they came.

She opened her door a crack, and then waited for two cars to go by before standing up on the high heels she'd bought at lunch along with the dress she had on.

Across the street, Danny was waiting by the door of the venerable establishment they had agreed to meet at for their date.

As he saw her, his smile, open and easy, faded quick.

And his eyes widened so much, the whites became the size of dinner plates.

Clearing her throat, Anne shut her door and locked her car—and then with each stupid-ass step she took, she made herself promise she would never, ever try to be a girl again. Obviously, her mother's advice, well intended though it had been, had missed the mark.

Stepping up onto the sidewalk, she shook her head. "Sorry. This was a dumb idea."

Danny's eyes went down to the stilettos, up the stockings, over the knees to the fairly short skirt and then to the cape that she had swung around herself like she was Lauren frickin' Bacall.

"Holy Mary, Mother of God . . ." he stuttered.

"I can go change—"

"No! No, don't change! You're . . . the most beautiful thing I've ever seen."

Anne blinked. Once. Twice.

Stop being a girl, she told herself. *Be a woman.*

Even though it was cold, she separated the cape's halves and flashed the dress that had been in the window of that shop at the strip mall. The thing was red, and it hugged her waist, and even dipped in between her breasts.

Danny lost the ability to talk again.

As she closed the cape back up, she started to smile. Well, looked like she was going to have to seriously thank her mother. Nancy Janice, it turned out, had skills. Mad skills.

"Your hair," he breathed. "Can I touch it?"

"Sure."

Danny's hand reached up and brushed the blonded streaks. "It's amazing. Not that it wasn't amazing before . . ."

"Should we go inside?" she said.

"Oh, yeah, sorry, sure, please. Thank you. What was the question?"

Danny tripped over his feet as he opened the door, and Timeout's raucous noise spilled out onto the street along with the warmth of its interior. As they entered, heads turned briefly—and then snapped right back.

The conversational din in the bar lowered.

And that was when Danny's chest puffed out and he put his arm around her, all proud caveman. Then he escorted her through the tables like he had won the lottery, the presidential election, a Nobel Peace Prize, and the Super Bowl at the same time. Especially as they went by the 617's booth and he nodded at Vic Rizzo.

As they came up to the 499's table, all the men started to stand. Duff even took off his baseball hat—and dropped it on his foot.

"Get over y'selves, it's just a little makeup," Anne said with a smile.

Danny helped her take off the cape and pulled out her chair. Then he leaned across the table and grabbed Duff's lapels. "Your eyes stay at head level. All you guys. I see one dip below the throat, and I'm going to use you as a cue stick."

Then he kissed her on the mouth and sat next to her, cracking his knuckles and glowering at the crew.

"Must you," she drawled.

"Yup. Absolutely."

And then it was drinks and it was wings, it was stories and it was jokes. It was the family she had worked with and the friends she had grown to love . . . and most of all, it was the big beautiful Irish man sitting beside her, his blue eyes shining.

Overcome with happiness, Anne stared at Danny. And when he

turned to her as if he wanted to know if she needed something, she put both her hands, the one that was flesh and blood and the one that was a tool, up to his face.

"Thank you," she whispered.

"For what?"

Anne tilted in and kissed him. "I haven't been to Timeout in a very long time ..."

a c k n o w l e d g m e n t s

There are so many people to thank in connection with this book. Over the last year, I have had the privilege of getting to observe many firemen and police officers in the course of their work. They have been unfailingly generous with their time, patient with my questions and inexperience, and incredible models of selfless heroism. In particular, I'd like to thank Captain Brian O'Neill, of the Louisville Fire Department, all of the officers of Louisville SWAT, and Sherriff's Deputy (ret.) Theodore Mitchell.

I'd also like to thank Meg Ruley, Rebecca Scherer, and everyone at JRA, and Lauren McKenna, Jennifer Bergstrom, and the entire family at Gallery Books and Simon & Schuster.

To Liz and Steve Berry, I can't thank you all enough for what you have done for me, and thank you also to our Jillian Stein (and BStein for the car advice!), who is the FB guru of all FB gurus.

Team Waud, I love you all. Truly.

And as always, everything I do is with the love and support of both my family of origin and of adoption. With special thanks to my husband, Neville, my mother, and Auntie Wow, Uncle Nath, and Uncle Darrie.

And I couldn't have done this without Naamah, my WriterDog II, who works as hard as I do on my books!

Don't miss J. R. Ward's Bourbon Kings series!

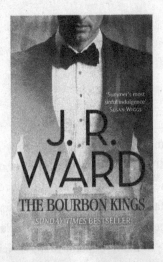

'Summer's most sinful indulgence'
SUSAN WIGGS

J. R. WARD

THE BOURBON KINGS
SUNDAY TIMES BESTSELLER

SUNDAY TIMES BESTSELLER

J. R. WARD

THE ANGELS' SHARE
'Summer's most sinful indulgence'
SUSAN WIGGS

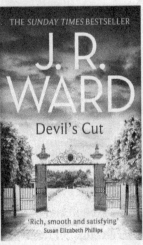

THE SUNDAY TIMES BESTSELLER

J. R. WARD

Devil's Cut
'Rich, smooth and satisfying'
Susan Elizabeth Phillips

Available now from Piatkus